Dacia Wolf

& the Wings of Change

A magical, dark paranormal fantasy novel

Dacia Wolf

AND THE
WINGS OF CHANGE

Book 6

Visit Mandi Oyster online at
www.MandiOyster.com

Facebook: https://www.facebook.com/MandiOysterAuthor
Instagram: https://www.instagram.com/MandiOyster/

*Once there was a girl who wanted
to see her dreams come true.
She never gave up,
and she never stopped believing.*

*This book is dedicated to her
and to everyone out there who keeps reaching,
no matter how impossible their dream may seem.*

Chapter 1

Caged

Troy shoved me down the spiral staircase, pressing his hand against the small of my back any time I slowed. The cells grew closer with each step. Looking down on them, they were more like cages bolted to the floor. There were no walls, no privacy. I hadn't done anything to deserve being imprisoned. I'd saved the world when the Nephilim hadn't. I'd saved the dragons when the Nephilim wouldn't. Yes, I'd befriended a demon, but he'd helped me more times than they had even considered trying to.

With every turn of the stairs, I glared at him. My fingers twitched, itching for some way to access my magic, even if it meant becoming more corrupted by Mavros' power. I tripped, barely catching myself before tumbling over the railing.

Troy laughed. "Please, fall and break your neck. Save us all the trouble of dealing with you." Before I'd completely caught my balance, he shoved me again.

When we reached the bottom, he thrust me forward, pressing the middle of my back hard enough to bruise. He led me to the central cell and threw me in. I fell forward unable to brace myself with my hands. My knees hit the ground, then my face smacked against the cement floor.

He stood above me, nudging me with the toe of his boot. I looked over my shoulder into his hate-filled brown eyes, and any hope that I might get out of this disappeared. "Little help," I mumbled.

Grabbing the zip tie, he hauled me to my feet and shoved me up against the cell. Then he spun me around and slammed my head against the bars.

Lights danced in front of my eyes, and I whimpered, hating myself for sounding so weak.

He cut the plastic binding my hands together. I grabbed my wrist, rubbing one, then the other. I thought he would leave, but instead, he pressed his body against mine, shoving me into the cold metal. My legs weakened, my heart pounded in my ears, and my breaths came in ragged gasps.

"Like I would want anything to do with a demon lover." His lips moved right against my ear. I couldn't see the expression on his face, but the disgust in his voice was obvious. He pinned my arm against the bars and clasped a manacle around my wrist. Then he grabbed my other hand and hung me from the side of the cage.

The tips of my toes barely touched the ground. I tottered, trying to hold my balance. My shoulders stretched, and I thought they might pull out of their sockets.

He took a knife out of his pocket. Holding it close to my face, he flipped it open. The blade skimmed past my nose as it snapped into place.

I looked around. Hoping to find somebody willing to help me, but there was no one. Why had the Nephilim gone through all of this trouble just to kill me? Why not do it before dragging me through the portals? I tried to focus on the tattoo on Troy's face, but the flash of his knife drew my attention away.

He waved the blade in front of me before slicing it through his forearm. Twisting his fingers in my hair, he yanked my head back, pulling my feet off the ground. I scrabbled around to find a place to put them to keep from hanging only from my wrists.

While I was flailing about, Troy pressed his arm to my mouth, forcing me to swallow more of his blood. It ran over my chin and down my neck. It spilled from my lips. I tried to spit it out, but he tugged my hair, jerking my head back farther.

The blood pooled in my mouth, and I held it there. The coppery taste and warmth of it threatened to gag me, but I refused to swallow it. I didn't want Mavros to be unbound to me. History wouldn't show how he could be if treated with kindness. It would only remember that he was a demon. Evil. Cruel. Malicious.

Troy lifted his arm from my lips and pinched my nose shut while covering my mouth. I stared up at the ceiling, trying to outlast him, but it was no use. By the time I swallowed his blood, my chest ached, and my vision had darkened.

He unhooked my arms, and I fell to the ground, greedily sucking in air. My tears fell freely, but I didn't care anymore.

Spinning on his heel, he sauntered to the cell door. It slammed shut with a loud clang. He turned a key in the lock and hung it just out of reach on the cage next to me.

Splashing his blood on the ground and murmuring something too softly for me to hear, he walked all around my cell, stopping several times to trace his finger through the gore.

Too scared to move, I watched from my position on the floor. Every time I turned my head, a new wave of dizziness crashed over me. I was terrified that if I moved from my hands and knees I would pass out. Then God only knew what Troy would do to me.

When he stood by the door again, he turned toward me. "Think of this as your home now." His lips curled into a sneer.

"Does it make you feel powerful to lock up a defenseless girl?" I imagined I looked feral with his blood still coating my face.

"I locked up a wolf in sheep's clothing." Disgust flickered across his features. He shook his fingers, and blood splattered the bars. Without the sun shining on it, I couldn't see the gold flecks in it anymore. "Your demon won't be able to get to you now." He pointed across the room at a giant crossbow. "If your dragons come, we'll kill them, and that won't hurt my feelings either." He turned away. "Sweet dreams, Princess."

The way he said it made a chill rush over my skin and stood the hair on my arms on end.

While he climbed the steps, I crawled to a hole in the floor and heaved, emptying as much of his blood as I could. When there was no more, I sank back on my heels and dragged my hand through my curls. I'd just gotten Argentum's blood out of my system. Would it be as difficult to get rid of Troy's? The thought made me queasy. I leaned over the hole and retched again. The smell wafting up from the darkness made it easy to purge the contents of my stomach.

Sitting up, I wiped my sleeve across my mouth and looked around my cage. Aside from the pit in the corner, it was empty.

I curled in a ball as far from the hole as I could get. My face throbbed. My knees stung. And my back ached. But worse than all of that was the pain in my chest.

Mavros stands in front of me. Seeing him is such a relief that my legs weaken. I sit down on the warm, sandy beach before I fall. His sleeves are rolled up, and I can't help but glance at his right arm. The damage done by my ice is completely healed. His skin is unblemished.

He kneels in front of me and stretches his hand out, stopping short of touching my cheek. "What have they done to you?"

"He made me drink his blood." I stare at the ground, unable to handle the look of despair on Mavros' face. Tears fill my eyes, blurring everything. "He said it will kill your magic, unbind us. Then … then they'll take me to the sanctuary."

He carefully tilts my chin up. "We'll rescue you, get his blood out"—his silken voice turns to a feral growl—"and make them all pay."

"You can't." I turn away from him. The turquoise water seems to go on forever with no end. "They warded it against you and plan to kill the dragons if they show up."

He slams his fist into his palm. The unexpected noise makes me jump. I twist around, looking for any sign of danger. When I turn back, I see several items appear on the beach beside him. He takes a washrag and dunks it into a bucket of water, then rings it out and gently brings it to my face, wiping the blood off. "I can heal you." His eyes turn down. "But I'd have to hurt you first to do it."

"I don't think Troy would like it if I woke up healed." I pull my legs up to my chest and wrap my arms around them. "He's deranged."

Mavros wipes next to my eye, and I cringe. "He doesn't need to know I healed you. Let him think your body can still do it on its own." He sounds so desperate, so broken. I wonder if this is how he'd been when he held me while I died. "Dacia, look at me, please."

"I can't." A sob tears out of me unexpectedly. "I can't let them hurt any of you."

"They can't hurt me." He continues wiping blood off of my face. His actions are tender, and once again, I'm amazed that he's supposed to be the evil one. "The dragons are ready to wage all-out war to get you back."

My gaze snaps to his. "No." I cover my mouth with my hand. "No. They can't do that. No."

"Dacia." He brushes my hair back. "Every one of us would gladly die to protect you." He watches my eyes. "Your pupils are huge." He points at the sky. "In this light, they should be tiny. Let me heal you."

I know what he's worried about. He's afraid I have a concussion. I wondered that the moment my head hit the ground, then again when Troy slammed it against the cage. I nod. My temples pulse in response, and the movement tugs at the bruises on my back.

Mavros' fingers become tipped with claws. I pull my arm out of my sleeve and hold it out to him. He grips my hand, squeezing my fingers. Then he swipes his paw through the air. His claws tear through my skin.

I jerk back, trying to get away, but he holds on. His fingers morph back, becoming human-looking, and he presses them to the gashes, drawing out the venom.

The pain throughout my body lessens. My heartbeat quits thundering in my ears. My vision clears.

"Remember when I pulled you out of your dream?"

I roll my eyes at him. "Of course." I'd almost died that night. Argentum had controlled Mavros, but he'd fought every one of the dragon's commands, doing what he could to keep me alive.

"I'd like to try." He lifts me to my feet and wraps his arms around me.

Hope blossoms inside of me, filling my chest. I lean into him and close my eyes. *Please, Lord, please let this work.*

We stand for what seems like hours but has only been seconds. I look up at Mavros' face. It's twisted in concentration. Sweat glistens on his forehead.

He growls, and the sound replaces my hope with despair. "The wards are blocking me."

My heart seems to plummet. I let go of him and sink to the ground.

He starts to walk away, but I grab his arm. "Please, please don't go." I hate the panic in my voice, the neediness.

Sitting next to me, he says, "Whatever you want."

"Stay with me—" I chew on my lip, pulling it into my mouth "—until I wake up, please. I don't wanna be alone."

He wraps his arm around my shoulders, pulling me against his side. Then he rubs his hand up and down my arm, caressing me, soothing me.

"Do you think Diana knows about this?" The thought makes my stomach twist. "Do you think she let them do it?"

He doesn't answer for a long time, so long that I begin to wonder if I asked the question out loud. "I don't think so."

"What would happen if she knew? What if Khione knew?"

☙8❧

Chapter 2

The Ghost Of A Chance

Somebody was kicking my foot. Part of me wanted to ignore whoever it was in the hopes they'd go away. The other part of me knew the kicking could be more painful.

I pressed my hand down on the ground and lifted myself up. The Nephilim with the scarred face who'd held the door open for Troy stood in front of me. His sword hilts stuck up above his shoulders, but his holster was gone. A bucket of water, towels, and a bar of soap sat on the floor beside him. "Get cleaned—" He sucked in a breath, and I wondered if he swallowed the toothpick that had been sticking out of his mouth. When I was about to ask, he flicked it forward with his tongue, then reached up and pulled it out, holding it between his thumb and index finger. He pointed it at me and looked around. "How are you cleaned up? And what's that smell?"

Mavros was gone, but the warm summer nights scent of him lingered. Breathing it in, I scooted back against the bars and held my hands out in front of me, flipping them over and staring at them like I was as surprised as he was. "I … I don't know. I was—" I rubbed my forehead. "I think I had a concussion. I was sleeping."

He shoved the toothpick back in his mouth. "Strip off your grubby clothes, wash the stink off, and put those on." He pointed at the stack of towels, and I realized there were clothes at the bottom of it.

"I'm good." I pulled my legs up to my chest and shook my head.

He bent down so that his nose nearly touched mine. "Do it, or I will." The look on his face was enough to send shivers racing down my spine.

I stared into his jade eyes, trying to find a way out of this, but there wasn't one. I imagined grabbing one of his swords and running him through with it, but the thought vanished as quickly as it came. Even though I had killed, I wasn't a killer.

Chewing on my bottom lip, I stared at the bucket. Just considering undressing in front of this man sent icy shivers of dread racing through my body. "Could you … could you at least make it seem like I have some privacy?"

He threw his head back and laughed. "Those days are over, girl." He walked toward the cell door, then turned around, leaned against it, folded his arms over his chest, and watched me.

My stomach dropped, and hot tears filled my eyes. I stood and searched through the pile. The clothes included a tan jumpsuit and a pair of men's boxer shorts. I dunked the rag in the freezing water and rubbed the bar of soap on it. I washed my face and ears first. When my hands touched the collar around my neck, I fought the urge to scream.

Turning my back to the guard, I kicked my shoes and socks off. The cement held no warmth at all. The chill spread up my body from my feet. I pulled my shirt down as low as it would go, then took my leggings and panties off. I washed as quickly as possible before pulling the boxers and jumpsuit on.

My fingers shook as I tugged on the zipper. It caught a couple of times before I got it zipped up to my waist. I hoped my hips would hold it on while I yanked my sweatshirt off. Slipping my hands under my shirt, I unhooked my bra. Then I slipped my arms out of my sleeves and tossed my bra to the floor. I washed the rest of my body, pulled the jumpsuit up, and zipped it to my neck, before slipping my shirt over my head.

The guard tossed my shoes and clothes out through the bars. Then he dumped the water down the hole in the floor, picked up the rest of the stuff, and left without another word.

I dragged my hands down my face as I watched him climb the spiral staircase. I couldn't smell Mavros anymore, and that hit me harder than I would have ever imagined. His scent had been a small comfort, something familiar. I sat in the corner of the cage. Fighting the stiffness of the jumpsuit, I pulled my legs up to my chest and rested my chin on my knees.

I wrapped my hands around the back of my neck, planning to rub some of the tension out. Cold metal reminded me that my freedom had been taken from me when the collar had been snapped on me without my consent. I tugged on it, running my fingers over the smooth surface, searching for a clasp. I sent several prayers to God as I pulled on it, begging for His help, imploring Him to get me out of this. Finally, I gave up.

My stomach growled, and I wished I'd gotten something to eat before going for a run. I licked my lips, hoping the moisture would keep the skin from breaking.

Hours or maybe only minutes passed before I saw another person. She was dressed all in white. White boots, white shirt, white jacket, and white, flowing skirt. A black belt was looped around her waist. I had no idea where she'd come from. She'd just appeared.

She glided across the floor toward me. Her feet didn't seem to touch the ground. Long platinum hair flowed in waves down her back. As she neared, I realized she was insubstantial.

I tilted my head, wondering what and who she was.

She passed through the bars and stood in my cell. The eidolon tilted her head, watching me. "You do not belong here." Her voice was like the quaking of aspen leaves on a breezy summer day.

"No." I shook my head, and tears sprung to my eyes. "I don't think I do."

She moved closer and reached for my hand. "Your heart is pure."

"I try to do what's right." I placed my hand in hers, like Mavros' vapor, somehow it felt solid.

She looked up toward the guardroom. "Why have they caged you, child?"

"A demon is bound to me." I lowered my chin to my chest, hoping she wouldn't judge me. "His power lies dormant within me."

She bent forward and lifted my chin. "Dormant? How?" The tendrils that made up her body shifted and flowed, constantly changing her appearance.

"By his doing." I had a hard time figuring out where to focus when looking at her. Normally, I looked people in the eyes, but hers were just dark, empty sockets.

She paced from one end of my cell to the other. "The demon willingly did that?"

"I summoned him to help me defeat Argentum." I pulled my legs up and rested my chin on them, staring across the floor. "I could've told him to kill Argentum for me, but I didn't think that would be right. I really hoped I could make Argentum see that I wasn't bad." The memory of his death wasn't as traumatic as it had been, but the guilt was still substantial. I had ended the life of an ancient being, and I'd hungered for his blood. "I wanted everyone to walk away. Nobody needed to die." I tugged my hand through my hair, still unsure if I'd made the right decision about fighting him myself. "Anyway, I commanded the demon to magnify my power, so I could do it myself. Apparently, demon magic doesn't play well with human magic." I looked up at her, hoping she could see what this meant. "He held back. He could've destroyed me. Whether it was to be free from the curse or to keep me from dying, I owed him for that. Instead, to pacify the Nephilim, I returned him to the Abyss with his blessing."

Her hair seemed to blow on an invisible breeze. She stared at me through hollow eyes. "You—" she tilted her head, looking at me like she couldn't quite fathom what I'd said "—have a demon who is loyal to you?"

"Yeah." I thought about how he'd come to me in my dream and somehow washed Troy's blood off of me and healed my wounds. A faint smile tugged on my lips. "I do."

She glided out of my cage, floating through the bars. Her form started to fade.

"Wait!" My chest tightened at the thought of being alone again. "Please. Who are you? Can you help me?"

She turned and for just an instant, her face looked like a skull. "I am."

I waited for her to say more, but she didn't. "You are who?"

"No." She shook her head. "I am. I always have been." Like steam rising from a pot, she disappeared momentarily. "I don't know if I will help you. Though you seem pure of heart and soul, the Nephilim are just. There must be a reason you have been imprisoned."

"It's because of my attachment to Mavros."

"He is the demon?"

"Yeah." I walked to the cell door and clutched the bars. "The silver-haired fairies, a gold dragon, a pegasus, and a unicorn all told the Nephilim to leave me alone."

"Then why are you here?" She faded and reformed.

I shrugged. "I believe this is a rogue band. A few of the Nephilim seemed to be on my side. Hopefully, they still are." I looked up, but I couldn't see inside the guardroom from here.

I wondered if they were watching me have a conversation with the phantom or if they were up there celebrating my capture and humiliation. "Sebastian and Troy fear my connection to Mavros. Can you do something to the blood on the floor, break the wards, so he can get me out of here?"

"I am … not sure what is right." Her form separated, then flowed back together. "I have always seen the righteous path. It spreads out before me like a sunbeam shining through the clouds." She floated away. "I must determine the honorable route and take it."

Then she was gone, and I was cold, hungry, and alone.

Chapter 3

My Captors

Something woke me. My eyes jolted open, and I stared into the unending darkness, listening. There was nothing, though. No hum from a furnace or air conditioner. No owls hooting or coyotes howling, no wind blowing. I suddenly felt more alone than I ever had.

Deciding it had been nothing, I closed my eyes and tried to go back to sleep. That was when I heard it.

A footstep.

Then another.

Somebody was cautiously edging toward my cage.

Pretending like I was still asleep, I rolled away from the bars. The steps stopped. As soon as I quit moving, they crept closer.

The key jangled as if it had been lifted from its hook.

My breathing accelerated. Whoever was out there had to have heard it. I tried to take deep breaths, but the terror rising inside me overruled my desires.

The key jiggled against the metal, and the lock clicked as it opened. I jumped to my feet, not wanting to be completely defenseless.

A flashlight shone in my eyes. I couldn't see anything but blinding light. "You heard me." Troy laughed. The sound made my heart plummet. "I'll have to be quieter next time." He moved closer, and I lifted my arm, shielding my eyes.

"What do you want?" My voice was raspy. I hadn't had anything to eat or drink since the night before my ill-fated run.

He grabbed my arm and yanked it, spinning me around and pinning my hand to the middle of my back. The light went out, and I was surrounded by complete darkness and Troy. "I want to know how you got my blood off of your face." He reached his other arm around me and tilted my head back until it rested on his shoulder. "I want to know how you healed yourself."

"I don't know." Panic cracked my voice.

"Liar." The word was breathed right into my ear and sent chills down my back.

I grabbed his wrist with my free hand, trying to loosen his hold on me, and he jerked my other arm, making my shoulder pop. "I dreamed—" a sob followed, and I hated that this man could make me cry. I wanted to be stronger, but without my magic and my guardians, I was nothing but a scared kid. "—I was clean and healed." Tears ran down the side of my face and into my ears. "When I woke up, I was."

He tossed me away from him, and I smacked into the bars. My lip split open on contact. I slid to the ground and gently pressed my fingertips to my mouth. "Why do you hate me?"

"Who were you talking to?"

"You." The word came out of me filled with more venom than I figured I could muster under these conditions. "Why do *you* hate me?"

I felt his breath on my face and realized he'd knelt right in front of me. "Don't test my patience." He grabbed my jumpsuit at the throat and yanked me toward him. "Who were you talking to earlier?"

Now, I understood. He wasn't about to answer my question. "An eidolon."

"A what?"

"A ghost, a spirit, a specter, an apparition."

"Tell the truth."

I grabbed his hands, and he slammed my head back. The crack echoed through the enormous room. I pressed my palm to the back of my skull and clenched my teeth, biting back the things I wanted to say, holding the pain and the tears at bay. "I. Am. Not. Lying."

He let go of me, and I assumed he stood. "A few days without food or water, and we'll see if you still feel like playing games." The cage door shut with a crash. "If I were you, Princess, I'd sleep with one eye open." He laughed as he walked off.

Rage, hot and furious, shot through my body. For just a split second, I thought I saw blue sparks flicker across my fingers, but it had to have been my imagination.

Once his footsteps were gone, I focused inside, thinking about my magic, hoping that even with the collar on, I could see it. The room was darker than normal. I glanced around and saw nothing. Cautiously, I stepped forward, feeling the ground with my foot before setting it down, not willing to hurt either serpent.

Even though they were bound, they should have been there. Coiled up somewhere, sleeping in the shadows. I kept searching, nearly giving up hope several times.

Finally, I found them. Their bodies were wrapped around each other. Their heads buried somewhere out of sight, protected from harm while they slept. Mavros' obsidian serpent sparkled slightly. As I strode closer to them, the light seemed to intensify, shining directly on the snakes.

Sharp pain sliced through my head, and I blinked back the brightness. Another concussion, then. I'd be lucky if I ever made it out of this place. I'd be even luckier if I left without permanent brain damage.

I sat on the floor and petted the vipers, letting the contact, imagined or not, help soothe me. I lifted the ebony serpent's tail. Gold flecked its obsidian scales.

"No, no, no," I whispered. My heart thundered in my chest. I needed to figure out how to get out of here before Troy's blood destroyed Mavros' power.

There was nothing I could do about it for now, so I focused on the pearlescent snake. The light made its skin shimmer. The color danced from blue to purple, to pink, and back again. No shadows writhed on its body. No darkness lingered under the scales.

"Two days," I whispered. Rayne wanted me to wait two days after the shadows disappeared before I used my magic. Could I make it that long? Would it come back to me when I called on it?

Not wanting to be caught off-guard by the Nephilim, I patted each of the serpents, then returned to the real world. I curled on my side and rested my head on my arm. I was terrified to sleep, afraid Troy would come back, but I also hoped Mavros would come heal me again. Not even to take the pain away, but just so I wouldn't be alone.

I closed my eyes, and the world swayed. As soon as I opened them, the spinning stopped. I stared across the room. The darkness was absolute. The silence was like a living creature, waiting for the opportune moment to strike.

I pictured Cody's face, hoping and praying that the Nephilim would leave him alone, that Russ would stay close and keep him safe.

Then I focused my thoughts on my parents. The first time Sebastian and Troy had tried to abduct me, they had threatened Mom and Dad. Hopefully, in my absence, the dragons were keeping my family safe, too.

At least Samantha and Dan were okay … or should be. My friends deserved a reprieve from my life.

Sleep eventually embraced me.

Cash and I jog down the road. My pace is slower than normal. For once, I don't feel like I'm being hunted. My breath puffs out in front of me, tiny white clouds clinging to the air for the briefest of moments. Our footfalls pound against the ground, a steady rhythm. We turn, and my steps slow. Without my magic, my energy drains faster, and I fall behind.

A bright light flashes in front of us. Then several more flare around us, separating Cash and me. Sebastian steps out of a portal. Lifting his hands, he stalks toward me. His honey-colored ponytail bounces against his back. "You used the demon's magic again."

My focus is entirely on him. I don't realize someone is behind me until a collar snaps into place around my neck. Cash had drained my magic before we left, but now, it's gone. There's an emptiness where it had been, a feeling of profound loss.

Troy slices his arm open and holds it to my mouth. Gold-flecked blood runs down my throat. Somewhere in the background, I hear Cash roar, and I hope they're not hurting him.

The Nephilim take me through one of the portals, then another.

Someone kicks the bottom of my foot.

I look around, but Troy is the only one with me.

"Wake up," someone said as they nudged my foot again.

I opened my eyes, then quickly pinched them shut. Pain, brought on by the light, pierced my skull.

He tapped my foot with his. "Get up."

I cracked one eyelid and assessed the Nephilim who stared down at me. I hadn't seen this one before. He had a friendly face framed by dark brown waves. He didn't look much older than me, but if they sent him to cozy up to me, it wasn't going to work. I didn't trust him any more than I trusted Troy, Sebastian, or the man with the scarred face.

I rolled over, and the world spun. I made it to my hands and knees before I heaved. Blood spilled out of my mouth, covering the man's boot.

"What the Hell?" He jumped back in time for me to hurl again.

My head throbbed, and there was a constant ringing in my ears. I lifted my hand to the base of my skull and, through the blood crusted in my hair, felt a huge lump. I winced and jerked my hand away. "Sorry." I looked up at the Nephilim. He was staring at his boot like an alien had given birth on it. "Concussion."

He shook his head, then reached his hand down to me. Like all the other Nephilim, he was muscular, but unlike the others, he didn't look at me like I was pond scum.

I slid my hand into his, and he tugged me to my feet. As soon as he let go of me, the spinning began again. I stumbled back against the bars of the cage.

He pulled a radio off of his belt. "The prisoner needs medical attention. She believes she has a concussion, and I'm inclined to agree with her assessment."

Static came across from the other side. Then a male voice answered. "Don't trust her for an instant. She's dangerous."

The Nephilim in my cage narrowed his steel-gray eyes at me and tilted his head. "Not today, she isn't. She's as pale as a ghost. She can barely stand."

"Don't let your guard down," the voice said, and this time I recognized it as Sebastian's. "I'll send a medic."

I leaned heavily against the cage, clutching the bars with one hand, watching the man out of the corner of my eye, waiting for him to turn on me like the others had.

Shaking some of my vomit off of his boot, he stepped toward me and stretched his hand out. I instinctively shrank back. He pressed his eyes closed and shook his head. "Whatever they did to you, I'm sorry." He lifted my arm over his shoulders, guided me away from the puke, and lowered me to the ground.

"He didn't come back." My voice was hoarse and weak, but he heard me.

"Who didn't come back?"

Somewhere in the back of my mind, I knew I shouldn't be telling him this. I knew that no matter what he looked like, no matter how he sounded, he wasn't my friend. "He didn't come back to heal me." I wiped my sleeve across my mouth. "I thought he would. I thought I'd be better." Tears dripped off of my chin.

The Nephilim reached out barely touching my lip. "Who did this to you?"

"Troy." My gaze darted around. I was afraid he would overhear and take it out on me. "He hates me."

The guy sighed. "Yeah, he does."

I clutched my head and bent over. The throbbing was the steady beat of a bass drum. The ringing in my ears was a screaming guitar solo.

"Close your eyes." He knelt in front of me, his guard completely down. "I won't hurt you."

I shot him a look that said I wasn't dumb enough to believe that.

He set his hand on my shoulder. There was no malice in the gesture. It was soothing. "I promise."

I lay on my side, pressing my face to the cold cement. "You need to act like I'm dangerous." My words were slow and slurred, but I needed to tell him. I needed more people like him to come into my cell and fewer people like Troy to. "You need to realize that I could take that sword and run you through with it. You wouldn't be the first."

A surprised laugh escaped from his full lips. "Yeah, you're a hurt, scared kid."

"It's true, though." I flattened myself on the ground. The pounding dulled slightly. "Besides, you're not much older than me."

He rubbed his stubbled chin. "But, I was never a kid."

He was one of them, but I was grateful to have someone to talk to, to not be alone for a little while anyway. "What's that supposed to mean?"

"We're trained, basically from birth, to fight evil." He looked me over from my head to my feet. "Which you are clearly not."

I rolled my eyes, then pressed them shut to stop the stabbing pain. "Troy and Sebastian will fight you on that one." I wondered where the medic was and if they would even bother to help me anyway.

He sat down and stretched his legs out, staring down them at his boot. "I'm gonna need new shoes."

"Sorry." I was surprised to find that I really was. "I wish I would've puked on Troy's instead."

He chuckled and flexed his foot. The look on his face turned to one of pure disgust. "You always throw up blood?" He tilted his head toward me, and his eyes softened somewhat. "You might have a problem."

I remembered feasting on Argentum's flesh, savoring the power in his blood, wanting to drain every drop, then puking it all over the place once I'd become human again. "More often than I'd like."

Footsteps approached the cage. I looked through the bars and saw Troy and Sebastian with a silver-haired Nephilim. "And, I have a lot of problems right now." I started to push myself up.

"Don't let her move, Liam." Troy's words were a command that the Nephilim with me couldn't disobey. "She's more dangerous than she looks."

"She can barely move right now, sir." Liam put his hand on my shoulder. Then he lowered his voice. "Stay down. Don't anger him."

I snorted. "Me being alive angers him." I remained where I was, though, not moving at all. I didn't want to give him any reason to slam my head into the bars again.

Troy opened the cell, and Sebastian swept his arm in front of him, indicating the woman should enter first. As soon as Sebastian stepped inside, he pulled the door shut. "Stay out, Troy."

The woman carried a medical bag. She inched toward me, waiting for Sebastian's okay. "Go ahead, Vicki. Give her what she needs."

I couldn't believe he approved treatment for me. Though he had never been as hostile toward me as Troy, it was rather obvious that he didn't like me either.

The woman started giving orders as soon as she had Sebastian's approval. "Troy, go get her a cot, a pillow, and a blanket. Liam, get her some crackers and water."

I wished she would have sent Sebastian away instead, but at least my cage was about to become more comfortable.

She knelt next to me. Sebastian nodded, and the other two left to obey the woman's commands.

"Hello." She pulled a blood pressure cuff out of her bag and wrapped it around my arm. When she finished with it, she took my pulse and shone a light in my eyes.

The pain in my head flared, and I winced in response.

She helped me into a sitting position, and the room spun again. My stomach lurched, and I gagged. Luckily for her, there was nothing left for me to throw up.

"Are you okay?" There was a business-like tone to her voice, but some sympathy was mingled in with it.

I pressed my hands to the ground to keep from toppling over. "I probably won't die yet."

She listened to my lungs, then grabbed my hand and slowly lifted it. Rolling my sleeve up, she pulled a syringe out of her bag and filled it with a transparent solution.

I flicked my gaze from the needle to her brown eyes. "What … what is that?" My lips trembled, and I swallowed hard, hating the fear that I felt.

"It will help fight the nausea. When Liam gets back, I'll give you acetaminophen for your headache." She wiped my arm off with alcohol and gave me the shot. Then she focused on Sebastian. "This needs cleaned up, or she needs moved to a different cell."

"She's not moving."

I jumped at the sound of Troy's voice. I'd been so focused on Vicki that I hadn't heard him come back.

He stood outside the bars with the supplies she'd sent him after. "The demon can't get past the wards I set." He pointed at the giant crossbow. "And, the dragons can't get past that. This is hers for the duration of her stay."

Sebastian nodded and pulled his radio out. "I'll call for Micah to clean it up."

"Nobody lays a hand on her." Vicki stared intently at Troy.

He pointed his finger toward his chest. "I don't make promises I can't keep. You know what she is, what she's done."

"I also know Khione said to leave her alone." Her voice hardened further, showing her disapproval. She nodded toward a clean area on the floor. "Set her bed up over there."

Troy grumbled the whole time, but he did as she ordered.

When Liam came back down, Vicki took the bottle of water from him and handed it to me. "Sip slowly." She waited for me to drink a little, then handed me the crackers. "You need to eat a couple of these so you can take the medicine."

While I chewed on a cracker, I looked at Liam's feet. The boots he was wearing were worn but free of my puke. "Nice shoes," I said.

He smiled at me but otherwise didn't respond.

The man with the scarred face clomped down the stairs, carrying a bucket and mop. He set them down while he unlocked the cage. "I am not a maid."

"Micah." Sebastian's voice was a stern warning.

Micah cleaned my puke up while I ate the tube of crackers. I couldn't help but smile. I was sure he and Troy would make me pay for it later, but for now, I was enjoying their annoyance.

My eyes kept drifting shut, but since I didn't want to sleep with these people in my cell, I forced them open again and again.

"The anti-nausea medicine makes some people drowsy." Vicki stood and stretched her hand out to me. Once I was on my feet, she pulled my arm over her shoulders and wrapped hers around my waist, leading me to the cot. "Get some rest. Someone will bring you lunch, then take you to the showers." She pointed to a door on the far end of the room past the crossbow.

"Thank you."

She pulled the blanket over me, and against my will, my eyes drifted shut.

I was in that place where you're not awake but not really asleep when I heard Troy ask, "Why are you taking care of her?"

"She's a kid." Vicki's voice was stern and agitated.

He huffed out a humorless laugh. "So was Draconian once." The cell door shut, and the lock clicked into place. "Look what he did without a demon's help."

Their voices floated off as they walked farther away or as sleep overcame me.

Chapter 4

A Little Slice Of Freedom

The scent of food woke me. My stomach grumbled in response, and I sat up gingerly, afraid of how my body would react to the movement. I was shocked when the world didn't spin. Even more surprising was the fact that they had let Liam bring me lunch. After he'd let his guard down this morning, I never thought I would see him again.

He handed me a tray. Then looked at my cot and said, "May I?"

"Sure." I scooted over, and he sat beside me.

I dipped my spoon into the thick stew and held it up in front of me. Steam rose into the air, so I blew on it before cautiously taking a bite.

"We're not going to poison you." He watched me. A crooked grin tugged at his lips. "You know?"

I swallowed the food in my mouth before saying, "I didn't want to get burned." I filled my spoon and held it above my bowl. "Besides, I don't think poison would work. Death would probably just send me back again."

"Again?" He choked on the bite he'd shoveled into his mouth. "What do you mean?"

"So, you really know nothing about me, huh?" I shook my head and took a bite.

He looked me over. "You're supposed to be dangerous, corrupted, and untrustworthy."

"That's all they told you?" I shook my head. "Figures." I wiped my mouth on the napkin from my tray. "I'm a … well I guess, I'm a witch. I saved the world from a demon just a coupla months after learning how to control my magic. I freed fifteen dragons from a crazed wizard."

"That's why they protect you?"

I nodded. "They feel like they owe me a debt that can never be repaid. Then I killed myself—"

"Wait." He held up his hand to silence me. "You killed yourself."

"I stabbed myself in the heart"—I mimicked the action with my spoon—"to keep Mavros, the demon who is now bound to me, from killing my friends or terrorizing the world. That's where you all come in."

"So, why are you here?"

I couldn't help but wonder if I was making a mistake by opening up to him, but this was all stuff I assumed Sebastian and Troy already knew. "Because a demon is bound to me, so obviously, I'm evil."

"Hmph." He waved at me to continue eating. "You need to finish, so you can shower and change. I even scrounged up a toothbrush for you."

That made my lips pull up in a smile. My mouth had tasted like blood or puke since they'd thrown me in here. "Did they send you to play good cop?"

"Maybe." He lifted his shoulder to his ear and shot me an impish grin.

"Well, your buddies know all of that stuff already." I scraped every bit of stew out of my bowl since I didn't know when they would deign to feed me again. As soon as I finished the last of it, I said, "Okay."

He moved my tray's contents to his, set his tray on top of mine, and put them on the floor. Then he stood. He turned his eyes downward. "I have to cuff you. I'm sorry."

A lump formed in my throat, and I swallowed hard, hoping not to cry, not to show any emotion at all. I stood and turned around. I should have foreseen this. After all, I was their prisoner, but I hadn't expected it from him. I'd been stupid.

He was gentler than Troy had been. The plastic band was nowhere near as tight this time. When he finished, he grabbed my arm at the elbow and led me to the cell door. I looked up at him while he pulled the key out and unlocked it. He was at least six inches taller than me and probably weighed close to a hundred and twenty pounds more than I did.

He swung the door open and held onto my arm as we strolled across the floor. The cement froze my feet, and I longed to have my shoes and socks back.

The room was bigger than it appeared from my cage. As we traipsed across it, the silence ate away at me. I felt like he was marching me to my doom. I didn't know what to say to him, but who knew how long it would be before I had company again? "You know, there are some Nephilim who actually like me."

"Oh." His eyebrows pinched together. "What brought that on?"

I looked at the enormous crossbow, realizing it stood nearly as tall as Malcolm did in dragon form. "The silence was too much, and I have no idea how to talk to people like you."

"Like me?" He cocked his head.

Maybe that hadn't been the best thing to say, but it was true. "Yeah. My captors."

He walked a few more steps, and when I thought he would just ignore me, he waved his other hand. "So, who are they?"

"Diana …" My voice trailed off, and I realized I had no idea what her last name was or even if Nephilim had last names. "Blonde hair, sky blue eyes. And, I think I was starting to grow on Olivia. Dark hair—"

"Pale green eyes." His voice had a faraway, star-struck sound to it.

"Yeah, that's her."

"For what's it's worth—" he opened the door and ushered me in "—I don't dislike you."

"Sure."

I stepped into the shower room and stopped, staring around. A jolt of panic shot through me. I wrapped my arms around my stomach as it plummeted. Sweat beaded at my temples. There were no enclosures, no curtains. A couple of sinks and toilets stood out in the open with no stalls. A bench sat along one wall with soap, towels, and a change of clothes on it. Tears filled my eyes. I couldn't do this. I couldn't shower in front of him.

He pulled a knife out of one of the many pockets on his pants. A cold chill spread through my core, and I backed away from him. He grabbed my arm and spun me around, slicing through the cuffs on my wrists. Then he pointed at the door. "This is the only way in or out. I'll wait on the other side." He tapped his radio. "Don't take too long or they'll make me come in and check on you."

Relief flooded my body, hitting me so hard that my knees weakened. I reached out to grab his arm but stopped short, afraid he'd take it the wrong way. "If you like me, really and not just good cop like me, tell Olivia I'm here. Please."

"I'd love to, Dacia." He held my gaze. His gray eyes filled with remorse. "But, I have to follow orders."

My shoulders slumped. I thought maybe that would be my escape route. I thought maybe Diana and Olivia could get me out of here to keep the Nephilim from going to war with the dragons.

"Ten minutes." He walked outside, and the lock on the door clicked into place.

The water was lukewarm at best, but I would've stayed under its stream all day to keep from going back to my cell.

However, since I didn't want Liam to come in while I was still undressed, I tried to hurry.

Washing my hair wasn't as easy as it should've been. Where Troy had slammed my head against the bars, dried blood clumped the strands together.

Praying I had enough time left to get dressed, I twisted a towel around my head and wrapped one around my body. Expecting another jumpsuit and pair of men's boxers, I looked down at the clothes they'd left for me. My chest swelled when I realized they were mine, and underneath them were my shoes.

I dried off quickly and was just starting to get dressed when the doorknob turned. Dropping my underwear on the floor, I snatched the towel up and held it in front of me. "Please." My lip trembled.

The door opened a crack. "Time's up." Liam stepped inside. As soon as he saw me, he looked down at his foot.

"Please, can I have a couple more minutes?" Panic filled my voice, making it crack. I felt like a teenage boy going through puberty.

"Make it quick." He didn't so much as sneak a peek at me on his way out, and even though I had promised myself I wouldn't let him get close to me, I found myself liking him a little more. As he pulled the door shut, he added, "Knock when you're ready."

I wiped the towel over my face. Then, before he changed his mind, I dressed as quickly as I could. Walking to the door, I dragged my hands through my hair, pulling out the tangles. After knocking, I stepped to the side.

When Liam opened the door, I turned around and held my hands together behind my back. I hoped that if I was on my best behavior the others might start treating me differently.

He bound my hands, grabbed my elbow, and led me back through the room to my cage. I took in everything as we walked across the vast space. Besides, the shower room, there were a few other doors on each wall.

The cell was too close. We'd be there too soon. My breaths quickened like I'd been running. My heart raced, and my stomach churned. I pulled against Liam, trying to slow him down.

"Dacia, don't." His voice was stern.

"Please"—tears welled up in my eyes—"can we take our time?"

He looked above the cages at the guardroom. They must have signaled him somehow because he said, "If you'll talk to me, we could make a lap around the room."

"Okay." I swallowed and bent my head toward my shoulder to wipe off my tears. "What?"

"Troy wants to know how you healed." He nodded to whoever was watching and turned us back around.

Though I was grateful not to be heading to my cell, my heart felt like it was shrinking. A bitter smile tugged at my lips. I dropped my chin to my chest and shook my head. "So, this is all good cop, bad cop." I lifted my hand just slightly before realizing I couldn't pull it through my hair. "I told him. He gave me a concussion, and I fell asleep. When I woke up, I was healed. I have no idea how. I can't feel my magic. There's this …" I wasn't sure how to explain what I felt. I looked up at the ceiling high above me. "This bottomless pit inside of me now.

There's nothing there." I looked into his gray eyes, hoping he'd believe me. "Maybe the healing is just part of me."

"Nah." He shook his head. "If it was, I wouldn't have to get new boots."

I couldn't help the surprised laugh that escaped from me. "No, that's probably true." I chewed on my lip for a second. "But, I really don't know."

"Next question then." He slowed down a little. "Why does the demon help you?" He looked at me like he was genuinely curious.

I wondered if it was a mask he could slip on like Cody used his expressionless one or if he really was. "Mavros appeared right before my eighteenth birthday. In order to break the dragon's curse on him, he needed to be bound to a mortal. He thought it needed to be a physical bond, so because of my power and because I'm a ..." Heat crept up my face, and I glanced at Liam, not sure what to say.

"Because you're what?" His nose scrunched up, confusion and curiosity mixed together. The result was an endearing expression that I didn't want to see on one of my captor's faces. I didn't want to like him.

I lowered my head and watched our feet. My voice dropped. "I'm a virgin."

He chuckled and wiped his hand over his mouth.

"What?"

Shaking his head, he said, "I thought you were going to say something horrible about yourself."

"Oh."

He squeezed my arm. "There's nothing wrong with being a virgin."

"Maybe." I looked around. "But, when you're being held prisoner by a bunch of men who hate you, it's not something you want made public information."

Anger darkened his expression. "None of us would—"

"What?" I stopped moving, and he nearly stumbled. "Bash a defenseless girl's head against the bars? Starve somebody? Give your prisoner nothing to drink? Make her strip down in front of you and wash with freezing water out of a bucket?"

He glared up at the guardroom. Then, as he turned toward me, his expression softened. "I'm sorry they did that to you, Dacia. I won't let them know that you're a virgin."

"Thank you." I stepped forward, walking slowly. "Anyway, Mavros thought I was what he needed. When I wouldn't give into him in that form, he came to me as Damon. He tried to befriend me, and I played along because when he was Damon he didn't try to control me." I pinched my eyes closed and remembered those days, the turmoil it created with Cody, and the friendship I'd gained with Damon. "When I killed myself, Mavros realized he didn't want me to die. He tried to save me."

He rubbed his chin. "But, why?"

"When Argentum summoned Mavros back to kill me, he told me nobody had ever treated him with kindness before, and until I was dying in his arms, he didn't realize what he felt for me. After what he put me through, I didn't believe him. It took me a long time to trust him again." I felt a pang in my chest and realized that talking about him and thinking about Cody made me miss my friends even more. I couldn't imagine what my parents and Cody were going through. I doubted Malcolm and Cash could hold their human forms for very long. If I ever made it back to them, I didn't think they would let me out of their sight again. If I didn't make it back, Cash would never forgive himself. "Mavros found ways to get around Argentum's commands to keep me alive long enough so I could find out his true name and return him to the Abyss. Then when I needed him to help me defeat Argentum, he was there. He could've let me die, you know?"

Liam just shook his head. I didn't think he'd expected me to tell him quite so much, but the cage was getting closer, and I wasn't ready to be thrown in there and left alone again. "Why didn't he? He's a demon."

"I changed him. When he loaned me his power, he became bound to me." I never realized how hard it was to talk without using my hands. My arms kept twisting and jerking. I imagined I looked like a fool, but I couldn't help it. "I didn't know it, though. The curse was broken, but he still let me return him to the Abyss." I watched the cage moving closer and hoped Liam would turn away from it again. When he did, I let out the breath I'd been holding. "When I killed Argentum, a piece of him stayed inside of me and merged with my magic. Mavros came back to help me destroy it. If not for that, he would still be sunning himself on a beach in another realm, and I would probably be free."

He lifted a single eyebrow, and his lips pinched together as he shook his head. "Is that what he told you?"

"He didn't need to. It's what I saw when I went to him to ask for help."

Chapter 5

Bad Cop, Good Cop

On the next round, Liam took me inside the cage. I knew it was coming, but that didn't make it any easier. While he cut my cuffs off, he mouthed in my ear, "Your secret's safe with me."

"Thanks." I managed a shaky smile before he picked up the trays off the floor and left me alone again.

Once he was gone, I looked around for something, anything to do, but there was nothing. I lay down on the cot and focused on my power. This time I knew where to find the serpents. They were still coiled together. I couldn't tell that they'd moved at all since the last time I visited them.

More gold glinted on Mavros' snake's body. How long would it be before he was no longer bound to me? What would happen to Mavros and the power he'd left inside of me?

I sat next to them and gently trailed my fingers over my magic's body. The pearlescent scales shimmered in the dim light that came from nowhere but my own imagination. I had no idea why I'd pictured my magic here. Usually, I was drawn to nature. Maybe I'd dreamed up a darkened room because my powers were trapped inside of me and not free to go where they wanted.

While I petted the serpent, I watched for any sign of lingering shadows. When I was sure there were none, I let out a relieved breath and stood. "One more day," I whispered.

When I opened my eyes, Troy stood above me. His posture was stiff. His gray t-shirt wouldn't have looked any tighter if it had been painted on him. His brown eyes narrowed as he glowered at me. "One more day 'til what?"

I tried to sit up, but he pressed down on my shoulder, holding me in place. "Don't. Move."

My heartbeat thundered against my chest. The desire to bolt like a scared rabbit pulsed through my veins, but I knew if I so much as twitched, he'd hurt me. Even so, I hated lying flat on my back while he stood over me.

"One. More. Day. What?" The tendons in his neck bulged.

I swallowed hard and hoped my voice would work. "I've been here one more day."

My head was knocked to the side when he backhanded me. I never even saw it coming. Blood shot out of my mouth, spraying the floor of my cell. I reached for my cheek, but he pressed my hand down.

He lowered his face until his nose nearly touched mine. Through clenched teeth, he said, "One more day 'til what?" His breath was hot and smelled like onions.

Tears streamed down my face, and I hated myself for crying in front of him. "Until nothing." I pressed my eyes closed. "What could I possibly have to look forward to here?"

He stood and walked away from me, clenching and unclenching his fists. "You have no idea how much I'd like to beat the truth out of you."

While his back was turned, I sat up and pressed my hand to my cheek. It was swollen already. My tongue ran along my lip. I jerked my head back and whimpered. It was split open and fat. "I think I do." I should've kept my mouth shut, but he brought out the worst in me. "It's not that hard to imagine."

"His hold on you is weakening. The demon taint isn't nearly as strong." He walked over to the cell door and looked over his shoulder. "You might wanna consider telling me the truth." He slammed the door shut behind him, then walked around the outside, checking the wards he'd set up.

When he neared the side I was on, I stood and moved to the center of the cage, out of reach.

He sneered at me. "Sleep good tonight … not too soundly, though.

Once he was gone, I pulled my cot away from the bars. Then I curled up on my side and cried into my pillow.

Mavros leans against an ancient oak tree on the top of a hill. Its branches are twisted and unruly. I have no idea where we are, but it's peaceful, secluded, and warm enough that I don't need a coat. The setting sun tints the sky in shades of pink and orange.

He stares out at a lake. His hands are shoved into his pockets with his thumbs sticking out over the top. He turns, and as soon as he sees me, walking toward him, his lips pull back, baring his teeth. "What have they done now?" The words are a low growl that makes chills dance along my spine.

He doesn't wait for me to answer. He strides toward me and tilts my head so he can see the bruises better. "I'll kill every one of them."

"No." I shake my head. "Some of them have been good to me."

He takes my hand in his, linking our fingers. "Do you want me to heal you?"

I start to nod but stop. "No, I can't let you. If I wake up healed again—" my voice catches on a sob. I turn into Mavros and press my undamaged cheek against his chest.

He wraps his arms around me and whispers, "It'll be all right, Dacia." Even though he's trying to be gentle, I can feel his rage in every movement he makes.

"Why hasn't Malcolm come?" I hate the brokenness of my voice. With the giant crossbow, I knew he couldn't come as a dragon, but he could teleport in invisible and then back out without them knowing until I was gone.

Mavros kisses my forehead tenderly, then steps back. "The Nephilim and dragons have not gotten along for centuries."

"Short answer, please." I cross my arms, gripping my biceps. "I don't know how long I have."

He nods, and flames swirl in his irises. "They have figured out a frequency that disrupts the dragons' magic. If Malcolm tries to teleport in, he will arrive in dragon form, visible. If we don't come up with a plan to get you out soon, he will come in with Cash, damn the consequences."

"No. He can't." Panic thrums inside me. My heart feels like it's banging against my ribs, fighting for freedom. I can't let him risk his life to save mine. I know the dragons think they owe me, but they don't owe me their lives. "If I can access my power, I can use it late tomorrow night. Tell him to wait." I drag my hand through my hair. "Unless you come up with a foolproof plan, wait to see if I can get out on my own."

He nods. I can tell that he doesn't want to wait. He wants to charge in and kill them all for what they've done. "I'll tell them, Dacia, but I don't know if they'll agree."

Something startled me awake. I jerked to a sitting position, expecting to find Troy standing over me, his ever-present scowl in place, but it was Liam. He walked down the stairs carefully balancing two trays. It smelled like dinner, if I got to eat it, would be more of the same stew that I'd had for lunch.

I crossed my arms over my chest, tucking my hands into my armpits. I figured that was about the least threatening position for me to be in.

He set one tray on the floor while he unlocked the cage, then he watched me vigilantly while he picked it back up. As soon as he was in, he kicked his foot up behind him, closing the door. He handed me one tray and set the other on my cot. Then he backed toward the door and locked us in together.

My heart plummeted a little. "Why so cautious now?"

"They're watching." He raised his eyes toward the guard-room.

I took a bite of the soup. When my teeth pressed together, pain shot through my face. I winced but tried not to let Liam see how much it hurt. "Weren't they earlier?"

"Yes." He looked at my face and rubbed his hand over his mouth. Anger flashed in his steel eyes. "Troy?"

"How'd ya guess?"

He shook his head and sat down next to me. "You were asleep when I brought the food last time. Then you were cuffed when we weren't eating. I don't want them to see me sloughing off and only allow Troy or Micah in here with you." He brushed his thumb along my cheek. "I'll get an icepack for you when you finish eating."

"Thanks." Even though it hurt, I scraped every last bite from the bowl.

He took my tray from me and set it on the floor. "If you don't mind being cuffed, I can take you to the shower room so you can, uh, relieve yourself."

I couldn't help but wonder how he would've worded it if I wasn't a girl.

"Otherwise—" he pointed at the hole in the floor before standing up.

I looked over at it and shook my head. Without a word, I stood and held my hands together behind my back.

As we neared the crossbow, I slowed. "What is that? I keep calling it a big crossbow thing in my head, but I know there's got to be a different name for it."

"Why do you call it anything in your head?" He looked down at me through the corner of his eyes.

"Because." I shrugged. "I have nothing to do but look around the room, get the crap beat out of me, and wonder what the ginormous crossbow thingy is called. I keep thinking trebuchet, but I know that's not right."

His head snapped back slightly, and he looked like I'd slapped him across the face. "It's a ballista."

"I'm sorry." My voice was soft. "I shouldn't have said that."

A humorless laugh huffed out of him. "Why not? It's true." He held the door open for me. A screen had been set up around one of the toilets, creating a makeshift stall. He locked the door, then cut the tie loose from my wrist. "It's hard to pretend I'm still one of the good guys when I find you bruised and broken." He nodded toward the toilets. "I was told to stay."

I nodded and strode across the room, pretending I didn't care, that it didn't bother me at all, but it did. No matter how hard I tried, I couldn't understand why the Nephilim wanted me caged. I wasn't bad. I hadn't done anything to deserve this.

When I finished, I trudged across the room toward him. My hair hung in front of my eyes, and I watched the ground instead of him. I felt like I'd been stripped bare for all to see. I knew it wasn't his fault. He wasn't calling the shots, but the last couple of days had been the most humiliating of my life. When I stood in front of him, I turned around and waited to be cuffed again.

"If you'll talk to me, we can walk for a while." He put the zip tie on even looser this time. I probably could've slid my hands out of it if I would have tried. When he finished, he spun me around. "I don't mean to make this uncomfortable for you."

"I'm a prisoner." I turned my face away from him. "I shouldn't expect anything else."

He squeezed my arm gently and led me out into the main room.

"So, I suppose you want to know what one more day means." I looked up at the guardroom. Sebastian watched us. His hands were clasped behind his back, and I imagined him in cuffs. The thought brought a smile to my lips. Troy stood next to him. His arms were folded across his chest, and it looked like his shirt might split along the seams if he flexed just a little more. All brawn, no brain.

Liam nodded. "That's what Troy sent me to find out."

"It means the same thing I told him." I tore my gaze away from the Nephilim above us. "I've been here one more day, and I'm no closer to getting out."

"You sure that's all?" He let go of my arm for just a moment.

I glanced up to see what kind of reaction that would get from the peanut gallery. They either didn't notice or didn't care. "You ever see the movies where prisoners mark down how many days it's been with a rock or chalk? It's because it feels like I haven't seen my friends or family for months. I'm bored out of my mind, I don't know if it's morning or night, if anything exists outside of this room, and I made it through one more day."

He put his hand on my back and turned me to make another lap. "Maybe I can find you a book or something."

"Really?" A smile spread over my face, and I cringed from the pain of it. If I could've, I would've pressed my hand to my cheek. Instead, I tilted it toward my shoulder.

Liam's eyes darkened, and he turned his head glaring up at Troy. "Have you heard from your friends?" He looked at me and tapped his temple.

My shoulders slumped forward. "No." I didn't know they knew the dragons could speak in my mind. "Not a whisper." I swallowed over the lump in my throat. "Maybe they're glad to be rid of me. They can go back to the lives they had before Draconian."

"Come on, now, Dacia." He stopped me and wiped the tears off my cheeks, careful not to hurt me. "You don't believe that."

On the next pass, Liam led me back into my cell. He picked up the trays and set them outside before cutting off my restraints. "I'll be back with an icepack for your face."

After he climbed the stairs, the silence pressed down on me. I considered checking on my magic so I wouldn't feel quite so alone, but I was afraid I would be caught off guard again. It seemed like hours had passed by before I heard footsteps on the stairs. I looked up, expecting to see Liam with my icepack, but it was Troy.

I scrambled to my feet and moved so the cot was between me and the cell door. As Troy neared the cage, my heart tried to flee from my chest. My breath whooshed out of me. When I tried to suck it back in, it caught in my throat.

He circled the outside of my cell, checking the wards. Then he stood near the door, not looking like he had any intention of entering. He held the icepack up. "Want this?"

I nodded slightly.

"Then come get it." He smirked, knowing he'd won.

I contemplated how badly I wanted it, how much relief it would really give me.

"Ten … nine …. eight …"

I strode toward the cell door with my head held high, staring into his hate-filled eyes. I stuck my hand through the bars, palm up. "May I please have the icepack?" My voice was so sugary sweet that I thought I might throw up again.

He stepped forward and turned the icepack over so that it looked like he was going to put it in my hand. Instead, he grabbed my arm and yanked me forward. "Put your other hand out here, too."

I tried to pull free, but he was too strong.

He jerked on my arm. "Other hand. Now."

If he tugged any harder, my head would slam into the bars again. Since I didn't want another concussion, I cautiously slid my hand out.

He dropped the icepack to the ground and held onto both of my wrists with one hand. Then he reached into his pocket and drew out a zip tie. He was not gentle. He tightened the strap until I yelped, staring me in the eyes the whole time, taking pleasure from my pain.

He drew me closer and bent my arms. Using another zip tie, he hooked my bound hands to a crossbar, making it so I could barely move. Then he unlocked the door, picked up the ice pack, and entered my cell. Panic rushed through me in waves. Each one crashed against me, threatening to drag me under.

I looked over my shoulder, but I couldn't see him. I turned my head to the other side and heard him move before I spotted him. A giant swell of fear rose inside of me. It pushed up from my stomach and crashed out of me as a terrified cry. "Please—" I dropped my chin to my chest and gasped for breath "—please, don't hurt me."

He clutched the back of my neck just above the collar. "If you would quit lying … if you would realize the evil inside of you, no one would ever hurt you again." He squeezed his fingers then released, again and again. With his mouth right next to my ear, he whispered, "Even Liam doesn't believe your story about one more day."

The way he said it, the feel of his breath on the side of my face, made it more menacing than if he'd yelled it at me.

He let go of my neck and stepped back. "He believes you don't know how you healed, but he's easily deceived by appearances." His gaze roved over me, lingering far too long in some places, before he stepped out of sight. "Maybe he doesn't find you as repulsive as I do."

My cot creaked, and I guessed that he'd sat on it. Believing he was that far from me, I relaxed slightly.

"I can sit here all night." He paused, and I wondered what malicious thoughts were planting themselves in his brain. "How long can you wait?"

I looked over my shoulder, but somehow he was still out of sight. "What do you want?"

"I want to know what one more day means." His voice blasted through the room, bouncing off the walls, reverberating through the open spaces.

Rolling my neck to release some of the tension, I asked, "What do you want it to mean?" I didn't have to try too hard to muster up some tears. "Tell me—" I sniffled "—and I'll give you that answer."

The cot creaked again, and his footsteps pounded across the concrete. He grabbed my hair and jerked my head back. His teeth were clenched, and anger radiated off of him. "Your tears aren't going to work on me. What does it mean?"

"Why are you harming her, Nephilim?"

Troy released me as soon as she spoke. I turned my head slightly and saw the eidolon standing outside of the cage. She tilted her head and floated through the bars, forcing him to back away from me. "Can you not sense her soul? Do you not see that she is good?"

"She … she's, uh—" he wiped his hand down his face "— she's bound to a demon."

The phantom moved between us, making it impossible for me to see what was going on. "She is, but she is not malevolent, and he is not wholly evil any longer either."

"You can't believe that." His voice was shaky.

She put her hand on my shoulder, and the gesture was comforting. "What I believe or don't believe has no bearing on this matter. What I know does."

"Who are you?" he asked.

I knew what she was going to answer, and Troy was not going to like it.

"I am." She let go of me.

"You are what?" Frustration edged his tone.

"I am. I always have been. I always will be."

I heard shuffled steps, and I wondered if the spirit was backing him against the far side of the cage.

"Do not harm her." She floated past me, then hovered outside the cell.

I bowed my head toward her. "Thank you."

As soon as she disappeared, Troy walked out of my cage. He took out his knife and cut me loose, nicking the back of my hand. He wiped my blood off on his pants and sneered at me. "Your icepack's in there."

I pulled my hands in and moved out of his reach before holding them out in front of me and looking down at them. The cuffs had cut into my wrists. Blood had seeped along the edges, but it was crusted now. I wondered how bad the cuts, bruises, and nick from the knife would look in the morning.

Chapter 6

Today's The Day

With nothing else to do, I had fallen asleep with the ice pack on my face. I knew there was a good chance Troy would come back while I was unconscious, but without my powers, my body needed more rest to heal. Hopefully, the eidolon had unsettled him enough to keep him away so I could get a good night's sleep. When I heard the creaking hinges, I jolted to a sitting position.

Liam pushed the door shut with his foot. "Morning."

"Hello." I smiled at him and quickly pulled the blanket to the head of the cot, setting my pillow on top of it.

He set both trays down. "Do you want to eat or use the restroom?"

"Bathroom please." The tantalizing smell of bacon made me consider changing my mind, but my bladder had the final say.

He pulled a zip tie out of his pocket. I turned around and put my hands together behind my back, hoping he would be gentle. When nothing happened, I looked over my shoulder. He was staring down at my wrists. A muscle jumped in his tightly clamped jaw. He glanced at me. "Troy?"

I barely bobbed my head. Liam had always been nice to me, but the fury welling up inside of him had nowhere else to go. There was no one else around to direct it to.

He grabbed my arm at the elbow and turned me around. "Pretend like you're cuffed. Don't make me regret this."

"Thank you." I sagged a little in relief.

He was quiet as he marched me across the room. Our footsteps slapping against the concrete were the only sound. I kept my hands close together, hoping nobody in the guardroom would be able to tell that Liam was breaking the rules.

As he turned the doorknob, he asked, "Why?"

"Because he can." I walked into the room in front of him. "People like him don't need reasons."

He stared down at his feet, and his grip on my arm loosened. "It's because I didn't believe your story. Isn't it?"

I didn't know how he'd react, but I slid my fingers under his chin, tilting his face up until his eyes met mine. "He doesn't need a reason to hurt me. He's told me more than once that the world would be better off without me."

Pulling my hand down, he nodded toward the other side of the room. "He might not need a reason, but I gave him one."

Just as I was slipping behind the screen, he added, "I hope you can forgive me."

My chest tightened as guilt clenched my heart. If I could access my magic and get away from them, Liam would come to hate me just as much as Troy did, but his reason would be justified. He'd hate me because I made him trust me, made him feel sorry for me, and then betrayed him.

The walk back to my cell started the same way. Liam's anger ate away at him. "Hey," I said, snapping him to attention. "I only get a little time that I can enjoy. Please, talk to me."

He grimaced, a weak attempt at a smile, but at least he tried. "What about?"

"I don't know." I shrugged. "Do Nephilim go to school? Do you have human friends?"

"Uh …" He glanced up at the window, and I wondered if these were questions I shouldn't have asked. "No to the first and not usually to the second. We have tutors and training. We don't get out among humans very often."

I chewed on my lip. Avoiding the tender spots, I pulled it into my mouth, wondering if I should ask more or just leave well enough alone. Curiosity had a habit of getting the best of me, though. "So, you just train and hunt demons and anyone who has anything to do with them?"

"Yeah, no." He blew out a breath. "We try to return demons to the Abyss. We also hunt fairytale"—he wiggled his fingers to put that word in quotes—"creatures who are breaking the laws and risk exposing all of us."

He held my cell door open for me, and I waited for him to pretend like he was cutting my hands free. Then we walked to my cot, picked up our trays, and sat down together. Breakfast was scrambled eggs that were fairly cold, bacon, and toast. I would have loved a big glass of chocolate milk to go along with it, but I had a bottle of water instead. At least they'd decided to feed me. After the first day, I wasn't sure if they would.

"So … Olivia? Is she your girlfriend?"

He choked on the eggs he was swallowing. "No." He shook his head, and pink tinged his cheeks. "I'm not sure she knows who I am."

"Too bad." I stabbed an egg with my fork. "You'd make a cute couple. How old are you anyway?"

His eyebrows pinched together. "Interesting subject change."

I shrugged.

"Twenty-three." He dipped his head toward his shoulder. "Well, in a couple days anyway."

"Happy early birthday." I bit into the bacon. It was cooked perfectly, crispy but not overdone. "I didn't know if you guys were like dragons or not. I figured you'd tell me you were eleven hundred and twenty-three."

For a second, he looked really confused. Then he said, "Yeah, that's what I meant. I figured you knew we were that old."

"No." I shook my head, and my nose crinkled. "You meant twenty-three. Didn't you?"

He chuckled. "Yeah. I don't look that old, do I?"

I slugged his arm playfully. "No, I figured you were pretty close to my age. I imagine that's why they sent you to play good cop." I ate the rest of my bacon, and after swallowing it, I said, "I'm glad they did."

"Yeah." He grinned at me. "Me, too."

I wiped my mouth with a napkin and winced. The pain was nothing like it had been yesterday, but unless I miraculously healed, it would hurt for a while still. "What day is it?"

He watched me closely for a few seconds. "Saturday," he said it like he was confused.

"What?" I asked.

He shook his head. "If you don't even know what day it is, one more day probably didn't mean anything more than what you said." He pressed his eyes closed and rubbed his forehead. "I'm so sorry. I didn't mean to cause you more pain."

"Liam, don't." I reached for his hand but stopped short. He wasn't Cody, Mavros, or one of the dragons. He was my captor. I needed to remember that he didn't really know me. He didn't know I wasn't going to hurt him. "Don't blame yourself for something somebody else did. He hurt me, not you. He was looking for an excuse. He could've decided just as easily that I wasn't grateful enough to him for bringing me the icepack."

He shook his head. "You might be right, but if I hadn't told Sebastian that I thought there was more to it than what you said, Troy might've let me bring you the icepack."

"Yeah." I smiled at him. "But, if you'd have brought it, Troy never would have met the eidolon, and I thoroughly enjoyed watching her scare the crap out of him."

Before Liam left, he grabbed something off his tray and tossed it to me. I caught it and pressed it against my chest. An elated grin covered my face. Even though I'd already read it several times, I was thrilled to have something to do. "Thank you."

I lay back on the cot and opened the book. *In a hole in the ground there lived a hobbit ...*

I was instantly transported away from my cell. The words pulled me into Bilbo's adventure. I forced myself to read slower than I normally would. I needed the book to get me through the day. I needed it to last until the lights were out and I could focus on my powers.

The smell of food wafting toward my cage drew my attention away from the book. I expected to see Liam with a tray for each of us, but it was the female guard from the first day. Her loose blonde hair fell past her shoulders. She only carried one tray.

I sat up, and she jolted.

"Don't move." Her voice was authoritative but edged with fear.

"Okay."

She stepped inside the cage quickly, keeping it open for only the briefest of moments. When she turned to lock the door, her hand trembled slightly, rattling the silverware.

"I'm not going to hurt you." I kept my voice soft and low like I was speaking to a frightened animal. "My magic is gone."

She stood back from me, stretched her arm out, and waited for me to take the tray from her. "Troy said you used your magic last night." Her aqua eyes darted to the side, then back to me.

I stared into them for a minute before grabbing the tray. "Troy's an idiot if he thinks I did that."

She glared at me, and I couldn't help but wonder if there was something more between the two of them. At the very least, she respected him.

Looking down at my lunch, I wondered if I would ever get to eat a solid meal again. I dipped my spoon into the chicken noodle soup and held it in front of me, blowing the steam off of it. "Thank you."

"Liam will pick up your tray and take you to the restroom when you've finished." She backed out of the door and turned the key. The lock clicked into place for what I hoped was one of the last times. She glanced around, and I wished the spirit would return. I wanted to see the guard's reaction.

She ran up the stairs, taking them two at a time. Her fear of me chasing her from my presence. Whatever they told her, I was glad they'd kept it from Liam.

When I finished eating, I made a few laps around the cage. Then I lay back down and picked up on Bilbo's adventure where I'd left off.

The tray sat untouched, as I read chapter after chapter. I looked at the hole in the floor, hoping I wouldn't have to use it, hoping Liam would come soon so that I wouldn't finish my book before I could see if my powers were strong enough to break through the collar.

When he finally showed up, he stood outside of my cell. "Dacia." His voice was harsh. "Stand by the door, turn around, and put your hands behind your back."

I set the book on the cot and walked over. At a total loss for words, I just looked at him with my eyebrows pinched together in confusion.

His eyes shifted toward the guardroom and then down again. "Turn around."

I did what he'd said, backing against the bars with my hands behind me.

He cinched the zip tie on more snugly than he ever had but still loose compared to how tight Troy made it. I gasped when it pulled on my wounds. As soon as my hands were bound, he opened the door, grabbed hold of my elbow, and led me across the room.

"Did I do something?" I whispered.

He reached down and turned a knob on his radio. "They know I didn't cuff you this morning."

"I'm sorry." I slumped forward. I didn't want to get him in trouble. He'd been nice to me since the beginning. "How?"

He lifted his shoulder slightly. "Cameras. Anyway … they're watching, so I have to follow the rules to a t." He squeezed my arm, not in a comforting sort of way, but in a you're-going-to-hate-this way. "They want me to stay in there while you shower."

"Why?" The word was barely able to scrape past the lump in my throat. Hot tears burned my eyes. The desire to wipe them away had me lifting my hands even though they were restrained.

He stared straight ahead at the floor, not even glancing my way. "You're a danger to us all, and I'm not taking it seriously enough."

When he opened the door, my eyes were drawn to the stack of towels. Realization thunked me in the head. "The towels. I never see anyone bringing them in here." I glanced behind me at the door we'd just entered. "There's another way in."

He nodded. "I lied." He cut the tie off of my wrists and pressed on my shoulder until I faced him. "I wanted to give you privacy."

I swiped at my tears. "Why you? Why not the girl who brought my lunch?"

"Lindsey?" He wiped his hand over his jaw. The stubble made a scratching sound. "I don't know. Because I'm stronger. Because I'm the one who screwed up. Because they're trying to toughen me up."

I huffed and turned away from him. "Because this is way more humiliating."

"Why?"

I clutched my stomach, wondering if there was any way out of this. "Cody hasn't seen me naked, and now, I'm supposed to shower in front of you? I've tried to do the right thing all my life, and look at where it got me." I stormed away from him. I wanted the privacy the makeshift stall had to offer.

When I finished, I gathered myself together and strode over to the bench without glancing at Liam. Tears blurred my vision. Pretending like the room was empty, I slipped my shoes off and pulled my hoodie over my head. The sooner I got this over with, the sooner I could go back to my cell and hide under the blanket.

A scraping noise pulled my attention away from undressing. I looked over my shoulder to see what was going on.

Liam dragged the screen away from the toilet. He stopped by one of the showerheads and positioned it so that it blocked the view from where I stood.

My knees wobbled, and I reached out to the wall, bracing my hand against it to catch my balance. "Thank you." The words were so quiet that I barely heard them.

He smiled as he strolled toward me. Clutching my shoulder, he said, "My job is supposed to be to protect." He lowered his head slightly and let out a deep breath. "How can I say I'm doing it if I can't even protect somebody's innocence?"

I set my hand on top of his. I remembered the way Micah had watched me wash off in the bucket and was grateful that for whatever reason they'd decided to make Liam my main guard. "Thank you."

"Don't thank me." He pulled away, positioning himself where he wouldn't be able to see behind the screen. "We both know that this is wrong. You shouldn't be here."

I picked up the clothes they'd left for me to wear, another jumpsuit, boxers, and a pair of mismatched socks. "Can I ..." I let my voice trail off. I shouldn't ask him for anything else. I shouldn't get him in even more trouble.

"What, Dacia?"

"Can I just wear my clothes again?"

He shook his head. "I can't break the rules. If I do, they'll stick you with Troy or Micah." He wiped his hand over his stubble. "I'll get your clothes back to you tonight if I can."

"Thank you." I grabbed the soap, towels, and clothes. Then I walked over to the screen.

Liam sat on the bench and stretched his legs out in front of him. "Ten minutes." He pushed a button on his watch.

The soap and water stung the cuts on my wrists, lip, and the side of my face. I imagined by now, the bruises were dark purple, green, and yellow, but the swelling had gone down significantly. I'd always resented my magic a little, but my time in prison was showing me all of the things I should have been grateful for.

I turned the water off and twisted a towel around my hair. Then I dried off as quickly as I could and pulled on the scratchy jumpsuit.

While I tugged my fingers through my hair in an attempt to tame my curls, Liam dried off the screen and moved it to block the toilet again. On his way back over to me, he stopped at the shower I'd used and turned the water on, soaking the floor, removing any evidence that he'd given me privacy.

When he finished, I turned my back to him and held my wrists together. Without eyes on him, he was gentler. His fingers were relaxed on my elbow as we strode to the door. As soon as we stepped through it, his grip tightened. There was no conversation on the march across the room. He held my cage door open and pushed me through it. I staggered forward surprised by his action. When I caught my balance, he said, "Back up against the cage."

Trying not to be hurt by his actions, I did as he said. He cut the tie loose and immediately turned away.

"If I tell you something"—he turned at the sound of my voice—"will they let you play good cop again? Will you stay with me while I eat?"

He walked to the stairs, pulled his radio out of one of the pockets of his cargo pants, and pushed a button. Holding it up to his mouth, he said, "The prisoner has information she would like to share with me." As he walked up the stairs, his tone turned snarky, and I could practically hear him roll his eyes. "She's lonely."

Chapter 7

I stared at the words, but no matter how hard I tried I couldn't get them to make sense to me. Did Liam really feel that way about me, or was his attitude necessary for Troy's and Sebastian's benefit? Had he known I could hear him? If I couldn't get out of here, it would be nice to think that I had one person I could count on, one person who didn't want me dead.

Since I couldn't focus on reading, I pulled my hair into a tight French braid, hoping that with nothing to hold it in place, it wouldn't unravel. Then I lay down and closed my eyes. If I was going to be awake all night, rest would do me some good.

Mavros in demon-form stares at me through the bars. Flames burn in his eyes. Three bolts from the ballista are buried deep in his long, muscular body. His midnight-black skin reminds me of a salamander's, smooth and greasy looking. Bat-like wings wrap around the cage, protecting me from any damage.

Another bolt slams into him. He lifts one of his angular heads and roars.

"Leave," I scream at him. "Please."

Not without you. He speaks into my mind, and I can feel his pain.

I fight to use my magic to help him. Nothing sparks on my fingertips. Nothing stops the Nephilim from firing at him again, but the collar burns my neck.

Another bolt flies through the air. It breaks through his wing and slams into the wall on the other side of my cage.

Black blood drips onto the floor, sizzling on the cement, burning away Troy's wards.

Mavros steps forward, reaches my cell, and grabs hold of the bars. Pulling them apart, he stretches his paw inside and snatches me, careful not to pierce me with his talons. He brings me close to his body, then teleports us to safety.

We materialize in a meadow. Mavros' body dissipates, leaving a black mist where he'd been moments before. When he reforms, it's as the man, not the monster. His injuries disappear with the beast.

He clutches my arms and stares at me. His expression is stony. Embers spark in his eyes, igniting them. The flames devour his obsidian irises.

"What's wrong?"

He lifts his hand to my cheek. His fingers delicately trail along the bruise. "Who?"

"It doesn't matter." I turn so he can't see it.

"Who?" His roar sends shivers through my body.

My eyes snapped open.

I held my head, replaying the dream over and over again. Could it have been a premonition? Even with the collar on?

Reaching my hands up, I felt my neck. Where the collar had burned me in my dream, it was tender. How? How could that part of my magic still work when nothing else did? What would happen if my dreams turned into nightmares? Would I heal by morning? Would I die?

I walked to the door and held onto the bars, looking out at the symbols Troy had drawn with his blood. I hadn't paid much attention to them before. They just were. But, now they could mean so much more. I stared at them, taking in every detail. As far as I could tell, they were identical to the ones from my dream. Was it possible that Mavros' blood could break the spell and free me?

Footsteps on the stairs pulled me out of the memory of my dream and back to my current situation. Liam walked toward me, carrying two trays.

Friend or foe?

I smiled at him, hoping his actions when we were alone showed the truth.

He lifted his gaze to the guard room. "I need you to back up."

I sat on the cot with my legs pulled up to my chest and wrapped my arms around them.

He set one tray on the ground while he unlocked the door. Then he slid it inside with his foot, never taking his eyes off of me. Once the cage was locked, he carried the trays over, handed me one, and sat next to me. "How's my favorite prisoner?" He twirled spaghetti around the tines of his fork and shoved it into his mouth.

I looked around, pretending not to know who he was talking about. Pointing at my chest, I said, "Me? I thought you meant one of the others."

"Sarcasm." He bobbed his head up and down. "Either I did something to hurt you or you're showing me your true colors. Which is it?"

"I'll let you know when I do." I took a bite of my garlic bread.

Pain flashed in his steel eyes.

"I heard what you said to them." I pointed at the stairs.

He tapped his fingers on his tray, then leaned down so his mouth was next to my ear. "It was the only way. They don't trust me. I thought you did."

"It might make me an idiot—" I held my face in my hands, wondering if I was making a huge mistake "—but I do."

A rakish smile lifted his lips. "How's the book?"

"I'm almost done." I wiped the sauce off of my lips. "I've read it before, but it's a good one."

We sat in silence and ate. I shoved another bite into my mouth, hoping I didn't have spaghetti sauce all over my face. Even though it was messy, I was grateful it wasn't soup.

Liam lifted his lips in a horrible imitation of a smile, pulled his radio out of his pocket, and set it on the cot on the opposite side of him. "I'll have to see if I can round up another one for you."

"That'd be nice." A grin tugged on the cuts and bruises on my face, and I tried not to wince.

He held the button on his radio, and I realized he was transmitting this to them. "So, what did you wanna talk about?"

I considered telling him that I wanted to wait until after I finished eating, but I was afraid Troy would come down to beat it out of me. "One more day did mean a little more." I wiped my fingers off, took a long drink of water, and set my tray next to me. Then I told him about the serpent that I visualized as my magic. I left out Mavros' snake, explained the shadows, and how the fairies told me to wait two days after they disappeared to use my power. Then I pointed at the collar. "As long as I'm wearing this, none of that matters, though."

Confusion was written all over Liam's face. He opened his mouth, then closed it. Scratching his jaw, he tilted his head. "Why let Troy hurt you? Why not just tell us?"

Not thinking, I bit my lip. "Ow." I rubbed it for a second. "Troy was going to hurt me no matter what. If I'd've told him that, he would've thought I meant to use my magic."

Liam nodded. "Yeah … probably."

"I can't, though. Not unless one of you takes this damn thing off of me." I tugged on the collar, but it wouldn't budge. "My magic is gone, my freedom is gone, my friends are gone, and after tonight, the corruption should be gone, too."

"Still—" he lifted his hand toward my face but stopped "—you should've told us." He stood. "Ready to walk?"

I turned my back to him and held my hands together. I hated that this action had become a habit already. If I ever got out of here, I wondered if I'd be able to leave a room without expecting to be cuffed.

As he escorted me to the door, I noticed his radio lying on my cot. I started to mention it, but he followed my gaze and shook his head. He gripped my elbow tightly as he led me across the room, not relaxing his posture at all.

When the door to the shower room clicked shut, he spun me around. "You're not planning something. Are you?" His face was pale, and I could count his pulse just by watching his neck.

"What?" I scrunched my eyebrows together. Pain shot along my right cheek, and I lowered it toward my shoulder.

He moved behind me and cut the restraint. "The way you were looking through the bars when I came down, and you can use your magic again." He dragged his hand through his hair.

"If I could leave, I would." I pressed my palm to the side of my face. "Can you blame me? Wouldn't you?"

He shook his head and looked down at his feet. "If you escape—" he grabbed my shoulders and made sure I was looking him in the eyes "—don't let Troy catch you again. He won't bring you back here."

"If I go back like this"—I pointed at my face—"the demon or dragons will kill him." I walked toward the toilet. Looking over my shoulder at him, I said, "I'll try to keep them from taking it out on everyone here, but they're overly protective."

His voice was soft, but I heard him say, "God help us all."

When I finished, Liam pointed at the bench. My clothes were folded and piled on it. "I'll turn around while you change."

Before we stepped out of the shower room, Liam cuffed me again. His grip on my elbow was loose until he opened the door. Then his demeanor changed instantaneously.

I glanced up at him. "You could tell Olivia or Diana. They could get us both out of here."

"They can't." He shook his head slightly but kept his eyes focused ahead of us. "They know already."

I felt like I'd taken another blow. My chest tightened, and I slumped forward. "Diana trusted me." Shaking my head, I looked up at him. "Olivia was starting to. I thought they would put an end to this."

"They're trying, but too many stand on Sebastian's and Troy's side." He squeezed my arm, an action that the others wouldn't be able to see from the guard room. "I'd ask for a transfer, but I don't want to leave you alone with them."

"Thanks." The thought of having Troy or Micah watch me shower or use the restroom made my skin crawl. "I, uh …" I cleared my throat and tried again. "I really appreciate your kindness." We walked past the ballista, and the memory of the bolts buried in Mavros' flesh made me shiver.

"You okay?" He looked down at me out of the corner of his eyes.

"Sure." I nodded at the giant weapon. "That thing just gives me the creeps."

His eyebrows pinched together. "Why? It didn't seem to bother you before."

"I had a dream about it."

His voice was soft, and his head was lowered. I wondered if it was to keep the others from reading his lips. "You're afraid the dream will come true?"

My eyes flicked toward him. I hadn't expected him to know about my premonitions. "I guess you know more about me now."

"They decided to tell me some things in my Dacia-is-dangerous briefing this morning."

I always wondered why they hadn't told him what a horrible monster I was ahead of time. If he would have feared me from the beginning, he never would have been nice. "With this on"—the urge to lift my fingers to the collar was overwhelming—"I don't know if I can have a premonition."

As we neared the cage, I realized someone had been in there. The trays were gone, and the bedding had been changed. I hoped they had left the book so I could finish it.

Liam held my cell door open while I walked in. As soon as it clicked shut, he freed my hands. I searched for the book, finding it under my pillow. I held it up and turned to face Liam. My smile dropped when I saw his face.

He stared at my bed. Sweat beaded on his forehead, and he clenched and unclenched his fists. "I don't know if they'll let me come back." He waved his hand toward the cot. "My radio's gone."

We both looked up when we heard footsteps on the stairs. Troy walked down them slowly, like a girl whose prom date waited at the bottom.

Liam grabbed my arms and whispered, "If you can get away, do it soon." He shook me. "Where's my radio?"

"I … I don't know." I didn't have to pretend to be surprised. I hadn't expected him to do this, but I understood why he was. "Hit me," I said so only he could hear me.

He shook his head.

"Or he will."

He pulled his hand back. "My radio." His voice was harsh, but the skin around his eyes was bunched, and his stare was pained.

I dipped my chin just slightly, letting him know it was okay.

His hand slammed into my cheek, knocking my head to the side. Tears sprang to my eyes, and I clutched my face.

Liam looked like he might throw up, and Troy clapped and laughed. "Well done. Feels good. Doesn't it?" He stood on the other side of the cage, waiting for an answer.

"Where is it?" Liam asked through clenched teeth, not even sparing a glance at Troy.

I could see the regret in his eyes. I wanted to be strong, to not let him know how badly he'd hurt me, but my voice wobbled. "I-I don't … have it."

Troy tapped something against the bars, and when Liam glanced over his shoulder, I could see it was the radio. "It must've fallen off your belt."

Liam pointed at me. "Sit." His voice was hard.

I sat on the cot and clutched my pillow, pressing it against my face.

He glanced at me, then took two steps toward Troy. "Thank you."

"No." Troy handed him the radio through the bars and smiled like a madman. "Thank you. That was quite entertaining." He tucked his hands into his pockets and strolled toward the stairs, whistling a song I didn't recognize. He bounded up the steps much quicker than he'd come down.

Liam dragged his hand down his face, then stared at his feet. "It's gonna be hard to play good cop now."

I grabbed his hand. "I told you to do it."

"I should've said no." He sat next to me. "I should've done the right thing."

I shook my head and backed away from him in case we were being watched.

Liam winced, but he had to understand what I was doing.

"They'll trust you now." I looked up at the guard room. "Get out of here before they realize you're trying to comfort me."

He stood in front of me, grabbed my shoulders, and leaned in so our noses nearly touched. From above, hopefully, it looked like he was yelling at me. "Get out of here as soon as you can."

I read until the lights went out. Then I lay down and pretended like I was going to sleep. Instead, I focused on my powers. The serpents were coiled together. I sat next to them and laid my hand on top of the pearlescent snake. I longed to feel the thrum of magic pulsating through its scales, but there was nothing.

I tightened my grip. "I need you." Remembering the rage I'd felt when Troy slammed my head against the bars and walked out laughing, I drew on my power.

Nothing happened.

I thought of Cody. My love for him. How happy he made me. I held onto those feelings and tried again to call on my magic.

There was nothing. Not a drop. Not a pinch. Not a whisper.

I opened my eyes, and a hand clamped down on my mouth, covering my startled scream.

Sebastian sat on the edge of my cot. He kept his hand over my mouth. "Is your magic responding?"

I tried to answer, but he just pressed down harder.

He leaned toward me, and his ponytail fell across my face. "Don't scream. Just answer my questions."

I nodded, and he let go. Even though I'd been able to breathe through my nose, I gulped down a breath.

"Magic … is it there?" He sat back up but held my shoulders down, keeping me from moving.

I stared at him, wishing I could call on my power to throw him off of me. I'd never wanted to hurt people before, but the longer they kept me here, the more I wanted them to know how it felt to be helpless and abused. "It's there, but I can't use it. I can't even feel it."

"What are you planning?"

I pinched my eyebrows together. "I'm hoping you'll realize that I've done nothing wrong, and you'll let me go—" my voice hitched "—home."

He pushed down on me, and I wondered if superstrength was something the Nephilim had to help them deal with demons. My shoulders would be bruised in the morning. "You're planning something."

"What?!" I clenched my fists at my sides. "What am I going to do? I'm trapped and powerless."

He grabbed my chin and turned my head from side to side. "Judging from the bruises, your magic hasn't returned." He stood and backed toward the door. Once he was outside of the bars, he said, "If you think you have it bad now, try to escape. Troy's chomping at the bit to take Liam's place, and I'll be inclined to let him."

After he left, I lay on the cot staring at the steps. How many more visitors would I have tonight? Did I dare try to check on my powers again? Would it even do any good anyway? Would I ever get my magic back? Would I ever go home?

Finally, I decided it didn't matter. If they were going to hurt me, I couldn't stop them.

I focused on my magic again. This time, I paid more attention to Mavros' power. The serpent's scales were obsidian and gold. I'd been trapped in this cage for three days. In three more, Mavros would no longer be bound to me unless I could somehow stop Troy's blood from taking it over.

Resting my hand on the snake's back, I hoped that Mavros could feel my desire to talk to him.

I slipped out of myself and back into the real world where sleep beckoned me. Resigned to my fate, I gave into its call without putting up a fight.

Chapter 8

Longing For Freedom

Mavros waits for me in my dream. He stands on a sandy beach, staring out at the water. His shoulders are slumped forward, his hair is tousled, and his usually impeccable shirt is wrinkled. "We've been trying to get to you, but we can't."

"The dragons can't." I walk to his side and slip my hand into his. The steady sound of the waves hitting the shore calms me. "You can, though."

He shakes his head and glances down at me. I'm shocked by his appearance. Deep bags frame his eyes. "I can't get past the wards."

I lift my hand toward his face, and he smiles sadly at me. "In my dream, I saw how you could." I take a deep breath of the fresh, clean air. The salty scent isn't familiar to me, but it's better than the stale air inside my cage.

"I don't think it's possible."

I explain what I had seen in my dream, hoping he would believe that it could work.

He squeezes my fingers, and his features morph until he no longer looks rumpled and sleep-deprived. "Can you make it through one more day?"

"Yeah." Trying not to let him see my disappointment, I wiggle my toes, burying them in the sand. "I'll try."

He turns toward me and brushes the back of his hand along my cheek. "I need to make sure the dragons can keep Cody and your parents safe while I free you, and my magic is stronger at night. The moon will only be about a quarter, and it'll be setting." I pinch my eyebrows together, and he says, "That'll help. A full moon high in the sky would be bad."

"Okay." I wrap my arms around him, needing to feel his warmth and comfort.

He pulls me close and rubs my back. "One more day, Dacia. You can do it."

The smell of breakfast woke me up. Liam stood just inside the door, holding two trays. He smiled when my eyes met his. "I can't believe you didn't hear me."

"Yeah." I sat up and tried to pull my hand through my hair. My fingers caught in my braid. "I'm kinda surprised to see you today."

He handed me my breakfast, then sat next to me. "I'm a little surprised by it, too. I thought you'd be gone."

"I wish."

Instead of eating, he stared at me.

"What?" I set my bacon down and turned toward him.

He lifted his hand toward my cheek, but I pulled away. "I'm sorry."

"Don't." I shook my head. "Just don't. I told you to do it, and it's probably the only reason you're here today and not Troy. Last night, Sebastian threatened me with him." I scooped some eggs onto my fork and shoved them into my mouth. "I need you here." My voice cracked a little. "It can't be Troy or Micah."

He nodded. "My conscience won't let me forgive myself for it, though." He took a couple of bites. Then he looked at me like he was about to say something.

I waited, but he just took another bite, then another. When I was nearly finished eating, he finally said, "They're going to try to send you through the portal again. I tried to talk them out of it, but they think the shadows are gone from your magic because you're ready."

My stomach plummeted, and I regretted eating breakfast. "Can I use the bathroom first?"

"Yes."

I waited until he was finished eating. Then I set my tray on the floor, stood, and turned my back to him. He cuffed me, then marched me across the room.

"What will happen if the portal works?" I didn't give him a chance to respond before asking, "What if it doesn't?"

He pulled away from me slightly, not letting go of my arm, but distancing himself. "If you go, you shouldn't need to wear the collar anymore. The sanctuary will keep you from accessing your magic." He rubbed his chin. "But, with you, I wouldn't be surprised if they made you keep wearing it."

"And … if it doesn't?" I felt like there was a better chance that I wouldn't be able to go. Mavros' power was still at least half his own.

This was the question that made his unease grow. "I don't know, Dacia. I really don't." He looked at me without turning toward me. "Troy will probably make you drink more of his blood. Hopefully, he won't hurt you." He let out a heavy sigh. "I'm so sorry about all of this."

"Take my collar off." The words rushed out of my mouth before I really had a chance to think about what I was asking of him. "Let me teleport out of here."

He held the door open for me. While he cut the tie from my wrists, he said, "I can't. Only Troy or Sebastian can remove it."

Suddenly, I felt exhausted. Not just on the surface but deep inside of myself. I wasn't sure how much longer I could keep fighting, not just the Nephilim but anything, whatever came next … if anything even did. "They never will." As I walked away from him, I looked over my shoulder. "Can you make them wait one more day?"

His head snapped up. "Why?"

"Because I'm scared." I stopped walking and turned toward him. "Because being forced to drink blood is disgusting. Because it won't work today."

"Why?" He strode toward me. "Why won't it work?"

I hadn't told him about Mavros' serpent. How could I explain without giving more of my secrets away? I looked down at the floor. "Mavros is still bound to me."

He put his hand on my shoulder and stared into my eyes. "How do you know?"

"I just do." I turned and walked to the makeshift stall. My limbs felt heavier with each step I took. If they were able to pull me through the portal, I would never be able to go home. I would never see my family or my friends. I would never touch my magic again.

After I washed my hands, Liam cuffed me and led me back across the room. Three Nephilim stood outside of my cell. My knees buckled, dropping me to the ground. Liam nearly tumbled over the top of me, but he caught his balance, then knelt in front of me. "You okay?"

"No." The word barely managed to push past the lump in my throat. My eyes filled with tears that I tried to hold back.

Sebastian, Troy, and Micah watched us. Troy started to step toward us, but Sebastian lifted his arm in front of him, blocking his path.

Liam hoisted me to my feet. "I'm sorry, Dacia."

"Yeah, me, too." I held my head high as I limped toward my cell.

He guided me into my cage. When he turned me around to cut my bonds, Troy said, "Leave 'em."

Liam kept hold of my arm. I hoped he knew how grateful I was for that. His touch kept me from feeling so alone.

The other Nephilim entered my cell, and Sebastian slammed the door shut. "Get on with it."

Troy waved his hands in front of him and repeated something over and over. A bright light flashed in front of him growing large enough for people to walk through. He reached for my arm, but Liam stepped between us. "I got this." He tugged me toward the portal, stopping right in front of it, then gently squeezed my arm. "Ready?"

I nodded, and Liam stepped into the light, pulling me along with him.

A scream pierced my skull, stabbing through my brain. I ducked my head down, tucking it into my chest.

Liam jerked me out, and the agonized yell silenced instantly. I rubbed my cheeks on my shoulders, drying my tears.

Sebastian nodded, and the others surrounded me. Sebastian and Micah grabbed my legs, and I flipped backward. Liam and Troy held my shoulders.

I stared up into Liam's face, sure mine was a strange mixture of fear and confusion.

His forehead was wrinkled, and he looked from me, to Troy, to Sebastian.

They carried me to the cot, and Troy said, "Hold her down."

Liam pushed down on my shoulders. Sebastian and Micah each pressed on my knees and ankles. The one I had just fallen on throbbed from the contact. Troy stood over the top of me, pulled his knife out, and sliced through his wrist. He watched the blood pool there, then bent over me.

I slammed my forehead into his.

He pressed his hand against it and staggered back. "You bitch!"

"Grab her leg," Sebastian said.

Micah moved so he was holding both of my legs.

I kicked, but my feet barely moved.

Sebastian grabbed one of my shoulders and pressed down on my forehead. He nodded at Liam, and Liam did the same.

Troy clutched my jaw in one hand, forcing it open. Then he smashed his wrist against my lips. My teeth sliced through my flesh, and his blood merged with mine.

The coppery taste coated my tongue. I opened my mouth further and bit down on Troy's wrist. He jerked back, and I spit his blood into Sebastian's face.

Sebastian lurched away and wiped at his eyes.

Troy lifted my head by my hair and slammed it down. It bounced off the pillow, and I sneered at him.

He leaned down next to me and whispered, "You disgust me." He tilted my head back, and while Sebastian forced my jaws open, he dripped his blood into my mouth. "If you were one of us, I'd like your fighting spirit. Hell, I'd reward it. But on you, I don't even respect it."

I choked on his blood, trying to keep from swallowing it, but it clogged my throat until I had no choice.

Troy backed away. Pulling a cloth out of one of his many pockets, he wrapped it around his wrist.

Micah and Sebastian let go. They joined Troy and left my cell. As soon as they were gone, Liam helped me sit up. "I can cut you loose or take you to get cleaned up."

"I'd—" As soon as I opened my mouth, my stomach rolled. I jumped to my feet and barely made it to the hole before throwing up.

Liam cut the zip tie so I could press my hands to the ground. I heaved until there was nothing left in me. Then I collapsed. The cool concrete settled my queasy stomach. I closed my eyes, hoping the room would stop spinning.

Liam bent down and rubbed my back. When I didn't move, he lifted me up and set me on the cot. Then he cuffed my hands in front of me. He stepped away and pulled his radio out. "The prisoner is covered in blood and puke. I'm taking her to the showers."

"Let her rot," Troy responded.

There was a loud sigh followed by Sebastian saying, "Be careful, Liam. Don't trust her."

He knelt in front of me. "On your feet, Dacia."

My head throbbed from knocking my skull against Troy's. My body shook from throwing up. I stood and stumbled forward.

Liam caught me before I fell and lifted me in his arms.

"Put me down." My voice wobbled almost as much as my knees had.

He shook his head. "You can't stand."

"You can't carry me like this." I fought against his hold. "They won't like it."

An unamused laugh spilled out of him. "They'll like seeing you helpless, though." He set me on my feet, then tossed me over his shoulder.

I hung limply. The fight had left me. I'd struggled against Troy, and he'd still won. More of his blood fought to expel Mavros, to break our bond. I could only hope Mavros would save me before that happened.

Liam didn't put me down until we were in the shower room. I swayed, pressing my hands against the wall to catch my balance. He held onto me and cut the cuffs off.

"Can you stand on your own?" He closed his knife and shoved it back into his pocket. "Or am I going to have to help you?"

Anger burned in my stomach. I turned and walked away from him, stumbling more than I would have liked.

"I'll get the screen then."

I let the fury build inside of me. It blazed through my veins. My heart pumped faster, harder, feeding the rage. I called my magic to me, expecting nothing.

A whisper.

Was it really there or had I imagined it?

I closed my eyes, centering myself, and focused on my power. The serpent's coils moved ever so slightly.

A hand clamped down on my shoulder, and I screamed. It jerked back, and Liam said, "Are you all right?"

"Yes." My voice was breathless and strained. I opened my eyes and looked at him.

"You were out of it." He rubbed his hand over his face. "I said your name several times."

I pulled the braid out of my hair and combed my fingers through it. "I was …" I turned my back and kicked off my shoes. He'd held me down. He'd helped them. Why should I trust him? I dropped my chin to my chest, hoping I was making the right decision. "I was focused on my magic, wondering if it would respond."

"Well, did it?" He sat on the bench and stretched his legs out in front of him.

Just in case I couldn't trust him, I shook my head. "Not yet." I grabbed the towels and clothes and walked over to the shower. When I was behind the screen and out of Liam's sight, I called on my magic again. Another whisper, but this time, I was listening for it.

I clutched the collar in both hands and pictured Troy's face. His hatred for me was etched into every line. I remembered all the times he had slammed my head into the bars. I let my rage and the powerlessness I had felt consume me. I coaxed my magic, nudging it, hoping it would respond. Then I sent all of my energy into crushing the collar.

Magic poured into my body, sparking on my fingertips. My hands sunk into the collar, and I pulled. The metal cracked. I yanked harder, and the pieces broke off in my hands.

Power surged through my veins, filling all the empty spaces inside of me. I felt whole for the first time since the Nephilim had kidnapped me.

"Dacia"—Liam's steps neared the screen—"what's going on?"

I shoved the collar fragments into the clean jumpsuit's pockets. Then, hoping I had created a convincing illusion of it circling my neck, I peeked around the screen. "Sorry. I'm still a little wobbly."

"Just hurry." He glanced toward the door, and I realized he was afraid somebody would come in and find the makeshift stall he had set up for me.

I saluted him with two fingers before ducking back behind the screen. I could teleport out of here right now, but they would suspect Liam had helped me. Whether he was my friend or not, he had been kinder to me than the others. I stripped my clothes off and showered quickly. I'd rather go home with the blood and puke washed off. It would be bad enough to return home with all of the cuts and bruises I had sustained.

I dried off, then dressed, stashing the collar pieces in the pockets, praying Liam wouldn't notice them.

While I pulled my shoes on, Liam moved the screen back. Then he ran the shower to make it look like the screen hadn't been there at all. As soon as he finished, I turned and held my hands together behind my back, hoping it would be the last time. He cuffed me and guided me toward the door.

Right before he opened it, he looked at me. His eyebrows pinched together, and he tilted my chin up.

"What?" I hoped the illusion of the collar appeared realistic enough to fool him. I hadn't ever seen what it looked like on me.

"Your face looks better." He let go of me and opened the door. Before stepping out, he clutched my elbow. "I'm glad. It makes me angry every time I see the bruises. We're supposed to be the good guys."

As we strode across the floor, I wondered if I would see him again after today. "If it's any consolation, I think you are."

"Thanks." He nodded at me.

"You should get away from them, though." I looked up at the guard room. Troy and Sebastian stared down at us. Neither of them had blood smeared over their face like warpaint, so I assumed they had both showered. "Don't let them change you."

We arrived at my cell sooner than I would have liked. I didn't argue this time, though. Now that I was closer to getting out, I didn't want to draw any unnecessary attention to myself. While I'd been gone, the bedding on my cot had been changed, and the blood and vomit had been cleaned up.

Liam cut my cuffs off and stepped toward the door. "Thank you for waiting to disappear. They would've blamed me."

My thoughts seemed to freeze, and I flinched my head back. "Wh-what?"

"The collar's a little off, not much." He stepped out and looked back at me. "Nobody else has spent as much time with you, so I don't know if anyone else would notice. Be careful." He smiled at me, and I could see his relief in it.

I plopped down on the cot and held up the book. "I've got to finish this. Then …" I lifted my gaze toward the guard room. "You should keep clear so they don't blame you."

"See you around."

I lay down, listening to him climb the stairs, hoping I'd never have to again. Hoping I'd been right to put my faith in him. Then I read the last couple of chapters.

My magic had built up enough that I felt it writhing under my skin, ready to be released. I closed my eyes and pictured my bedroom. The sky-blue walls. The blue and purple comforter covering my bed. The window seat where I'd spent so many days reading.

My body stretched in and pulled out. The cool air of the Nephilim's prison was replaced by the warmth and comfort of my house. I opened my eyes, and an unexpected sob broke free from me.

I fell to my knees and sent a thought out to Cody, my parents, the dragons, Mavros, and Liam, *I'm home.*

Chapter 9

My phone rang, my parents knocked on my bedroom door, and Malcolm, Cash, and Mavros appeared in my room. I opened my door, waved my parents in, and answered the phone. "Hello."

"Dacia." Cody's voice broke.

Mom and Dad wrapped their arms around me, and the air whooshed out of my lungs.

"I'm home," I said for all of them and also to reassure myself. I'd waited for this moment for too long. I needed to say it out loud, to know that it was real.

Mom's fingers brushed my face. "Oh, baby, what did they do to you?"

I clutched her hand. "I'm okay."

Malcolm and Cash inspected me. The more bruises and cuts they noticed on my skin, the closer they came to looking like they were about to transform. Mavros' lip curled, Dad's face filled with rage, and Mom clung to me.

"Now that the collar's off, I'm healing." I couldn't hold anyone's gaze. I hated what my imprisonment had done to them. Before I came back, I should have healed myself. I shouldn't have let them see me like this.

"I'm coming over." Cody's voice left no room for argument.

My heart raced. I imagined the Nephilim taking him, holding him until I turned myself in. "Is Russ with you?" Panic surged inside me. If my parents hadn't been holding onto me, I don't think I could have kept standing. "Can he bring you?"

"If that's what you want."

My relief was instantaneous. "Yes, please." I glanced down at myself. "The living room I'd like to change into my own clothes."

"Five minutes." He paused for a second. "Don't disappear."

The phone clicked, and I hung up. I tossed it onto the bed, then returned my parents' hugs. Pulling away from them, I said, "Cody'll be here in a few minutes. I'd like to change." I pulled the pieces of the collar out of my pockets and handed them to Malcolm.

He took them without saying anything, turning them over in his hands.

"Okay." Mom stepped away. "Okay." She glanced over her shoulder like she was making sure I was still there. Her eyes were red-rimmed, and I doubted she had slept at all since I was taken.

Dad hugged me again. "Don't disappear." His clothes were wrinkled. Black circles, darker than the Abyss, crouched beneath his eyes, dulling the green of his irises.

"That's what Cody said." I tried to laugh, but it sounded off. "I'll be out in just a minute."

He started to walk away.

"Oh, Dad."

He turned.

"Cody's just going to appear." I pulled my hand through my hair. "Maybe with Russ."

He nodded and pulled the door closed.

I turned toward the others. Cash dropped to his knees and lowered his head.

Before he could say anything, I put my hand on his shoulder. "Please. Don't apologize. Just keep me safe." I went to my dresser and pulled out leggings, underclothes, a t-shirt, and an oversized hoodie. "Can I have a minute?"

Mavros smiled at me. "Don't disappear."

Not wanting to be alone, I changed quickly and hurried out to the living room. Everyone watched me without being obvious about it.

Malcolm sat next to me on the couch. He kept his eyes downcast. "We failed you, Dacia."

"No." I patted his leg. "I sent you away. I thought it was over. None of us realized the Nephilim would do this."

Before he could say anything else, Cody and Russ appeared in the middle of the room. Cody looked at me like he wasn't sure if I was real or an apparition. He stepped forward, and I stood, meeting him halfway. He stretched his hands toward my face but didn't touch me. "What'd they do to you?"

"It doesn't matter." I wrapped my arms around his waist and pressed my forehead against his chest. "I'm so glad you're okay."

He held me out from him. "You're glad I'm okay?" He brushed my hair off my face. "Oh, Dacia."

Dad cleared his throat. "Tell us what happened."

I sat on the couch between Cody and Malcolm and pulled my legs up, tucking them inside of my sweatshirt, hoping to feel the sense of security that had been missing for the last several days. Cash, Russ, and Mavros stood behind me. I shoved my hands into my pocket and stared at the floor while I told them about my imprisonment.

The whole time I talked, Cody's hand ran up and down my back to soothe me or reassure himself, or maybe both.

Mom stopped me at one point. "He made you drink his blood?" Her voice shook.

"Yes." I nodded. "A few times."

When I told them where the bruises had come from, all of the dragons growled. My parents' eyes widened, and they cowered back.

"Sorry." Malcolm nodded at them and made a point of not savoring their emotions. "Your fear was not our intent."

Mom smiled uneasily at him.

I finished by saying, "They want to break my bond with Mavros so they can take me to their sanctuary and never let me leave." I pressed my eyes closed, and Mavros rested his hand on my shoulder. "I think it's working."

He walked around the couch and knelt in front of me. "If you wish me to remain bound to you, we will find a way."

"They tried to take me through the portal again." My voice wobbled at the remembered fear. Rehashing all I had been through was too much, but at least I only had to do it once. "I'm afraid your powers woke up again."

He held his hand in front of me, and I set mine on top of it. Our powers writhed underneath my skin. The serpents came closer to the surface than I'd seen in a long time. Mavros focused on them and ran his finger along my vein. Shivers of desire tingled through me, following his gentle touch.

Cash, Malcolm, and Russ snapped their heads toward Mavros and sucked in deep breaths. Their bodies were taut, ready to spring into action at any moment, and I wondered why Mavros would choose now to mess with them.

He smiled at me and lifted his eyebrows mischievously before his magic blasted into me. The obsidian snake coiled its body up and disappeared. My powers slithered after it.

"Check later." Mavros stepped back. "Make sure my magic is dormant."

I nodded. "Thank you."

Russ stared out the window. "They're out there, Dacia."

I stood, and Cody reached for my hand. "No. Please … don't go."

"I have to." I let out a deep breath. "I have my magic back, and I can use it if necessary."

Dad went to the door. "Sit down, Dacia. You're not going anywhere." He grabbed his coat. "We're not losing you again." Shoving his arms into the sleeves, he stepped outside. "Leave! You can't have her."

Malcolm, Cash, Mavros, and I walked to the door. Sebastian and Troy stood in my driveway in front of about thirty or forty other Nephilim.

Sebastian held his hands out and stepped toward the house. "Sir, your daughter is a danger."

"To whom?" Dad crossed his arms over his chest and widened his stance.

Troy's face reddened, and he stormed past Sebastian. "To everyone. To you. To us. To the world. She's a demon lover. A menace."

Portals appeared between my father and the Nephilim. Diana, Olivia, Liam, and several others stepped out. Khione cantered across our snow-covered yard. Her fur gleamed in the sun. A beam of light reflected off her horn.

Aurelia and Arion appeared on my sidewalk. Arion folded his wings against his sides and bowed to me. Then he turned around.

"Sebastian, Troy—" Diana strode closer to them with every word she said "—by the power granted me by the Angelic Tribunal, you are under arrest."

Troy's stance turned menacing. "For what?"

Something next to Liam moved. Under the bright light of the sun, it was hard to make out the specter at first. She glided forward, and Troy's eyes widened.

"False imprisonment," the eidolon said, "assault and battery, inhumane treatment." She turned toward me. "I am sorry that I did not free you. I discovered my path too late."

Troy started mumbling, and his hands weaved through the air.

I pressed the handle on the door and dashed out onto the porch.

"Dacia, no." Cody's voice trailed behind me.

I had to go, though. I had to try to stop him.

Cody followed me, grabbing my arm. He pulled me behind him so that I was shielded by his body.

"He's creating a portal." I pointed at Troy.

He glanced up at me just as a light blossomed in front of him. The smile that spread over his lips was feral.

Khione and Aurelia rushed toward him. Sebastian sprinted over and dived through the portal before it was fully formed, and Troy followed him, never taking his eyes off of me.

The Nephilim who had stood behind them dropped to their knees. I recognized Micah, Lindsey, and a few of the others.

Liam strode toward me, and the dragons stepped outside, surrounding me.

I put my arm on Cash's shoulder. "It's okay. I trust him."

He relaxed his stance slightly but stayed in front of me.

I held onto his arm and nodded at Liam. "I'm glad to see you left."

"Likewise." He cleared his throat, and his gaze darted between me and the dragons. "You shouldn't stay here. You're in danger until we catch them."

Dad looked at Liam through narrowed eyes. "You're one of my daughter's kidnappers?"

"Yes." He lowered his head. "I tried to keep her safe. I failed."

Cash huffed. "Join the crowd."

Stretching his hand out to Liam, Dad said, "Thank you. We're indebted to you for that."

"No," Liam said as he took Dad's hand. "I should've done more." He glanced at my face, and I saw his Adam's apple bob.

I shook my head. "Forgive yourself." I stepped toward him, and Cash moved with me. "I told you to do it."

Malcolm's head snapped up, and a menacing growl permeated the air.

"He didn't beat me." I dragged my hand through my hair. "I told him to hit me so they wouldn't make Troy or Micah take me to the shower room."

Dad's jaw tightened, and his fists clenched.

I put my hand on his arm and sent soothing energy into him. "Liam was a gentleman. The others wouldn't have been." Once Dad seemed calmer, I turned my attention back to Liam. "I can't leave here. They threatened my parents before. I've got to keep them safe."

While we'd been talking, the Nephilim who had arrived with Liam had cuffed Sebastian's and Troy's followers and pulled them through portals. I watched Olivia drag Micah into one. He glared at me and clamped down on the toothpick so hard that I wouldn't be surprised if it had shattered into tiny slivers in his mouth.

Liam turned and followed my gaze. "I should help them."

"Wait." I pulled away from Cash and strode toward Liam. "What will they do with them?"

He rubbed his scruffy beard. "They'll be questioned. The ones like me will be released. I don't know about the others."

"How do they know who to believe?" A chill ran up my spine at the thought of them releasing somebody as fanatical as Troy.

Tapping his forehead, he said, "We have our ways." He started to turn again, but I pulled him into a hug. His hands hung loosely at his sides for a few seconds before he returned it. "I wish we could've met under better circumstances."

I pointed at the people gathered on the porch. "Malcolm, Cash, and Russ wanted to kill me and my friends. Mavros wanted to bind himself to me and take over the world." I turned back to Liam. "None of us met under optimal circumstances, but I wouldn't know what to do without them."

He nodded at them. "I don't know what's going on in Sebastian's and Troy's minds, but I don't think they'll stop." He smiled apologetically. "Keep her safe. I won't be there to protect her next time."

Malcolm stretched his hand out. "Stay here. Help us guard her."

Liam cautiously slid his hand into Malcolm's. "I cannot just abandon my duties."

"No." Diana strolled toward us. "You can be restationed and reassigned if this is what you want." She lowered her eyes.

"I am truly sorry, Dacia, for everything. I never dreamed my people would do something like this."

"Yeah." I dragged my hand through my hair. "I seem to have that effect on everyone." A humorless laugh spilled out of me. "Do you know how many times I heard that Argentum was good and just? That he'd been righteous?"

Aurelia strode closer. "Power does not only have the ability to corrupt those with it. It can also corrupt those who desire or fear it."

I huffed out a long sigh. "Yeah."

Cody stepped up beside me. We watched the rest of the Nephilim prisoners disappear through the portals. Once they were gone, he stared at Khione and Arion. "Britny'd be in heaven."

"What did you tell your parents?" I wrapped my arms around him. His presence comforted me and made me feel whole.

He cupped my cheek in his hand, rubbing his thumb along my eyebrow. "Everything."

My stomach dropped to my feet so quickly that I stumbled forward.

He tightened his grip on me.

"Do they—" I clutched his shirt "—are they afraid of me?"

"Don't think so." He stared into my eyes. "I hadda tell 'em."

"I thought about it." I pressed my head against his chest. "I just hope it doesn't change things."

We sat at the dining room table eating tacos. Khione's magic had settled over all of us after the Nephilim had taken their prisoners away. My parents had been fairly relaxed since, but I wondered how long that would last.

Liam smiled at Mom. "Thank you for dinner and your hospitality."

She nodded. "Thank you for trying to keep Dacia safe."

Cody glanced across the table at Liam. His face was expressionless, and I couldn't help but wonder what he thought about Liam being here. Of all my guardians, at least he didn't have to worry about him being in my room with me at night. My parents, knowing the dragons watched over me at night, had offered him the spare bedroom.

Mavros ate without saying a word. He watched Liam, occasionally glancing over at me. His face darkened every time he looked at my cheek. I knew the bruises were gone, but it would take a long time for the memory to fade.

After supper, I helped my parents with the dishes before leading Cody downstairs. I curled up next to him on the couch. "I didn't know if I'd get to see you again. They tried to pull me through the portal into their sanctuary this morning."

"You said that. Why?" He leaned back, looking down at me with his eyebrows pinched together. "Wouldn't the other Nephilim have freed you?"

"Oh." My head snapped back a little. I hadn't thought about that. "I don't know. Maybe they planned to hide me somewhere there, or maybe once I was there, everyone would've decided it was for the best."

He trailed his fingertips over my arm. His touch was featherlight and as smooth as silk. "So … uh … is your magic under control?"

"Yes." My eyes drifted shut. "It's my own again." I thought about ingesting Troy's blood and hoped that wouldn't change. I hoped it wouldn't have any effect on my magic, but I also couldn't help but wonder if his blood was why the shadows had disappeared so quickly.

Cody pulled me so I was straddling his lap. Then he swung his legs onto the couch and lay back.

My hands flattened on his chest, and I gazed down at him.

His sapphire eyes sparkled as he trailed his hands along my sides to my waist. "Thought I'd lost you."

"I thought you had, too." The memories stole over me. Fear and hopelessness pulled the air from my lungs.

Three dragons surrounded the couch. A black mist weaved between them, forming into Mavros. They all stood in defensive positions. The dragons' features were caught somewhere between human and beast. One of them growled low, menacing.

"What?" I sat up. "Are they here?"

Malcolm looked over his shoulder at me. Confusion contorted his face. "We smelled your terror."

"Oh." I dragged my fingers through my hair. "I'm sorry. It wasn't real … just memories."

Cody cupped my cheeks and made me look at him. "Those're real."

"But, I'm home now." I set my hand over the top of his. "I'm with you. I need to let them go."

Liam thundered down the stairs. "What's going on?"

"What did you do to her?" Cody jerked upright, holding onto me to keep me from falling. His mask was gone, his eyes narrowed, and his jaw was clenched.

Liam's gaze dropped to the floor, and his shoulders hunched. "We can sense evil." His voice was so quiet that I strained to hear it. "I knew the first time I saw her that she was good. Troy and Sebastian convinced the others that it was a trick. They reminded us over and over that she was friends with a demon. They asked us how a creature of light could be."

"You did nothing wrong, Liam." I pointed at the rocking chair.

He shook his head at me while he sat. "You know I did."

"I told you to." Instinctively, my hand shot up to my cheek.

The dragons growled, and Cody said, "You hit her."

"I told him to."

"Don't care if you told him to." Cody's fingers tightened on my waist. "He shoulda known better."

I thought of the way Troy had looked when he'd sauntered down the stairs. He knew he would finally get what he wanted. "It—" my chest tightened like the air was being sucked out of me.

Malcolm sat next to me and grabbed my hand. "You're okay." His energy soothed me.

"It was the only way to keep Troy or Micah from being my main guard." I stared at the hunter carpet without seeing it. Instead, I saw Micah watching me wash in the bucket. The toothpick stuck out of his mouth. Troy's body pressed against mine as he chained me to the cage. He stood over me. Hatred and disgust mingled together on his face. "If Liam hadn't hit me, Troy or Micah would've been watching me shower, and I wouldn't have gotten the collar off."

"He"—Cody pointed at Liam—"watched you shower?" His other hand tightened into a fist.

I ran my fingers over Cody's leg, hoping to calm him. "No. That was one of the many rules he broke for me."

"Troy went to her cell several times." Liam stared at his hands folded together in his lap. "He was sure he could beat the truth out of her. Luckily, Sebastian decided to let the medic see her. She insisted that we feed Dacia and take care of her."

"I wondered."

Liam nodded. "Troy fought for bread and water once a day, but Vicki knew, like I did, that keeping you prisoner was wrong."

"I guess I owe her for more than just fixing me up then." I smiled at Liam. "At least, I didn't puke on her boots, too."

He shrugged. "If someone made me drink their blood, I'd have probably done the same." He glanced in my direction but wouldn't meet my eyes. "I didn't know until later that was why you were puking blood. I thought Troy had given you more than just a concussion."

I traced my finger along the side of Cody's face, getting him to focus on me. "Liam knew I'd gotten the collar off. He warned me to run and never allow Troy to capture me again."

Liam sighed and pinched the bridge of his nose. "I should've done more."

"As much as I love you all—" I looked around the room at all of my guardians "—I need some time alone with Cody before he has to leave."

One by one the dragons disappeared. I could still feel their auras. Malcolm's felt closer than the others', but after I'd been kidnapped, I didn't think they'd leave me alone again for a while, and I wasn't sure that I wanted them to.

Mavros waited next to the door for Liam to leave. Liam turned at the bottom of the stairs. "Thanks for trusting me."

Cody and I lay on the couch together. His arms were wrapped around me, and I traced patterns over his t-shirt, watching the fabric darken and lighten. I didn't want to talk. I didn't want to think about what I'd been through. I just wanted to feel safe and loved.

"Can you come over tomorrow?" Cody's voice was a soft murmur.

My stomach clenched. What would his family think of me? "Probably." I propped myself up. "Who knows?"

"Mom, Dad, Josh, and Dawson."

I pressed my eyes shut. "Do they know about Malcolm, Cash, and Russ?"

"Uh." He held his hand out and wobbled it from side to side. "That they're your guards."

I lay back down and let his heartbeat soothe me. "Will they hate me?"

"No."

Chapter 10

Finding My Way Back

Something moved. My eyes shot open, and my heart thudded against my rib cage. An arm wrapped around me, and my terrified scream pierced the silence. I thrashed about, trying to free myself from the grip, but it only tightened.

"Dacia, you're okay," Mavros whispered. "You're home. No one's going to hurt you, not on my watch."

I rolled over and flipped on the light on my nightstand. "I'm sorry." I sat up. "I'm a mess."

"No." He brushed his hand over my hair. "You're going to be fine."

I wanted to believe him, but I couldn't. I thought I would be fine after defeating Nefarious. I thought I would be fine after killing Draconian. After returning Mavros to the Abyss. After killing Argentum. But now I knew, I would never be fine. I would wear all of my invisible scars forever. *Malcolm.*

As soon as his name ran through my head, he was standing in front of me. He lifted his hand toward my face. Talons tipped his fingers.

"Can you go with me to Cody's?"

He nodded. "Thank you for asking and not just leaving."

As I stood, Mavros said, "Be careful, Dacia."

I smiled at him. "I want you to know, having you come to me in my dreams … it meant more to me …" I swallowed a lump in my throat. "It saved me. Thank you."

His eyes softened, and he nodded at me.

I grabbed hold of Malcolm's hand. Then I imagined Cody's room. My body stretched in and pulled out. Darkness surrounded us. When we appeared, Russ jumped to his feet, scanning us.

Malcolm kept his voice low. "Dacia needed to see Cody."

"You okay?" Cody's voice was hoarse from sleep, but he seemed alert.

I tilted my chin toward my chest. "I just needed you." I pointed at his bed. "Can I?"

"Always, Dacia." He pulled the covers back, and I climbed in next to him. Snuggling against his side, I laid my head on his bare chest. His hand brushed over my arm from shoulder to wrist, soothing, reassuring.

I drifted off, knowing this was where I belonged.

It was still dark outside when I opened my eyes. I lifted onto my arm and looked over Cody at the bright red numbers on his alarm clock. 5:35. I needed to be back in my room before my parents came in to kiss me goodbye. I brushed my lips over Cody's, and he pulled me against him. "Stay."

"I can't, Cody." I rubbed my thumb along his stubbled cheek. "It'd kill my parents to find me gone again."

"You'll come back?" He brushed my hair off my face. "Stay for dinner?"

Even though I wasn't sure how his parents would feel about me, I nodded. "I will, Cody, but—" I glanced at Malcolm, hoping he would agree "—I need to work on building my magic back up first."

"Don't take too long." He pulled my mouth onto his, kissing me softly. I started to pull away, but he followed, nipping at my lip. He grabbed hold of me and flipped us over.

I slid my leg along his while kneading his back.

His fingers slipped under my shirt, tracing my sides.

I arched up into him, tilting my head back, and moaned.

One of the dragons growled softly, and heat rose up my neck and over my face. I pushed against Cody's chest. "I need to go."

"Stay safe." He rolled onto his side and watched me while I slipped my hand into Malcolm's. "Love you."

"I love you, too."

Malcolm used his magic to take us back. I couldn't make myself do it. I didn't want to leave Cody.

As soon as we were in my room, Malcolm looked at Mavros. "You got this?"

Mavros inhaled deeply, grinned at me, and nodded. "Go hunt."

"I'm sorry." I went to my dresser and pulled out clothes. I could hear my parents moving around in the kitchen, getting ready for work, and I was glad I'd gotten back before they left.

Malcolm disappeared, and Mavros chuckled. Wiping his hand over his nose and mouth, he turned toward me. "It'll be like this for a while. Their beasts want blood."

"What about you?"

His expression darkened, and flames spread through his irises. "I want so much more."

Not for the first time, I was glad he wasn't my enemy anymore.

I set my clothes on the bathroom cabinet and went out to the kitchen. Mom and Dad sat at the table, drinking coffee and eating breakfast. Mom did a double-take when I walked into the room. "You're up early. Everything okay?"

"Yeah." I pulled a glass out of the cabinet.

Dad drummed his fingers on the table, a sure sign that something was bothering him. "I could call in today if you're worried about the Nephilim or being alone."

"No." I pulled the milk out of the fridge, then set it on the counter, and faced them. "Magic is kind of like a muscle. It needs to be trained. I haven't used it much lately, so I need to build it back up. The dragons are going to help me with that today."

"Not just the dragons." Mavros leaned against the door-frame, gauging my reaction.

I picked the milk back up. "I guess Mavros is, too." I held out the jug, and he walked closer. "Want some?"

"No." He reached over me and pulled down a coffee cup.

While I stirred in my chocolate, I said, "The last thing you need to worry about is me being alone. My guards won't give them another chance to take me."

"Please"—Mom focused on Mavros—"do whatever you need to to keep her safe."

The smile he shot her was wicked. "You don't need to ask me twice."

"Cody would like me to go to his house for dinner." I slid into a chair at the table. "Malcolm, Cash, Russ, and Liam will be with me."

Dad hooked his thumb over his shoulder at Mavros. "Why not him?"

"I cannot enter homes I haven't been invited into." Mavros sat across from me.

Mom paled slightly. Most of the time, I didn't think they thought about what he was, but every once in a while, they were reminded.

"Cody's parents have a right to know who they're letting in." I spun my glass between my palms.

Dad cocked an eyebrow. "And, we didn't?"

"I needed his help." I glanced across the table at Mavros. His perfection no longer entranced me. He stared into his coffee, and I couldn't help but wonder what he was thinking. "I still do."

The smile that spread over Mavros' face was real and honored.

"Mavros will be here to protect you." Arianna and Val had been in charge of keeping them safe while I was imprisoned. Even though I hadn't seen them yet, I was sure they were still filling those roles.

Liam walked into the kitchen dressed in his standard uniform. Black t-shirt, cargo pants, and work boots. He glanced around at everyone and rubbed his chin. "Morning."

Mom and Dad said, "Good morning," at the same time. Then Mom pushed her chair back. "Can I get you something for breakfast?"

His weight shifted, making him appear really uncomfortable.

"I was going to make something for Mavros and me." I walked to the fridge and looked inside. "I'll get it for Liam, too." I pulled eggs, bacon, and cheese out. "I can make omelets or waffles. Which would you prefer?"

"Protein." Mavros walked to the cabinet and pulled out the skillet. "You need protein, not sugars, if you're going to train."

Liam strode to the sink and washed his hands. "Let me help, please."

"Sure." I got out the tongs and covered a plate with paper towels. "What do you want in your omelet? We've got spinach, peppers, onions, mushrooms, tomatoes."

He pulled the bacon apart and put it in the skillet. "No mushrooms or onions, please."

"Whatever you want in yours," Mavros answered. "I've never had an omelet."

I nodded. "Okay, if I make them all the same, it will be easier."

Mom and Dad put their cups in the dishwasher. Then each of them gave me a hug. "Stay safe," Dad said.

Mom kissed my cheek. "Let us know when you'll be home."

"I will." I smiled to let them know I was okay. "Have a good day."

As soon as they left, Cash appeared next to me and chuckled softly. "Only you, Dacia." He squeezed my shoulder.

"Only me what?" I turned toward him, glad to see his guilt had been replaced with amusement.

He pointed at Mavros and Liam working side by side, making breakfast. "Only you could make that happen."

They both seemed to be at ease. Mavros chopped vegetables while Liam fried the bacon. I wasn't surprised by Mavros, but I thought Liam would be a little leerier of spending time with a demon.

"Is Malcolm still hunting?" I sat at the table and watched them cook.

Cash pulled out a chair next to me. "Yes. When he gets back, we'll start training again." He stared down at the table, and I knew without asking that he was thinking about me being captured.

I set my hand on top of his. "It wasn't your fault. Aregentum's power was gone. We thought it was over." I sent a jolt of calming energy into him and hoped it would work.

I held onto his hand until the bacon was nice and crispy and the veggies were all cut. Then I took over and made the omelets.

Cash watched us eat. His lip turned up in disgust. "Do you really enjoy human food, demon?"

"When I'm in this form." Mavros held his fork in front of his lips, waiting for Cash to say something else.

"I don't even like to eat in this body." Cash pointed at himself. "I will, but it needs to be meat, preferably raw."

I wrinkled my nose at him. "Don't gross me out. I'm trying to enjoy my breakfast."

"So, what's training going to be?" Liam took my cue and changed the subject.

I looked at Cash and smiled. "I was thinking flying."

"Yessss!"

I laughed at his response.

Liam looked from Cash to me. "Why is that so exciting?"

How much do you trust him? Hearing Cash's voice in my head startled me.

I showed him some images of Liam helping me while I was imprisoned.

Have you read his aura?

I shook my head.

Liam watched us, and from one of our conversations in my cell, I figured he probably realized we were talking.

"Liam—" I turned in my chair so that I was facing him "—all of my friends have allowed me to read their auras."

His eyes flicked to Mavros, and Mavros smiled mischievously. "Yes, even me, angel-boy."

"I trust you implicitly, but it would put them at ease if you'd let me read yours."

He pushed his plate away from him. "Sure. What do I need to do?"

"Sit there. Open your mind to me." I stared into his gray eyes and was met by a wall of light. Instead of blinking, I kept my eyes wide open and pressed through his defense.

I saw Liam as a child. He was dressed all in black and had a sword in his hand. Troy stood opposite him. "Never drop your guard." He swung his blade, and the scene changed. Liam kissed Vicki on the cheek. "Goodnight." Then he looked down at me. I was sleeping on the floor of my cell. He nudged me gently with his foot. Struggling, I made it to my hands and knees before puking all over his boot. In that instant, he went from seeing me as a threat, to seeing me as an innocent kid.

Pulling away from his memories, I felt his aura. Strength, discipline, honor. Just as I was about to let go, a sense of deep, overwhelming sadness struck me. For a second, I thought it was something from inside of me, but then I realized it was part of his aura, part of something I knew nothing about and didn't want to interfere with.

"Vicki's your Mom?" I wiped my hand over my eyes.

He shook his head. "No, she's my grandma."

"Did she leave with you?" I turned back to my breakfast. I wasn't hungry, but I knew that neither Cash nor Mavros would let me leave it on my plate.

Liam took his dishes to the sink and started filling it with water. "She wanted to leave sooner, but I told her I wouldn't leave you alone with them. As soon as we found out you were gone, we portaled out of there." He grabbed the cutting board, pans, and utensils and set them beside the sink. "So, what did you decide?"

"What I already knew." I took a drink of milk to wash the eggs down. "You're trustworthy."

Cash nodded. "Dacia doesn't fly as a human." He waved his hand. "Well, she can, but she is *ours*." The last word was spoken by Cash's dragon. The voice was deeper, richer. "She flies as one of us."

Liam shivered, then turned toward us. "You allow her to be a dragon?"

"Yes." A few scales dotted Cash's face.

I scooped the last of my breakfast into my mouth and walked toward Liam. "Their dragons didn't want to accept it, but when I could breathe fire without using magic, they did." I shrugged. "It's my true alternate form. Just like the man at my table is Cash's."

"Wow." He took my plate from me and shoved it beneath the suds. "As far as I know, no other human has survived becoming a dragon."

Cash's beast was still near the surface. "None."

"What should I do while you're training?" He rinsed the silverware off.

Mavros set his plate on the counter, then grabbed the towel from me. "Go get ready for your training."

"What do you want to do?" I let Mavros take the towel, but I didn't leave.

He lifted his shoulder. "I'd like to be useful while I'm here."

"There are imps and lesser demons hiding in the forests surrounding her house." Mavros didn't look at me, giving me the impression that they didn't want me to know I was still being hunted. "We have been clearing them out, but more come every day."

Chapter 11

As soon as the kitchen was cleaned up, Malcolm appeared. He looked a little less tense than he had when he dropped me off this morning. Liam, however, looked disheartened that he couldn't come along with us.

I patted him on the shoulder. "Tomorrow, I'll do some training you can join in on, but today, I want to spread my wings."

The smile that stretched over Malcolm's face matched Cash's, but his fangs made it appear a little more menacing.

"There's a spare key by the garage door." I pointed at it. "Please lock the house whenever you step out." I pulled a shaking hand through my hair. "Who knows what'll come after me next?"

He glanced at the dragons, and I wondered if the three of them had some idea. If they did, I didn't want to focus on it right now anyway. The sky was calling me.

Malcolm held his hand out palm up. I placed mine on top of it. Mavros and Cash followed suit. Malcolm put his other hand on top of the pile and said, "3 … 2 … 1."

We fell through the sky. Mountain peaks reached for us, but we were high above them. I called on my dragon form, and it responded instantly. Wings sprouted from my shoulders as my body lengthened and my bones reformed.

The wind caught my wings, and I rode the current. My companions, a black dragon, a purple dragon, and a three-head-ed demon, flew next to me.

I closed my eyes and allowed myself to feel at peace for the first time in a long time. One of the dragons roared. Instinct kicked in, and I responded. Flames blasted from my maw. I flapped my wings, racing to catch up to the fire. Then I pulled them against my sides and dove.

Even from this height, I could zero in on deer standing near a stream in the valleys far below us.

I spread my wings and soared over the tops of the peaks. Cash flew beside me. "Race?"

I turned my head toward him and marveled at the beauty of his scales. With my human eyes, he was purple, but up here, closer to the sun than I'd ever been, and with my dragon eyes, he was purple, lavender, lilac, amethyst, violet, plum, heliotrope, wine. Each scale contained all of the shades of purple I could imagine.

Pulling my attention away from the magnitude of colors, I asked, "Where to?"

"See those trees with the boulder in the middle of them?" He nodded to a distant mountain. It must have been twenty miles away.

"Yes."

Mavros and Malcolm lined up beside us, obviously wanting to join in on the fun.

"Ready?" I asked.

"Set," Malcolm added.

"Go," the four of us said at once.

All of them had more experience flying than I could fathom, but I held my own against them. Their bodies were bulky. Mine was streamlined.

I bolstered the wind, calling it to me, propelling myself forward.

Malcolm's laugh followed behind me. "That's cheating."

"No." I glanced over my shoulder. "It's using what God gave me."

Malcolm and Cash zipped past me, using magic of their own to drive them on. Mavros flew next to me. One of his three heads focused on our destination while the other two searched the land and sky, assumedly for threats to me.

"There's no way they could know I'm here." I hoped that I sounded as sure as I felt.

"Did you bleed?" Unlike the dragons, his voice didn't change when he did. Even as this creature, it was as silken as it was in his human form.

I swallowed hard. The peacefulness I'd felt earlier disappeared completely. The serenity was replaced by a sense of unease that grew with every flap of my wings.

The dragons slowed, looking back at me. *What is it?* Malcolm's voice penetrated my thoughts.

They can track my blood? Spots danced across my vision, and the world tilted.

"They can't fly." Malcolm tried to make his voice sound soothing, but it didn't cover the growl.

A heavy weight settled on my chest, stopping my airflow. My wings stuttered, and I dropped. I knew I needed to stretch them out to catch myself, but there seemed to be a disconnect between my brain and limbs. My heartbeat pounded in my ears, drowning out all other sounds.

I should have heard the air whooshing by me, my guards' worried voices, my thoughts.

The mountains stretched their serrated cliffs, reaching for me, ready to pluck me from the skies.

Dacia! Cash's voice tore through my skull, scattering the haze.

I snapped my wings into place. The wind snatched me, jerking me back, and I lifted. The peaks withdrew, and while my guards observed me, I surged forward.

The boulder was the size of my house. I stretched my feet out, ready to clutch it in my talons. Mavros zipped past me at the last instant, claiming victory for himself. His heads twisted around, scenting the air, and I realized he would have risked everything to beat me there.

I rotated my wings so they were perpendicular to the ground and clasped a jagged edge in my claws. It wasn't graceful, but I'd only successfully landed one other time.

Malcolm and Cash flanked me. They both transformed into their human avatars as soon as they landed. Malcolm put his hand on my foreleg. "How much of your blood do they have?"

"I don't know." I jerked my head from side to side, searching for the danger that was stealing my breath and making my heart race. "There was some on the bars, some on the floor, some on the bedding, some on my clothes." My tail swished from side to side like an agitated cat's. "Oh … and Troy nicked me with his knife."

"Did he wipe it off?" Mavros asked.

I turned toward him, expecting him to have changed back into his normal body.

All three sets of his eyes stared at me. "Did he wipe it off?" Hearing his voice come from the demon form of him was an affront to nature. A voice so rich and silky shouldn't come from something that was born of nightmares.

I tipped my head to the side. I couldn't remember if I'd seen him wipe it off. Closing my eyes to focus on my memory, kicked my other senses into overdrive. I could hear blood pumping through their bodies. I could smell every creature in the surrounding forest.

"Did. He. Wipe. The. Blood. Off?"

"I'm trying to remember." The voice that came out of me shocked me. It was a guttural growl reminiscent of the other dragons I had been with. "I think he wiped it on his pants before he folded it up."

The demon disappeared, and a black mist floated where he had been. It undulated, twisting and curling around until it formed Mavros the man. He stepped toward me. "Think or know?"

"Think." I lowered my head, still not willing to retake my own body. The mountains here were cold, and even if they hadn't been, I felt safer in this form. "I was in a bad place … mentally and physically. I can't be sure, but I think he wiped it off."

Cash rubbed his chin and paced a few steps away from me, then back. "I can't imagine they can get back in there to get her blood off the bars or floor. There would've had to have been a lot of blood on the cloth for it to be useful, but if it is on the blade still, they'll be able to use it."

"It was on the zip tie." The words escaped on a breath. "He pulled it so tightly that it made my wrists bleed."

Malcolm growled, and his fangs extended.

I couldn't focus on his reaction right now, though. The terror that had risen in me, knowing they might be able to track me, was all-consuming. "I don't know what he did with it. There was nowhere for him to dispose of it around me."

Mavros strode toward me. "Do you want me to remain bound to you?" He stopped in front of me. I couldn't read the expression on his face or the scents coming off of him. "I will accept whatever you choose."

I looked at Cash and Malcolm wondering what they would think of me if I said yes.

As if they knew, they both nodded at me. "You need him." Malcolm sounded as surprised to say it as Mavros looked to hear it.

"Yes." There was no way they couldn't hear the relief in my voice. I had been terrified that my decision would upset the dragons.

He knelt in front of me and put his hand on top of my foot. "Let me see your power."

I focused on my magic, and Mavros and I stood in the darkened room with light illuminating nothing but the serpents. The pearlescent snake had grown again. It slithered over to me.

I am free.

"Yes." I rubbed my hand over its head. "I will do everything I can to keep it that way."

While it nuzzled its head against my palm, I looked at Mavros' power. The obsidian snake was more gold than black now. Its scales shimmered, and prisms danced along the walls and floor.

Mavros sat on the ground next to it. He ran his hand along the creature's back, and everywhere his fingers touched the gold deepened, slowly morphing to ebony.

"This won't keep me from using my magic." My words echoed, bouncing off the walls. The worry in them increased with every reverberation. "Will it?"

He glanced up at me. "No, I will not awaken my power." When he finished the snake was as black as a moonless night.

All hints of gold were gone. He stood in front of me. "Thank you, Dacia."

"For what?" My arms hung limply at my sides, and I tilted my head.

"For allowing me to stay." He lifted his hand to my cheek, gently rubbing his thumb over it. "For letting me protect you."

I backed away from him. Here where we were the only two people, it felt way too intimate. Nodding at the serpents, I asked, "Will it last?"

"I believe it will, but you should keep an eye on it." He took my hand in his, indicating he was ready to go back to the real world. "Let me know immediately if anything changes."

Cash and Malcolm watched us. I nodded my head, and Mavros said, "It is done. Thank you."

"She still belongs to us." Malcolm's pupils were thin slits, and smoke billowed from his nostrils. It seemed his dragon wasn't as sure about his decision as Malcolm had been.

Surprisingly, Mavros didn't argue this time.

Cash's voice was soft, but as a dragon, I would have picked up his words from ten miles away. "Transform, Dacia. We will keep you safe while we train."

"No." I backed away from them. Fire built up inside of me, ready to blast at my unseen enemy. My tail smashed into a tree, knocking the centuries-old pine to the ground. Guilt riddled me as it tumbled to its death.

Malcolm strode forward. "I will hold your hand the whole time, Dacia, if that's what you need. I will do whatever you want to ensure that we won't be separated." He pressed his hand to my scales, and soothing magic poured into me. "We will keep you safe." This time it was his dragon that spoke to me.

I nodded and let go, transforming back into myself. I stood in front of my three sentinels, feeling inadequate. Shivers racked my body. The trembling was uncontrollable.

Malcolm wrapped his arms around me, pulling me against his chest. His body heated until I stopped.

Mavros slid his arms out of his jacket and handed it to me. "You need this more than I do."

"What are we going to do?" I held Mavros' coat in front of me, wondering if I should bother with it.

Malcolm pointed at a trail through the trees. "We're going to run up the mountain while you use your powers to exhaustion."

"Are you sure?" I looked at each of them. "Are you sure you want my magic used up? What if something happens?"

Cash had been hanging back, but he walked over to me. "Nothing's going to happen, but we will refuel you before we leave."

I could see the sorrow and guilt in his eyes, and I hated myself for making him keep reliving it. It hadn't been his fault that I was captured, but there was no way he would ever believe that.

The wind ripped through my sweatshirt, chilling me as soon as I stepped away from Malcolm, so I pulled on Mavros' coat. Then I ran toward the trail Malcolm had pointed to. I felt him running closer to me than my own shadow.

Mavros cut through the timber and appeared on the path in front of me in his panther form. The beast was corded muscle covered in midnight fur. Powerful, deadly, magnificent.

My steps faltered, and he matched his stride to mine. Once the pace was set, I lit a fire in the palm of my hand. The spark grew until it was the size of a softball. The blue flames soared ahead of us, and I chuckled.

Mavros looked back at me. Curiosity filled his fiery eyes.

"I'm blazing the trail." I nodded at my fireball.

He chuffed and turned back around, following my flames up the twisting path. Running behind him, with the sun shining on his ebony fur, I realized for the first time that he had spots like any jaguar or leopard would.

"What else do you have, Dacia?" Malcolm moved alongside me, and Cash took over his place as my shadow.

I focused on my hair, turning it a deep purple with teal highlights.

I could hear the laughter in Cash's voice when he said, "Purple suits you."

"I thought you might like that." Like Cody's little sister, Britny, I had always admired the purple streaks in Cash's hair.

As I continued running, the long, straightened strands blew over my shoulder and into my face, so I shortened my hair into a pixie cut. Then I concentrated on my shoulders. Wings erupted, bursting through Mavros' jacket. They were fairy wings in the same colors as my hair. I fluttered them and felt myself lift off the ground.

Malcolm slid his hand into mine, keeping me next to him.

I dropped back down and continued running. The longer I held the unnatural transformations, the quicker my power drained out of me. After several minutes, my breathing came in harsher gulps. The air here was thinner than I was used to, and my magic use was taking a toll on me. I slowed, and my guardians instantly matched their pace to mine.

"Doing okay?" Cash asked.

I placed my hands on the top of my head and slowed to a walk. The wings disappeared, and my hair became my own. "I think I'm done." I ambled to the edge of the cliff and looked out over the world.

Lakes, rivers, and forests covered the ground as far as I could see. There were no roads, no houses, no telephone poles, and no cell towers. Snow-covered mountain peaks surrounded a lush, green valley. At first glance, the rocky outcrops appeared gray, but as I stared at them, I noticed pink, green, brown, and white stone mixed in to make up the range that stretched out in front of me.

Malcolm stood beside me with his hand on my shoulder. *You shouldn't give up yet.*

I can't use it all. Tears pooled in my eyes. When I looked up at him, his face looked distorted. *I can't be powerless.* I wrapped my arms around my body, trying to hold in the fear and emptiness I felt at the thought. *I can't.*

Cash and Mavros lifted their noses to the air, trying to figure out where my panic was coming from.

Malcolm pulled me against him, and I buried my face in his chest. "I know I'm supposed to be stronger than this, but … they broke me, Malcolm."

His growl rumbled through his chest and into my body. "I'm taking Dacia back to her house."

I looked up at his face. His fangs were easily twice as long as normal. I remembered a time when it would've scared me, a time when I thought dragons were the nastiest creatures on the planet, but I knew better now. They were like any predator. They didn't kill just to kill. They didn't look for fights. They protected their own, and for the most part, they just tried to survive.

He tightened his grip on me and teleported us back to my house. We stood in my room, and even though I wasn't wobbly or disoriented, I held onto him. I sensed when the others arrived, but I didn't let go. Malcolm's hold on me softened, and he ran his hand from the top of my head to the middle of my back, over and over until I finally stepped away.

I lifted my sweatshirt collar to my face and wiped my eyes. "Sorry."

"Don't apologize." It was his dragon that answered, and I realized my emotions were pushing him over the edge. "You are but a pup, and they tortured you." He turned toward Mavros. "Keep her safe, demon."

Mavros bowed his head at him. "With my life."

Then Malcolm and Cash disappeared.

I pulled Mavros' jacket off, handing it to him. "I'm afraid I ruined it." My lip quivered, and I pressed my palms to my face.

"It's okay." He tried to pull my hands down, but I held on tighter.

I heard the coat hit my bed. Then he wrapped his arms around me. "Dacia, it's not a big deal. How many of my jackets do you have lying around here? If I need a pristine one, I can always take one of them."

"When's it going to end?" My voice sounded tiny. "When will I feel safe again?"

Chapter 12

*L*iam sat next to me in my truck. I gripped the steering wheel until my knuckles turned white. The tension ran up my arms and into my neck. I tried to loosen my hands, but somehow, I kept ending up in this same position. Even though it was only a short drive to Cody's, I felt vulnerable.

It had crossed my mind to teleport there, but since Britny and Brandon didn't know about me yet, I decided it would be best to drive. They would be at school when I arrived, but I didn't want Cody to have to pretend to give me a ride home. I didn't want him to be out on his own. He'd already been used as leverage to get me too many times. I couldn't keep putting him in danger when he couldn't protect himself from all the diabolical beings that wanted to harm me.

When I pulled into Cody's driveway, I pried my fingers from the steering wheel and flexed them several times to get the blood flowing back into them. Malcolm and Cash appeared outside of my truck. A startled yelp escaped from me, and my heartbeat crescendoed.

Liam settled his hand on my shoulder, a small comfort. "You've got this."

Malcolm opened my door and held onto my arm as we walked to Cody's porch. Each step we took toward the house made my knees weaker. Cody's parents were going to hate me after this. There was no way they could accept the threat I was to his life.

Malcolm wrapped his arm around my waist, lifting me slightly. "You're okay," he murmured. "You're okay."

The door opened before we reached it. Cody stood inside the house still. He had on a blue t-shirt that made his eyes more vibrant than normal and jeans. He must have just gotten out of the shower because his hair was wet, and his feet were bare. Had they not been, by the look on his face, he would have rushed outside to rescue me. "What's wrong?"

"They're going to hate me, Cody." My voice cracked. I stopped walking and folded my arms over my stomach. The thought of going in there and seeing them look at me with disdain was more than I could handle. Malcolm's energy poured into me, numbing me.

As soon as I was inside, Cody cupped my face in his hands. "They don't. They won't."

I clutched his shirt but didn't say anything.

"They know you're it for me, Dacia." He leaned his forehead against mine. "They knew before we did." He bent down and pulled my boots off. Then he took my hand in his and led me through the house.

Malcolm, Cash, and Liam followed us. Bo, Josh's dog, didn't try to chase them off, so I assumed he'd been locked up before we arrived. We went to the dining room where Susan and Brent were already sitting.

Susan hopped up, flipping her light brown hair over her shoulder, and walked over. Hugging me, she said, "I'm so glad you're safe. We were so worried about you."

"Thank you." Cody hadn't let go of my hand, so I hugged her with one arm.

When she pulled away from me to look at Malcolm and Cash, tears brightened her blue eyes. "Thank you for getting her back to us."

Cash ducked his head down, hiding his guilt, and Malcolm's jaw tightened before he said, "She freed herself." His voice was a growl.

As soon as she let go of me, Brent hugged me. "We were worried about you." He stepped back, and I realized how much of Cody came from him. They had the same blond hair, the same sapphire eyes, and the same expressions. "You've got another friend."

"Yeah, uh—" I nodded at Liam, not quite sure how to introduce him "—he's, uh, helping protect me."

He stepped forward and shook each of their hands. "Liam."

After introductions were made, Susan brought drinks out for us and said, "Well, sit down."

Susan sat at the head of the table with Brent to her right. I sat between Cody and Malcolm. Without Josh here, there was nobody to look disapprovingly at how close Malcolm was to me. Cash and Liam sat across from us, scrutinizing every move I made.

"So"—Susan folded her hands on the table in front of her and glanced between Cash and Malcolm—"was Britny right about you two?"

Cash shook his head and wiped his hand over his mouth. "We are not fairies."

"But you're not human either?"

"Mom." Cody's voice held a warning. "You can't un-know."

"Nor do we want to." She smiled at me, and it lit up her entire face. "I believe Dacia will be part of our lives for a long time to come."

Malcolm waited for her gaze to return to him. Then he shook his head and took my hand in his. "We are not human. Dacia freed us, and we owe her our lives."

"You don't." I squeezed his fingers with mine. "You've repaid your debt."

I failed you. Cash stared across the table at me. His purple eyes bored into mine.

Brent nodded at Liam. "And how do you fit into this?"

"I, uh … I was Dacia's guard while she was imprisoned." His chin dropped to his chest. "I tried to keep her safe from the others."

Cody's parents looked at me in confusion. Then Brent turned back to Liam. "Are you human?"

"Half."

"Okay, then." Susan stood and leaned on her chair, taking each of us in. "So is Dacia safe?"

A startled laugh spilled out of me. "Probably not."

Cody ran his hand down my leg, and Malcolm let soothing energy flow into me.

"The Neph—" Malcolm stopped and stared at them. "How much do you want to know?"

Brent reached for Susan's hand. "I, uh, I think we'd like to know it all." He looked at her, and she nodded before sitting down again.

Malcolm's finger skimmed my chin, tilting my face up to his. *How much do you want them to know?*

"They're talking." Cody tapped his temple. "With their minds."

I guess what my parents do. I pressed my eyes shut, hoping I was making the right decision. *Then they can talk to each other about it when we're back at college.*

Can you show them your magic? Worry seeped into his expression before he hid it behind a veil.

Yes. I pushed my chair back and stood in front of it. "Malcolm wants me to give you a sample of what I can do."

Brent and Susan leaned forward and watched me eagerly.

Holding my hand in the air with my palm facing up, I lit a spark. It grew into a blue ball of fire the size of a baseball. I didn't want to look at Cody's parents' faces and see fear or disgust on them, but I couldn't not look either.

They stared at the flames. Wonder lit their eyes. Their mouths were slightly parted.

I slid my hand out from beneath the fire, letting it hover in front of me. Then I blasted it with ice. Frost crawled over the flames, engulfing them. Through the smooth surface, I saw when the last of the light inside flickered and went out.

Never having tried it before, I pictured the kitchen sink, then waved my hand. The sphere disappeared, but I heard it clunk against the stainless steel.

Liam knew about my magic, had witnessed it being used, but his mouth hung open. "You just used what? Four different powers? Without even flinching?"

"Yeah." I tilted my head and changed my hair to purple tipped with teal like I had on my run earlier today.

"No wonder why you were able to break the collar so easily." He leaned back in his chair and stared up at the ceiling.

I pinched my eyebrows together and looked from Cash to Malcolm. I didn't know what Liam was getting at, but I didn't want to delve into that subject right now. Letting my hair color go back to normal, I sat next to Cody again.

Susan recovered first. "That was amazing. Is that all you can do?"

"No." Heat crept onto my cheeks. "I can do—"

"Anything you can imagine," Cody finished for me.

I pulled my hand through my hair. "Pretty much."

"Wow." Brent rubbed the back of his neck and looked around excitedly. "Cody told us, but wow."

Their reactions loosened the knots my stomach had been tied in. Cody draped his arm over my shoulder and tucked me against his side. He had a smug what-did-I-tell-you look on his face.

Malcolm squeezed my fingers. *Would you like me to tell them your story?*

Please. I lowered my chin and nodded.

He held his hands in front of him with just the tips of his fingers touching. "Dacia is … recovering from her latest incident. Some of the things she's been through may cause her to have panic attacks, so she would like me to tell you most of her story." He pointed at Liam. "Some of his people, the Nephilim, are still after Dacia. They believe she is a threat. She's not."

"Half human. Half?" Brent asked Liam.

"Angel." His lips pinched into a bitter smile, and his shoulders slumped. "Though, some of them aren't acting very angelic."

I snorted but otherwise kept my mouth shut.

Malcolm started at the beginning, explaining my dreams, my training with Sarah, and my battle with Nefarious. Then he told them about the dragons and Draconian. He didn't tell them how the dragons had harmed Cody, my other friends, or me. He didn't tell them I was a murderer who ran Draconian through with a sword, then watched as the light faded from his eyes.

Susan's gaze shifted from Malcolm to Cash. "Britny was right? You two are dragons? How?" Her eyes were wide, and her foot bounced up and down.

"It's okay," I said. "They won't hurt you."

Russ materialized in the doorway. He folded his arms over his chest and leaned against the frame.

"You, too?" Brent asked.

Russ tilted his chin toward his chest. "I'm here to make sure Cody stays safe."

Susan relaxed a little. Russ had been staying with them for a good chunk of Christmas break. He hadn't harmed anyone or caused any trouble. "Dragons? Really?" She looked from Russ to Cody.

Blood-red scales dotted Russ' skin, and his amber eyes became those of his dragon's. "Yes, really." The voice that came out of him was deeper, richer than the voice they were used to hearing.

"Okay, then." Brent clapped his hands, then rubbed them together. "Dragons."

Please ... don't tell them everything about Mavros. I sent my thoughts to all of the dragons in the room. *Don't tell them how he made me feel, how he wanted Cody out of the way.* I pulled my lip into my mouth, trying to come up with a way to justify my request. *They might meet him someday.*

Malcolm held onto my hand. *I won't, Dacia. I don't want them to fear for their son's life.*

Russ lifted his nose and inhaled deeply before disappearing.

Brent and Susan stared at the space where he had been standing.

"We are not without our own powers," Cash answered their unasked question.

Malcolm told them about Mavros, leaving out his plan to kill my friends and how I had defeated him. I didn't want my parents to find out I had killed myself. Of all the things I had gone through, that was the one I was certain they wouldn't be able to handle.

He moved on to my first encounter with the Nephilim, Argentum, and how Mavros came back into my life. Without telling them that I had killed Argentum and that my magic had tried to kill Cody, he explained why the Nephilim wanted me captured.

"Wait." Susan held her hand up. "If Mavros is one of your guards, why haven't we met him?"

I stared at her, going through Malcolm's story in my head, trying to remember everything he had told them. Finally, I pinched the bridge of my nose and said, "Mavros is a demon."

Both Susan and Brent sucked in deep breaths. Brent crossed himself, and I wondered if he had been raised Catholic.

My chest tightened. Would this be the part that made them fear me? "He cannot come into your house without being invited, and even though I trust him with my life, it was not right to bring him into your home without you knowing."

"Why?" Susan looked around the table at everyone before settling her gaze on me. "Why would you trust a demon?"

"He saved me." My voice was soft. I knew everyone thought I was crazy for befriending him. "More than once. He healed me. He fought Argentum's control for me."

Liam cleared his throat. "As a Nephilim, I can sense evil." He folded his hands together on the table. "It's there in him, but it's not like it is in other demons. It's buried deep inside. I didn't even notice it at first."

I stared at him. My mouth fell open. No wonder why he had been so at ease cooking with Mavros. He should have told me, though. He should have let me know that I wasn't being fooled by Mavros' act.

"If it's safer for you to be with him—" Brent paused, making sure I was paying attention to him "—you may invite him in."

I nodded. "We'll see. I have the power to rescind his right to enter, but I don't want to command him unless I have to. I'm not sure where that would leave us."

"Think about it," Susan said.

Malcolm continued with my story. He was just finishing telling them about my imprisonment and the standoff in my front yard when Brandon and Britny were dropped off by the school bus.

Susan leaned over the table. Even though the kids hadn't come inside yet, her voice was low. "They know none of this." She looked directly at me. "The older boys know about you and that you have bodyguards, but that's it."

The door opened and closed, and a minute later, Britny and Brandon tore around the corner. "Dacia!" Britny's voice was higher than normal. I could feel her excitement. "You brought your fair—dragons!" She clapped her hands and ran to Cash, hugging him while bouncing up and down on the balls of her feet.

"Hello, little one." The smile that spread across his face was filled with adoration.

She narrowed her eyes at Brandon and whispered in that way six-year-olds have, "Brandon says you can't be dragons."

"What does he think we are then?" Cash asked while he lifted her onto his knee.

"People." He sat next to Cody and pulled books out of his backpack. "And Dacia's bodyguards."

Cody laughed, but it sounded forced. "Bodyguards? Why?"

"Ask them." Brandon's hand fluttered through the air in a dismissive wave. "Something about magic."

Brent and Susan looked at each other, and without making a sound, something passed between them. "You cannot say a word to anyone outside of this house." Susan pierced him with her gaze. "It will put Dacia's life in even more danger."

He looked at her like she was trying to pull a fast one on him, but he wasn't about to take any part in it. "Really? You really think I believe that?" He grabbed a pencil and a worksheet. "Next, I suppose you'll tell me they're dragons." He looked at Cash. "My what big teeth you have."

Cash smiled at him, showing fangs he didn't usually have in human form. "You're thinking of a wolf, boy."

Britny looked around the table like we were all stupid. "Dacia is magic, and they are dragons." She looked at Liam with one side of her mouth puckered up. "But not him."

"What am I then?" He leaned closer to her. His steel eyes sparkled with mirth.

She tapped her finger on her chin. "You could be a fairy … or an elf."

"Nope." He chuckled and sat back.

Her eyes widened, and her voice turned dreamy. "Or an angel."

Before Liam could say anything, I asked, "Why do you think I'm magic?"

"Because you are, sillyhead," she said it like it was the strangest thing she had ever been asked. She glanced around and leaned toward me like she wanted to share a secret. Holding her hand beside her mouth, blocking her words from Brandon, she stared at him while she whispered, "You always have been." She tapped her chest. "I can feel it."

Brandon laughed. "And you guys think I have an imagination."

"So, are you?" Britny focused on Liam.

He winked at her. "Only half the time."

Brent and Susan both got up. "We need to get supper started. The boys will be starving when they get home from basketball practice."

"I can help." I started to stand, but Cody held onto my hand, keeping me in place.

"No, Dacia." Susan shook her head at me. "You're our guest." She stopped by my chair and gave me a hug. "Thanks for the talk."

"Yeah." I hugged her back, then whispered, "Russ, Malcolm, and Cash don't eat."

"Good to know." She walked into the kitchen with Brent, and I heard pots and pans clanging together.

"I feel like I should be helping."

Brandon set his pencil down and stared at me. "If you wanna help and you're really magic, finish my homework for me. I have other things to do."

"That'd be nice." Cody laughed. Then he stood, reaching one hand down to me, while he ruffled Brandon's hair.

Brandon picked his pencil up. "Thought so."

Cody led me into the kitchen. I could feel Malcolm's gaze on me, but he didn't get up and follow us in.

"He won't quit," Cody said to his parents.

"I know." Susan set her knife on the cutting board and turned toward us. "Could you do something at dinner to show them all?"

"What you did with the fire and ice was amazing"—Brent continued cooking hamburger without looking at me—"but something simpler would probably be better for this."

"Uh … okay." I sagged against Cody. I had spent my whole life trying to keep this secret, and so many people knew already. What would happen when more did? Would their lives be in danger, too?

My chest tightened, and I clenched Cody's hand. Sweat beaded on my forehead. My legs weakened until I slid to the floor. I pulled my knees up and wrapped my arms around them.

Dacia. Malcolm's voice rang through my head at the same time a chair was pushed back.

I felt everybody looking at me. The walls seemed to close in around me, sucking the air out of the room as they pressed closer.

Malcolm knelt in front of me and lifted my chin so I was looking at him. "Dacia." He scooped me up and said, "I'm taking her to your room."

While he carried me, he sent soothing power into me. The panic died down, but I felt wiped out. He set me on Cody's bed and waved him over.

Cody stretched out next to me, tucking me against his side. He rubbed my back, waiting for my muscles to loosen as tension released from my body.

"I'm sorry." I snuggled against him.

His hand stopped moving for a moment. "For what?"

"Your parents probably think I'm a nutjob."

Malcolm growled. "No, they do not." He stepped toward the door and pointed at it. "There's too much emotion. Do you mind?"

"You're not leaving. Are you?" My heartbeat ramped up as I lifted my head and looked at him over Cody's shoulder.

He held his hand over his mouth and nose. "I'll be in the hall."

I lay back down and closed my eyes. I needed to get my emotions under control before I chased Malcolm and Cash away again. I needed them here with me.

A soft knock sounded on the door, and Malcolm was instantly back in the room. He stood by the open window with his face pressed up against the screen.

"Come in," Cody said without pulling away from me.

Susan stood in the doorway, wringing her hands. "I hope we didn't upset you, Dacia." She walked in and sat on the edge of the bed.

"It's—" the word latched onto something in my throat, and I couldn't force it out.

Malcolm turned away from the window and waved his hand toward me. "This is why I told you her story. The panic comes over her, and she can't let go of it."

"I can't imagine how you handle it at all." She rubbed my arm. "You've been through so much."

Tears leaked out of the sides of my eyes, dripping onto Cody's arm. I bit my bottom lip and nodded. I knew I couldn't say anything right now, so I didn't even bother trying.

"We're here for you if you need us." She stood and walked to Cody's door.

As soon as she stepped into the hall, Malcolm disappeared again.

Cody held onto me, not saying anything, just letting me figure out how to cope.

I pulled myself closer to him and kissed the bottom of his chin. "I'm sorry."

"No, don't apologize." He pulled back from me and stared into my eyes. "Please. Gonna take time for you to deal."

I pressed my head into his chest, and his arms tightened around me. "I don't know if I'll ever be able to. I don't think I'll ever be who I was."

"I'll love you no matter what." He held me until we heard the front door open. "If you don't wanna show them, don't."

I sat up and wiped my hands over my face. "They know. They might as well see it."

I walked out into the living room with Cody following me.

Josh was setting his boots to the side of the door. He looked up and saw me with Cody, Malcolm, and Cash and stood up straight. "I guess I owe you guys an apology." I shook my head, but he held his hand up. "I do. I should've known you wouldn't cheat on my brother. I shouldn't have jumped to conclusions. I'm sorry." He held his hand out to Malcolm.

Malcolm stepped forward and shook it. "It takes a big man to admit he's wrong."

Josh walked over to Cash and said, "Thank you for watching out for her. Cody'd be a mess if something happened to her."

"It's our pleasure." Cash shook his hand.

"Speaking of—" Josh turned toward me "—he's been one for the last several days, so what happened to you?"

Cody wrapped his arms around me and pulled me against his body. "Told you she was outta town."

"You need a better story." Josh snickered and pushed past us. "Something happened."

"Dinner's ready," Susan called from the kitchen.

Britny ran through the hallway to the dining room. "I get to sit by Cash."

"Someone's got a crush." Dawson smiled at us as he walked by.

"Do you need help?" I asked as I walked into the kitchen.

Susan shook her head. "I have five kids. They can help. Go on in and sit down."

The Hawks boys carried in meat, cheese, tortillas, and everything you could imagine topping tacos with. Then they brought in chips and salsa, rice, and salad.

Brent stood at the head of the table and held his hands to his sides, taking Susan's in one and Cody's in the other. The rest of us followed. I slipped mine into Cody's and Malcolm's, and unlike last time I was here, Josh didn't shoot a dirty look our way. Brent said grace, then as we were sitting, he said,

"Dacia, why don't you and your friends start since you're our guests."

"Okay." I nodded. I was about to ask for the shells when I decided to make a spectacle of myself instead. Focusing on the tray they were on, I lifted them into the air and brought them to me. I carefully peeled two shells off the top and sent the tray to Liam.

He smiled. "Thank you."

Without meeting any of Cody's sibling's eyes, I did the same with the meat and cheese. My hands shook, not from the effort, but because the room was silent.

Malcolm draped his arm over my chair and touched his thumb to the back of my neck. *You're okay. Look at them.*

A wide smile covered Britny's face. When my gaze met hers, she said, "I knew it!"

Brandon stared at me. His napkin was held in his hands like he'd been planning on spreading it over his lap but hadn't quite gotten there yet. "Are you sure you can't use it for homework?"

I shook my head. "I wish I could." My grades had dropped significantly since starting college. Between fighting monsters, training, and hiding out from Nephilim, school had taken a backseat. "Believe me."

"Whoa." Brandon dropped his napkin and waved his hands. "Wait. Does that mean they're dragons?"

I glanced at Cody's parents. I didn't know how much they wanted their kids to know, and it wasn't my place to make that decision for them.

Brent pointed at Susan, and she nodded. "Yes. Cash and Malcolm are dragons."

"Don't forget Russ, Mommy." Britny knelt on her chair and reached for a tortilla. "He's one, too."

Cash laughed and handed her the meat. "Yes, he is."

Dawson stared long and hard at Cash. Then he focused on Malcolm. His eyes were narrowed, and his head shook so slightly that I wondered if he even realized it. "Dragons. Is that like a special division of bodyguards or something?"

"No." Malcolm leaned back with his hands behind his head. "It's what we are. These bodies are our avatars."

Josh laughed. "Nice try." He scooped rice onto his plate. "But, I ain't buying it."

"May I?" Cash asked.

"Sure," Brent said, "but pass the tortillas first."

Cash did as he was told. Then he stood, facing Cody's family. Purple scales covered his arms, neck, and face. His pupils turned into thin slits in his amethyst eyes, and horns jutted out from his head.

I remembered when he had shown up in the cave where Cody and I were hiding from Argentum and the Nephilim. When I found him with Malcolm, his features had looked similar to this, but he had been filled with rage. He had sworn to protect me, and even though he had never been nice to me, he had begun to respect and like me against his better judgment.

Brandon's eyes widened, and he looked around the room, assessing everybody else. Britny stared at Cash with a satisfied smile lighting up her face.

Josh shot him a crooked grin. "I guess dragons are much smaller than I imagined."

"Careful, boy." Cash's voice was the deep, rich timbre of his dragon's. "If I transformed fully in here, you'd have to rebuild your house."

Dawson smirked at Josh and elbowed him in the side. "That's what I'd say, too."

"Don't." Cody handed me the tomatoes. "He's not transforming in here."

Britny patted Cash's hand. "He can show us later." She turned to Liam. "Can we see your angel?"

"This is me." He waved his hand in front of himself. "I don't have wings or a different body."

She pursed her lips, then nodded, accepting his answer. "Can I have cheese, please?"

"Aren't you gonna eat?" Josh waved the spoon from the meat at Cash and Malcolm.

Malcolm shook his head. "We can eat your food, but we prefer not to." He let his features morph a little, not enough to look like a dragon but to look more menacing. "Dacia's magic and our identities must remain secret."

Each of the boys nodded, and Britny said, "Okay."

As soon as we finished eating supper, I thanked Cody's family for their hospitality. "I should go." I chewed on my lip. "I don't want to stay too late. Mom and Dad will be worried enough."

"Oh, dear—" Susan pulled me into a hug "—we understand."

While I put on my coat and boots, Cash and Malcolm started my truck and made sure it was safe for me to leave. Once I got the okay, Cody walked outside with me. The quarter moon brightened the evening sky. I shivered and wrapped my arms around myself.

"Can I come back tonight … if I need to?" I stared up at the stars. They made me feel like my problems were just tiny blips, and the thought soothed me. A lot of people would have been depressed by that, but to me, it was a relief knowing there were bigger things than me to worry about.

Cody brushed his fingers over my cheek, drawing my attention back to him. "Whatever you need, Dacia." He pulled me closer and kissed the top of my head.

Needing to be closer to him and needing to not feel so alone, I wrapped my arms around his neck and stood on my tiptoes, drawing his mouth down to mine.

Chapter 13

Broken

ootfalls sound in the darkness. They edge closer. With each quiet step, my heart pounds against my chest.

I know it's Troy.

I know he's coming to terrorize me.

I know that if I had my magic he would be no match for me.

But I don't.

And he's stronger than I am.

The key jangles, then slips into the lock.

My eyes dart back and forth, searching for an escape, but there isn't one. There's no place to run or hide. There's nothing for me to do but take the beating he's about to dole out.

He steps toward the cot, and I roll off, keeping it between us. He laughs, but it sounds menacing, not amused. "One of these nights, you won't hear me coming." His knife swipes through the air between us. "After that, you might not wake up again."

"You're supposed to be a good guy." Fear clings to my voice, making it louder than normal. It echoes through the chamber, and I realize how pathetic I sound.

Troy backs away, and I ready myself to dart to the opposite end of the cot. He moves back another step. Then he dives over the bed and grabs my arm.

He yanks it behind me, twisting it, making me turn my back on him. I whimper, and he tugs it harder. With his feet on either side of mine, he walks me toward the bars.

The cell presses against me, but he keeps pushing, keeps moving forward, squeezing me between them and him. When there is no way for me to move at all, he says, "Call your demon."

"No." With my face squashed between the bars and his muscled chest, the word sounds muffled.

He steps back slightly, grabs my hair, and slams my head against the cage. "Summon him. Now!"

Blood trickles down my cheek from my hairline.

A fierce growl fills the room, and hot breath blasts my face.

My eyes snapped open and without conscious thought turned into a dragon's. No light filtered in through the window. I stared up at Malcolm. Anger etched his features. He brushed my hair off my face. Then he looked at his fingers. His eyes dilated, and his fangs descended.

"Malcolm." Mavros' voice was a warning.

Malcolm jerked his head to the side to glare at Mavros. While his attention was diverted, I slid back. One of my legs slipped out from under the covers. I was just about to put it on the ground when Malcolm grabbed my arm.

I stared into his dragon's eyes and saw my reflection in them. Blood covered the left side of my face. "You vowed not to hurt me."

He blinked, loosening his grip on my arm.

Mavros leapt, morphing into his panther before he landed between us. He lowered his head and arched his back, growling at Malcolm.

I pulled away and teleported into the bathroom. By the time I got the blood cleaned off of me and went back to my room, Malcolm was gone.

Mavros lay stretched out on my bed in human form. "Looks like it's just you and me." He patted the mattress. "I'll keep you safe."

"I—" I stared at Mavros lying on my bed. It was tempting to snuggle up next to him and be held. I felt broken and alone and needed human contact. Turning away from him so he couldn't read my expression, I looked out the window and wrapped my arms around myself. "I'm going to Cody's."

The bed creaked when he got off of it. "I can't keep you safe there." He put his hands on my shoulders, and his touch filled some of my empty places.

"His parents gave me permission to invite you in if I need to." I set my hand on top of his.

He let go of me, backing away. "Stay safe, Dacia."

I turned invisible and teleported to Cody's room. The light was on, and he was still awake, propped up on one arm with a book on the bed in front of him, but it didn't look like he was reading. I walked over to the light switch and turned it off.

He looked toward me and smiled. "Wondered if you'd come."

I pulled the covers back and lay down next to him before making myself visible. "I broke Malcolm."

He moved his book to his nightstand before wrapping his arms around me. I snuggled against him and fell asleep feeling safe and loved.

Tuesday morning, Cash, Mavros, Liam, and I sat at the kitchen table. I wasn't ready to be awake, but as soon as we heard movement at Cody's, I had teleported home.

"I don't think Troy will try anything while you're here." Liam poured syrup over his pancakes. "Khione is still guarding your house."

The chocolate in my milk had settled to the bottom. I grabbed my spoon and stirred it, focusing on the brown specks, watching them disappear into the milk. "So … when? On my way to college? While I'm there?"

"Diana and I have been discussing whether or not he'll try to take you again at all." He held a forkful of food in front of his mouth. "He's on the run now. It won't be as easy for them to hide you."

My stomach sank, and I pushed my plate away from me. "He'll come. He's not the kind to let his quarry escape." I looked into Cash's amethyst eyes. *Where's Malcolm? Is he okay?*

"Neither of our dragons took your capture well." He stared out the window, refusing to meet my gaze. "He'll be here if you need him, but he needs some time."

After breakfast, Liam showered and went to bed. Apparently, unlike dragons and demons, Nephilim needed to sleep. Even though he didn't believe Troy would come after me here, he'd stayed up all night patrolling.

Cash and Mavros took me high up into the mountains to spread my wings and use my powers. Then I spent the day packing. Friday, as long as nothing happened to delay us, Cody and I would be driving back to Phlox University. Hopefully, once I was gone, I wouldn't have to worry about my parents' safety anymore.

Wednesday and Thursday followed the same pattern. During the night, I snuck off to be with Cody. Early in the morning, I teleported back home, trained, did laundry, packed, and spent the evenings with my parents. Malcolm stayed away.

Friday morning, I teleported to my room just in time to hear a knock on my door. I hurriedly slipped under the covers and clutched my extra pillow, hoping my act would be convincing. I peered at my parents through barely slitted eyes.

Mom sat on my bed. "Would you like us to take the day off and go with you?"

My first impulse was to tell her that would be wonderful, but I stopped myself before the words escaped. "No." I sat up.

"No?" Her eyebrows pinched together, and she sounded like I had slapped her.

Dad stepped closer, folding his arms over his chest. "Why not?"

I hadn't handled this right. I'd upset them when all I wanted to do was protect them. "It's not that I don't want you there. I'm afraid they'll—" Troy's hate-filled face skittered through my mind; I swallowed hard, hoping I would never see him again but knowing I probably would too soon "—they'll use you against me. You'll probably be safer here."

"Oh." Dad rubbed his jaw. "It is a long drive with lots of open space. I could see that."

"Will you be safe?" Mom clutched my hand, squeezing my fingers tight enough to show me the depth of her concern.

Safe. Would I ever be safe? Was that even a possibility for me? I kept my mouth shut until I had time to think. I didn't want to make them worry more than they already would. "I should be. I'll have Liam with me."

"Liam?" Dad's voice shot up at the end.

I nodded. "He can't turn invisible and fly." I tugged my hand through my tangled curls. "So, he'll be with me. Mavros and all of the dragons will make sure Cody and I stay safe."

"You'll call us as soon as you get there," Mom said.

It wasn't a question, but I answered anyway. "Yes."

Shortly before Cody showed up, my phone's notification went off. A text message from Sarah said, "See me before you go to your room. Cody too."

A ton of questions popped into my head at once. I thought about responding with several of them, but I settled on, "OK."

As soon as I heard wheels crunching over the gravel, Liam and I went outside. Cody pulled up in his parents' SUV with Russ riding shotgun, and I wished I could trade places with him. They parked next to me, and Cody rolled his window down. He took his phone out of his pocket and read the message from Sarah. "Whadda you think that's about?"

"I don't know, but I doubt she'll answer." I folded my arms over the ledge and leaned in. "Hey, Russ."

He smiled and waved at me.

"Don't let me forget to call as soon as we get there." I kissed Cody on the cheek. "Mom and Dad are worried."

He reached out and brushed my hair back, tucking it behind my ear. "Yeah, supposed to call, too. Ready?"

"Sure."

Holding my face so that I stared into his eyes, he said, "Be careful." Before I could respond, he pressed his lips to mine.

I could feel his fear in the kiss, and it was unsettling. Placing my hands over the top of his, I pulled away. "It'll be okay."

Liam stood outside of my truck until I got in. We hadn't been alone much since I'd escaped the Nephilim's prison. While I drove, I drummed my fingers on the steering wheel to the beat of the music, glancing at him occasionally and feeling really uncomfortable.

"It's weird. Isn't it?"

His voice made me jump. I laughed awkwardly. "Yeah."

The silence loomed on, filling the cab of my truck, making it stuffy. He cleared his throat. "I've never studied like humans do, and now, I'm going to college." He turned his steel-gray eyes on me. "What'll it be like?"

Telling him about college helped ease some of my tension. When the next break in conversation happened, I said, "So, uh—" I pulled my lip into my mouth and wondered if I should stay quiet.

Liam dipped his chin slightly. "Go ahead. Ask."

"How big can they make their portals?" I twisted my hands on the steering wheel, making a terrible rubbing noise. "Could they make me drive through one?"

He tilted his head and stared out the window. Lodgepole pines zipped by on both sides of the road, blocking the view of anything else. "If Sebastian and Troy joined theirs … probably."

"Great." The word was little more than a breath, but somehow he heard it.

"The tribunal is doing everything they can to find the rogue Nephilim." His fingers tapped against his thigh, not to the music, but like he was agitated. "They'll bring them in."

I hadn't thought about it before, but now that I was talking to Liam, I could hear the longing in his voice, the desire to hunt his former comrades. "If you want to go after them, you don't need to stay with me." I raked my fingers through my hair. "I've got more than enough eyes on me." I thought about Cody and how I was never actually truly alone with him. I knew it had to wear on him, but it probably wouldn't change anytime soon. "All of the time."

"If you want to get rid of me, you can just say it." His mouth was pulled down, and his eyebrows were bunched up. "Looking at me has to be hard for you."

I shook my head, trying to clear it. "Why?"

"I've gotta remind you of being locked up."

I huffed out a humorless chuckle. "Everything reminds me of being a prisoner." I waved my hand at the window. "Looking outside, waking up in my own bed, taking a shower, driving, seeing my friends and my parents, going to the bathroom when I need to and not when they tell me to. All of it makes me wonder when it will be taken from me again." The thought of being captured made my stomach harden, and a hollow feeling spread through my chest. "You were the only bright spot." I took my eyes off the road long enough for him to see that I meant what I was saying. "It doesn't bother me to look at you."

Silence filled the truck, but this time, it wasn't uncomfortable. "I think I'll talk to Diana about it. I want Troy and Sebastian locked up for what they did to you." He stared out the window, clenching and unclenching his fists. "They could tell you weren't evil."

Chapter 14

few miles before Althea, I pulled off the road in an area truck drivers used to put chains on their tires and picked up my phone. Liam reached for the doorknob. "You can stay if you want. I'm just letting Mom know we're about there."

"Oh, good," Mom said without saying hello.

I pointed at the phone to let Liam know I was about to talk to Mom. "I'm outside Althea. Sarah wants Cody and me to see her before going to our rooms." I paused for a minute while several scenarios played out in my head. "I don't know what that's about or how long it will take."

"Okay, honey. Be careful on the rest of the trip." She sniffed, and I couldn't help but wonder if she was crying. "Don't be a stranger."

"I won't, Mom. Love you."

"I love you, too, Dacia."

I hung up and looked in the rearview mirror. As soon as I saw Cody put his phone down, I pulled out onto the road. The Snowfire Mountains rose in front of us. The peaks were hidden behind gray clouds that held the promise of snow.

A half-hour later I sat in my truck in Cacomistle Hall's parking lot. The three-story building looked like it had grown out of the earth. It was stone and timber surrounded by centuries-old pine trees. Enormous boulders peeked at us through the snowdrifts.

Liam looked around like he expected to see somebody. "Do you want me to go in with you?"

"That's totally up to you." I watched Cody pull into the spot next to me. "I imagine all my other guards will. If you want to talk to Diana, though, you can."

He shook his head. "That can wait."

I opened my truck door, and the passenger doors on Cody's SUV opened at the same time. Even though Russ had been the only one to ride with Cody, Cash, Malcolm, and Mavros all appeared to step out of the vehicle, too.

Malcolm held onto my door and the side of my truck, effectively keeping me from stepping away. "Forgive me." His voice was rough and deep, his dragon's.

I set my hand on top of his. "Always."

"Val and Arianna will watch over your parents for the next several days." His eyes morphed into his human's. As he talked, his words became less feral sounding. "Once we deem them to be safe, they will join us here."

Hearing that my parents wouldn't be on their own was a huge relief. "Thank you."

He lowered his arm and pressed his hand against the small of my back, leading me inside.

As soon as the door opened, Sarah's assistant, Alicia looked up. Her spiky hair was hot pink with purple tips today. A small diamond shone at me from the side of her nose. She held a manicured finger up and nestled the phone between her shoulder and ear. "Dacia and her entourage are here to see you." She paused while listening to whatever Sarah was saying. "Will do." She hung up and said, "She'll see you now."

We climbed the massive, open staircase, and Sarah met us at the door, pulling me into a hug. "I hope your break was relaxing."

"No." I snorted. "Not even a little."

She stepped back still holding onto my shoulders. "What kind of monster this time?"

"Some of the Nephilim kidnapped me and threw me in a cage." I tried to sound blasé about it, but it came out broken.

She scanned the faces of the people with me and stopped when she saw Liam. "You're new, so are you," she said to Mavros.

"Ahh—" he morphed into Damon "—you know me as him."

Cody clenched his jaw and pulled me against his side. No matter how much time passed or how used he had become to seeing Mavros, he would never be okay with Damon. It didn't matter that they were one and the same. Damon's face forced Cody to recall memories that he wanted to remain buried.

Noticing Cody's reaction, Damon smirked and changed back to Mavros.

Liam stuck his hand out, and Sarah shook it. "Liam."

"Liam." Her eyebrows puckered together. "Liam Fox? New student?"

He looked from her to me. "Maybe."

"Maybe?" She moved out of the way so we could go in. "How do you know Dacia anyway?"

"I, uh—" he rubbed the back of his neck and stared at the floor "—I was one of her captors."

She closed the door and pointed at the couches. "That's a story I'll have to hear."

I sat in my usual spot and stared out the window at the mountains. The clouds covered more of them. "If we're gonna unpack before it snows, it'll probably have to wait."

"You're right." She sat across from me. "Two apartments opened up. They're both four-bedroom, four-bathroom. There is a waitlist"—she tipped her head toward her shoulder—"but under the circumstances, your names could make their way to the top of it." She glanced sidelong at Mavros, and I wondered if one of the reasons she thought of it was because he could enter my dorm room now. What would she think of me if she knew he'd been holding me while I slept, keeping my dreams away?

"That'd be great." A huge smile brightened Cody's face. "No more hiding. No more Marcy."

I nodded my head in agreement. "My own bathroom for nights when I wake up injured from my dreams. I think it's a good idea."

Sarah pulled out lease papers. The information for Cody and I had already been entered into them. "You need to decide who you want the other rooms to go to, whether you want your guardians or some of your other friends to live there."

"We will take the other apartment," Malcolm said before I could answer. "That way we can be there if you need us. If you don't, you will have some privacy."

"I'll talk to Samantha and Dan." I chewed on my lip. "If they don't want it, I suppose I could ask Cassandra and Bryce, but I don't want anyone else to know about my nightmares or my magic."

She handed us the keys. "I told Samantha and Dan to see me. They'll be here tomorrow afternoon."

I nodded. I knew they weren't coming today. Even though I hadn't talked to Samantha much over break, we had texted. I had kept everything light, hoping she wouldn't see through my responses and worry too much. They would find out soon enough how my break had been and how it had affected Cody.

Before we left, Sarah pulled me into another hug. "I'd like to know what happened when you have time to tell me."

"Yeah." It wasn't a conversation I was looking forward to having, but for everything she had done for me, she deserved to know.

While we'd been inside, the wind had picked up, and the temperature had dropped. I shivered as I pulled my truck door shut. The apartment building was across the street from Cacomistle Hall, so we didn't have far to drive. Cody pulled up next to me, and while my guards got out, I stared at the building. The open apartments were on the top floor, 501 and 502. Even though it would be nice to be out of the dorms, I wasn't looking forward to carrying our stuff to our new room.

Tiny snowflakes sprinkled the windshield. I got out and grabbed a couple of bags, hoping to get everything unpacked before the storm began in earnest.

After climbing five flights of stairs, Cody unlocked the door, and we stepped into the living room. It was open to the kitchen. The walls were cream-colored. The carpet was tan, and the couch and chairs were brown leather. There were two doors on each side of the rectangular room.

I walked toward the kitchen. The tile was several shades of brown mixed together in a way that would make it difficult to tell if the floor was dirty or not. The window above the sink had a spectacular view of the Snowfire Mountains and Falcon Lake.

"I'll take that room." I pointed to the one with two outside walls. "That way my screaming won't bother our neighbors."

Cody's eyes filled with sadness for me. I knew he wished he could take the nightmares away. Until I came to college, they hadn't been part of my life, but so far, they showed no signs of letting up. Hopefully, they would disappear as suddenly as they had arrived, but I doubted it.

I walked into the bedroom and dropped my duffle bag on the floor. Taking in the room, I said, "We're going to have to buy some things."

"Beds're bigger." Cody walked back out into the kitchen and opened all the cabinets. "Need dishes and pans. Food if we're gonna cook."

I turned toward the living room, and Mavros stared at me from the hallway. He looked like a puppy who had been left outside in the rain. His eyes were opened wide, and his brows pulled together.

I felt a pang of remorse in my heart at seeing him look so forlorn.

"Will you invite me in?" He sounded like he didn't dare hope.

I glanced at Cody, and he nodded. "Mavros, you may enter," I said.

He nodded at us, and a smile softened his features. "Thank you."

With the help of my guards, Cody and I were moved in in no time. They turned invisible and teleported in and out with our possessions. Cody, Liam, and I carried some of the boxes up the five flights of steps so that anybody watching would see us moving in.

Once our vehicles were emptied, we teleported to our old dorm rooms and brought back almost everything that belonged to the two of us. I left Cookie Monster behind in case Samantha wanted to stay in our old room. Malcolm promised to take it to my house if we didn't need it.

I stood in the middle of the room, taking it in. So much had happened here. Since coming to college, my life had changed exponentially, and a lot of those changes had happened in this room.

Slipping my hand into Cody's, I teleported us back to our apartment.

Snow fell steadily, forcing Cody to use the wipers as he drove us all to Althea. I stared out the window remembering how Grandma had always told me that if the flakes started small the accumulation was larger.

"Don't know about you guys"—Cody glanced in the rearview mirror at the passengers—"but I'm starving. Mind if we eat first?"

Liam smiled back at him. "Sounds good to me."

With that decided, he drove to The Avalanche. There were seven of us, so we were seated at a table in the middle of the room. I sat where I could watch the door. Cody and Malcolm positioned themselves to either side of me.

About the time our food arrived, a blast of cold air hit me. I looked up and watched as Troy, Sebastian, Micah, and several other Nephilim strode inside. Troy's brown eyes sliced into mine, and he flashed a cruel smile at me that was anything but friendly.

Malcolm grabbed hold of my hand. His grip was like a vise, clamping my fingers to his with no hope of pulling away. His pupils were thin slits, and his fangs lengthened.

I wanted to tell him to calm down before someone else noticed, but I couldn't think. I couldn't move. They were going to take me. A war between them and my guardians was going to break out right here in the restaurant. Whoever didn't get killed or seriously injured would see Troy feed me his blood, then drag me off.

Would they kill me this time? Would Cody get hurt in the fight? Would any of us survive this?

Air entered my lungs through ragged gulps. Tremors rattled my body.

Malcolm turned toward me. He sucked in a deep breath before sending soothing energy flowing through me.

The Nephilim were seated at a table near ours. Troy crossed his arms over his chest and stared at me the entire time I ate. His shirt was pulled tight over his bulging muscles. His lip was curled in disgust.

I fought to hide my terror, but I was sure he could see the way my hands trembled with every bite I brought to my mouth. I wanted to push my food away and leave, but I didn't want him to know he had that much control over me. I took another bite of my burger even though the thought of swallowing it made me want to puke.

As soon as we finished eating, Malcolm, Liam, and Mavros surrounded me. Russ walked with Cody. His hand rested on Cody's shoulder. Cash glanced back at us multiple times on his way to pay the bill.

My legs trembled so badly I could barely walk past the Nephilim's table. I kept my eyes focused ahead of us, not sparing a glimpse at any of them, and wondered if I was about to lose control of my magic.

"Soon." Troy's promise followed me through the door.

When I stepped outside, I released a deep breath and shuddered.

Soon.

He wouldn't stop until I was imprisoned.

The trembling in my legs increased until they could barely hold my weight. Malcolm tightened his grip on my waist, guiding me over the snow-covered parking lot. The falling flakes were huge. I watched them pile on the ground and mumbled to no one in particular, "Hopefully, Dan and Samantha can make it okay tomorrow." My voice sounded lifeless. Seeing Troy and his buddies had brought the hopelessness of prison back to the center of my thoughts.

Malcolm opened my door for me, and as soon as I was inside, he pushed the lock down and closed it. I stared at The Avalanche waiting for Troy to come out, wondering how he would get me away from my guards, praying no one I cared about would be hurt.

The door pushed outward. I clutched the handle above the glove box. My fingernails bit into my palms. Far off in the distance, I heard Malcolm growl, but I couldn't tear my attention away from the restaurant.

Cash stepped outside, and my shoulders slumped forward.

As soon as he was inside the SUV, Cody drove back to campus. We needed to buy things for the apartment but not with the Nephilim around.

I turned in my seat, focusing on Liam. "How was Micah with them?" My voice was thick with unshed tears. "I watched him get shoved through a portal in cuffs." I closed my eyes and pulled my finger and thumb across them, pinching the bridge of my nose. "And, how could they just walk in there? Aren't Diana and Olivia and some of the others watching for them?"

"I don't know." He rubbed his chin. The familiar sound of his calluses scratching against his stubble filled the vehicle. "They can't confront them in public."

"Micah." Cody's voice was harder than his grip on the wheel.

Liam shook his head. "I don't know. Someone must be working with Troy."

One of the dragons growled, and Mavros' chuckle sent shivers running up my spine. "Angels … you'd think you could trust them."

My guards surrounded Cody and me until we were safely in our apartment. Then Malcolm handed me a notepad and pen. "Write down what you need, and I'll get it for you."

My stomach seemed to settle somewhere around my knees. I couldn't do this. How could I live constantly in fear, constantly hiding? Somehow this needed to end.

Chapter 15

Since being captured, I had avoided my reflection, afraid of the terror I would see lurking behind my eyes, but there were two mirrors in my bathroom. A full-length one and one above the sink. I stepped out of the shower, turned away from one, and ended up staring into the other.

I couldn't look away.

Sitting on the counter with a towel wrapped around my body and one twisted over my hair, I tried to remember what my irises had looked like before. Before the darkness of Mavros' eyes had settled into them. Before the Nephilim had torn me from my friends and family.

I couldn't remember the exact shade of green they had been. I couldn't picture them without the lingering sadness. But I knew they had never looked like this.

They were haunted.

Looking into them, I imagined I could see all the shattered pieces of my soul. There was no way I would ever be able to put myself back together. No amount of glue, no amount of tape, no amount of healing would ever fix me.

I focused on my irises again. Gold mingled with the green and black.

A piece of Troy.

Extracted from his blood.

My heart dropped. I didn't need another reminder of my time with the Nephilim. I didn't need to remember his blood pouring down my throat. I didn't need to dredge up my fear or humiliation.

Bang, bang, bang. I fell off the counter, clutching my towel in one hand and pressing the other to my heart.

"Dacia." Malcolm's voice was a snarl. "Let me in."

I opened the door a crack and peered out at him.

He looked over my shoulder. His gaze darted from side to side, searching for the cause of my turmoil.

"It's nothing." Tears pooled in my eyes.

He stepped back, giving me space.

I waved a hand at my face. "I'll never be—" A sob broke free. I shut the door and got dressed. When I opened it again, Malcolm was leaning against the wall with his arms folded over his chest. His veins pressed against his skin, looking like they might burst through it. His jaw was so tightly clenched that a muscle in it jumped.

I should have been wary, but I rushed toward him without thinking twice about it.

He wrapped his arms around me and held me against his chest. His power leeched into me, helping stabilize me. He ran his hand down my back. "You're safe here, Dacia." His voice was too harsh to be soothing, but his actions and energy made up for it.

Without pulling away from him, I said, "I can't look at myself without seeing Troy."

Stepping back, he tilted my chin up and looked into my eyes. "I'm sorry, Dacia."

"Why didn't it go away when Mavros changed his magic back?" I stepped into his embrace again and hoped my emotions wouldn't be too much for him to handle.

He held onto me without complaint. "Have you checked on your powers lately? Has Troy's blood taken over again?"

I opened up my mind to Malcolm and focused on my magic. The serpents were illuminated as if by a spotlight. My snake sparkled like a zircon in the sunlight, and Mavros' was as dark as an overcast, moonless night.

Malcolm knelt next to the serpents. His gaze roved over their scales. "Dacia." His voice was soft, and somehow it felt more ominous than if he'd spoken loudly.

I pressed my eyes closed and breathed in deeply. "What's wrong?"

"Mavros' power is free from the corruption." He took my hand in his. "Yours, however, is not."

I sank to the ground and curled up, trying to hold my panic inside. Why hadn't I even considered this predicament? Why wouldn't his blood infect me, too?

Malcolm's hand gently rubbed the middle of my back. "Mavros may be able to tell you how to purge it since he removed it from his own."

A tiny ember of hope ignited inside of me. Maybe this wouldn't be the trial that eradicating Argentum's blood had been.

I sat up and set my hand on top of my serpent's head. "What is his blood doing to you?"

It is not changing me. The snake nuzzled into my fingers, rising higher. Its tongue flicked out, scenting the air. *It has not made me stronger. It has not corrupted me.*

I slowly released the air from my lungs, relaxing a little as I did. My serpent didn't say us. I pressed my hand to my chest. Troy's blood wasn't doing the same thing Argentum's had. Maybe it wasn't sentient.

My magic lowered itself back to the ground and curled around Mavros' ebony serpent. I slid my fingers into Malcolm's and pictured us back in the real world.

He pointed at my bed. The bedspread, blanket, and sheets he had picked up for me were piled on top of it. "I thought you needed something bright and cheery."

"Thank you." The comforter he'd picked out for me was hot pink and purple brushstrokes. He got me a set of sheets in each of the colors. The blanket was bright blue. "They're perfect."

We walked out to the living room together, and everybody very obviously didn't stare at me. Cody and Mavros sat on opposite ends of the couch. Liam and Cash each sat on one of the chairs. I plopped down next to Cody, and he draped his arm over my shoulders.

"Okay?" he asked.

I shrugged. "I've been better." I curled into his side, hoping to fill some of my emptiness with his presence. "My eyes have gold flecks in them. Troy's blood is consuming my magic, but so far it's having no effect on it." I pulled my hand through my still wet hair and turned toward Mavros. "I need to know how you stopped it from transforming your power. Your snake is still black. Mine is shimmering."

"I'm a demon." Mavros shook his head. "The angelic part of Troy's blood recoiled at my touch. If my power hadn't been dormant, his blood would never have taken hold."

Liam tilted his head and pinched his lips together. The look said, "Whatever."

"It's true, angel-boy. I'm not one of the demons that you can exorcise." He grinned, and it was savage. "Not even twenty of you could send me back."

"Who are you?" Liam's voice was filled with disbelief.

"Mavros Malkin." He held his hand out like they were meeting for the first time. "Prince Mavros Malkin, if you're so inclined to kneel to royalty."

"Royalty?" I sat up straighter and stared at him. "Seriously? Royalty?"

"Yes, ma'am."

I looked at the dragons, wondering if they knew this.

"I knew he was powerful." Cash ran his hands down his face and stretched his legs out. "Only the strongest demons can take human form."

Malcolm stared at Mavros. The intensity in his gaze made me expect his dragon to surface, but it didn't. "You?" He laughed.

"What's so funny?" I looked from Malcolm to Mavros, trying to figure out what I was missing.

Malcolm shook his head. "Only you, Dacia."

"Only me … what?"

"Only you could make a demon prince and dragons get along." Cash leaned forward, resting his elbows on his knees. "Only you could befriend us all."

Malcolm leaned against the wall, folding his arms over his chest. "Well, Prince, how does Dacia stop Troy's blood from contaminating her further?"

"If I try to stop it, my magic might taint hers." Mavros lowered his gaze to the ground. When he looked up again, he stared into my eyes. "The gold flecks are pretty, Dacia. You could leave them." I shook my head, and he ran his hand down his face. "I don't know how many more black flecks you can add before the fairies can't help you."

My eyes burned with unshed tears. "The black ones … they come from my friend." I chewed on my lip. "The gold flecks—" I sucked in a deep, shaky breath "—remind me of an evil, hate-filled monster. I can't look at them without losing another piece of myself."

"If that's what you want." Mavros reached for me, but Liam jumped up.

He shook his head. "Don't decide yet. Maybe Khione or Aurelia knows a way to purge it … maybe even the fairies."

Mavros grabbed my hand. His touch was tender, concerned. "You don't want to be without your magic again unless it's the last resort. Let him see what he can find out."

"Okay." I squeezed his fingers and turned my attention to Liam. "What did you decide?"

He sat back down. "Before dinner, the plan was to hunt Troy and Sebastian. Now, I think the more people watching you, the better." He rubbed the back of his neck. "I can still search for them while you're in class or sleeping, but I can see that they won't stay away. I should've known."

"Tomorrow"—Cash stared out the window—"I will take you to Khione. Tonight, with this storm, the risk is too high."

Cody and I took our bedding and searched for the laundry room. We finally found it in the basement. It looked and felt like we were alone, but I knew at least one of my guards was with me. We sat and watched the sheets tumble through the soapy water.

"Why didn't you tell me?" I couldn't look at Cody when I asked it.

His chair scraped across the floor. "Tell you?"

"About my eyes." I waved my hand in front of my face.

"Thought you knew." His next words came out broken and barely audible. "Been that way since you came back."

I slumped forward, holding my head in my hands. "I couldn't look at myself." I dragged my fingers down my face, pulling my skin with them. "I was such a coward … a baby.

Without my magic—" I stared at the tile floor and forced the words out "—I'm nothing."

The full moon hovers high in the sky, shining down on everything below. Its light reflects off the snow. A handful of stars are bright enough to be seen.

I stroll across campus, alone for the first time in weeks, but for some reason, I'm not afraid that the Nephilim will try to snatch me. Pine trees surround me, but I don't search them wondering if Troy is waiting for me.

I hear the clippety-clop of hooves on the sidewalk behind me. My heart leaps into my throat, and I spin around.

A black horse trots toward me. Its long mane and tail flow through the air. Nothing seems abnormal about it until I notice its eyes.

Yellow.

Not the yellow gold of a cat's eyes, but a luminescent, bright yellow that could never belong to a mortal.

It steps close enough to me that I could reach out and pet its silky nose, but I force my hands to stay tucked into my pockets.

Tossing its head from side to side, it whinnies. The sound soothes me, and I find myself stretching my arm out. My hand glides over fur that's softer than any I've ever felt before.

The horse seems to smile at me. I stare into its eye, and memories dart through my mind too quickly to hold onto, but I catch glimpses of them.

A brief flash of Nefarious. Floating off Cody's hospital bed when we decided to date. Aurelia walking along the beach. Flying through the night sky with Arion. Draconian sneering at me. His dragons fall in behind him. I feel Malcolm's talons slash through my back. I remember the rotten smell of his breath. I see hatred burning in Cash's eyes and feel terror rise up inside of me.

Then I see myself staring into Mavros' obsidian irises. He's perfect, beautiful, and I'm drawn to him, before I step into his embrace, I plunge the knife deep into my heart. Everything fades to black. Then I stand before Death.

For a moment, I wonder if the memories will start up again or if this creature will stop whatever it's doing.

I stare at the tree. Imagining Draconian's body beneath it. Seeing myself run him through again and again. Watching the light in his eyes dim, then extinguish. When I turn around, the dragons stand in front of me in human form. Malcolm, Val, Arianna, Russ, Cash, and Tye.

Nephilim follow me. They trap me on the side street. The dark-skinned Nephilim reaches into his jacket, but I never find out what he has hidden there. I lie on the ground, staring up at Mavros. My chest is torn open, and blood spills out of me. Argentum's rheumy eyes focus on me. He won't give up, no matter what I do. I tear into his flesh, wanting more, savoring every drop of his ancient blood.

The creature holds my gaze, not letting go until it has seen every detail of my life. My battle with the darkness inside of me, my capture, and torture.

The memories stop replaying, and the horse trots off.

„178‘’

Chapter 16

The snow fell steadily through the night. By the time the sun peaked in through my curtains, nearly two feet blanketed campus.

Cody was propped up on his arm, staring down at me. The covers were only pulled up to his waist, leaving his torso bare. His blond hair was mussed from sleep. He looked perfect. "Morning."

I dragged my finger down his sternum, not taking my gaze from his. "Morning."

"We alone?" He smiled at me, and it was filled with mischief.

I shook my head. "I doubt it."

A black mist coalesced in the corner of my room, slowly forming into Mavros. "She really hasn't been alone since she defeated Nefarious." He sauntered toward my bed, positioning himself on the edge of it. "Someday … maybe." The look he shot Cody was meant to antagonize him, but if Cody took the bait, he didn't let it show.

Mavros strolled out into the living room, leaving my bedroom door open. I pressed my hand on Cody's chest until he lay back. Then I snuggled against him with my head over his heart. "Do you think they'll take the other rooms?" I traced circles over his bare skin.

"Think so." His eyes fluttered closed. "Why not?"

Flattening my hand, I said, "They've been kidnapped and tortured because of me. Why wouldn't they want to distance themselves?"

"They're friends." He wrapped both arms around me.

I pinched my eyes closed. "For how long, though? How long can they deal with all of this? How long can you put up with being watched all of the time? When are you all going to say enough's enough?"

"Never." He kissed the top of my head. "No amount of time with you will be enough."

As soon as they could, Mavros, Malcolm, and Cash whisked me away for training. Russ and Liam stayed behind to make sure that Cody was safe from anybody who might try to use him against me.

Once again, Malcolm teleported me to the distant mountains. I held out my arms and legs and freefell through the sky. The ground rushed to greet me, but for once, I felt no fear. The trees stretched toward me, and I morphed into my dragon. Scales burst through skin. Wings exploded from shoulder blades, snapping into place. I flapped once, lifting myself a little higher, and let the drafts carry me where they wanted.

My guards … no, my friends surrounded me, letting me set the pace and direction. I felt their concern for me, rippling along this body like a sixth sense. It took me a while to realize that it wasn't intuition. It was their scents, blowing toward me with every change of the wind. I could smell their unease, their desire to make things right, their fear that I would be taken again.

I pointed my nose toward the cobalt sky high above and flapped my wings hard and fast. The wind rushed over my scales. My tail held rigid, keeping me from veering off course. I burst through a fluffy cloud with Malcolm and Cash right next to me.

Heat settled in the pit of my stomach, and I roared. Blue flames blasted through the air in front of me. Malcolm and Cash followed my lead, and I smelled their concern shift to excitement. We raced across the sky, aiming for the mountaintop where I would transform and use my magic as a human.

When we neared the boulder, Malcolm pulled away, increasing his lead. This was a race they would never let me win. One of them always wanted to get there first to make sure no danger awaited me, but this time, it was my turn. I focused on the stone, remembering how it had felt gripped in my talons, and teleported to it.

Mavros' roar tore through the sky. As soon as I clutched the stone, Malcolm appeared next to me. His bronze eyes were narrowed, but he turned away from me. Lifting his snout, he sniffed the air.

Cash landed on the ground in front of me, pulling his wings in as he transformed into a human. Mavros, the three-headed demon, alit next to me. Two of his heads searched for danger while the third glared at me. "What the hell, Dacia?"

I curved my neck over my back, instinctively protecting my jugular. "I'm tired of losing."

"We're trying to protect you." The silken voice filled with venom.

Morphing into my human body, I said, "Sorry, Prince."

His heads snapped back as though I'd slapped him, and I couldn't help but wonder about the story hidden behind his normally cocky exterior. His body vaporized. A black mist hung in the air. A few minutes later Mavros, the man, stood where the beast had been. His hair was perfectly combed. His clothes were black and wrinkle-free. He held his coat out to me. "Please"—his voice was softer than I could ever remember hearing it—"don't call me Prince."

I nodded and accepted his jacket. "I didn't mean to upset you."

He brushed the back of his hand along my cheek. "There are things you don't know about me. Things you don't want to know."

"Yeah." I snorted. "I don't know much at all."

"It's better that way." He lowered his hand and stepped back.

A chill ran through my body, and I turned toward the path. I started out in a slow jog, not sure if the others were ready, but my pace gave them plenty of time to catch up even if they weren't.

Mavros shifted to his panther form and loped in front of me. Looking over his shoulder, he matched his speed to mine. Cash and Malcolm jogged alongside me. Malcolm glanced at me, and it was his dragon that looked out. "Don't do that again."

I turned my gaze away from his and stirred up a gust that blew snow from the treetops. Anger burned inside of me. How could they tell me how strong I was and then act as if I would never be able to protect myself? Did they really have so little faith in me, and if so, should I?

The wind whipped harder. Gray clouds rolled across the sky. I ran faster, sprinting past Mavros. He growled as I bounded by and sped up to stay next to me.

Cash ran along my other side. "What's wrong?"

I clenched my teeth and stared straight ahead. My feet pounded against the trail. With each stride, I saw Troy standing over me, hatred and disgust etched in every line of his face. I heard his voice telling me that I disgusted him. I imagined him saying that I was nothing. That I was weak and pathetic and insignificant.

Cash grabbed my arm. I tried to jerk away, but he held on, slowing us down. Coming to a stop, I bent over with my hands on my knees. My breath came out in ragged pants.

"What?" he asked again.

I pulled my arm out of his grip and walked a few steps away. Staring out over the snow-covered mountains, I said, "I'm nothing without my magic." I tugged my hand through my hair. "I know that now."

Mavros transformed into his human form. Malcolm moved closer to me. A low growl rumbled over me. Cash turned me around. "You are not nothing."

"I am." I couldn't look at any of them, so I studied my shoes. The path we ran along was essentially just crusted snow. In the summer, it was probably a nice trail, but at this time of year, it was inaccessible to most people. "When I won, your reactions made me realize that even with my magic, I'm a liability. I'll never be as strong as any of you." Tears dripped off of my chin, but I didn't have the energy to wipe them away.

Malcolm shook his head. "As long as you can access your magic, you will be stronger than us within a year."

Disbelief must have flashed across my face because Cash stepped closer to me and brushed the tears from my cheeks. "Had your magic not been tainted by Mavros and Argentum, you might already be stronger than us." His voice had an edge to it that made it sound like he was fighting his dragon for control. "Even if that were the case, you could be overpowered or taken by surprise." His dragon broke through. "You could be taken from me … from us again. We won't let that happen."

I could see they felt that way, but I didn't. "Maybe … but I need to learn how to defend myself without magic."

Cash made a rumbling noise that sounded a lot like a purr. "I'll go with you."

I kicked at a clump of snow. "I can't guarantee I'll have my powers next time someone tries to take me, and I—" the rest of my words got caught in my throat. I turned away, finding strength and serenity in the scenery. "I can't let that happen again."

I teleported to the apartment completely exhausted. My legs felt like wet noodles, and my magic was nearly depleted. Malcolm held onto my hand. His energy flowed through me, replenishing mine enough for me to get cleaned up. I shot Cody a half-hearted smile, grabbed a change of clothes, and took a long shower.

Even with the blinds closed, the window filled the room with light. I stood at the sink and twisted my hair into a Dutch braid. I suspected the others were anxious for me to join them, but I needed some time to myself.

Sitting on the cabinet next to the sink, I focused on my magic. The serpent had nearly doubled in size since I left the Nephilim's cage. Its pearlescent scales shimmered with flashes of gold.

Mavros' snake lay coiled in the same position. Its scales were the endless black of the Abyss, so dark it seemed like no light had ever shone upon them.

I squatted next to my serpent and trailed my hand along the top of its head and down its back. Its scales were smooth and glossy. I stretched my fingers out as wide as they would spread, and they didn't span even half of its girth. What would it be like when my magic was as vast as the dragons kept telling me it would be? Would I keep picturing the snake growing larger as my magic increased?

"Is his blood affecting you?" I swallowed hard, not ready to hear the answer but needing to know.

The snake puffed up, slowly turning its copper gaze to me. *My power is my own.*

I let out a long, drawn-out sigh. I could handle my eyes having gold flecks in them as long as my magic had not been compromised. "Thank God."

Letting go of the serpent, I looked in the mirror. If I was being honest with myself, the gilded highlights in my eyes made them look more like they had before being muddied by the black flecks. It wouldn't be easy, but maybe I could learn to live with them.

I remembered Cody standing in my kitchen, cooking tacos, and asking me to tell him something good. My magic was its own. I needed to focus on that.

Stepping into my bedroom, I glanced around, expecting to find at least one of my guards, but it was empty. There was a time that I would have enjoyed the solitude, but I'd had enough of that in the Nephilim's cage. I hurried through the door. As I stepped into the living room, I saw Samantha and Dan carrying bags into their rooms.

It shouldn't have surprised me, but it did. My knees buckled when the tension released from my body. I gripped the doorframe until I was sure I would be able to walk.

Malcolm appeared in the middle of the room holding a stack of boxes. "You okay?" He tilted his head to the side and breathed in my emotions.

"Yes." I pointed to their rooms. "Relieved."

He nodded and walked to Dan's room. "Where do you want these?"

I heard Dan's voice but not what he said.

There had been no reason for me to wonder if Samantha and Dan would share the apartment with us. Over the past year and a half, Samantha hadn't complained much about her lack of sleep because of my nightmares, and the only time she had avoided me was when Mavros had returned. As soon as she'd figured out that he wasn't controlling me, that he was protecting me, she had stood by me.

She had been kidnapped by dragons and Mavros, yet she never left my side. She cheered me on and was there for me whenever I needed her.

Samantha stepped out, and when her eyes met mine, a wide grin lifted her lips. There was no part of her face the smile didn't touch. "This is amazing." She practically sang the last word. "I love it!" She strode toward me and pulled me into a hug. "How was break?"

Troy's hate-filled face flashed through my mind. The helplessness of being imprisoned followed it. My arms tightened around her.

"Not great, huh?" She stepped back. "I was worried about you, but I figured you'd let me know if anything terrible happened."

I couldn't hold back the tears that welled up in my eyes or the terror that spread through my body with each beat of my heart, seeping into the empty spaces, filling them with dread.

Cash was suddenly standing next to me, clutching my hand. "You're okay, Dacia." His voice was soft, but his dragon shone through his amethyst eyes.

Peacefulness flowed into me, and not for the first time, I wondered if I would ever feel that way on my own again.

The doorknob turned, and I clenched his hand. My eyes widened as I stared at it. The next few seconds contained several lifetimes. My heart pummeled my ribs. The sound thundered throughout my body, drowning out all other noises.

Cash's mouth moved, but his words were lost in a thick forest of fear. *It's Cody.* He sent the words directly into my head.

Cody walked into the apartment at the same time that I collapsed into Cash's arms. A sob tore through my throat and out of my mouth before I could stop it.

The bags Cody had been carrying fell to the ground, and he rushed to me. "What is it?" His voice was a strange mix of concern and horror.

"Panic attack," Cash answered for me.

Samantha rubbed my back. "Did I say something wrong?"

Cody lifted me up, and I clung to him like a lion trying to bring down its prey. He carried me to the couch and held me, trailing his hands up and down my arms while whispering, "You're okay," over and over again.

I heard Cash tell Samantha about my break, but I tried not to listen, not to think about it, not to picture the cell with Troy's blood scattered about the floor surrounding it, not to remember his expression as he tightened the zip ties on my wrists, not to remember the malice in his voice.

Malcolm sat next to Cody. The bronze of his irises covered his scleras, his pupils were thin slits, and smoke drifted out of his nostrils. He grabbed hold of my hand without saying anything. He tried to send calming energy into me, but it was mixed with anger and hatred.

I jerked my hand away, and his head whipped toward me. The movement was more dragon than human.

I held his gaze even though I knew I shouldn't. "I can't take anymore rage." I bit my lip. "It covers the fear, but it builds inside of me."

He closed his eyes and breathed in deeply. Something shifted in his posture, and when he looked at me this time, it was his human gazing at me. "Let me try again."

After the panic and fear dissipated enough that I could breathe, I squeezed Malcolm's hand and said, "Can you take me to Khione?"

His head dropped toward his chest. "She cannot help you."

"Oh." I clutched Cody's shirt in my hand and recoiled into him. "What did she say?"

Cash sat in the chair and leaned forward with his elbows on his knees. He folded his hands in front of him and stared at them instead of looking at me. "She wants you to keep an eye on your powers and make sure nothing changes." He finally glanced up, and I could see grief in his eyes that hadn't been there before. "She thinks it may emphasize some of your powers but not try to control them. She thinks that with Mavros' interjection, your dragon nature, and Troy's power you are becoming more."

"What's that supposed to mean?" My stomach seemed to drop to my feet, and I was glad that I had been sitting when it happened.

Malcolm pulled his hand out of mine and dragged it down his face. "We don't know."

Chapter 17

Snow twirls through the air, catching in my curls, sticking to my eyelashes. It muffles the normal sounds of campus. As I near the lights, everything brightens significantly. Each snowflake is illuminated, tiny prisms dancing through the night sky. Stepping beyond them, darkness surrounds me.

I heat my skin enough to keep the night's chill off. I should hurry back to the apartment, but I need a few more minutes of solitude, a few minutes where I won't be looked at like a victim.

Neither Samantha nor Dan have known what to say to me since Cash told them about my imprisonment. I catch them sneaking glances at me. I'm sure they talk about me at night when the doors are closed and the lights are out.

As I walk, I kick at the snowdrifts, watching those flakes mingle with the ones falling from the sky. For just an instant, the path in front of me is obscured from my view. When the snow settles, a massive black dog stands in front of me. It's easily three times my weight, and it looks me in the face without raising its head at all. Its eyes are a bright, vivid yellow.

I take a step back, not sure whether it's friendly or not. It yips excitedly and wags its tail, dropping its body down over its front legs. It looks like it's ready to play fetch, but I have nothing to throw.

Its luminous eyes stare into mine, and suddenly, I'm not scared. I pat my leg, and the enormous dog bumps its head against my side, nearly knocking me to the ground. I right myself and ask, "Who's a good boy?"

For some reason, I'm not surprised when it grins mischievously at me and says, "I'm not."

My eyes snapped open, and I stared into the darkness careful not to wake Cody. I'd seen those eyes before. Hadn't I? I searched through my memories, trying to place them, but nothing came to mind. I drifted back to sleep thinking about the massive, talking dog.

Cody's fingers were soft and gentle as they trailed over my arm. The tips barely grazed my skin.

As I left that stage between being asleep and being awake, the fogginess cleared from my head, and with it, all traces of my dream disappeared. I tried to grasp it, but it was like holding onto vapor. Whatever it had been was gone. I rolled onto my side, facing Cody.

He smiled at me. "How'd ya sleep?"

"All right." I placed my hand flat on his chest. "I had a dream"—my eyebrows pinched together in concentration—"but it slipped away." I dragged my fingers down his sternum, and he leaned into my touch. "How about you?"

He cupped my face. His thumb brushed my cheek, and his sapphire eyes sparkled. "With you here?" He leaned in until our mouths were only a whisper apart. "Great." The word brushed against my skin, making me shiver.

I slid my hand over his abs and around his back, pulling our bodies closer together. Like a butterfly landing, I touched my lips to his.

His mouth answered mine, tiny light kisses that built upon each other. He scraped his teeth over my bottom lip and clutched me to his body as he rolled us over.

I dragged my fingernails over his skin and tilted my head back.

His kisses trailed over my chin and onto my neck. He nipped at my earlobe.

Bang, bang, bang.

My eyes sprang open, and I stared at the door. My heart seemed to have leapt into my throat, blocking any words from coming out. *It's not him. It can't be him.* I tightened my hands into fists, digging my fingernails into Cody's back. He winced, but I couldn't loosen my grip. All I could think about was Troy. The loathing in his eyes. The black tattoo running from his scalp, down his face, and beneath his shirt. *He wouldn't knock. It can't be him. He'd barge in.*

My chest tightened, and I thought I might puke.

"Use your magic, Dacia." Cody ran the back of his knuckles over my cheek. "Who is it?"

I closed my eyes and breathed in deeply. As I released my breath, I focused. Strength, discipline, honor, and sadness pelted my awareness. "Liam." The word scraped past my heart, forcing its way out of my mouth. Spots continued dancing in my vision, but the flood of emotions that had blocked out my thoughts subsided.

He knocked again. This time, it didn't sound quite so menacing.

"Yeah?" Cody rolled onto the bed, propping his head on his arm, looking across me.

The door cracked open just enough for Liam to peek in. "Malcolm says training starts in five minutes." His gaze kept shifting to the side, never settling on Cody or me.

"Why'd he send you?" I asked as I flipped the covers back and sat on the edge of the bed. I dragged my hands through my hair, tugging out the knots as I did.

Red splashed across his cheeks, and he cleared his throat. "He, uh … said you stink of—" he lifted one shoulder toward his ear while wiping his other hand over his mouth "—doesn't matter." He bumped the door, opening it farther. "Anyway, I'm training you today."

"Oh." I snapped my gaze to his. "Why?"

"Self-defense." He stepped into the room, reaching for the doorknob. "They'll be there, too."

I pulled leggings and a sports bra out of my drawer and started toward the bathroom. "I'm probably about out of time."

"Cuttin' it close." He stepped back and shut the door.

For a minute, I felt like I was there again, being locked in my cell with no one, no escape, no hope.

"Dacia." Cody's voice was soft, but it was enough to break the memory's hold on me.

I lifted my lips in what I hoped would pass for a smile. "I'm okay."

"Want me to come?" He stood up, and when he stretched his arms over his head, I couldn't help but admire his physique, lean, sculpted muscle. He chuckled. "Like it when you look at me like that."

I turned away, embarrassed at being caught. "Why, uh"—I had to get my thoughts back in order—"why do you want to come?"

"Wouldn't hurt for me to know." He walked up behind me and turned me to face him. "Maybe I wouldn't be a liability."

I could see it in his eyes. This would mean a lot to him. "Sure. Better hurry. Malcolm doesn't like to wait, and my five minutes are probably already up."

While I was braiding my hair, somebody knocked on my door again. This time, fear didn't overtake me. I focused on the aura. Determination and concern. "Come in, Cash." When the door opened, I didn't turn around but watched him in my mirror. "I'm just about done."

He breathed in deeply, and his eyes fluttered shut. Rolling his neck from side to side, he met my gaze and pointed at my bed. "May I?"

"Sure."

He sat on the edge of it and held his head in his hands. "Liam has been trained in Krav Maga."

My eyebrows pinched together, but I didn't say anything.

"It's probably the best option for you." His words didn't match his body language. It sounded like he wanted me to learn it, but his shoulders were tense, and every time he paused, he clenched his teeth together. When he spoke again, the words were growled. "It can be used against one attacker or many."

I wrapped the band around the end of my plait and walked over, sitting next to him. "What is it?"

"You're going to get hurt." His dragon looked out at me. "It may even be me who does it."

I shook my head, not sure what he meant. "Why?"

"That's how you learn self-defense." His hands tightened into fists. Purple scales reflected the light coming in through my window. "You defend yourself."

I patted his arm, hoping to give him some assurance. "I heal quickly, Cash. I'll be fine." Standing, I stretched my hand out to him. "Cody wants to come along. He thinks he should know self-defense, too."

He slid his fingers over mine, and I was reminded of how big he was in comparison to me. There was no doubt in my mind that he could hurt me if he wanted to, but I knew he wouldn't. His determination to keep me safe was one of the things I could sense in his aura.

He nodded. "That will be good for both of you." He looked at my outfit. "Grab a sweatshirt."

I stood in a clearing surrounded by Cody, Malcolm, Liam, Mavros, and Cash. The wind blew through the trees, but I couldn't feel it here. Someone had created an invisible dome to keep the weather from freezing Cody and me. Snow fell from the branches and was whisked off the barrier almost instantly.

Malcolm handed me a mouth guard and some protective gear. He looked at Cody and lifted his hands apologetically. "I didn't realize you would be here, too. I'll get you something before tomorrow."

"No worries." Cody watched me pull off my sweatshirt and slip on a long-sleeved spandex shirt. "Doesn't look like it'll do much."

Liam nodded. "It's a rash guard. It'll protect her skin from scrapes and scratches." I couldn't tell if he had one on or not. He was wearing a black jacket and black cargo pants. Even though he wasn't my prison guard anymore, he still looked the part of a soldier.

I strapped on shin guards, then pulled on gloves. Liam wore none of the padding. Seeing that, I couldn't help but wonder if he saw me as a fragile doll. That thought had me glaring at him. "You know I'm not that breakable, right?"

"You will be." Mavros was suddenly next to me. He snapped a collar around my neck, and my magic disappeared as if he had flipped a switch.

"What … why?" I couldn't say anything else. I couldn't believe they would betray me like this. I scanned the area, wondering if the Nephilim were there, wondering if they were about to hand me over to Troy or Sebastian and why.

Cody blocked me with his body, standing in front of me with his arm back, protecting me, but against the people here, he was as helpless as I was.

Liam stared at his feet. "You told Cash you wanted to learn self-defense in case your powers were taken."

"So, you took them?" I swiped my tears away. "Without telling me. Without giving me any say in it."

Malcolm's hand clamped down on my shoulder, and I jumped, bumping my elbow into Cody's back.

"It's the only way." Black scales lined Malcolm's face, making me realize this was hard enough on him.

"Fine." I pulled away from him. "Fine. Whatever. Tell me next time." I folded my arms over my chest and stared at Liam. "So … what do I do?"

"Troy and Sebastian are scared of you."

I couldn't keep from rolling my eyes. The collar seemed to take away all of my self-control, too.

"They are." Liam rubbed his stubbly chin. "So are their followers. Most likely, when they come after you, it will be from behind."

I noticed that he said *when* they come after you, not *if* they come after you. That should have scared me more, but for some reason, it seemed to settle me. At least I knew to expect it, instead of wondering if it would happen.

Liam waved his hand as if to say let's go. Cash stepped behind him and wrapped his arms around Liam, lifting him off the ground. Liam slipped his left leg behind Cash's. Then he mocked slamming his palm into Cash's groin multiple times. Cash let go and bent over as if he'd really been hit. While he was in that position, Liam said, "Here, you have two choices." He swung his elbow toward Cash's nose. Then he kicked his right leg back, slamming it into Cash's chest.

Liam made it look so easy as he showed me two more times. Then Cash moved away, and Liam pulled on a helmet and slid the face shield down. "Your turn. Stand in front of me."

I walked over and looked up at him. "Am I really gonna be able to do this?"

"Yeah, why not?"

I shook my head and waved my hand, emphasizing his height. "I'm at least six inches shorter than you. I weigh half as much."

"Krav Maga was created for people of all shapes and sizes to be able to defend themselves." He tapped the shield in front of his lips. "Now, put your mouth guard in."

I did as he ordered, then turned around and waited for him to grab me.

"Don't be afraid to hit me. I heal quickly, and I'm wearing protective gear."

I nodded, and he wrapped his arms around me, lifting me off my feet. I could feel his chest protector pressing into my back, and I wondered how I hadn't realized he was wearing one. I swung my leg back but didn't get it hooked around his.

"Try again." He squeezed me tighter, and my fingertips tingled from the blood circulation being cut off.

Fear sprouted in my stomach, vining out until it spread throughout my body. I remembered Troy hanging me on the cage, his chest pressed against mine, and how helpless I'd felt. I flung my leg around, hooking it on Liam's. It pulled my body to the side enough that I could swing my hand back. I struck him three times in rapid succession, and he lowered me as he bent over. I threw my elbow into his mask, and he staggered back.

"Good," he said. "Again."

"Again?"

He nodded. "Until it's second nature." He looked at Malcolm, then Cash. "Will one of you work with Cody?"

"Sure." Cash stepped forward and waved Cody on.

I must have gone through the maneuver with Liam twenty or thirty more times. Finally, he stepped away from me. "Good job." He reached into his duffel and pulled out a couple bottles of water. He threw one to me and drank half of his before I even had mine open. "Now, I'm going to show you what to do if they don't lift you up."

Cash stepped away from Cody and wrapped his arms around Liam. Liam dropped down quickly, lowering his center of gravity. Then he moved his hips to the side and struck at Cash's groin. As Cash let go, Liam swung his elbow back, stopping the movement before he made contact with Cash. Then he kicked back into Cash's knee.

The actions looked so obvious, like anybody would realize to do them when seized, but I knew from experience that wasn't the case. I'd let the Nephilim capture me and didn't fight at all when Troy led me away.

Never again.

Liam and Cash walked through each step in slow motion, showing Cody and me different angles. Then Liam waved me over.

I stood in front of him and closed my eyes. I imagined the Nephilim surrounding me. When his arms wrapped around mine, I imagined them more muscular.

Dropping my center of gravity, I shifted my hips and slammed my hand into his groin. When he moved to the side, I slammed my other hand into him. As he doubled over, I swung my elbow into the face shield, then kicked his knee.

He fell back, landing on the ground, clutching his leg. I dropped to my knees next to him. Snow soaked into my leggings. Its chill spread through me. "Liam." I covered my mouth with my hand. "I'm so sorry. I was picturing Troy."

His face was twisted with pain. He sat up slowly, still holding his leg. "It's all good." He tried to smile, but it came off as a wince. "At least we know you can do it." He rocked back, lying on the snow-covered ground. "I'll be good as new in a few minutes. Then we can try again."

By the time we finished, I felt like I could get away from Troy or Sebastian if they grabbed me in a bear hug.

Liam patted my shoulder and handed me another bottle of water. "You did good." He smiled. "You're a natural at this."

"Thanks." I stared at my water bottle. "Only because I can't let them take me again," I said as the dome we were standing inside disappeared. The wind whipped through the clearing, and my sweat-dampened skin chilled.

Russ appeared next to Cody. "Ready?" he asked.

"For what?" Cody looked as confused as I felt.

Malcolm slapped his hand down on my shoulder. "We've got training to do still."

"Oh." I unintentionally slumped forward. My elbow throbbed, my palm stung, and every muscle in my body ached. I wanted to soak in a hot bath, then spend the rest of the day lounging in my pajamas.

Mavros strode toward me. His hands were shoved into his pockets, and he wouldn't look me in the eyes.

My fingers shot to the collar around my neck. Part of me wanted to hold onto my earlier anger at him, but I knew I wouldn't have been able to resist using my magic to protect myself if I would've had access to it. I dropped my hands and pushed the betrayal aside. "I forgive you," I said when he stood next to me.

His head jerked up. Shock and relief flashed across his face before his usual cocky expression resumed its place. "Let me get it off of you."

As soon as the collar was gone, my powers rushed through my body, begging to be released. I kissed Cody on the cheek. Then I stepped away from everyone and transformed into my dragon.

Liam whistled and looked at my other guards. "You told me, but I didn't really believe they'd let you be one of them."

"She is *ours*." Malcolm extended himself to his full height and crossed his arms over his chest. His lip curled up, and he glared at Liam in challenge.

Liam backed away a step and lowered his gaze.

Cody stared at me, slowly striding toward me. His sapphire eyes were wide. His mouth hung open slightly. He stretched his hand up, and I lowered my head to nuzzle against it. His fingers trailed over my scales, but all I could feel was them shift under his touch. "Amazing," he whispered.

I studied him. Through these eyes, I could see that his blond hair was made of a multitude of shades. Bruises and scrapes covered his skin. Rage burned within me, and smoke drifted from my nostrils.

"What?" Cody's eyebrows pinched together, drawing my attention to his eyes.

His irises were a unique blend of colors. Aqua bursts shot out from his pupils like lightning bolts cutting through a cobalt sky.

I shook my head. "You're bruised all over."

"So were you." He waved his hand at me. "Before this."

Russ took a step toward us, drawing my attention. "I will heal him, Dacia."

Mavros, Malcolm, and Cash transformed. Three full-grown dragons and a three-headed demon stood in the clearing.

Cody glanced at each of them. A shiver ran down his spine, visibly shaking him, and he suddenly smelled better than a t-bone steak cooking on the grill.

"Keep him safe, Russ." I launched into the overcast sky before my senses overwhelmed me. Cold air smacked against my face, forcing the smell of Cody's fear out of my nostrils.

Mavros flew next to me. One of his heads turned toward me. The smile that crossed the beast's face was one I'd seen Mavros and his panther wear before. "Now you know why the dragons leave sometimes."

"Yeah." I quit flapping my wings and let the wind currents carry me. "I imagine actually being a dragon would make it even worse."

Cash laughed, sending flames spewing through the air. "And, don't forget, your magic makes you smell even more appealing."

Chapter 18

Voices blasted through the dining hall doors, bombarding us before we even stepped inside. "Sure about this?" Cody asked.

"I'm not cooking tonight." My trainers had kept me out a lot longer than I'd anticipated. Malcolm said it was because classes were about to start, but something told me there was more to it. "My muscles are killing me."

Samantha lifted her gloved hands. "Don't look at me. I don't even know how to boil an egg."

"Really?" Dan's head jerked back.

She smacked his arm. "No, not really, but pretty close."

"I can teach you." He rubbed his bicep.

As soon as Cash opened the door, the aroma from all the different foods hit me, and my stomach growled in response. I'd been starving since I'd smelled Cody's fear, and even though I hated to admit it, nothing here was quite as tantalizing as that had been.

I settled for a cheeseburger and fries. Then I searched the packed room for a place to sit. Cassandra and Bryce were at a table in the middle of the room. I hated the idea of sitting with my back exposed, but the tables along the walls were all taken.

"Hey." Cassandra smiled at me as I approached. "We didn't think you were here yet."

I studied the faces of the people at the surrounding tables before sitting next to her. "We, uh—" I felt guilty for not offering her the apartment across the hall, but I really needed my guards to have their own place "—got an apartment. Sarah offered it to us yesterday." I lowered my voice. "Because of everything that happens to me."

Cody plopped down next to me, and Liam set his tray in the spot next to Cody's. He stretched his hand over the table. "Liam Fox."

"Cassandra." Even though she shook his hand. She looked at me. Her eyebrows were pulled into a question.

"Bryce." He bumped his fist against Liam's. "Nice to meet you."

"Soooo?" Cassandra asked.

Cody shook his head. "Not here." He peeled the wrapper off of his straw and stuck it through the hole in the lid. "Come by the apartment after."

Bryce nodded.

Samantha, Dan, and Malcolm joined us while Mavros and Cash went in search of chairs to add to our table. It was crowded, but I was glad to have my friends surrounding me.

"Did y'all have a nice break?" Bryce asked when he finished eating.

I let the others answer. I tried to pay attention to what they had to say, but my thoughts kept circling back to my break.

The flames that could have burnt the church to the ground. Nearly killing Cody. Having my leg stuck inside of a demon. Fighting Argentum's blood. Being kidnapped and tortured.

Everything disappeared. The roar of the other students faded into nothingness. The people around me seemed to pop out of existence.

My pulse ratcheted up, taking my breathing along with it. I was alone in a sea of white. No sound. No smells.

"Dacia." Cash's voice was right in my ear, but when I turned nobody was there.

"Dacia." It was louder this time.

I blinked several times, hoping to clear the nothingness.

Dacia, Cash roared inside my head, and the room slowly came back into existence.

Everyone at the table stared at me. Their bodies leaned toward me like I had some sort of gravitational pull on them.

Cassandra set her hand on top of mine. Her fingers were soft and cold. "I'm sorry, Dacia. Whatever happened. I'm so sorry."

I tried to blow it off and make it seem like everything was all right, but I couldn't. I couldn't catch my breath. I couldn't get my heart to stop racing.

Tears welled in my eyes, and I looked around the table at everyone, shaking my head.

"Take her," Mavros practically growled at Cash. "I'll make it look like the two of you walked out of the door."

Cash grabbed my tray and wrapped his arm around my waist. Then without another word, we disappeared, reappearing in my apartment. He set my food on the table, then held me while I cried on his shoulder.

"I'm sorry I failed you, Dacia." He brushed his hand over my hair and down my back.

I pulled away. "It's not your fault." I swiped at my tears, wishing I could be stronger. "I've gotta figure out how to get over this."

"It's going to take time." He walked to the window and pushed it open. "That's the only cure."

"How come you guys don't panic and break down all the time?" I sat on the couch and tucked my legs up underneath me. "You were prisoners a lot longer than I was."

Cash brought me my burger. "You need to eat." He scrubbed his hand down his face. "Draconian's dead."

The cold tone of his voice and the harshness of his words made me wince. "I know." I set my burger down and looked him in the eyes. "I killed him."

"That's why we don't share your fear." He sat next to me. "Your captors are still out there. Ours is dead."

While we waited for the others to show up, I choked down my dinner. I'd completely lost my appetite, but Cash was right. I needed to eat. I needed to keep my strength up. I needed to be ready next time Troy showed up to haul me off. I couldn't let it happen again. There would be no Liam or Vicki to keep me safe. With Troy's rage, I would be lucky if I made it through the first night without him killing me.

I watched Cash out of the corners of my eyes. He seemed to be stuck in his head. "Does it ever get easier?" I finally whispered.

"I don't know, Dacia." He wrapped his arm around my shoulders and pulled me closer. "I hope so."

My friends were somber. As they stepped into the apartment, each of them shot me a sympathetic look. Cash stood up, and Cody immediately sat next to me. "You okay?"

"Sure." I was as okay as I was going to be. There was no simple fix for what was wrong with me. Time was the only cure.

Cassandra and Bryce piled into one chair, and Samantha and Dan took the other one. Cash, Malcolm, Mavros, and Liam stared at each other for several minutes before Malcolm made Cody and I scoot down. Then he sat on my other side.

"Am I really that bad?" I asked as I moved.

Malcolm shook his head. "We were trying to decide who could best keep your emotions under control."

"So … you got the short stick."

He smiled at me, showing fangs that were longer than normal. Then he grabbed hold of my hand and started explaining everything to Cassandra and Bryce. I listened to him tell them about the beginning of break. He was explaining how Mavros had come back into my life when I stopped him.

"I think I need to do this." I looked down at the tan carpet and chewed on my lip. "If I don't face it, I'll never be able to come to terms with it." Aside from feeling guilty about how my magic had lashed out at Cody, the first part of the story was easy enough to tell.

When I got to the part about killing Argentum's power, Cassandra leaned forward. Her ice-blue eyes were wide. "It's gone then?"

"Thank God," Cody mumbled.

I nodded. "Yeah. Mavros helped me get rid of it, so—" I closed my eyes and breathed in deeply. I needed to figure out how to cope with having been held captive, but the thought of talking about it made my chest tighten.

"I can tell them, Dacia." Malcolm's words brushed across my ear.

If I smelled like Cody had earlier, how could he be so close to me? How could any of the predators in the room stand to be near me?

His strength flowed into me, and I shook my head. "I need to." I rubbed my hands down my legs, wiping my sweaty palms off on my jeans, before twining my fingers with Malcolm's again. "The Nephilim"—I noticed Liam duck his head—"some of them, anyway, decided I didn't deserve freedom."

Several times throughout my story, I had to stop. Each time, Malcolm poured his strength into me, taking the edge off of my terror.

"Why?" Cassandra asked when I finished. "Why do you trust him?" She sliced her finger through the air, aiming it at Liam.

There was a part of me that wanted to laugh like a crazed woman at that. Neither she nor Bryce were people I had ever expected to trust, let alone like, but here I was spilling my darkest secrets to them. I lifted one shoulder toward my ear. "For the same reason I know I can trust anyone."

"So, why'd you do it?" I hadn't heard Bryce sound so angry since he'd been trying to figure out what I'd done to Cassandra.

Liam looked at me, and I could feel that sadness that was so deeply ingrained in his aura resonating from him. "At first, I was following orders." He pulled out one of the kitchen chairs and straddled it, folding his arms over the back. He stared at the floor in front of him. "As soon as I saw her, I realized she wasn't evil, like we'd been told. It's the Nephilim's job to protect, so I tried to keep her safe … keep the others away until we could get her out."

I pulled my hand out of Malcolm's and snuggled into Cody's side. He automatically wrapped his arm around me, drawing me against his body.

Malcolm watched me, keeping his jaws pressed firmly together. Finally, he nodded and walked to the window. He pushed his hands down on the counter, leaned as close to the screen as he could, and breathed in the fresh, mountain air.

The room is dark. A single bulb down the hallway spills dim, yellow light along the walls. Shadows stretch out, covering most of the room, keeping me from being able to tell where I am. I lie on the cold, cement floor. My shirt is pulled up slightly on my back. I want to tug it down, but I can't seem to drag my hands from the collar. It feels like a noose around my neck. Each breath I take seems to tighten it.

Troy stands above me, and I stare up into his face. The rank smell of his body odor makes me want to turn my head to the side, but I'm terrified of what he'll do if I look away.

I want to be brave and ask him if it's been hard finding a place to bathe now that he's on the run. I want to kick his feet out from under him. I want to show him that I'm stronger than I seem. But, it's all I can do to keep my eyes focused on him.

My head throbs. Another concussion. Even though I heal quickly, I wonder what long-term effects I'll sustain from all of these head injuries.

His face blurs, and I see three of him above me. I blink, and when things come back into focus, there's only one of him there again. I don't want to see the hate in his eyes, so I stare at the tattoo running along the side of his face. As I focus on it, I realize that it covers a horrific scar.

"What are you looking at?" He kicks me in the knee, and when I reach for it, he steps on my hand. He takes out his knife and slices it down his arm. "Lucky for you, they want you alive still." He squats down, places his knees on my arms so that I can't move, and presses his wrist against my mouth. With his other hand, he runs the back edge of his blade along my hairline. "Not me, though. I'd love nothing more than to send you back to your demon one piece at a time."

I shiver, and his blood pours down my throat. Coughing and spluttering, I choke on it, but instead of pulling his wrist away, he presses it down harder, smashing my lips against my teeth. I twist my head to the side, and the tip of his knife nicks my temple. He smirks and twists the blade.

A whimper escapes from me even though I try to contain it.

Holding the knife above me, he lets the blood on the blade drip onto my face. He looks down his nose at me, holding my gaze, almost daring me to do something.

When nothing happens, he presses the back of the blade against his leg and snaps it closed. Then he lifts his wrist off my lips and dips his finger into his blood. He bends over, and his knees smash my arms against the cement floor. Chanting something under his breath, he draws on my forehead, dabs his fingers in his blood again, and traces a symbol on both of my cheeks.

When he finishes, he waves his hands through the air, and a portal opens up next to me. He rocks back on his heels and grabs both of my wrists in one hand. Then he yanks me to my feet and tosses me through the gateway.

For a moment, the bright light blinds me. I press my eyes shut and wait for the screaming, but it doesn't come. Lush grass tickles my skin. Somehow, he has managed to get me inside their sanctuary.

Chapter 19

New Semester

Cody's arm was thrown over the top of mine. I had gone to sleep, hoping he could keep my nightmares at bay. I listened, making sure his breathing stayed even. Then I slipped out of bed. As I walked to the bathroom, I slid my hand over the back of my skull. My fingers met with a tender spot that must've come from my head being slammed into the floor.

I stood in front of the mirror expecting to see blood on my face from a small wound at my temple. What I saw in the reflection made my breath catch in my throat and stopped my thoughts.

I stared at my face. Troy's gold-flecked blood sparkled like glitter on my skin. Besides the wound, three strange symbols were drawn on my forehead and cheeks. *Mavros.* Even in my head, my voice shook. *Malcolm. Cash.*

Two dragons stood in my bathroom with me. Malcolm grabbed my shoulders and turned me toward him. "What happened?"

"Troy." The word was little more than a whisper. "Nightmare." My gaze slid from Malcolm to Cash. "Where's Mavros?"

"Here." The word came from behind me.

I pulled out of Malcolm's grasp and threw myself into Mavros' arms. "I thought you were gone. I thought he'd taken you from me."

"I'm here." He pulled me against his body. He was warm and strong, and I savored the feel of his arms around me.

The familiar smell of warm summer nights soothed me.

"Dacia." Cody stood in the doorway in only his shorts. His hair was tousled, and his blue eyes were filled with dread. "Why didn't you wake me?"

I stepped away from Mavros. Even though he no longer tormented Cody like he used to, Cody didn't need to see me in his arms. "I thought I would just have a cut here." I turned so they could see my temple. Then I waved my hand over my face. "I didn't know I would have all this."

"What's all this?" Cash stepped toward me. He tilted my face to the light so he could see the symbols better.

I stared up at the ceiling while he studied my face. "Troy fed me more of his blood, drew these, and pulled me through the portal. It worked." I chewed on my bottom lip. "When I saw them on my face, I thought maybe he'd broken my bond to Mavros."

"Check your magic." Malcolm's voice was low and dangerous.

I pulled my chin out of Cash's grasp. "I wanna wash my face first." I turned toward the sink. "I'll be out in a minute."

I stared at my reflection. I looked like I was being prepared for a sacrifice to some heathen god of old. Blood splatters covered my face and dripped down from my temple to my chin. The symbol on my forehead looked like a backward cursive E with two vertical lines through it. On one cheek, there was something that looked like a cursive L that was mirrored. The other side had a script Y with three diamonds along the tail.

These weren't just random designs that he'd drawn on my face. There had to be a meaning to them, a reason Troy had chosen these symbols and not others.

I pulled a washrag out from under the sink and ran warm water over it. As soon as I got all the gore cleaned off of my face, I walked into my bedroom. I knew before I opened the door that they were all there, waiting for me. "Do you know what any of that meant?" I asked the immortal beings.

"They're angelic symbols." Mavros waved his hands before tucking them in his pockets and staring at me.

I tilted my head. "How do you know that?"

"All greater demons do." He shrugged like it was no big deal. "Know thine enemy and all that." He pointed at his left cheek. "Willingness." Tapping his forehead, he said, "Order out of chaos." His finger slid to his right cheek. "Sacred place. They were wisely chosen."

Cody sat on the edge of my bed. He had thrown a shirt on while I'd been in the bathroom. "Can he take her?" He raked his fingers through his hair.

"With those symbols … and his blood, probably, yeah." Mavros pinched the bridge of his nose.

His words weren't what I'd wanted to hear, but I'd been pretty sure of the answer before Cody asked. I plopped down next to Cody. My leg was pressed against his. The warmth of his skin seeped into me. I twined my fingers through his and waited for whatever my guardians would say next.

"I know it's not what you want, and I'm truly sorry, but your best protection against them is me. They can't abolish me." When Mavros looked at me again, there was genuine sorrow in his eyes. "I can be Mavros or Damon. I can be someone else, but I need to be with you until we can figure out another way to keep you safe."

Cody's head snapped up, and he narrowed his eyes at Mavros. "Not Damon."

I knew that would be Cody's reaction, but no matter what form he was in, he was still the same, and he still wanted me in the end. "Just be yourself. Lots of people have seen you around here anyway. If you change, I'll just have to explain why I have another guy hanging around me all of the time."

Cody rested his hand on my shoulder. "Should sleep."

"I need to check on my magic first." It was hard to concentrate with four pairs of eyes staring at me. I finally closed mine and pretended to be alone. Just before I slipped into the room where my power resided, I felt Mavros' consciousness rub up against mine.

He took my hand in his. "I thought you might need a friend with you."

"Thanks." I tugged him across the floor to where my serpent lay coiled around his.

The pearlescent snake was a monster compared to the onyx one. It was like seeing an anaconda curled around a rattlesnake. With its venom, there was no doubt in my mind that a rattler was capable of killing an anaconda, but next to it, the ebony snake appeared delicate.

For the first time, I realized that it probably wouldn't take much to drive Mavros' magic out of my body. If the Nephilim had known how little of his essence was there, could they have forced it out in those few days that I'd been their prisoner? Would it be gone if Troy had fed me his blood every day?

"Dacia." Mavros' voice was soft and reassuring, but I still jumped at the sound of it.

I glanced up at him and saw a gentleness in his eyes that he reserved only for me. "Right." I slowly lowered one knee to the ground and reached out my hand.

As soon as my fingers touched the serpent, it jerked its head up and struck. I fell back, and its fangs sunk into my shoulder instead of my neck.

Mavros grabbed hold of the snake and pulled its head forward to dislodge its curved teeth from my shoulder. Its copper eyes stared into mine, a challenge in them that I hadn't seen since Argentum tainted my powers. Its fangs were still descended.

I lowered my gaze, hoping to avoid a confrontation. Pain pulsed through my shoulder, and blood ran down my arm, dripping from my fingertips. I pressed my hand to the wound.

I am my own. The serpent lowered its body to the ground. *Do not sneak up on me again.*

I laughed at the irony of that statement and shook my head, trying to get some order to my thoughts. How could I sneak up on something that was a part of me?

Mavros looked at me like I dropped my marble bag, and the contents spilled out all over the floor, some of them lost forever.

I wanted to tug my hand through my hair, but both of them were coated in blood. Instead, I closed my eyes and took a deep breath, settling myself. "I didn't mean to startle you."

If a snake could smirk, I would say this one did. *I am my own.* It curled around Mavros' power and looked up at me through half-lidded eyes. Its scales shimmered but no more than the last time I'd seen it.

I focused on Mavros' serpent. "What about his?" I pointed at Mavros. "Is it still its own?"

My snake's tongue darted out, scenting the air. *Yessss.*

Some of the tension drained out of me, but the fear stayed behind. I pushed myself to my feet and stood next to Mavros. He slid his hand around my waist, and I opened my eyes on the real world.

The dragons stared at me. Cody jerked his arm down and held his hand out in front of him. My blood coated his fingers. He looked into my eyes. "What happened? Are you okay?"

Mavros slipped his hand under my elbow and stood me up, walking me into the bathroom. "Her magic attacked her."

"Why?" Cody asked at the same time Mavros turned the water on.

He tugged my hands under the faucet and washed the blood off of them.

I watched everything as if it was happening to somebody else. I saw the blood on the back and front of my shirt. I saw the vacant expression on my face, the emptiness in my eyes.

Mavros tore my shirt so that my shoulder and the bite marks were exposed.

The dragons observed us from the doorway, moving aside to let Cody in with us. He took the rag from Mavros and cleaned my wound. As soon as the blood was gone, he grabbed bandages and antiseptic ointment. Then he looked around the room and ended up guiding me to the bathtub. He helped me sit on the edge of it. "She needs a new shirt."

He knelt in front of me, tending to my wound. His hands were gentle. His face was an unreadable mask.

Cash brought a clean shirt in for me. Cody pushed off the tub and stood, taking it from him. "Give us a minute."

The door closed, and just the two of us were in the bathroom. He held my shirt out. "You or me, Dacia?"

He bent down and tilted my chin up.

The tears that had pooled in my eyes spilled out, running down my face and dripping off of my chin.

He brushed my hair back, then ran his knuckles along my cheek. "Ya gotta change. Me or you?"

I stared at him. I knew what he was saying, but I couldn't find my voice. It was lost somewhere inside of me, wondering if Troy had somehow infiltrated my magic and what the cost would be.

Cody slipped his hands under my shirt and began lifting it.

"No." Panic filled my voice, and I pressed down on his hands. "I got it." I blinked several times, trying to clear my head. "I got it. I'll be out. Okay?"

As soon as he left, I pushed myself to my feet and stared into the mirror. If the gold flecks had increased, I couldn't tell.

I changed clothes and burned my bloodied shirt.

When I opened the door, Malcolm and Cash quickly assessed me before disappearing.

Mavros dipped his chin. "I'm here if you need me, Dacia."

I climbed into bed with Cody and prayed the rest of the night would be uneventful.

Starting between my eyebrows, Cody trailed his finger down my nose. "Wakey, wakey." His voice was as soft as his touch.

I pulled the covers up over my head and moaned into my pillow, rolling over as I did. Pain tore through my shoulder, reminding me of last night's dream and the events afterward. I whimpered and flopped onto my back.

My shoulder should have been healed. Maybe my powers hadn't worked because morning just came far too early, but I thought there was more to it.

"Dacia?" Cody propped himself up, looking down at me. "You okay?"

I shook my head slightly, but even that sent pain shooting from the snake's bite. Pinching my eyes shut, I tried to focus on life and healing. Magic tingled inside of me, coursing through my body until it converged in my shoulder.

I pulled my collar to the side, ripped the bandages off, and watched as the skin drew together. Scabs formed over the punctures. They dried up and fell off, leaving scars where the snake's fangs had pierced my flesh. Almost as soon as they showed up, they disappeared, and my skin was once again un-marred.

"Why?" Cody rubbed his hand over his mouth. "Shouldn't that have happened overnight?"

I let go of my shirt and sat up. Sitting on the edge of my bed with my back turned to him, I said, "I have a feeling my magic was showing me who's in control."

"Doesn't make sense." He rubbed my back. "You're the same person."

I stood up. I didn't want to think this, but what other explanation could there be? "Are we still?" I walked to my dresser, trying to keep from saying what kept running through my head. "Or is it Troy, too?"

Cash, Malcolm, and Mavros waited for me by the door. Since none of my friends were in any of my classes this semester, I was worried about keeping them safe when we were so spread out, but I also hoped that without me around their lives wouldn't be in danger.

The four of us stepped outside, and sleet pelted my face. The cold wind burned my exposed skin. Malcolm walked in front of me, blocking me from the worst of it. Cash threw his arm over my shoulders and tucked me against his side.

I stared into the faces of everyone we walked past, expecting to see a black tribal tattoo running down the side of one of them. Expecting Troy to lunge out at any moment.

Cash growled low enough so no other humans around us would be able to hear it.

"Sorry," I mumbled.

Redirecting my thoughts, I studied my guards. Neither of the dragons seemed bothered by the weather. Cash just had on a dark gray t-shirt that said, "Do not meddle in the affairs of dragons for you are crunchy and taste good with ketchup." The dragon on it was, of course, the same color of purple as the streaks in his hair.

Malcolm looked a little more reserved in his sweater. It was several shades of brown, black, and gray knitted together. He looked over his shoulder at me, and I realized the sweater brought out the bronze of his eyes, making them seem even more otherworldly than normal.

I turned my head toward Mavros long enough to take in his appearance. He looked like he did every day. He had on a long-sleeved, silk shirt, jeans, boots, and his customary leather jacket. All of them were his standard-issue black.

My eyebrows pinched together, and my head tilted toward the side. I'd never really thought about it before, but did he always dress in black for the same reason that I turned blue in dragon form? Did it strain his magic to wear a different color?

As soon as my thoughts wandered to his powers, I felt myself being drawn into the fear that Troy was taking over my magic. I shivered, and Cash pulled me closer still.

Glancing up at him, I noticed faint stubble on his cheeks and chin. I reached up but dropped my hand before touching his face.

"What?" His gaze briefly met mine before going on high alert again.

"How does it work?" As soon as the words came out, heat blossomed on my cheeks.

His eyebrows pinched together. "You're going to have to be a little clearer. How does what work?"

"This." I waved my hand, encompassing his whole body. "Being a dragon in human form. Are you … do you…" I couldn't find the words I was looking for.

Mavros smirked at me. "She wants to know if your body functions like a human's when you're human."

"Yeah." Students from the dorms merged onto the sidewalk near us. *It's no different than when you're a dragon.*

I chewed on my lip. *But I don't stay a dragon. If I did, what would happen?*

That, I don't know. His eyes flicked to me. "You're the only one of your kind."

"Okay, then, so what about you?"

He looked around. "When we were with Draconian," he said the words slowly like he was weighing each one, "we didn't change at all. We were instinctual."

Malcolm's shoulders were tight. His steps faltered.

"Now, we're this most of the time." He nodded at a few passing people and waited a minute to continue. "If we hold it longer … for more hours than not, we take on more of the traits."

"Eventually—" Malcolm glanced over his shoulder and grimaced "—your food will even become appetizing."

A chuckle slipped out of me. "No, not that." I held my hand over my mouth. "Oh, the horror."

Mavros held Quartz Building's door open, and as we stepped inside our conversation stopped.

Troy stood in the hallway leaning against the wall next to the classroom door. A backpack was slung over his shoulder, and he watched every step I took.

My hands trembled. The air was pulled from my lungs, and they refused to refill. I saw him standing behind me, slamming my head into the cage, forcing me to drink his blood.

Malcolm moved between us, blocking him from my view while Cash sent soothing energy flooding through me. He dragged me into the room. The whole time, he whispered something to me over and over again, but the words couldn't cut through the fog that had engulfed me.

Dacia. His voice was harsh.

I blinked up at him, but I couldn't pull myself out of my memories. I was stuck in the prison cell, reliving every encounter I'd had with Troy. I could taste his blood rushing down my throat, feel his hot breath on my skin, see the hatred in his eyes.

Cash directed me to a desk at the back of the room and set me in the chair. I saw him kneeling in front of me, but he was distorted by the superimposed images of Troy.

He held my hands, and his strength poured into me. The fog dissipated, and sound flooded in all at once. Students talking over each other, chairs scraping across the floor, the blast of the furnace, zippers being pulled down, people taking books and pens and paper out of their bags, the whir of computers coming to life, and the blood rushing through my veins.

It was too much, too overwhelming.

Troy strode toward me, and tears pricked my eyes. My stomach tightened, and I thought I might throw up. I wrapped one arm around my belly and held my mouth with my other hand.

Mavros moved in front of me, blocking Troy's path. "Not another step." Mavros' voice was smooth and silky, but the threat was clear.

"I can't wait 'til I can send you back to the Abyss." Troy's eyes narrowed. "Kicking and screaming the whole way."

One side of Mavros' mouth lifted in a malicious mockery of a smile. He strode right up to Troy and whispered, "Is God himself going to come down and help you with that?" Backing away, he added, "That's the only way you can banish me."

Something flashed across Troy's face too quickly for me to make sense of it.

He sat at the desk directly in front of me, turned to the side, and threw his arm over the back of the chair so that he could watch me throughout class.

Mavros scooted as close to me as he could and draped his arm over my shoulders. Troy's lip curled in disgust, but he kept staring at me. The look on his face told me he had no doubt that he would be able to capture me again, even with my guards by my side and vigilant. His confidence was more intimidating than his presence.

How can I fight him? I sent the thought to Cash. *I can't even breathe when he's nearby.* I wanted to press my palm into my chest, to clutch my hair, and bow my head in defeat, but I didn't want Troy to know how broken I was. I didn't want him to know that his presence here made me feel more powerless than I'd been inside the Nephilim's cage.

Cash didn't say anything. He just took my hand in his and gently rubbed his thumb over mine. The whole time, his power trickled into me.

Mavros looked around me at Cash and Malcolm. "If you want to remove the trash, I can make it look like he got up and left."

"You could"—Troy didn't try to mask his hatred for Mavros—"but do you know where her friends are and who's with them?" He held his hand in front of him staring at his fingernails. "You'd be surprised by the number of new students this semester."

Malcolm growled, and a few students turned in their seats to look at us. Both dragons inhaled deeply. Malcolm kept his voice low. "Your choice, Dacia. I can drop him off a mountain peak if you'd like."

I imagined Troy dangling from Malcolm's talons. His normally smug face was riddled with fear. "No." Grabbing my bag, I pulled out my book and a notepad. My hand shook.

Troy laughed. "Your guardians aren't going to last much longer." He scooted his chair back, bringing himself closer to me. "Your fear has to be driving them nuts."

"I'm not afraid of you." There was no way he didn't hear the lie in my voice.

The smirk he shot me was evidence I hadn't fooled him. "You never could tell the truth."

"Hello." A man stood at the front of the class wearing a tan tweed suit. He had brown, curly hair and wire-rimmed glasses. He sat on the edge of his desk. "I am Professor Natterjack, and this is Arthurian Legend." His accent was distinctly British.

I tried to take notes, but I couldn't focus with Troy staring at me. Liam had told me that Troy was afraid of me, but if that was true, he was better at hiding his emotions than I was.

When class ended, Troy stood right in front of my desk, holding a piece of paper. "Looks like creative writing is next." He smirked at me. "Save me a seat—" he held his hand out in front of him with his palm up "—or you could just come with me now."

I shoved my stuff into my bag, then twined my fingers through Mavros'.

Troy looked at our joined hands. Disgust and anger battled for dominance over his expression. "Have it your way." He turned and jogged out of the room.

I practically collapsed into Mavros' hold. "They're going to take me."

"We're not going to let that happen." Cash's dragon was too close to the surface. "I won't fail you again."

Chapter 20

As soon as Russ and Liam walked Cody back from class, we all teleported to the clearing. Mavros snapped the collar around my neck, stealing my magic from me. I clutched Cody's arm until I felt steady enough to move. Then I walked away from everyone, hoping that whatever Liam planned on teaching me would give me the confidence to face Troy.

I made it another two steps before somebody wrapped their arms around me. My chest tightened, and fear froze my body.

"You know what to do." Liam's voice was right next to my ear, and I realized it wasn't Troy who had grabbed me.

I dropped my head. If it had been an enemy, the collar would have been slipped around my neck without me putting up a fight. Somehow, I needed to make my body react and not freeze with fear. I swung my leg, hooking it behind Liam's. Then I slammed my hand back three times, hitting my mark. I smashed my elbow into his face, then kicked him in the knee before running off.

Malcolm shook his head at me. "You've got to react faster."

"I didn't realize we were starting." I stood with my hands fisted on my hips and glared at him.

There were no whites in his eyes. "And, you're going to know exactly when you'll be attacked?"

My arms were clamped to my sides, and I was lifted off the ground. This time, my reaction was instinctual. Liam was lying on his back before I had time to think about what I had done.

"Good job." He looked up at me, clutching his knee. He turned his head to where Cash was working with Cody. Then he let go of his leg and flipped up onto his feet. "Cash, can you train with Dacia for a while? I'd like to see how Cody's doing."

After Cody dropped Cash, Liam and Cash traded places. "Do your worst," Cash said when he grabbed me.

For the next hour and a half, Cash and Liam attacked us from behind, and Cody and I practiced escaping from them. By the time Mavros took the collar off of me, my body was bruised, and my muscles ached.

Magic rushed through my veins. Flames danced over my skin. I was afraid that if I didn't release it, I would end up hurting someone. I focused on transformation.

Wings tore from my shoulders, but they weren't the ones I had expected. I spread them out and stared at the pristine white feathers. Light radiated through my skin.

Mavros tucked his hands in his pockets. "Is she still yours, dragon?"

"Why?" I knew it had to have something to do with Troy, but why would I change into this when the dragon was my alternate form? Where were my blue scales? Where was my fire?

Liam rubbed his beard and strode toward me.

Smoke rolled out of Malcolm's nostrils. "She is ours." His roar thundered through the clearing.

A distant whumph drew my attention. I turned toward the sound, my wings all but forgotten. A low, rumbling followed it. I pinched my eyebrows together trying to figure out if a storm was moving in. The slope of a mountain broke into a slab. The whole thing slid down the peak, racing toward the valley below. Trees toppled beneath the rush of snow.

Cash grabbed my shoulder and turned me around. Scales dotted his face. "Try again, Dacia."

I'd never had to think about becoming a dragon. It had always just happened, but this time, I focused on scales, talons, fangs, and fire. I thought about the ice-blue color I became as a dragon. My body expanded. My bones broke and reformed.

I opened my eyes. The world was sharper, clearer. The colors were more vibrant. The sounds and smells were magnified. I could sense Malcolm's and Cash's pleasure without even looking at them.

Lowering my face so that I was at eye-level with Liam and Russ, I said, "Keep Cody safe, and heal him please."

"We will, Dacia." There was no animosity in Russ' voice. His dragon wasn't riled by mine anymore. He clamped his hands down on Cody's and Liam's shoulders, and they all disappeared.

The rest of us leaped into the skies. I flapped my wings as hard and as fast as I could, hoping to leave my fear and helplessness far behind me.

Mavros flew next to me. "Don't use it all, Dacia. Troy will be in your class this afternoon."

Between one beat of my wings and the next, I changed from a confident dragon to a shaky, dizzy mess. I landed on an outcrop, not sure if my wings would keep me aloft any longer. I stumbled to the side. My breath came in harsh, ragged gasps. In this form, I needed more air. The risk of hyperventilating was stronger, but I wasn't willing to become human again. My human body was too vulnerable, too fragile.

Malcolm, Cash, and Mavros landed next to me. Malcolm's wing folded over the top of me, and soothing energy flowed through it, calming me. "We'll be with you. He will *not* take you today."

"He's going to try." I didn't know dragons could cry, but giant tears splattered on the ground at my feet. "He'll use those symbols and take me."

Mavros stood in front of me. All three of his heads were focused on me, and when he spoke, it was like listening to a symphony. "I will not leave your side. With me next to you, you have nothing to fear."

"I wish I could believe that." I stared into the trees. I had no idea where we were. No idea if the Nephilim had enough of my blood to track me. "They won't give up. Ever."

"Neither will we." Fire burned in Cash's throat.

Malcolm and Mavros sat on either side of me in creative writing. Cash took the seat directly in front of me. I didn't think Troy would be brave enough to sit next to him, but I was wrong. He angled the chair, then plopped down, smirking at me.

Mavros scooted closer to me and draped his arm over my shoulders. He was my friend, and he was protecting me, but I didn't want to seek comfort from his touch. I didn't want to need him. This was already hard enough on Cody. He didn't need constant reminders that Mavros could keep me safer than he could.

Professor Fisher strolled into the classroom. He stroked his goatee as he looked around the room. "I see some faces I recognize, and some that I don't." He sat on the edge of his desk. "I'm Professor Max Fisher. You can call me Professor, Max, Fisher, Fish, or any combination of those." He rubbed his hand over his shaved head. "You have thirty minutes, starting now, to write a one-page introduction of yourself."

Troy didn't touch his pen or paper. He just stared at me while I tried to write something. My penmanship looked worse than a first grader's. The letters were shaky and hard to read.

Malcolm rested his hand on my thigh and sent a calming wave of energy rushing through me.

Refusing to look at Troy, I finished writing my introduction. Professor Fisher had raved about my final paper, so I hoped I could pull off a good grade this semester, too. However, if I had to deal with the Nephilim for very long, I doubted I would do well in any of my classes. Without Malcolm's help, my fear was the only thing I could concentrate on with Troy around.

"Dacia—" Max smacked his hands and rubbed them together "—why don't you read your introduction?"

Maybe it wasn't a good thing that he had liked my final last semester. I stood, no longer feeling Malcolm's soothing energy or Mavros' protection. Troy stared up at me. My hands shook as I lifted my paper so that it blocked out his face. My voice trembled, but I managed to read the whole thing without having a panic attack and crumbling in front of everyone in the room.

"Does anyone have any questions for Dacia?" He paced in front of the class with his hands folded behind his back.

Troy shot me a phony smile, then raised his hand.

"Yeah, you there, in the back." Max pointed at Troy.

Troy stood up. His lip curled when he looked down at me. "What's with the bodyguards? Why are they always touching you?"

Heat blasted my face. Malcolm pinched his eyes shut, and I wondered if they looked human at all.

I stared into Troy's hate-filled face. "I'm filthy rich, and they think it will rub off on them."

Several students laughed. Others whispered amongst themselves.

Max folded his arms over his chest. With his muscles flexed, I realized he might have been more muscular than Troy. "Not cool." He looked at the rest of the students. "Does anyone else want to ask Dacia something?" He strolled from one side of the room to the other. When nobody spoke up, he pointed at Troy. "Okay, then why don't you read yours? While he's doing that, the rest of you can come up with totally inappropriate things to ask him."

"Don't think too hard." Troy sat back down and stared at me. "I didn't write a paper. I'm just here for her." He hooked his thumb at me.

When class ended, Troy hustled out of the room, pushing past the other students. I shoved my stuff into my backpack and breathed easily for the first time since he had shown up. Maybe seeing him constantly would eventually break my fear's hold on me, but I didn't think it would resolve quickly if at all.

"Dacia," Max said as I walked by his desk, "are you okay? Do I need to worry about that guy?"

Malcolm put his hand on my shoulder and shook his head. "He's what we're here for." His voice wasn't low enough to hide the savageness in it.

Max's eyes widened, and his face drained of all color.

I felt sorry for him. He was obviously concerned about my safety, but Malcolm had been pushed too far today. "You don't need to worry." I smiled at him, hoping it looked sincere. "I'll be fine."

He pushed his chair back and stood up. Genuine concern shone in his blue eyes. "Do you need a restraining order? Do the cops need to be involved?"

"No." Suddenly, the room felt too hot. The air was too thick. "It's under control. Dean Aspen is aware of the situation, and we're working on it."

He tugged the hairs on his goatee. "Let me know if you need anything. Someone to talk to. Someone to watch your back while they sleep." He nodded at my guardians. "Anything."

"Thanks." It was nice to know that so many people cared, but I couldn't involve anyone else. I couldn't risk anybody else's life, and I couldn't risk anyone else finding out about my magic. "I really do appreciate it."

Malcolm clutched my arm, and Mavros slid his fingers through mine. Cash walked in front of me, blocking me from view. If Troy was waiting for me in the hallway or on the path back to the apartment, they weren't going to give him a chance to take me.

When we stepped into my apartment, I expected them to relax, but Malcolm turned toward me and said, "Training in five minutes." His nostrils were flared, and his fangs hung over his bottom lip.

"What kind?" My shoulders inadvertently slumped forward.

Cody sat on the couch with a thick textbook on his lap. He glanced from me to Malcolm, waiting to hear the answer, too.

"Self-defense."

Cody shoved his book into his backpack and stood up. "Somethin' happen?"

"Just Troy being Troy." I shrugged and walked into my room to change into my training gear.

Liam didn't seize me as soon as I turned my back on him. I wasn't really expecting him to, but I was ready just in case. I took my position and rolled my neck as I turned to face him. Training was not how I had expected to spend my afternoon, but if it would settle the dragons, I would do it.

"I've got something new for you." Liam stood with his feet shoulder-width apart, and as soon as he waved Cash over, he put his hands behind his back. A soldier clear through. I had no doubt that he was fully aware of everything happening around him. "We worked on how to escape bear hugs. Troy is bigger than you and will be inclined to use strength and the element of surprise against you. What I want to show you now is how to escape if he puts you in a headlock from behind."

He stepped in front of Cash, and Cash wrapped his right arm around Liam's neck. "Your first instinct is going to be to push the arm away." He lifted his hands and pressed against Cash's arm. "You only have about six seconds to get free before you pass out, so this isn't going to work. You're not strong enough." He dropped his hands.

I stared at my feet. He was right. I wasn't strong enough. Nothing I had done had any effect on my captors. I'd fought, but it wasn't enough. Without my magic, I wasn't good enough. I wasn't strong enough.

"Instead of using force, I want you to use motion." He tapped Cash's arm. "He used his right arm to hold me, so I'm going to step forward with my left leg." He slowly mimicked what he'd just told me. "Then I want to swing my right leg between our bodies and dip my shoulder down. He'll probably still have hold of me, so I'm going to use both of my hands to shove against his chest as hard as I can." He did the whole technique several times, showing me exactly what I needed to do. Then standing in front of Cash, he said, "Ready, or do you want me to show you one more time?"

"Ready as I'll get." I didn't feel very confident about this. Liam and Cash were built similarly. Compared to me, Liam was a giant. I didn't see how I could get away from him when we were just practicing, let alone escape Troy when he came for me.

Liam wrapped his arm around my neck. "Do it slowly at first."

As I stepped forward, I noticed Malcolm walk off. His shoulders were pulled tight.

"Dacia?" Liam's breath was hot against my ear.

I pushed against his arm, trying to get some air. "Sorry." I went through the motions, but when Liam released me, I didn't feel any more confident about it.

"Faster." He grabbed me again.

With each attempt, I felt my assurance rise. Troy wasn't quite as tall as Liam, but he was more muscular. I would have to aim lower and push harder when shoving away from him.

We practiced until the sun sank behind the surrounding mountains. Orange and purple light spread across the sky, setting the clouds on fire.

"Take Cody." Malcolm's voice was still a growl. His dragon had only gotten closer to the surface as our training had gone on.

Russ stood between Cody and Liam with a hand on each of their shoulders. He nodded at me, then they were all gone.

Mavros pulled the collar off, and as soon as he did, Malcolm said, "Transform." He held up his hand in a stop motion. "Into a dragon."

A shiver rushed down my spine. *Cash, what will he do if it isn't a dragon that answers?*

I'm here. His voice was steady and soothing. *I won't let anything happen to you.*

Since I didn't want angel wings to explode out of my shoulder blades, I closed my eyes and focused on blue scales and flames. My body expanded. My bones cracked and re-formed. The smell of burnt food assaulted my nostrils, and I realized how deep Malcolm's anger ran.

He grinned, a feral imitation of a smile. Then, almost instantly, his dragon stood in front of me. He spread his wings and leaped into the sky.

Cash, Mavros, and I followed him. The cold air soothed my aching muscles and gave me a sudden burst of energy. I wanted to glide on the breeze, but Malcolm must have had energy to burn. He raced ahead of us.

Mavros stayed right next to me, close enough to touch me if anything happened. "He doesn't like it when your powers are bound. His dragon yearns to protect you. It can't bear to watch Liam attack you."

He was far enough ahead of us that he looked like a large bird soaring through the clouds. I looked from him to Mavros. "Don't hate me." I teleported to Malcolm's side. "I'm okay."

He turned his gaze on me. His eyes flashed, and I couldn't help but wonder what was going on in his head.

"Troy will take you." The words ground over each other, forcing themselves out of his mouth. "Soon."

I flapped my wings harder and faster than I ever had and still struggled to keep up with him. "I figured as much."

"Why didn't you let me take him?"

It took me a minute to realize what he was asking. Why hadn't I let him kill Troy? That was what he meant. "It wouldn't solve anything. If Troy disappeared more of them would come after me. They wouldn't believe that I don't want to hurt any-one. If I kill one of their own, they will never stop hunting me."

A low rumble started deep inside of him. It burst out of his mouth surrounded by an inferno. Red flames lit up the night-darkened sky. "If he takes you again, I'll kill him, Dacia. Damn the consequences."

Chapter 21

Slipping Through My Fingers

*T*roy hasn't shown up to class yet. I keep staring at the door, unable to pull my gaze away, wondering when he'll saunter in and plop down next to Cash. Maybe he has finally realized that he's pushed Malcolm just about as far as he can. There's only so much a dragon can take before incinerating everyone in his path.

The door opens, and my heart leaps into my throat. A guy with shaggy, black hair steps into the room and looks around. As soon as he sees the empty chair next to Cash, he grins and bounds toward it. The whole time, he stares at me.

His eyes are a vivid yellow. His smile is filled with mischief, and there is no way he's human.

Mavros pulls me closer. "Stay away from him," he hisses right in my ear.

The warning in his voice pulls my attention away from the carefree stranger. I turn and stare at Mavros, but he doesn't look at me. Flames dance in his eyes.

I startled awake. Staring at the ceiling, I tried to remember what Mavros was so upset about. What would have annoyed him so much that he forgot to hide his eyes?

Cody slipped his hand around my waist. "You okay?" His voice was thickened with sleep.

Except for Mavros' eyes, I couldn't remember anything about the dream. I didn't know if I needed to be even more concerned about Troy taking me or if there was some new monster, waiting in the shadows to drag me off. "Yeah." I rolled onto my side and settled my hand on his shoulder. "I had a dream, but it faded away."

"Happening a lot lately." Suddenly, he was wide awake. He lifted his head, propping it on his hand. "We need to worry?"

My hand slid from his shoulder, and I flopped onto my back. "Probably."

What's wrong? Malcolm's voice thundered through my head, making me jump.

Cody's gaze darted around the room, searching for whatever had startled me.

I tapped my finger against my temple. *Another dream I can't remember.*

Another? The word was little more than a growl. *How many?*

I tugged my hand through my hair and tried to remember how many times I'd woken to have my dreams disappear before I could grasp them. *At least three.*

No sooner was the thought out of my head than Malcolm stood at the foot of my bed. He pulled out my desk chair, sat, and stretched his legs out next to mine, making sure he touched me. "You need to tell us these things."

I nodded. There was no use in making excuses. His dragon wouldn't cope well with them. It was too riled.

"I'm staying here—" he gripped the arms of the chair, showing exactly where he meant "—until I see what these dreams are."

Cody lay back down. "Goodnight." He slid his body closer to mine and wrapped his arms around me.

I stared into Malcolm's eyes until mine were too heavy to keep open any longer. Then I drifted off to sleep.

Malcolm nudged my foot with his. "Wake up." His voice was still rough but not as bad as it had been.

With some effort, I managed to peel my eyelids apart. "Something wrong?"

"I need to hunt before you go to class."

I sat up and pulled both hands through my tangled mass of curls. "Were my dreams that bad?"

His eyes flicked to Cody, and my face felt hotter than a three-alarm fire. "Don't leave the apartment without Mavros."

He disappeared, and I stared at the chair he'd vacated. Even though they were getting along better, it couldn't have been easy for him to say that.

Cody rolled over and braced himself above me. "What'd ya dream?" A thousand emotions sparked in his sapphire eyes. Desire, love, mischief. Those were the ones that stuck out the most, but I also saw fear and concern flash through them.

I held onto his biceps and stared at him. A million possibilities darted through my head, but I had no idea what I'd dreamed. "Malcolm didn't let them through. I wish he would have. I could use some good dreams."

Cody lowered himself slightly, still keeping most of his weight off of me, and nudged my nose with his. His lips were softer than velvet. He brushed them across mine, and I pulled him down on me. My fingers trailed over his skin, exploring his back. I twisted my leg around his, needing him closer. I slid my hand up his body until it rested on the back of his head. Then I pressed down and nipped at his lip, intensifying the kiss. He wrapped his arms around me and rolled over, pulling me on top of him. Holding my waist, he ran his thumbs over the bare skin on my stomach. I moaned, and somebody cleared their throat.

I rolled off of Cody and looked around the room. Mavros stood by the door. "Malcolm sent me over to keep an eye on you." He waved his hand. "Continue if you'd like."

I grabbed my pillow and threw it at him. "Knock next time."

He darted out of the way and dipped his chin. "As you wish."

As soon as Mavros left, Cody huffed and flopped down, making the bed bounce. I laid my head on his chest and traced circles over his abs. "I'm sorry, Cody."

"Yeah." He squeezed my shoulder. "Know he wants you, but he's gonna have ta wait."

I didn't want to think about that. As long as Cody was alive, I would choose him over Mavros. I didn't want to think about the day when Cody was gone from my life. I didn't want to worry about how long I would live after he died. I wanted him by my side. Always.

Malcolm hadn't returned by the time we needed to leave for class. Before we even stepped out of my apartment, Mavros wrapped his arm around my shoulders and tucked me against his side. "You'll be safe with me, Dacia."

Cash nodded, then opened the door. Neither of them took more than a couple of steps away from me on our way to my Introduction to Fiction class.

I wanted to be stronger than this. I wanted to be independent, but until I could let go and not be so afraid, that wasn't going to happen. Until I stopped jumping at shadows, I needed my guardians with me.

We walked into the classroom, and I headed straight for the back of the room. I set my backpack on the desk next to me, hoping Malcolm would show up before Troy tried to sit there.

Mavros sat next to me and held my hand. Cash stood in front of me, ready to deflect Troy if he tried to sit beside me.

I leaned to the side, peaking around Cash, and watched the door. Several students entered, filling up the empty spaces. I recognized a few of them, but the majority were perfect strangers. My gut twisted a little more as each of them strolled in. Any of them could have been Troy's and Sebastian's minions, but none of them seemed to pay any attention to me.

"Where is he?" I asked Cash.

His eyebrows squished together. When I'd first met the dragons, they hadn't shown very many human expressions, but the more they were with me, the more human they seemed. "Malcolm or Troy?"

"Malcolm." My gaze shifted toward the door, like Cash saying his name aloud might have summoned Troy.

His features softened. "He said he'd be here."

The next person to step into the room pulled the door closed behind her. Her long, black hair hung to her waist. Where the light hit it, it shone, reminding me of a raven's wings. She turned toward the class and started talking, but I didn't hear a word she said.

I stared at the door, hoping Malcolm was okay and wondering what Troy was up to. I hated having him around me, but not knowing where he was or what he was doing was disconcerting.

Mavros grabbed my hand and stroked my thumb with his. He didn't send soothing energy into me like the dragons did, but his touch helped center me and reminded me that I wasn't alone.

Turning away from the door, I smiled at him, then tried to focus on what Dr. Yarrow had to say. The squeak of the hinges made my head jerk toward the door. Malcolm strolled into the room followed by Diana and Olivia.

I picked my bag up off the chair, and he slid in next to me. "Sorry," he whispered.

Everything okay?

He nodded. *Just lost track of time.*

Having him next to me helped settle me enough that I was able to pay attention to class. Diana and Olivia glanced at me a few times. They didn't stare at me like they had in the past, and they didn't seem overly vigilant.

When class was over, I took my time putting my stuff away. If Diana and Olivia planned to talk to me, I thought it would be better to have fewer people around.

Diana's blonde hair bounced as she walked toward me. "Hey, Dacia."

"Hello." I hefted my bag onto my shoulder.

Olivia stood off to the side, watching Mavros. Her lip was curled, and her nose wrinkled. Mavros slipped his fingers through mine, and she turned away as if she couldn't bear to watch.

"Liam told us Troy showed up in your classes yesterday." Diana didn't seem to notice Olivia's disgust. "We'll follow your schedule, and if he shows up, we'll nab him."

Students started filing in like lemmings. They all looked like they were being led to their deaths, but they just didn't have the will to care.

Cash cut a path through them. His shoulders were stiff, and his movements were jerky. As soon as we were in the hall, he spun around. "Will he stay in your custody longer than Micah did?"

Diana flinched. His words hit their mark. "You didn't do a great job of holding Argentum either."

"One of ours didn't free him." Malcolm had been unusually silent. The rage in his voice explained why. Even though he'd hunted, his dragon was still too close to the surface.

Olivia crossed her arms. "That won't happen again."

"We need to train." Malcolm clamped his hand on my shoulder.

I shook my head. "I need to eat. I didn't have breakfast."

"An hour, Dacia." His fingers loosened, letting me know it was my decision. "Then we'll eat."

For whatever reason, it was obvious that he needed this. "Okay, sure." I stepped outside and shivered. While we'd been sitting in the classroom, it had somehow gotten colder. The wind whipped between the buildings, throwing snow up into the air. I used a little of my magic to warm myself on the walk to the apartment. When we got to the outside door, I turned toward Diana and Olivia. "I have Graphic Design at 1:30."

"We'll be there." Diana held the door open and watched us step inside.

I was surprised they didn't follow me all of the way up the stairs to the fifth floor. It made me wonder if I should feel safe here. If they weren't worried enough about Troy being in the building, maybe I didn't need to worry about it either.

Unlocking the apartment door, I stepped inside. Samantha sat at the table, working on homework.

She waved at me and pulled her earbuds out. "How was class?"

"No Troy"—I set my backpack on the floor—"so that was good." I pulled my coat off and hung it on a hook by the door. "I'm going to train for an hour, then go to lunch."

"Do you mind if I join you?" She looked like she was ready to be disappointed, and I realized I needed to be a better friend, not just a better daughter.

"Of course, I don't mind. If Dan's back, he can come to."

The smile that lit up her face let me know I'd said the right thing.

"Ready?" Malcolm took ahold of my hand.

I nodded, and in the blink of an eye, we were falling through the clouds. Fear didn't consume me as it once had. I knew I could transform with little more than a thought. I knew that once I opened my wings the air would catch them, and I would soar on the breeze.

Wings burst through my shoulder blades, unfolding as they did. The wind still beat against my exposed skin. My legs dangled in the air. I looked behind me. The angel wings were beautiful. They reminded me of Arion's, and for just a moment, I wondered what it would be like to transform into a pegasus.

My thoughts were disrupted by Malcolm's angered growl. "Why, Dacia?" He narrowed his bronze eyes at me.

"I didn't mean to." I shivered. In this form, I could freeze to death. "I meant to be my dragon."

"Change." The word was a command that I couldn't ignore.

This time I concentrated on my transformation. My skin hardened into thick scales that the cold wind's bite couldn't penetrate. My wings grew, morphing into my dragon's.

Mavros flew on one side of me and Cash on the other. *Think about it next time.* Cash's voice echoed through my skull. *His dragon is too riled. It's beginning to doubt your true avatar.*

Why is this happening? I could hear the tears in my voice even though they weren't falling yet. *This is what I should become. This is me.*

He turned toward me, and I could see sorrow in his amethyst eyes. *Khione believed you were becoming more.*

Chapter 22

More

By the time we returned to the apartment, Malcolm had calmed down enough to be around people. His dragon peeked out at me a few times on the walk to Sedum Student Center, but I pretended not to notice. Eventually, if he needed to, he would confront me. It wasn't something I was going to rush into, though.

When everyone else split off to get their lunch, Mavros stayed right next to me. "Don't you want to get something to eat?" I asked him.

"I'll have whatever you're having." He grabbed a tray. "I wasn't kidding when I said I was your best hope of staying safe."

Suddenly, I wasn't as hungry as I had been. "I know, but—" I looked around the vast space, then lowered my voice "—do you really think he'd try to take me here?"

"I think he's getting desperate." He nodded. "I think he'll do whatever he needs to."

I didn't want to eat, but I knew nobody would let me get away with that. I grabbed a grilled cheese sandwich and a glass of water. Mavros shook his head, then heaped his plate full.

We walked together to a table against the wall. He sat next to me with his leg pressed up against mine.

Cody strode toward us. He pulled out the chair on my other side. His eyes drifted toward Mavros, but he didn't say anything. Samantha and Dan plopped down across from me, leaving the chairs closest to me open for my remaining guards. Liam sat next to Mavros. I thought about the way Olivia had looked at Mavros this morning and was glad Liam had a more open mind about him. Russ pulled a chair over from another table and sat next to Liam.

Malcolm and Cash were surprisingly the last ones to get to the table. I looked from them to Mavros and wondered if they had finally decided to trust him. Malcolm set his tray down, looked at my plate, and growled.

I lifted my shoulder. "I lost my appetite."

"You have to keep your strength up." His eyes flashed to his dragon's and back again so quickly that I wasn't sure if I had actually seen it.

Not wanting to argue, I lifted my sandwich and took a bite of it. It may as well have been ash for all I noticed of the flavor.

"I ran into Cassandra earlier." Samantha stabbed at her salad multiple times, making sure to get lettuce, cabbage, carrots, tomato, and chicken onto her fork. "She wanted to know if we'd all like to go to Althea with her and Bryce Saturday."

Cody shrugged. "Sounds good."

Justin and Bryce walked over and stopped behind Dan. Napkins were thrown over empty plates on their trays. Dan turned and bumped his fist against both of theirs.

Bryce nodded toward the rest of us. "Anyone up for a game?"

Please. I sent the thought to Cash and Malcolm.

Malcolm sucked in a deep breath. I was sure he wanted to train more, but I needed a break. "Sure. When?" He pointed at himself, Cash, and me. "We have class until 3."

Justin tilted his head to the side. "Meet ya there at 4:15?"

"Yeah, okay." My chin unintentionally dropped to my chest. With an hour between class and going to the court, I'd be lucky if Malcolm didn't insist on training.

Cash finished his lunch, then pushed back from the table. I watched him walk away, wondering what he was doing.

Malcolm tapped his finger on the table in front of me. "Eat."

I took another bite and listened to Samantha talk about her schedule. Unlike the lemmings I'd seen trudge into class earlier, she was excited about learning. There had been a time when I felt that way, but now it was a struggle to make it to class some days. When I did make it, I spent most of the time wondering when I would be ambushed.

Cash strolled back to the table with a new tray in his hand. He set it down in front of me before taking his seat. Fruits, vegetables, and cookies covered the plates. *You need to eat something healthy.* His amethyst eyes bored into mine. *You need to keep your strength up.*

I looked at the food, and my stomach recoiled at the thought of eating anything else.

Please, Dacia.

I stabbed a chunk of pineapple with my fork and shoved it into my mouth. The tangy, sweet juice coated my tongue and ran down my throat. I pushed my grilled cheese away and pulled the tray closer.

Cash smiled at me, and the tension released from his shoulders. "Thank you."

I ate most of the vegetables and all the fruit. Then I wrapped the cookies in a napkin and stood up. Mandarin Arts Center was one of the farthest buildings from the apartments. If we didn't leave, we wouldn't make it on time.

Mavros tugged my hand, pulling me back into my seat. "We're not walking." He kept his voice low enough that I doubted Samantha or Dan heard what he said. "We'll turn invisible and teleport."

"There are too many places for an ambush." Malcolm's words were a nearly indecipherable growl.

My stomach churned, and I wished I wouldn't have eaten so much. Nefarious and Draconian had both waylaid me there. I pushed my tray forward and rested my head on the table.

Cody rubbed my neck. "Want me to skip?"

"No." I peeked up at him. "I'll have plenty of guards." I sucked in a deep breath. "Just be careful. Stick with Liam and Russ."

He kissed my temple and stood. "Will do."

"We need to head out, too," Samantha said.

I sat up and looked at her. "See you later."

"I'll probably take my stuff and watch you guys play." She tugged her coat on and hefted her bag onto her shoulders. "Be safe, Dacia."

I nodded. "Thanks."

As soon as they were all gone, Cash took the trays and dumped them. Mavros grabbed my elbow and guided me toward the restrooms. Malcolm and Cash followed close enough that I imagined I could feel their breath on my neck. Between the bathrooms, there was a supply closet. Mavros looked over his shoulder, opened that door, and guided me inside. The dragons followed. The room was cramped. Our shoulders pressed together.

"What if somebody saw?" I narrowed my eyes at Mavros. All I needed was to be seen going into the supply closet with three guys.

He reached for my face, but I jerked away, hitting my bag against a shelf. "If anyone was watching, they saw you go into the women's room and us go into the men's." He dropped his hand. "I won't do anything to tarnish your reputation. Not anymore." His voice softened so much that I barely heard the last two words.

Malcolm held his hand out and waited for us all to put ours on it. He stared at me. There was no hint of the human persona in his eyes. "Do not show yourself until we do."

A heavy weight settled in my chest. Sandwiched between Malcolm's, Mavros', and Cash's hands, my fingers were freezing. Troy's face flashed through my mind. He was going to take me. He wouldn't let me get away this time. Liam wouldn't be there to keep me safe. There would be no one. No one to help me, to comfort me.

I imagined his blood trickling down my throat. The warm, coppery taste of it. I saw him standing above me. Revulsion filled his brown eyes.

I wouldn't escape again. He'd kill me if he couldn't take me to the sanctuary.

My knees buckled. Malcolm and Mavros slid their free hands around me, catching me before I hit the ground.

Scales dotted Malcolm's face. "Breathe, Dacia." He dropped his hand, and the rest of ours fell. Wrapping his arms around me, he pulled me against his chest and ran his hand over my head. "You're safe."

I clutched him, terrified to let go and find myself alone. His energy flowed into me, and I felt Cash's influence over my emotions. Stepping back, I swiped at my eyes.

Malcolm held onto my shoulders and stared into my soul. "Do you want to skip?"

"It's the first day." My lip quivered a little, but I was able to get the words out.

He slid his hand down to my elbow and held the other one out. "It's going to be okay."

I placed my hand on top of his, then turned invisible. All three of them could scent my emotions, which was bad enough, but I didn't want them to watch me fall apart anymore.

The others followed suit, and our bodies were stretched in and pulled out guided by Malcolm's magic. We stood under the cover of the pine trees. If we became visible right now, nobody would see us.

Malcolm's hand dropped out from beneath ours. "Stay," he whispered.

As soon as he let go of me, I felt utterly alone again. I couldn't see anybody around me. I couldn't hear Mavros or Cash breathing. Wrapping my arms around my stomach, I tried to hold my panic in, but I felt it taking over me. My breaths came in quick, shallow gasps that clouded the air in front of me.

A hand clamped down on my shoulder, and I screamed.

Chapter 23

"Dacia." Mavros' breath caressed my ear.

I jumped back, but he held onto me. I clutched the hair on the side of my head and tried to get myself under control, but every sound made me jerk.

Mavros pulled me against his chest. The scent of him filled my nostrils. My breathing slowed to normal, and my heart quit racing. If he was here, holding me, I was safe. The adrenaline fled from my body, and I collapsed against him.

He pressed his lips to my forehead and wrapped his arms around me more tightly. "You're safe."

I looked up into his obsidian eyes and realized he was visible. Putting my hands flat against his chest, I tried to push back, but he clutched me against his body, refusing to let me go. "Make sure you're steady first." He slowly released his grip on me.

"Thank you." I looked anywhere but at him.

Cash stepped in front of me and tilted my chin up. "You have no reason to be embarrassed."

I wanted to believe him … so badly, but I felt pathetic and hopeless. How would I ever be able to stand against Troy when I couldn't even face the ghost of his memory?

Mavros threw his arm over my shoulders, and the four of us walked onto the path together. Every step that crunched on the snow made my heart leap. I looked over my shoulder, ready to flee like a frightened rabbit.

Cash and Malcolm were uneasy. Their dragons were too close to the surface, and until Troy disappeared, I didn't see that changing.

"Can you take the edge off?" My voice sounded hollow. "Or make me mad."

Malcolm flashed his fangs at me. It was a feral look that would have scared me when we first met. "I don't think we'll be done training in time for you to play basketball." He pressed his hand against my lower back, keeping me moving. "You're too short to compete against us anyway."

I sped up and tried to spin to the side to get away from him, but like a good defender, he stayed right with me. I faked to the left, then pivoted right. When he grabbed me, I jabbed my elbow into his ribs.

He ruffled my hair and laughed. "Mad enough?"

"For now." My chest felt tight. I clenched and unclenched my fists.

Cash held the door open and ushered us inside. I strode in first. Mavros caught up to me and grabbed my hand, twining his fingers through mine. I jerked away, but he held on. "Sorry." He tilted his head and lifted one side of his mouth in a sad smile.

I tightened my fingers, hoping he would let go, but he didn't even seem to notice.

"Why didn't you paint me?" He pointed at the picture I'd done of Nefarious bursting out of Falcon Lake. "Didn't I scare you?"

I tried not to look at the red and black-skinned beast rising from the water. I tried to hold onto my anger. "For different reasons." I turned my back on the painting and glared at him. "And instead of being so vain, maybe you should be grateful that I forgave you."

"I am." He rubbed his thumb over my hand.

Malcolm growled. "Not now, *demon*. She needs to hold onto that anger."

Diana and Olivia stood outside of the classroom, waiting for us to show up. Olivia's dark hair was pulled into a French braid. She backed up so that she was half of a step behind Diana. Her pale green eyes were narrowed at Mavros, and she watched every move he made.

Diana nodded at the door. "He's not here."

Hearing that should have settled my nerves, but it didn't. If he wasn't here, where was he?

We stepped into the classroom, and a man in his mid-forties held his hand out, indicating the chairs. "Please sit."

Mavros led me toward an open table in the front of the room. The idea of having everyone behind me made my skin crawl, but there was nowhere else for us to sit together.

There were two stools per table. Mavros pulled one out and pointed at it. Then he sat next to me. Cash sat at the table across the aisle from me next to a dark-haired guy. Even without my dragon senses, I could feel his unease. Malcolm stared at him until he mumbled, "I'll … uh … sit back there." His hands trembled as he hurriedly shoved stuff into his backpack, then stumbled to a table in the middle of the room.

The teacher pulled the door shut, and I jumped at the sound. "I'm Shane Shrike, and this is the last time any of you will be late for my class. Understood?"

With anger still churning in my gut, I wanted to tell him that not everyone lived a life as easy as his. I wanted to tell him that I would be on time if monsters didn't exist. I wanted him to know that my monsters were real. They weren't just some internal struggle that I fought every day, but actual physical beings. Instead, I stared at the computer screen in front of me and hoped I could make it back to my apartment in one piece.

We were expected to follow along with what Professor Shrike demonstrated. I missed large chunks of what he'd done while I fought against my desire to turn around and scan the other students' faces. The longer I sat there, the more my anger faded, and fear and hopelessness filled the spaces that were left behind.

When Professor Shrike came by to look at our monitors, mine looked just like his. I turned toward Mavros, and he smirked at me.

"As soon as I look at your project, you are excused." Professor Shrike was a couple tables behind me now. "Remember to get here on time Thursday. You know how far away this building is now."

I leaned back in my chair and stared up at the ceiling. Sucking in a few deep breaths, I tried to work up the nerve to leave.

Cash stood beside my table. A peaceful feeling washed over me. I tugged my hand through my hair and pushed my chair back.

"No hurry, Dacia." His eyes were dark, and his mouth was set in a grim expression.

I brushed the back of my hand against his. "The sooner we go, the sooner I can quit worrying about it."

He grabbed my backpack off the floor and slung it over his shoulder. Mavros held his hand out, and I twined my fingers through his. When we stepped into the hall, Diana and Olivia joined us. We all walked outside together. Malcolm strode toward the group of trees next to the door. As soon as we were under the cover of their branches, he held his hand out.

Mavros lifted our joined hands onto it. I tried to pull my fingers away from his, but he shook his head. Cash set his hand on top of ours, then looked at Diana and Olivia. "We'll be at Lupine at 4:00. Dacia has class at 8:00 tomorrow morning."

They distorted, fading into nothing. Malcolm teleported us into the living room of his apartment. It looked just like the one across the hall, except cleaner.

"Why here?" I asked.

Malcolm shrugged. "No one will be here … ever, but in your apartment, there could be people around."

"Makes sense." I nodded. "I'll let Sam and Dan know they don't need to worry about us teleporting in."

Mavros finally allowed me to pull my hand out of his. I backed up a few steps, planning to go to my place. Malcolm's voice stopped me before I got very far. "We have time for more training."

"Yeah." My body slumped forward, and my chin dipped to my chest. "Can we not, though?"

He clapped his hand down on my shoulder, and I jumped. "Why?" his dragon asked.

"I know I need to train. I need to learn everything I can to keep Troy from capturing me again." I tugged my fingers through my hair, then clutched my hand at the base of my skull. "I really need a break, though. I need some time to focus on other things. The more I think about Troy and all of this, the worse my panic attacks seem to get."

The dragon faded back behind Malcolm's eyes. "Okay, Dacia. No more training today, but tomorrow we're back at it. Liam has a few more moves he'd like to show you, and you need to keep practicing the ones you already know."

Laughter from the hallway came through the walls. The sound of it was like a punch in the gut. The voices were all achingly familiar, but none of them had laughed around me for so long. I wanted to be a part of it. I wanted to feel carefree, but I was too broken.

I backed up against the door, then slid to the floor. Pulling my legs against my chest, I wrapped my arms around them and rested my head on my knees.

"What is it, Dacia?" Mavros' voice was soft and right next to me.

Tears glided over my cheeks. "It's nothing. It's stupid."

"It's not nothing." He skimmed his finger along my face, and I imagined him licking my tears off like I'd seen him do before.

I raised my head just enough that I could see him. "I'm never alone, but I am lonely no matter who I'm with." I lifted one hand and pointed at the door. "I don't think I'll ever have that again."

"You will." He set his jaw and gave me a curt nod.

A key turned in the lock. Mavros held the door shut while I scampered out of the way.

As soon as Mavros let go, Liam slowly pushed the door open, peering around it. "Oh, hey, Dacia."

"Hey." I didn't look at him. I didn't want him to see that I had been crying.

"Cody's back." He sidled past me. "I'm gonna change." He went into one of the rooms and shut the door.

"I suppose I should go." I held my hand out to Cash, and his eyebrows puckered together. "You have my bag."

"Oh, yeah." He pulled it off his shoulder and handed it to me. "Troy would be a fool—"

I shot him a look that made it clear what I thought of Troy.

"He's many things, Dacia"—Malcolm put his hand on my shoulder and squeezed gently—"but a fool's not one of them."

Cash nodded his agreement. "Try to relax and have fun playing basketball. He won't attempt to take you with all of us around."

"I'll try."

Mavros opened the door and stepped into the hallway first. He held onto my elbow and led me across the hall. I could hear voices coming from the apartment, but as soon as I opened the door, the conversation came to an abrupt halt.

Samantha, Dan, Cody, Russ, Cassandra, and Bryce stood in the living room, looking at me.

"Did I interrupt?" I pointed at my chest. "I can go."

Cody stepped toward me. "No."

I backed up.

"Don't go." He dragged his hand down his face. "We were just talking—"

"It's okay." I strode to my room, trying not to let them see how hurt I was. "I need to change."

Soft footsteps hurried toward me. Samantha grabbed my arm. I wanted to pull away and hide in my room, but her voice stopped me. It sounded almost as distressed as I felt. "We were talking about break, but we didn't want to upset you. Then we did anyway." She let go of me and stared at the carpet. "I'm so sorry." Her gaze slowly lifted to mine, and I could see she meant it.

"It's okay." I hoped the smile I gave her looked sincere. "You can talk about your breaks in front of me." I turned to face them. "I hope all of you had a good time. I should've asked." I sucked in a deep breath and slowly let it out. I really needed to be a better friend. "Just because mine was awful doesn't mean I hope yours was."

Dan walked over and threw his arms over mine and Samantha's shoulders. "Group hug. Come on guys, get in here." As the others joined us, one of his brilliant smiles covered his face, showing off his dimples.

Half an hour later, we stepped into the hallway where my guards were waiting for me. I looked at Liam and Mavros and couldn't stop the giggle that burst out of me. I was so used to Mavros wearing black jeans and shirts and Liam wearing his uniform that it was weird to see them in athletic shorts, t-shirts, and sneakers. At least Mavros was still dressed in all black. I really couldn't imagine him in another color. "Man, Liam, when was the last time your legs saw the sun?"

"Never?" He tilted his head to the side and tapped his finger on his chin. "Yeah, I'm going with never."

An image of Mavros lying on the beach in nothing but a speedo flashed in front of my eyes. *I didn't ask you,* I thought to him.

I thought you could use a reminder. His voice was like a soft caress that sent a shiver up my spine.

Cody's hand tightened on mine. Even though he wasn't involved, he must have realized something was going on.

We stepped outside. The sun sat low in the bright blue sky. It looked like a picture-perfect day, but the wind brutally beat against our exposed skin. The chill settled deep inside of me. I warmed the air around us, and my friends stepped closer.

Footsteps pounded against the sidewalk, moving toward us rapidly. Mavros grabbed hold of my arm, pulling me out of Cody's grasp.

"Hey, guys, wait up." Justin sounded out of breath.

Dan looked over his shoulder. "Nah, man. It's too cold. Gotta keep moving." His gaze lingered on me for a moment.

"Thanks," I mouthed before he turned back around.

When we got to the gym, Malcolm and Cash decided to be captains again. Justin was the only one who didn't know why they were, but he didn't seem to mind. Cash chose Mavros, Liam, Dan, and Bryce. Malcolm chose Justin first this time, then Cody, Russ, and me.

I pulled my coat and sweats off and threw them on the floor next to Samantha and Cassandra. Then I watched Cash's team toss their t-shirts off. Since they picked first, my team got to bring the ball in.

Mavros guarded me, standing closer than my shadow. I could feel the heat coming off of his bare chest. It was too distracting. "Back off a little," I said so that Justin wouldn't hear me.

"Sorry." He grinned, enjoying my discomfort.

I pressed my hand to his chest, trying to push him back slightly. Cody passed to Justin, then came to my rescue. He set up a pick, and I ran around Mavros. Justin passed me the ball, and I shot, bouncing it off the rim. Russ got the rebound and rocketed it back to me. I shot again, and this time, one of my favorite sounds filled the gym … swish.

Malcolm ran down the court next to me. "You're guarding Mavros."

"I thought we weren't worried."

He glanced down at me. "We're not. We're precautious."

I stood an arm's length away from Mavros between him and the basket. Sweat glistened on his abs, and it took all of my concentration not to stare at him.

Dan passed the ball to Liam, but Cody deflected it, knocking it toward our basket. We all ran after the ball. Justin reached it first, and Malcolm cut toward me. He set up a pick behind Mavros. "Quit toying with her."

"Seriously?" I shook my head. I should have known he was doing something to me. In this form, he was the epitome of perfection, but I didn't want him.

Mavros grinned at me. "Kept your mind off things." *Besides, I know you like looking.*

"Don't do that to me." I threw my elbow into his ribs and ran past him. Cody passed me the ball, and I immediately tossed it to Justin.

When he tried to pass it, Dan stole it, and Samantha cheered. I ran down the court behind Liam. Like all the Nephilim, he was tall and muscled, but deep scars ripped down his back. Scars where wings would be.

We ran up and down the court, exchanging baskets and wearing ourselves out physically. Finally, Dan called it. "Good game." He walked off the court.

Cash's team picked their shirts up off the floor and put them on. I picked up my water bottle and drank half of it in one gulp. I was hot and worn out, but for the first time in days, I didn't feel the need to look over my shoulder.

Justin stood next to me. "Cody said you're learning self-defense. How's that going?"

Before I had a chance to answer, strong arms wrapped around me, lifting me off my feet. My reactions were instinctual. I twisted my leg around my attacker's. Then I swung my hand back three times. The sound of my knuckles banging against his cup filled the gym. He grunted and released me. I kicked back, connecting with his knee, before running toward the top of the key.

Justin stared toward the area I had just vacated. His eyebrows were pinched together, and his mouth was pulled up in a grimace. I turned around to find Liam lying on his back, clutching his knee.

"Sorry." I ran toward him and knelt by his side. "I didn't think. I just did."

He nodded and rolled up into a sitting position. The smile he shot me was infused with pain. "That's what I've been training you to do."

"Remind me never to sneak up on her." Justin shook his head and shot the basketball into the cage with the others.

"I don't recommend it." Bryce patted my shoulder.

I glanced up at him, afraid of what I would see on his face, but there was no animosity in his pale eyes.

"So"—Justin took off across the court—"are you apartment dwellers too good to eat at Sedum?" He spun on his heel and kept walking backward. "I'm starving."

Cody's arm was comfortably draped over my shoulders. He looked down at me and shrugged. "I'm hungry."

"That's different." Samantha laughed. "Cody hungry, who'd have thought?"

Justin held the door open for all of us. As Dan walked by, he said, "Sounds like we're going to Sedum."

I stepped outside, and my body instantly stiffened. The sky was black. The air was still. It was quiet. The kind of silence where even the animals hold their breath.

Mavros nudged Cody out of the way and grabbed my arm. Malcolm took hold of the other one. Cash stepped right in front of me, and judging by the hot breath on my neck, Russ must've positioned himself behind me.

As they marched me forward, Justin said, "What's going on?" His voice was filled with uncertainty.

"There are people who would hurt Dacia." Russ kept his tone softer than either Cash or Malcolm would have.

I expected Justin to respond, but he must have been deep in thought or shocked to have gotten an answer. I tried to look over my shoulder at him, but Malcolm and Mavros held me too securely to even turn my head.

Finally, when I thought he would disappear, never having anything else to do with me, he asked, "Why?"

"Saw something she shouldn't've," Cody answered before I had a chance to even think of a response.

"Aw, man, that's gotta be rough." Justin sounded both understanding and sympathetic, but I didn't deserve it. It wasn't strictly a lie, but it wasn't the truth either.

Malcolm let go of me for long enough to turn around. "Keep it quiet. We've worked hard to keep people guessing."

Chapter 24

The only good thing about having an early morning class was that the dragons didn't try to convince me to train before it. I woke up in Cody's arms with Malcolm's foot touching mine. He looked into my eyes, made sure I was okay, and disappeared. His pupils had been thin slits, and his scleras were bronze instead of white.

Cody lay on his side, looking down at me. His finger gently trailed over my arm. Goosebumps followed in its wake. "How'd ya sleep?"

"Good." I looked to where Malcolm had been and wondered what he had seen while I slept. "I must've had some interesting dreams."

"He'll be okay."

I tossed back the covers and sat up. "I'm sure he will." I tugged my hand through my hair. "But that doesn't mean I want him to see my dreams … especially when I can't." I got out of bed and grabbed my clothes.

By the time I was ready to go to Arthurian Legend, Malcolm was back. He walked in front of me. His movements were stiff, and his pace was brisk.

I tapped Cash on the arm. When he met my eyes, I nodded at Malcolm. The question was obvious without me saying anything. He lifted his shoulders in response.

I jogged to catch up to Malcolm and slid my fingers around his bicep.

His arm tensed, and a low growl escaped from him. He glanced down at me. His lips were pulled tight to cover his fangs. His eyes were inhuman.

I pulled my sunglasses off, squinting against the light, and handed them to him. "Wear these." While he put them on, I thought to him, *What did I dream?*

Images flashed through my mind. Visions of me flying on angel's wings. Then I saw Mavros guarding me while we played basketball. Sweat glistened on his chest and abs.

You are ours. His voice was possessive, angry, and maybe a little hurt.

I squeezed his arm. *I am.* I showed him my memory of our first flight, the happiness I had felt when I'd soared through the air with him. Then I showed him my shock when I had sprouted angel wings. My fear at what Troy's blood was doing to me.

The tautness of his muscles eased somewhat. "We are training after your classes today."

Mavros took hold of my hand as we walked past a large group of students, and Malcolm edged in front of me.

"I know." I moved back between Mavros and Cash again.

As soon as class ended, Malcolm led me into a less-trafficked stairwell. He made sure the coast was clear, then teleported us to his apartment. I set my backpack next to the door, and he grabbed my hand, transporting us again. We fell through the sky, high above the mountains. This was a test, one I didn't dare fail. Malcolm might be able to forgive me if I did, but his dragon wouldn't.

I thought about leathery wings. Horns curving from my angular head, twisting like antlers. Icy-blue scales shimmering even in the dim sunlight.

Falling through a cloud, water collected on me, soaking through my clothes, spreading a chill throughout my body. And, still, I plummeted. The mountains stretched their rocky peaks toward me, hoping to pluck me from the sky.

"Transform." Malcolm flew next to me, the massive dragon, darker than the pits of Tartarus that used to plague my nightmares.

Wings burst from my shoulders. I couldn't tell if they were dragon or angel. Fear settled in my stomach, making it impossible for me to concentrate.

Praying that when I glanced back, I wouldn't see feathers, I pinched my eyes shut. As I turned my head, a rumble tore through the air next to me. I couldn't tell if it was Malcolm's excitement or his dismay. Taking in a deep breath, I looked.

Blue.

Small … but blue.

The rest of my body transformed. Breaking, lengthening, recreating. The wings grew with it.

My senses sharpened. The scent of Malcolm's relief, happiness, and exhilaration rushed through me, stoking the fire inside me. I roared, and flames burst through the overcast sky.

Flapping my massive wings, I climbed high above the clouds. Mavros, Malcolm, and Cash all stayed beside me. Vigilant. Determined to protect me, but whether it was fear or a sixth sense, I knew their defense would fail. Something was going to happen soon, and whatever it was, they wouldn't be able to keep me safe.

I sat in the Creative Writing classroom, listening to my stomach growl. Malcolm had kept me out too late to eat lunch. He glanced at me and lifted his lips in an apologetic smile.

Shrugging at him, I refocused my attention on the door, expecting each person who walked in to be Troy, Sebastian, or Micah. I hadn't seen them since Diana and Olivia had shown up, but I knew they wouldn't stay away for long.

When class was over, Malcolm led me to the same stairwell and teleported me to his apartment. We walked across the hall, and Malcolm went straight to the kitchen, smeared peanut butter over bread, and handed it to me. "We're leaving as soon as Liam gets here."

I took a bite of my sandwich and swallowed my disappointment along with it, knowing it wouldn't do me any good to argue. I needed to learn Krav Maga, but when the time came, I didn't know if I would be able to defend myself anyway.

As soon as I finished my sandwich, I changed into my training clothes. A small part of me considered leaving while no one was watching, but besides knowing I would never have another second to myself, the fear of Troy finding me alone was nearly debilitating.

I stepped out into the living room to find everyone waiting for me. Cody stepped forward. His gaze swept over me, and when his eyes met mine, there was a question in them. "Missed you at lunch."

"Yeah." I tugged my fingers through my hair. "Sorry about that."

Malcolm held his hand out, waiting for all of us to place ours in it. "She needed to train." His voice was a low rumble.

"Needs to eat, too." Cody's retort surprised me. He was a human with no powers, no defense against the dragons, but there he was standing up to one for me.

I pressed my hand against Malcolm's. "I had a sandwich, Cody. I'll be fine."

He slid his fingers through mine and squeezed. Everyone but Russ stepped in. I looked at him with my eyebrows pinched together.

"You've got all of them." He waved toward my guards. "I'll be back to go to Cody's classes with him."

I nodded, and Malcolm teleported us.

The clearing he took us to wasn't the same one we had been training in. Instead of snow, purple, red, yellow, and pink wildflowers covered the ground. They rose up the slopes, becoming sparser the higher they climbed. White boulders were strewn about as if they'd been thrown by an angry giant. The mountains weren't as tall as the ones we'd been frequenting, but they were warmer and no less beautiful.

As soon as Mavros snapped the collar on me, Liam grabbed me in a bear hug. I expected him to lift me off the ground, but when he didn't, I swung my leg around, trying to get out of this hold the way he had shown me. Instead of pulling myself to the side and leaving him open for attack, his body moved with mine. I tried again with my other leg.

"Put your feet down, and bend your knees." His arms were like steel bands wrapped around my body. "Then move your hips to the side."

I did what he said, knowing that what came next would be the same as what he had already taught me. I swung my arm back, and he groaned, immediately letting go. I jogged forward a couple of steps before I turned around.

Liam looked up at me from the ground. He was lying flat on his back with his knees pulled up to his chest. "I wasn't expecting that."

"Sorry." I pulled my bottom lip into my mouth with my teeth. "I thought it seemed logical."

"It was." He put his hands by his head and flipped up. It was amazing to see such a big guy move like that. "I just wasn't expecting it." He held his hand out with his finger pointing at the ground and spun it around.

As soon as I turned, he grabbed me, pulling me back against his body. When I bent my knees and moved my hips, he shifted with me. "Now what?" I asked.

"Push my hands against your body." He waited while I followed his instructions. "Now, drop down explosively."

I raised up onto my toes and then plummeted.

"Good." He held on just as tightly. It didn't seem like the movement had done anything at all. "Inhale and inflate your chest. Fill it as full as you can. Then exhale and raise your elbows. Hold onto my hand and arm. Otherwise, I can move you into a chokehold."

I slid my hands where he was telling me to put them. My gaze met Malcolm's, and I saw his humanity slipping. I smiled at him, hoping he would see that I was okay, but I wasn't sure how convincing it looked.

Liam, either not knowing about Malcolm's turmoil or not caring about it, said, "Lift your shoulder, and rotate under my arm. Keep your shoulder pressed into my elbow. Then push down at the same time as you pull my hand up."

I followed his instructions, leaving us both in rather awkward positions.

"You're doing good, Dacia, almost there." He pulled the shield down on his mask. "Slam your knee into my face, then pretend to punch me in the back of my neck two or three times." His gaze met mine. "Please don't really do that, though."

I went through the motions, escaping from Liam's hold when I kneed him in the face. I started to run away, but he grabbed my hand. "In this move, always punch the neck. It will keep your attacker down."

He let go of my hand, and I mimicked pounding his neck three times before running off.

"Good." He stood up.

"Did you get that?" Cash asked Cody.

He raised one shoulder. "Think so."

"Always try the first one I showed her before you do the last one." Liam grabbed my hand and spun me around, locking his arms around me. I went through the moves again and again until they were second nature, and I was dying of thirst.

Liam pulled sports drinks out of his bag and tossed one to everybody. Then he sat on the ground and opened his bottle, gulping down half of it. "You're doing really well, but now we're going to see what you remember."

I wiped my arm across my mouth. "I hope this will help me when he makes his move."

"I'll keep working with you every day until you know it as well as I do." Liam's eyebrows pinched together. "Even after that, we can keep training."

I finished the strawberry-banana-flavored drink and stood up. "Yeah." I moved my neck from side to side, cracking it. "I just hope it's enough."

Cody slid his hand into mine, gently rubbing his thumb over my knuckles. "She has feelings … intuition, premonitions. Whatever." He pivoted, moving in front of me, and tilted my chin up so that I was looking at him. "Happening soon?"

"I think so." I swallowed hard, trying to push down my fear.

Malcolm's growl filled the clearing. All other animal sounds stopped, silence brought on by deep-rooted survival instincts. "They will not take you again."

"I hope not." I tugged my hand through my hair and tried to cover my terror. If Malcolm's dragon didn't calm down, he would end up hunting Troy or taking me to a cave and hiding me until everyone else died of old age. "What now?" I asked Liam.

Liam looked at the sun, judging its position in the sky. "If you think he'll attack sooner, not later, I'd like to show you how to get out of a choke-hold from the front and back." He rubbed his hand over his stubble. "Then I'd like to see you run through all of them."

"All right." I massaged the tender spots on my arms. At least, when I got my magic back, I'd heal quickly.

This time, Liam had Cash help him demonstrate the moves. Then Cody worked with Cash, and I trained with Liam until the actions were instinctual. My muscles ached, and my strength was waning, but as soon as I finished freeing myself from a chokehold, Liam grabbed me in a bear hug, and we went through all of the maneuvers a few more times.

When Liam finally patted me on the shoulder, I nearly collapsed. *Another reason to be grateful for my powers,* I thought.

Mavros walked up and reached for my neck. Before he could grab me, I raised my arms and swung my elbows around.

Liam let out a hearty laugh, and I dropped my hands to my sides. Heat flushed my face. "Sorry. It was …"

"What you need to do," Mavros finished for me. Then he stepped closer and slowly raised his hands to my neck. He pulled the collar off, and magic flooded my system. The onslaught of power made me sway on my feet. I stretched my arms out, catching my balance. Everything was still spinning, so I pinched my eyes shut.

The pearlescent serpent rose up in front of me. Its head loomed over me. Its black and gold-flecked copper eyes stared down into mine. *Why do you allow them to bind me?*

I stretched my hand out, hoping it would let me touch it, praying it wouldn't strike. "I'm trying to learn how to protect myself, so the Nephilim can't take you away again." I chewed on my lip. "I need to know how to defend myself without magic … just in case."

They would not bind me if we killed them. It nuzzled its head against my fingers.

I ran my hand along its smooth scales, wondering how this part of me could be so different than I was, not understanding how it could want me to kill when the very idea was abhorrent to me. "If I kill Troy, they'll all come for me."

Then we'll kill them all. It lowered its body, coiling around Malcolm's power as if protecting it. *Do not bind me for too long.* It glared up at me. *I will not permit it.*

I nodded. "Is his magic affecting you?"

I am my own.

I opened my eyes, and everybody was staring at me.

"You okay?" Cody looked like he wanted to reach for me but was scared he might break me.

"Yeah." Realizing my arms were still outstretched, I folded them over my chest. "My magic wanted to talk." I chuckled at how ridiculous that sounded. It had to seem even dumber to all of them, but each of them pretended to understand.

Cody lifted his arm to drape over my shoulders and winced. Bruises ringed his biceps.

Anger burned inside of me. Everything sharpened, and I could see farther. My teeth lengthened into fangs, puncturing my bottom lip.

"Dacia." His voice was soft, and fear lined his expression.

The emotion smelled delectable. My mouth watered in response. I leaned closer and breathed deeply. He took a step back, but I tucked my fingers into his belt loop to keep him close to me.

My guardians surrounded me, and Liam pointed at my face. "Her eyes aren't human."

I grabbed Cody's hand with my other one. His eyes flicked from our linked fingers to my face. "What's wrong?" His words shook.

"You're hurt." Sending healing energy into him, I pressed my body against his. I tried to think about anything but the wonderful aroma wafting off of him and what it was doing to me.

He stood perfectly still. A deer trying not to be seen by a cougar.

I stood on my tiptoes and pressed my lips to his throat. His pulse ratcheted up as I skimmed my teeth along his flesh.

Chapter 25

Strong hands clamped down on my shoulders and jerked me backward. A growl tore loose from me. The sound was wild, angry, and shocking. The snarl of a cornered beast defending its kill.

I stumbled back, falling into my captor. My body went limp. My fangs retracted. I ran my tongue along human teeth. My vision diminished, and as it returned to normal, I realized Cody's bruises were healed, but I feared the damage I'd done might not ever be.

He stood rigid, but the pulse in his throat sprinted. He stared at me without blinking.

My chest tightened. I replayed what I'd done. Smelling him like he was a juicy steak. Skimming my fangs over his flesh. Would I have sunk my teeth into his neck? I looked over my shoulder.

Cash still held onto me. Sympathy shone in his amethyst eyes.

"I'm okay." I patted his hand, then stepped toward Cody.

All the color drained from Cody's face, and he swept his hand over his forehead. It looked like it was taking all of his nerve to keep from stepping back.

My heart plummeted. "I'm s-sorry." I reached for his hand, and he let me slide my fingers through his. "I just wanted to heal you." A lump blocked my throat, making it nearly impossible for me to speak. "I saw the bruises, and I got so angry."

He squeezed my fingers, then let go. "Yeah." He folded his arms over his chest, tucking his hands into his armpits. "I need a shower." He looked over my shoulder at Cash. "Can you take me?"

Cash patted me on the back, then walked around me. He grabbed Cody's arm, and Liam said, "Wait. I'll go with you."

The three of them disappeared, leaving me staring at the spot where Cody had been moments before. My eyes burned. My throat and lungs ached.

Mavros pulled me against his side. I leaned into him even though I shouldn't have. I didn't deserve to be comforted. "What have I done?"

"You scared him." Malcolm stepped next to me. "He needs some time to come to terms with it." He held onto my arm and teleported us directly into my room.

I pulled away from the two of them, gathered my clothes, and went into the bathroom. After shutting the door, I slid down the wall to the floor and pulled my knees up to my chest, listening to the water run in Cody's shower.

Resting my head on my legs, I closed my eyes. Cody stared at me. Sheer terror drained the color from his face, held his body rigid, and made his pulse race.

Even now, the remembered scent of his fear made my stomach growl.

I tugged my hand through my hair. I couldn't let myself think about that.

Since getting my powers, he had looked at me in a lot of different ways: love, admiration, sorrow, sympathy, hurt, betrayal, pride, and astonishment, but not dread. Dread had never been one of them … until today.

I pressed my hands against the floor and pushed up. My legs shook, but I made them move. I walked out into the living room, took the phone out of the cradle without looking at my guards, and went back into my room. I flopped down on my bed and pressed the buttons without thinking about them. It had been my phone number for as long as I could remember.

Mom answered on the second ring. "Dacia." She sounded so excited that I wondered if I should lay any of this on her.

"Hi, Mom." I tried to inject some enthusiasm into my voice, but it still seemed lifeless.

"Aaah, what is it, dear?"

I wanted to go home. I wanted her to wrap her arms around me and tell me it would be okay, but if the Nephilim were tracking me, they would know I had been there. My parents wouldn't be safe. "I think I broke Cody." The words came rushing out of me after that, and somehow, Mom understood everything through my sobs.

"Oh, honey." The compassion in her voice brought fresh tears to my eyes."He loves you. I've seen the way he looks at you."

The fear I'd seen in Cody's eyes erased any other looks he'd ever given me. Every time I pictured him, it was what I saw. "You didn't see how he looked at me today."

"Dacia, your magic is vast and overwhelming." She sounded a little exasperated. "You need to understand that. You need to give him a little time to cope." Her voice softened. "I'm sure it's not quite as bad as you're making it out to be."

I didn't want to argue. I wanted to feel better. I wanted Cody to plop down next to me. I wanted to know we were going to be okay, so I let Mom change the subject. She asked me how college was going and what I had been doing. She asked about Troy and the dragons.

I tried to focus on our conversation and answer her questions, but my mind kept wandering back to Cody's fear. I remembered how scared I had been of the dragons. The horror I'd felt when Aurelia had told me that they would be my guardians. The terror that had gripped me when I realized that Cash would be one of them. I remembered the way I had felt when Malcolm told me he had tasted my blood, kissing his fingers and flicking them away as if he had enjoyed a mouth-watering meal or a tantalizing wine.

Even now, sometimes when their beasts were near the surface, fear rose up inside of me. I tried to hide it, but there were times I failed miserably.

There was a soft knock on my door. I could feel the auras of everyone who was in the apartment, so it could have been any of them standing on the other side. Warmth blossomed in my chest even though I tried to push it down. I didn't want to be disappointed if it wasn't Cody.

"Mom"—I heard the nervousness in my voice, so I was sure she did, too—"I need to go. I love you."

As soon as she said goodbye, I dropped the phone onto the bed and hurried to the door. Wiping my sweaty hands on my leggings, I opened it, and my heart plummeted.

Liam looked down at me, no doubt seeing my disappointment. The sadness in his gray eyes was the same as I had seen in Cash's before he had teleported back here with Cody. "Diana and Olivia think they found where Sebastian and Troy have been hiding." He paused like he expected me to say something, but I had no words. "Unless you want me to stay, I'd like to go with them."

"G—" I cleared my throat, hoping to get the word out "—go."

He smiled one of those sad, I-wish-I-could-make-things-better smiles and patted me on the shoulder. "It'll work out."

I returned it with an I-don't-believe-you-but-thanks-for-trying smile. "Be careful."

When he stepped away, my gaze flicked across the room, taking in the faces of my other guards. "Where's Cody?"

"His room." Malcolm nodded toward Cody's closed door.

I backed into my room and shut the door. Pulling my hand through my hair, I stared at the wall. Would he forgive me? Could he? The paint faded away. Cody sat on his bed. His towel was wrapped around his waist. Water dripped off of his hair, running along his face, down his neck, and onto his bare chest. His elbows rested on his knees, and he stared at the floor but didn't seem to see anything.

I blinked, and the wall was back in place again. Maybe Malcolm and Mom were right. Maybe he just needed time to come to terms with it. Maybe he would forgive me, but what if he didn't? I stared at the wall until everything blurred together, wondering if I should go to Cody and try to make things right or if I should wait for him to come to me. I finally decided that I stunk and should shower before either of those things happened.

When I finished, I walked out into the living room, hoping I would find Cody out there. Even though I wasn't surprised when I didn't see him, my breath hitched, and my heart seemed to shrink. Hot tears pricked my eyes.

Cassandra and Samantha sat in the chairs. Malcolm stood by the open window. Mavros sat on the couch. Cash was nowhere to be seen. The tension in the room was so thick that it was a wonder I could walk through it.

Cassandra smiled at me, then in a sugary sweet voice said, "Can you give us some time alone? Girl time."

Both of my guards turned their stares on me. Part of me wanted them to stay. Cassandra and Samantha must have wanted to talk about Cody and what had happened, and I didn't know if I could do that. Would they end up fearing me, too? I let out a deep breath and shrugged. "You can watch me from your room, right?"

Malcolm walked up to me and held onto my shoulders, making sure I was looking into his eyes. "Don't leave," he growled.

I stared at the dragon. "I won't."

His movements were stiff as he followed Mavros into the hallway.

"So … girl time?" I sat on the couch and looked between my friends. "What's up?"

"Dan and Bryce went to Sedum with Cody and Cash." Samantha shot me one of those smiles like Liam had given me earlier. "We've got the oven warming up and chocolate chip cookies ready to bake."

For the first time since scaring Cody, I felt a little lighter. "Thanks. You guys are the best."

"Do you need to talk?" Cassandra leaned forward. Her ice-blue eyes held both curiosity and sympathy.

I pressed my fingers against my temples and slowly massaged them. The last thing I wanted was to think about what I had done, let alone talk about it, but I didn't want to push them away either.

"If you don't want to, it's no big deal." Samantha got up and put the cookies in the oven.

I waited until she sat back down to say anything. "When I train with Liam, Mavros puts one of the Nephilim's collars on me and takes my magic away. When it came back today, I saw Cody's bruises, and the dragon instincts …" My stomach churned, and my throat felt thick. I stared at the tan carpet. "They're overpowering. He smelled so good."

The couch pressed down on both sides of me, and my friends wrapped their arms around me. The scent of cookies baking filled the apartment.

"I haven't seen him since he left the clearing." My lips trembled, but I couldn't start crying again. If I did, I wasn't sure I would be able to quit. "I don't know if he can forgive me for this."

The timer buzzed. Before Samantha got up, she squeezed my shoulder. "Give him some time."

"Yeah—" my mouth turned upward half-heartedly "—that's what everyone says."

When she came back, she held a plate covered in cookies out to me. I took it from her and breathed in deeply. The aroma lifted my spirits. I picked one up and tore it in half, burning the tips of my fingers. The outside was golden, and the inside was gooey. Perfect. "Thanks." I looked between the two of them. "Don't you want any?"

"No." Cassandra patted her stomach. "I don't have a hunk teaching me self-defense, and I don't like to sweat."

Samantha shook her head. "I did the freshman fifteen last year. I'm watching it this year."

"Okay, then." I shoved half a cookie into my mouth, savoring it. "I'll try not to eat them all at once."

We talked and laughed until I felt Cody's aura. Chewing on my lip, I stared at the door.

Samantha set her hand on my knee. "What is it, Dacia?"

"They're back." I looked over my shoulder at my bedroom. "I'm not going to make him see me unless he wants to. Thanks for cheering me up." I hugged each of them before I got up, walked into my room, and pulled the door shut. Then I sat on the edge of my bed and stared through it into the living room. My leg bounced up and down, making the springs in the bed creak.

Cody walked in with Bryce, Dan, and Cash. His posture was more relaxed. A slight smile still hovered over his lips. He scanned the room, then said something. Since I could only see the side of his face, I couldn't tell what it was.

Cassandra nodded at my door.

Cody looked at it and, taking a play from my book, pulled his hand through his hair. He turned toward everyone else, and I imagined he was saying something to them.

Taking a deep breath, he sauntered toward my room and lifted his hand as if to knock. He held it there unmoving, rolled his neck, and took a half step back.

I wanted to run to the door and pull it open, but I couldn't force him to see me. This needed to be his choice. I was afraid that if I pushed myself on him, I would just end up scaring him away.

His head dropped forward, and my heart fell with the motion, slamming to a stop, waiting to see what he would do next.

Samantha said something, but I was too focused on Cody to make it out.

He lifted his hand and rapped so lightly on the door that I barely saw the movement.

"Come in." I grabbed a book off my dresser so it looked like I was doing something besides watching him and waiting for him to come to me.

He looked from my face to the book and chuckled. "Easier to read when they're not upside down."

Heat crept up my neck, then rushed over my face. "Yeah, I, uh … I wasn't reading. I was watching, hoping." I tossed the book down and tugged my hand through my hair. "It had to be your choice." I stood slowly, giving him the chance to stop me or to back away.

He tilted his head to the side and watched me. There was no fear in his eyes, but concern darkened their blue depths until they appeared to be deeper than the oceans.

"I'm so sorry, Cody." I stood in front of him and bowed my head. I couldn't bear to look at him, to see hatred or fear or disgust on his face. I pressed my eyes closed and remembered the way he had looked at me. Standing motionless. His pulse racing. Terror holding him rigid.

Fingers slid under my chin, tilting it up. They were still cold from being outside, and I shivered in response.

"Look at me." Cody's voice was soft, steady.

I shook my head ever so slightly.

"Please." He brushed his knuckles along my cheek. "Know it was instinct. You wouldn't'ta hurt me."

I stepped back, away from the comfort of his touch. I didn't deserve to be consoled. Not from him. Not after what I'd done.

"Scared me." He backed me up against the wall, putting his hands on either side of me, caging me in. "I got over it." He pressed closer. "Imagine it'll happen again." He stood so close that I could feel the heat of his body. "May take time, but I'll get over it then, too."

I lifted my hands, pressing them against his chest to keep him from stepping any closer. "Why? How?" I clenched his shirt. "How can you keep forgiving me? I don't deserve it. I don't deserve you."

"Played this game." Even with my hands on his chest, he drew closer. His breath caressed my face. "I don't deserve you."

I was having trouble thinking with him surrounding me like he was. "I put your life in danger … almost every day."

"You save me." He kissed the corner of my eye, then the tip of my nose. "Scare me from time to time." He kissed my other eye. "But you'll never scare me away." He nudged my nose with his, tilting my head back. Then he crushed his mouth down on mine.

All my arguments, all my insecurities, they all disappeared. I twisted my fingers into his t-shirt and pulled him closer.

He held the back of my head with one hand and slid the other around my waist. His tongue flicked against mine, and a moan escaped from me.

I slid my hands under his shirt, trailing them over his back.

He lifted me, and I wrapped my legs around his waist, clinging to him, never wanting to let go. Maybe I didn't deserve him, but I had him, and I would never willingly give him up.

Chapter 26

Missing

The alarm went off, and I forced my eyes open. As soon as I did, I blinked back the early morning light seeping in through the window. I reached for my phone, stopping the annoying sound without looking at it.

Cody tightened his hold on me and nuzzled into my neck. "Stay."

I said a silent, "Thank you," to God, not believing that Cody's forgiveness could have happened without some sort of divine intervention.

Malcolm stood, drawing my attention to him. "Liam has not returned. Jax agreed to accompany you to your classes." He focused on Cody. "Russ and Cash will stay with you."

"Jax is still here?" I propped myself up.

Malcolm stared down at the foot of the bed. "After your … capture, Aurelia appealed to the dragon council for help. The others requested that their presence not be divulged unless absolutely necessary."

"What about Mavros?" Cody's voice was rough with sleep.

A black mist undulated next to my bed. The vapor solidified, and Mavros stood where it had been. "I will be with Dacia. She is safest with me."

"Right." Cody rested his chin on my shoulder. "With Jax."

Mavros' smile was all teeth, meant to antagonize Cody. "He's fully aware of what he agreed to."

"I'll be back before you leave." Malcolm disappeared.

I turned back to Mavros, trying to figure out how to ask him to go away before he riled Cody up.

His obsidian eyes softened as he looked into mine. "I won't do anything that will bring you harm. Malcolm's presence should soothe any unease that Jax has about being with a demon."

As soon as he left, I rolled over and rested my head on Cody's bare chest, listening to the rhythmic beating of his heart. His arms wrapped around me, and he traced patterns over my skin. I thought over the conversation. I had been so focused on Jax that I had missed the most important part.

Liam.

My stomach dropped, and at the same time, a gasp exploded out of me.

"What?" Cody's grip tightened.

"Why isn't Liam back?" I sat up, dropping my head into my hands. Troy and Sebastian wouldn't go easy on him if they captured him. They wouldn't be able to forgive him for guarding me, for taking my side, and turning his back on them.

Cody's shoulder lifted. "Stakeout, waiting to ambush them, waiting on reinforcements."

"I don't think so." I pinched the bridge of my nose. "I think something bad happened."

"Don't go looking for trouble."

I swung my legs over the edge of the bed. My back was to him. "I won't, Cody." Guilt tore through me, tightening my chest. I clutched the hair on the sides of my head. I should help Liam. I was supposed to be the hero, but I couldn't let them capture me again. I couldn't let them render me powerless. "I can't let them throw me in another cell." I pictured Micah leering at me. It didn't take a lot of imagination to figure out what prison would be like without Liam to help protect me.

"Not gonna happen." The bed shifted, and he massaged my neck. When he spoke again, the anger had fled from his voice, replaced by desperation. "Come back, okay?"

I stood, and his hand trailed down my back as I walked to my dresser. "I hope to." I pulled out a hunter-green, long-sleeved t-shirt and skinny jeans. "I need to get ready." I kissed him quickly, then went into the bathroom to change.

When I finished and stepped back into my bedroom, Cody was gone. I stood with my hand on the doorknob and sucked in a deep breath, holding it in my lungs, hoping today would be a better day than my intuition was telling me it would be. I strode out into the living room and was surprised to see Jax.

His dark skin was a few shades lighter than Malcolm's and was set off by his blond hair. He turned toward me, and for the first time, I noticed his eyes. I stared into them entranced, wondering how I'd missed them the only other time we'd met. They usually drew me in. With most people, there was a better chance I would remember their eyes than their names.

Jax's were mesmerizing, a pale lilac that was nearly white.

I blinked, hoping I hadn't angered him by staring into his eyes as long as I had. "Thanks for volunteering. I really didn't think I would ever see you again."

"Only when the need is dire." He smiled. Instead of softening his features, it made him look menacing.

Trying not to acknowledge the shiver that crept down my spine, I said, "I am indebted to you."

"No." He shook his head, and rage flashed through his eyes, darkening his irises. "My debt will never be paid."

I turned toward Cody's door and knocked on it. "I'm leaving," I said.

"Hang on." His voice was muffled. I heard footsteps. Then he opened the door, pulling his shirt over his head as he did. It clung to his damp skin on one side, leaving his ribs exposed. I slid my hand over the uncovered skin, and he reached up and cupped my face. "Be careful."

"You, too, Cody." I stepped closer and gave him a quick peck on the lips. He tried to deepen the kiss, but I pulled back. I had no idea how well Jax would handle the scent of my emotions, and I didn't want to test him yet.

Stepping to the side, I waved my arm. "Cody, you remember Jax."

I could see the second he realized why I wouldn't extend our kiss. His eyes widened slowly, and he tipped his chin toward his chest. "Jax. Thanks for watching her."

"We have been observing her for weeks." He didn't sound perturbed or like he wanted to kill me, but those seven words brought about a new kind of fear.

I focused on my breathing, trying to keep it steady. Everything else faded into the background.

A hand clamped down on my shoulder, and I jumped.

"Dacia"—Cody's eyebrows pulled together—"what's wrong?"

I couldn't say anything in front of Jax, so I forced out a humorless laugh and asked, "What isn't?" I turned away from him. "Malcolm said he'd be back before I left, but I need to go."

Mavros strolled across the room. With his hands tucked into his pockets, he exuded confidence. He didn't spare a look at Jax as he passed by him. Once he stood next to me, he draped his arm over my shoulder. "I won't let anything happen to you."

Jax slid his hand under my elbow, and I wondered if he would try to pull me away from Mavros. "Malcolm will be here any—"

"Now." Malcolm stood in front of the door. Blood still coated his teeth.

Another chill shuddered down my spine.

Jax sucked in a deep breath. "Does she always smell this delectable?"

"Almost." Malcolm stood in front of him. "You can take the rear. It's your choice whether you are seen or not."

On the long walk to Stellaria Hall, Mavros never moved his arm from my shoulders. I suspected it had more to do with Jax than the Nephilim. No matter what his motives, it was comforting.

I concentrated on projecting my thoughts to Malcolm and him alone. *Jax said he's been watching me for weeks. Does he know?* The urge to glance over my shoulder was nearly irresistible. I didn't even know if I would see Jax there or if he had turned invisible. *Has he seen me as a ... a dragon?*

No. Malcolm's growl rumbled through my head. *Don't tell him.*

I swallowed hard, knowing Mavros and Jax would wonder what had me so on edge. *What will he do?*

We can't afford to find out right now. He slipped his hand into mine and squeezed my fingers gently. *Until Liam returns, we can't risk losing more guards.*

I chewed on my lip. "Are Ariana and Val still watching Mom and Dad?" My voice came out tiny, but I knew they would hear me.

He nodded. "They will until this mess is cleaned up."

I figured that would be the answer, but I blew out a relieved breath anyway. "Is Liam okay?" This time my voice shook.

Mavros pulled me closer, and the heat from his body seeped into me.

I breathed in his warm summer nights scent, allowing him to comfort me. If Troy could get Liam with all of his training and expertise, how long would it be until he came for me? How could I protect myself with only a tiny fragment of Liam's knowledge?

Mavros and Malcolm looked over the top of my head at each other. Finally, Mavros said, "We have no way to contact him."

I stepped over an icy patch on the sidewalk. "Do you know where he went at least?"

"No," Malcolm answered. "He knows what he's doing, Dacia. He'll be fine."

I wanted to believe him. I wanted him to be right, but doubt had wormed its way into me, and I couldn't shake it.

Malcolm held the door to Stellaria Hall open. While he did, his senses were on high alert, searching for anything that might harm me. His eyes darted from side to side, dilating and contracting as he searched for dangers.

As soon as I was inside, he took his place next to me. Holding onto my elbow, he led me through the hallway and up the stairs.

I glanced over my shoulder. I knew Jax was behind me, but he had chosen to remain unseen. It amazed me that in a building filled with people, nobody walked into him. It was almost as if people's self-preservation instincts kept them from stepping too close.

Malcolm stopped in the doorway for just a second before heading to empty seats in the back of the room. He seemed to be more on edge than normal. I wondered if it was because of something I had dreamt, because of what I'd asked, or because of Liam not returning.

I took my coat off and threw it over the back of my seat. Then I sat down. My chair shifted, and I jerked around, looking over my shoulder, wondering who was pressing on it. When no one was there, I tried to calm my breathing. *Jax? Is that you behind me?*

His voice in my head was like the distant, rolling thunder. *Yes, it is.* As if to emphasize his words, his breath ruffled my hair.

I pulled my notebook and pen out of my bag, determined to pay attention in today's class. Staring at the teacher, I tried to come up with her name. She sat on the edge of her desk, seemingly examining her fingernails, but I noticed that her eyes tracked the students as they entered, taking their measure. Her tawny complexion made her look like she had a deep, summer tan, the kind that would never touch my pale skin.

My eyes pinched together as I studied her. Her name had to be buried somewhere in my memory, but I couldn't come up with it. Tuesday in class, I had been distracted, but I didn't realize I had been that out of it. I pulled my itinerary out and said her name aloud a few times, hoping to commit it to memory. "Doctor Yarrow, Doctor Yarrow, Doc—"

Troy stood in the doorway. The tattoo on his face seemed to draw all of the light into it. He tucked his hands into his pockets with his thumbs hooked over the lips of them and stared at me.

I couldn't hold his gaze.

My stomach rolled, and I leaned over my desk, contemplating throwing up.

Mavros' fingers trailed over my spine, comforting, warm, protective. "He will not take you, Dacia."

His words were meant to soothe me, but I knew they were a lie. Troy wouldn't be standing here if he thought Diana and

Olivia were still watching for him. He would not give up until he had me in his clutches.

You need to be strong. Malcolm's voice held barely suppressed rage. *Give him a reason to fear you instead of the other way around.*

I peeked up at him. He had to know how Troy's presence affected me. There was no way he didn't smell my terror.

Pretend. The word was ground out. His hand replaced Mavros' on my back. Soothing energy flowed into me, and I sat up. My focus was immediately drawn to the door. Troy wasn't there.

I jerked my head toward Malcolm, hoping he could tell me where Troy had gone. I followed his gaze and found Troy. He edged his way through the students, angling for the empty chair in front of me. He stared at me, and I didn't turn away from him. He smiled, but it didn't touch the anger in his brown eyes.

He reached for the chair, pulling it out slowly, making it scrape against the black-flecked tile floor. "Liam sends his regards." He tilted his head and tried for an innocent look. "Well, at least he would if he could speak."

My heart battered my rib cage, fighting to be released. The sound reverberated through my skull. There was no way Troy didn't hear it, no way he thought I was unafraid. "What did you do to him?" My voice trembled. *So much for looking strong.*

"Not enough." His eyes narrowed, and he clutched the chair so hard I thought it would break. "He's a traitor." His anger ran deeper than it had when I was his prisoner. I thought about when I'd read Liam's aura, how Troy had been in his memories, and realized that Troy had cared for Liam, that Troy probably felt betrayed, and he blamed that betrayal on me now, too. "He deserves more than a broken jaw."

Mavros hooked his foot around my chair and pulled it back. He leaned toward me, putting himself between Troy and me. "Some would argue that you're the traitor. Your superiors told you to back off. You went rogue."

Troy's lips pulled back as he focused on Mavros. His words came out in a harsh whisper that I hoped nobody else heard. "Only because my superiors have been deceived by a demon. Once you have been returned to the Abyss, they will forgive me."

"We'll see," I said.

He shook his head slowly, letting his disgust show on his face. "We can pick your guards off one by one, or you can make it easy on yourself. Come with us. Let us end this standoff."

A fierce growl filled the classroom. Everyone stopped what they were doing. The silence was like a living thing. Almost as one, students gathered the courage to look over their shoulders. I joined them, not wanting to be singled out but knowing I wouldn't see anyone behind me.

"What the hell was that?" Sound came back to the classroom as students tried to decide if they should run for their lives or if they were hearing things.

"Looks like you've got someone guarding your back." Troy stared at the wall above my head. "No matter. You'll be ours in the end."

He sat down, turned his chair sideways, and glared at me throughout the entire class. I didn't hear a word of Dr. Yarrow's lecture. It was drowned out by the drumming of my heart. I stared into Troy's eyes and imagined the perverse pleasure he had derived from torturing Liam.

Rage burned inside of me. My senses sharpened. The room smelled like a locker room after the big game and made me scrunch my nose up in disgust. Everything was brighter, but unlike in the sunlight, things became more detailed.

Troy's eyes widened, and the intoxicating aroma of fear made my mouth water.

A hand clamped down on my shoulder, and serenity crashed over me, washing away my anger. My heightened senses diminished. I leaned back in my seat and closed my eyes. *Too close,* I thought. *I've got to get ahold of myself.*

Troy's chair creaked. He got up and sauntered through the door. The teacher's gaze followed him as he walked out, but she didn't seem to have any other reaction.

When class ended, I stayed in my chair. The idea of walking in a group of people was too much. Students bumping into each other and stepping on each other's feet would give me a sense of claustrophobia. I wouldn't be able to keep an eye out for the Nephilim. I couldn't allow myself to be that confined. I couldn't guarantee I could keep the tenuous grip that I held on my powers.

Somehow, I needed to figure out how to tamp the dragon down. It couldn't surface every time I was agitated.

As soon as everyone but us was gone, Jax showed himself. His lilac eyes were all dragon. "What the hell was that?"

"Calm down, Jax." Malcolm's voice was steady. His posture was rigid. He stared into Jax's eyes until Jax lowered his head. "I will explain everything at the training grounds."

He placed his hand under my elbow, guiding me to my feet. "We're teleporting to my living room." He nodded at Mavros. "Can you make it look like we're leaving here … just in case someone is watching?"

Mavros nodded at him but kept his attention focused on Jax.

I picked up my things, and Malcolm teleported us. As soon as we solidified in his apartment, I heard his voice in my head. *You're going to have to show him.* He opened the door and ushered me across the hall. "We'll wait here for Cash. If you need something to eat, get it now."

The thought of eating made my already upset stomach churn. How many dragons would accept me? Hadn't I already exceeded the limits? My luck wouldn't last forever. Would it? I dragged my hand through my hair and shook my head. "I'm not hungry."

"I've heard fear will do that to humans." Jax leaned in closer and took a big whiff of me. His eyes rolled back like it was pure bliss.

I couldn't stop the shiver that shook my body.

His answering laugh made me want to run and hide. Cash's determination and concern filled me, holding me in place. When the door opened, his amethyst gaze met mine, and he offered me a small, apologetic smile.

Cody followed Cash into the room and swung the door back. Russ pushed against it, forcing it open again. Cody shot him a sheepish grin. "Sorry."

"No worries." Russ shut the door. "What's the plan? Am I with Cody?"

Malcolm nodded. "Fill him in. Keep him safe."

"Aye. Aye." Russ snapped his heels together and saluted.

The action was so human that it caught me off guard. I couldn't help but chuckle.

Jax narrowed his eyes at me. "If this is what I think it is, there is nothing to laugh about." He turned toward Malcolm. "We leave now. Show me where."

Malcolm stared at Jax for a minute, then Jax disappeared.

Cody looked from the place Jax had just vacated to me. "What's going on?"

"Liam, Troy, my dragon …" I let my voice trail off. I needed to be strong. I needed to be prepared for a battle, even though I hoped it wouldn't come to that. Pulling my hand through my hair, I focused on my breathing. Once it was under control, I walked to Cody, grabbed the opening of his coat, and pulled him toward me. My lips crashed against his hard enough that I was afraid I might have hurt him, but he returned the kiss with the same urgency.

Malcolm cleared his throat. When I didn't pull away, he said, "Jax is waiting." His voice was soft and soothing. It reminded me of somebody who was trying to coax a scared kitten out from under the bed. "We don't want his dragon riled up any more than it already is."

Cody pulled away. Lifting my chin so that my eyes met his, he said, "Whatever this is, come back to me." Then he looked over the top of my head at my guardians. "Bring her back … please."

Chapter 27

Malcolm held my hand. His grip was too tight, but I didn't say anything. The sting in my fingers helped keep me focused. He teleported us to a valley that I had never seen before. A frozen waterfall hung from the rocky side of a mountain. The ice was clear, white, and pale green. It shimmered in the late morning sun, reminding me of a crystal chandelier.

I looked down at the ground and realized we were standing on the river. "Is this the best place to do this?" I imagined the ice shattering into giant sheets that bounced and churned with the current.

"We're here." He nodded toward the tree-lined shore. "They're here. We must make the best of it." *I will not let them harm you.*

"They?" I looked to where he was indicating. The four hidden guards stood together. Jax, Mara, Mortimer, and Seth. They were as different from each other as they could be, but their expressions were identical. Rage and disgust.

Mavros stepped forward, shaking his head. "Dragons." He made it sound like they were the lowest form of evolution. "Shall we get on with this?" He led the way, positioning himself directly in front of me.

The top layer of snow had been crusted by the sun. My footsteps crunched over it. I kept expecting my leg to sink through, but it didn't.

Forcing my fear down, I let anger roll over me, covering the more appetizing smell. Malcolm never let go of my hand, keeping pace with me whether I slowed down or sped up. Cash stayed one step behind me, protecting my back.

Mara pointed her finger accusingly. "How could you?" She spat the words out. Murder darkened her green eyes.

"I felt the same." Malcolm kept his voice steady. Of the dragons who watched over me, it was obvious that he was the alpha, but even he had to tread carefully here.

Seth's eyes flicked to mine. The rich cobalt color of them reminded me of his dragon's scales. "Then why?" He looked from Malcolm to Cash. "Why is she still alive?"

Seth was the soft-spoken dragon who had seen Mavros' grief when I'd killed myself to escape him. Icy fingers trailed down my spine at hearing that question come from him. My legs trembled, and I wasn't sure if I could take another step.

"I saw her transform." Malcolm squeezed my fingers. *Stay strong, Dacia.* "It is her true alternate form. Just as this is mine and those are yours."

"It can't be," Mara said. "She has deceived you." She stepped forward.

Malcolm growled, long and low. A warning.

She dropped her eyes, but the tension in her body was clear. If I didn't transform soon, this wouldn't end well. Like Russ and Cash had been, their dragons were already too riled up. The difference was Russ and Cash had spent time with me. They knew me. They didn't want to hurt me. These dragons had only watched me from afar. They had promised to protect me, but they hadn't learned to care about me.

I focused on my magic. The pearlescent serpent slithered toward me. It was massive. Its black and gold-flecked copper eyes stared into mine.

I stretched my hand out. "I need to turn into a dragon just like I did before. I can't think about it. I can't become anything else. Can you help make sure that happens? Don't allow me to transform into anything else. Especially not an angel."

They needn't scare you. The snake nudged its head against my palm. *We could end them all.*

"Yes … but I won't." I sighed. "I need as many allies as I can get. I need to free Liam and probably Diana and Olivia. I need to keep my friends and family safe."

You don't need any of those things. Its pink tongue flicked out. *You only need me.*

I petted the serpent's head. "Will you help me?"

Of course.

Opening my eyes, I blinked back the light. Then I stepped forward. "I will open my mind to you so that you can see how my transformation comes about without any conscious thought of what form I will take."

They didn't respond, just stared at me through their dragons' eyes.

Please. I sent up a silent prayer. Then, I opened my mind to everyone and thought about transformation. Like Malcolm had told me to do, I imagined a caterpillar creating a cocoon, then sleeping while it somehow transformed into a magnificent butterfly.

My body shifted, pulling, stretching, and breaking. Muscles tore. Bones broke. Wings shot from my shoulder blades, heavier than angel wings. I fell onto four legs.

The dragons stared at me. Their eyes were wide. Surprise mixed with their rage. Mortimer ran his hand over his shaved head. He was almost a foot shorter than Mara, but he was solid muscle. "It can't be." He looked at Malcolm like he was hoping for an explanation, but there wasn't one.

This was what I was meant to be when Dacia Wolf wasn't enough. This was the other version of me, the scarier version.

"That doesn't mean anything," Jax yelled. A purple mist swirled around him. When it cleared an amethyst dragon with bat-like wings and twisted horns stood where he had been. He darted toward me.

My fear was gone. Dragon instincts took over, and I prowled toward him. Lowering my head, I stared into his lilac eyes.

He opened his mouth. Flames burned inside his jaws.

I stopped and watched him, hoping the others would stay back. Hoping this could just be between Jax and me.

We circled each other. I felt exposed when my back was to the others, but I knew Malcolm, Cash, and Mavros would protect me if need be.

A blast of fire exploded out of Jax, hurling toward me.

I could have flown over it. I could have used my magic to stop it, but neither of those things would have proven anything to the dragons.

An inferno ignited inside of me, heating my belly. Blue flames blasted out of my maw. They collided with his purple ones, knocking them back.

His wrath subsided like Russ' had. "How?" He looked from me to Malcolm and Cash and then to the other dragons. "It shouldn't be possible."

"It isn't." Mara stepped forward. "It's a trick." Her focus darted around the valley, searching for someone or something to blame. Her gaze landed on Mavros, and her eyes hardened. "The demon's doing."

Mavros smiled sadly and shook his head. "It is not."

Mara sprinted forward, transforming into the massive emerald dragon that had haunted my nightmares.

I could taste her fury. Charcoal and ash.

She whipped her tail at me. The move was unexpected, but in this form, my reactions were quicker. I jumped over it, feeling the air shift below me. Spreading my wings out, I hovered above her, waiting for her next move.

She lowered her body and sprang up. Flapping her wings, she launched into the sky like a rocket, exploding past me.

Spinning around, I searched for her shadow behind the fluffy, white clouds. As I turned back, she plunged toward me. Talons and teeth ripped into my scales.

I roared my frustration, letting her believe she had hurt me worse than she had. Flapping my wings like it was a struggle to keep my body in the air, I waited for her to come closer, to strike at me again.

It didn't take long. Victory flashed through her eyes as she lunged for my throat. I spun to the side and slashed my claws through the thin membrane of her wing.

She screamed and tumbled through the air, spinning out of control. I hovered above her and drew on my magic. It was harder in this form, but I slowed her fall, gently laying her on the ground at Malcolm's feet.

"Anyone else?" I growled.

When neither Seth nor Mortimer challenged me, I landed next to Mara. "I don't want to hurt you, but if I have to, I will." I loved the rich timbre of my dragon's voice and how confident it made me feel. "I didn't choose this form. Knowing how dragons feel about it, I wouldn't have." I willed her to hear the sincerity in my voice.

She started to stand, but Malcolm's growl stopped her. Instead, she transformed back into her human avatar. She looked up at me in confusion. "Why did you stop my fall?"

"You've watched over me. Helped keep me safe." I changed back into myself. Without my senses threatening to overpower me, I could think better. "I understand how hard it is to fight the instincts." I tugged my hand through my hair and a bitter chuckle escaped me. "Yesterday, I wanted to eat my boyfriend."

This time when she started to stand, Malcolm allowed it. As soon as she was on her feet, he grabbed her arm and held her back from me. "I will keep your secret." She bowed her head. "I will wish you well, but I will not guard you any longer."

"Why?" My heart sank, leaving a dull ache behind it.

"In your moments of weakness, I would not be able to guarantee your safety." Her shoulders slumped forward. "I cannot guarantee that my dragon wouldn't take advantage of the situation."

I looked around the valley at the others, wondering if they would feel the same way, hoping I could trust them when I needed their help.

"You gave me my freedom—" she smiled at me "—and for that, I am eternally grateful." She backed away from me, and Malcolm let her go.

Then he wrapped his arm around me and pulled me against his side. "What about you?" He studied each of their faces. "She freed us. She belongs to us."

Mavros' eyes flashed from obsidian to flaming orbs and back to black. Even in my human form, I felt his annoyance, but he kept his mouth shut. He'd made it clear that he didn't think I belonged to anyone. There was no sense in fighting about it now, though.

Seth stepped forward, and Malcolm clutched me tighter. Seeing his reaction, Seth stopped and lifted his hands. His soft voice seemed to carry over to us on the breeze. "My dragon didn't take offense to hers once I saw her transform." He met my eyes then. His pupils elongated, and the blue of his irises spread out, covering his scleras. "I vow on my honor to protect you with my life if necessary."

"I apologize for my ire." Jax bowed his head. "I should not have involved the others." He looked up at me through his eyelashes. "My stupidity has cost you a guard and put your life in danger." He went down on one knee. "Please accept my sincere apology."

I nodded. "Of course."

Malcolm turned me so we were facing Mortimer. "I'll keep her safe. I told the council I would. I told you I would." He rolled his head like he was trying to crack his neck. "Now, if you don't mind, I need to hunt."

"Thank you." I looked at each of them, holding their gazes, making sure they knew I meant it. "For watching me, for keeping me safe. Hopefully, you'll be able to get back to your lives soon."

Mortimer nodded and disappeared. Seth said, "We have no lives to return to. Draconian stole them from us."

"We will protect you as long as you need us." Jax stood but kept his head bowed.

I sat in class, trying to listen to Professor Shrike, but all I could focus on was my growling stomach. I should have eaten when Malcolm had told me to, but just the thought of food had made my gut churn.

Jax stood behind me still opting to remain unseen. Seth grabbed a stool from the front of the room and sat in front of me. His spiky hair kept drawing my attention. The blue strands shimmered in the light, reminding me of his dragon's scales. It transformed from a turquoise to a rich cobalt every time he shifted.

I had been surprised when he returned to my apartment with us. He'd knelt down in front of me. "I have remained hidden in the shadows for far too long. It is time for me to step into the light."

"If he is seen with you—" Jax smiled, showing a mouth filled with sharp teeth "—Troy may not realize I am still guarding you."

I shivered, and Mavros looked at me, lifting his eyebrows in a silent question. I shook my head. Even if we weren't sitting in class, I didn't know if I would tell him how just the thought of Troy sent terror racing through me.

While I was still focused on Mavros, Professor Shrike called my name. I turned and stared at him, trying to figure out what he had asked. "I'm sorry." Heat crept over my cheeks. "Could you repeat the question?"

"When working on photos, what color mode should you use?" He enunciated each word carefully, making it clear he didn't think I could answer him.

"RGB."

He rubbed his chin, clearly surprised. "Correct."

When he turned away from me, I glanced at the clock. Only fifteen minutes had gone by. I slumped back in my chair. The room suddenly seemed too warm, and the air felt stuffy.

Sweat beaded on my forehead. I tapped my foot, hoping the movement would hide my trembling. My heart pounded against my chest, and the room spun.

From across the aisle, Malcolm turned to me. His posture made it obvious that he was ready to defend me at all costs. *What is it?*

I don't know. I shook my head. *Claustrophobia?*

He pressed his lips into a thin line and lifted one of his eyebrows.

Seriously.

As soon as class was over, I grabbed my stuff and rushed for the door. The thought of breathing in cool, fresh air hurried my steps. I turned to the side and slipped between other students. The crowded hallway constricted my breaths, making my lungs burn.

Dacia. Malcolm roared in my head.

But I couldn't stop. The doors were only a few feet in front of me. I sped toward them, shoving them open. Then I stepped to the side, gulping down deep breaths.

A hand clamped down on my shoulder too hard. Fingers dug into my skin even through my coat.

Troy! The name burst through my thoughts, sending fear crackling through my body.

There were too many people around me. He couldn't take me, and I couldn't throw him off. Not here.

"What were you thinking, Dacia?" Mavros' voice was filled with venom.

I sank back against him. My fear washed away, and the adrenaline that was left behind made me shake violently. Tears streamed down my face, and sobs racked my body.

Mavros turned me around and held me, letting me cry into his silk-clad chest. When I finished sobbing and pulled away, we were surrounded by dragons.

"What happened?" Malcolm fought to keep his beast at bay.

I remembered the panic and the feeling that the air was being pulled from my lungs and that the room was shrinking. "I don't know. I needed to get out of there. I couldn't think. All I could do was run."

My guardians turned toward each other. Their expressions told me that they had some idea of what had happened.

"What?" I asked.

Malcolm shook his head. "This isn't the place. We'll talk in your apartment."

Mavros didn't let go of me on the walk back. When I tried to pull away, he clutched me tighter and shook his head. Malcolm led the way, not moving at all when we came across others on the sidewalk. Seth trudged through the snow next to me, and judging by the wide path people took around Mavros, Jax must have been next to him. Cash brought up the rear. He was close enough to me that I could feel his breath ruffle my hair.

My mind raced with possibilities. Had the Nephilim come up with a way to draw me out like Mavros had? Were they doing something to me to make my anxiety fly off the charts? Was it something my magic was doing? Was it because of Troy's blood in me?

Each new question made my heart race faster. The pounding of it blocked out all other sounds. My vision thrummed with each beat.

Malcolm held the door open to the apartment and ushered us all in. Then he hurried us to the stairway. I stumbled on nearly every step I tried to ascend. My feet didn't want to lift up high enough. Panic stole my breath and along with it my strength.

Cash pulled my backpack off, and Mavros lifted me into his arms. His mouth moved, but the words were lost somewhere in the rhythm of my heartbeat.

What could be so bad that Malcolm hadn't even thought it to me?

The apartment wasn't empty. Cody, Dan, and Bryce all sat on the couch with video game controllers in their hands. At the kitchen table, books were spread out in front of Samantha, and Cassandra had her laptop in front of her. Russ watched us from the armchair.

They all stopped what they were doing and stared at us. Cody jumped to his feet and ran over to me. I focused on him, hoping to clear the thrumming from my ears so I could let him know that I was okay.

He held my hand, and Mavros' words broke through all the noise. "… think she's having a panic attack."

"Why?" Cody's voice was steady, but fear shadowed his features.

Malcolm pointed at a chair. "Sit." Then he turned to Mavros. "Put her down."

Mavros stood me on my feet. I clung to his arm until I knew for sure my legs were steady. Then I sat on the floor in front of Cody, leaning back against him.

Malcolm looked at me, and the sorrow I saw in his eyes filled me with fear. "Last night, Dacia finally had the dream I've been waiting for."

"Why didn't you tell me?" I tugged my hand through my hair, catching my fingers in tangled strands.

He gave me that look that adults give to children when they ask questions without thinking them through first.

"So … what is it?" Samantha pushed her chair back and came into the living room, sitting down next to Dan. Cassandra quickly followed suit.

"A phouka."

As soon as Malcolm said it, images of a black horse with luminescent yellow eyes flashed through my memory, immediately followed by ones of a massive black dog, then a guy with shaggy, black hair. "Can they …" I let my question trail off. I didn't need to know.

"Dacia"—Cash stepped closer to me—"finish."

I chewed on my lip. I didn't want to know how badly I had messed things up before I knew better. "Can they see what happens in my dreams?" I waved toward Mavros. "Like he can?"

Malcolm nodded. "What did you tell him?"

"Nothing."

Seth stared at me, seeing right through my answer. "What does he know?"

"Everything."

Chapter 28

$\mathcal{B}$ryce raised his eyebrow and tipped his head to the side. "Everything? How could it know everything?"

"In my dreams—" I folded my legs up and, bracing my elbows on my knees, clutched the hair above my ears "—it looked through my memories. All of them." I chewed my bottom lip and laced my fingers together to keep from pulling my hair out. "It was a horse then. Black with bright yellow eyes. I couldn't look away. I didn't even want to."

Cassandra tugged on the sleeve of her sweater. It was a slightly darker blue than her eyes and form-fitting. Her jeans looked like she had painted them on this morning. She rarely ever wore sweats or t-shirts and always had her make-up done up like she was ready to walk the runway. She looked around the room, then asked in a voice softer than normal, "What exactly are we talking about?" She flipped her long, black hair over her shoulder. "What's a phouka?"

"It's some kind of faerie, isn't it?" I looked up at Malcolm for confirmation.

He nodded. "He is. Some bring good fortune."

"Not this one." Cody put his hands on my shoulders, gently rubbing them.

"No." Malcolm's pupils turned into thin slits. "Not this one. This one likes to cause trouble. He enjoys mischief and mayhem."

Samantha pulled Dan's arms tighter around her. "You know him, then?"

"I know *of* him." He leaned against the door and folded his arms over his chest. "Kieran Tormey."

Cash dragged the kitchen chairs into the living room. When he finished, he straddled one, folding his arms over the back of it. "Not his real name of course. If you could get that, you could control him." He waved at the other chairs. Seth and Mavros each took one, but Malcolm stayed where he was.

"So, he's like Mavros?" Samantha asked.

"No." Mavros' voice was low. Anger seared the word. "He is free to terrorize people. He does not need to be bound to stay here. He just needs an opening in the veil."

"He's probably the reason for your claustrophobia." Malcolm rolled his neck, and I could hear it crack from where I was. "He knows I intercepted your dream last night, and I imagine he thinks it would be fun for Troy to capture you."

My breath caught, and my knuckles whitened.

Cody slid onto the floor and wrapped his arm around me. I wanted to lay my head on his shoulder and allow him to comfort me, but there was too much tension in my body. I just sat there as rigid as a statue.

"There's a chance"—Seth's voice normally had a calming effect, but this time, I couldn't feel it—"that he wants to take you for his own. To play a game with the Nephilim."

Black mist swirled around Mavros. His edges looked hazy. "This changes nothing, Dacia. We will keep you safe."

"How?" I wanted to believe him, but I had escaped all five of them earlier without even consciously trying.

Jax's voice came from the other armchair. "I will do better. Unseen, I can push my way through people or teleport next to you."

"Won't that give you away?" Dan asked.

Jax showed himself. "The human mind has a way of covering up these—" he waved his hand through the air "—indiscretions. None of you realized I was here, and yet, none of you tried to sit in this chair. When I walk with Dacia to class, students veer out of my way as if they can see me. Maybe it's survival instincts. Maybe it's a sixth sense. Who knows?"

"Okay." I stood up, needing movement to help me think. "My life is in even more danger." I raked my fingers through my hair while I paced from armchair to armchair. "That's really nothing new, but what do we do about Liam? And, if Troy's got him what about Diana and Olivia?"

Malcolm reached out and grabbed my arm on my next pass by him. "Stop." He stared down at me. "If Troy wants to rejoin the Nephilim, he can't—" he pursed his lips while he thought about what to say next "—permanently damage them."

"Maybe not on the outside." I folded my arms around my stomach. "But I don't know if I'll ever be the same." My voice faded a little with each word.

He pulled me against him. His hand ran down my spine. "Do you want to train?"

"You're giving me a choice?" I took a step back and looked up at his face.

He squeezed my shoulder. "It's been a rough day. I thought you might want a break."

Turning toward my friends, I said, "Anyone up for basketball?"

Kieran Tormey stands in front of me in the center of a ring of trees. His grin is lopsided and all fox. "You know who I am." He shoves his hair out of his eyes, but it flops right back down.

"Yes." The air thrums against my skin as if it's electrified. "Kieran Tormey."

His smile widens, and he dips his head toward his shoulder. "Yes … but no. Not really." He circles me. His lithe body suddenly seems inhuman. The movements are wrong, too smooth. It's almost as if he's liquid.

I turn with him, not wanting him out of my line of sight for even a second. "What do you want from me?"

He leaps and lands with his toes touching mine. "Oh, we're going to have so much fun together, you and I." He grabs my hand, kissing the back of it like a gentleman from days gone by. Then he turns it over and presses an acorn into my palm before disappearing.

A growl tears through the clearing. I turn, trying to figure out where the sound came from and what kind of animal made it.

"Open your hand, Dacia."

I popped up in bed and smacked my forehead against Malcolm's. He jerked his hand off mine and pressed his palm to his scale-lined face.

"Ow." Rubbing my forehead, I swung my legs over the edge of the bed. "What was that about?"

"Open. Your. Hand."

I spread my fingers out. A perfect acorn sat on my palm. I pinched my eyes shut, hoping that when I opened them again it would be gone. I didn't need a phouka trying to have fun with me. I needed to find Liam. I needed to figure out how to get Troy to leave me alone. I didn't need whatever this acorn meant.

I peeled my eyelids back slowly, peeking through them. The acorn was still there, and without all my attention focused on it, somehow it was different … other. A faint green light radiated out from it, spilling over my hand. Tiny sparkles like pixie dust floated into the air from the cap. "Take it, Malcolm. Get it out of here."

He reached for it, but his hand passed right through it like it was an illusion.

My stomach clenched. Fear spread through my body. I poked at it, but the acorn was as insubstantial as the eidolon had been.

"What is it?" Cody's breath blew along the side of my face.

I had been so focused on the acorn that I didn't even realize he'd woken up. "A gift from the phouka."

"Not a gift." Malcolm's fangs bit into his lip. His voice was more dragon than man. "A curse."

I stood up. My legs were unsteady, but I tried not to let my fear show. I walked into the kitchen and grabbed a glass out of the cabinet. I filled it from the sink. My hand trembled as I lifted it to my lips, and water spilled down my pajamas.

I set the glass on the counter and reached for the towel to mop up the mess I'd made. The acorn glowed in the dimly lit kitchen. I tightened my fingers into a fist and wished it away, but beams of light penetrated through the cracks between my fingers.

I shoved my hand into my pocket and stomped back into my bedroom. Cody lifted the covers, and I slid under them, burying my hand beneath my pillow.

Malcolm sat at the end of the bed watching us. "Do you want me to try to keep your dreams away?"

"I thought you were." I pressed my body against Cody's, hoping contact with him would take away some of my fear.

Malcolm's eyes reflected the light like a cat's. "So did I."

"Please." I tried to smile at him, but it only brought my tears closer to the surface.

Cody wrapped one arm around me and brushed my hair back with the other. Eventually, his eyes drooped, and sleep overcame him, but even with Malcolm's help, I tossed and turned for the rest of the night.

Every time I closed my eyes, I saw Kieran whispering in Troy's ear. I watched my guards get picked off one at a time until there was only me and the Nephilim. The giant, black dog chased me through the forest, nipping at my heels, driving me into the Nephilim's trap.

When I couldn't handle it anymore, I slid out of Cody's embrace, grabbed a book, and went to the living room. I curled up on one end of the couch, and Malcolm watched me from an armchair.

I opened the book, and the glow from the acorn shone up at me. Slamming the book shut, I got up and went to my coat hanging by the door. I rummaged through my pockets and pulled out a glove, slipping it on as I walked back to the couch.

Malcolm nodded at me. "You might be able to cover it up with magic."

"Maybe." I opened the book again. "But that will take energy, and I should probably reserve as much of that as I can."

I forced myself to concentrate on the words. My mind kept wandering to Kieran, but every time it did, I read out loud until thoughts of him were shoved into the background. The chapters flew by until I could no longer make out the blurred words. I set the book on the floor, and Malcolm sat down next to me, pulling my head onto his shoulder.

Sleep finally found me, and this time, I was too exhausted to dream.

Chapter 29

Playing Games

"What's with the glove?" Dan pointed his spoon at me before dipping it into his cereal.

I shrugged. "New fashion trend." It came out sounding more like a question than the witty answer I was trying for.

"What happened?" Samantha set her hand on top of mine.

I leaned back, staring down at my toast. The thought of eating something as simple as that made my stomach roil. "Kieran visited my dream last night." I really didn't want to see if the acorn was still emblazed on my palm, but I slowly peeled the glove off, one finger at a time. My heart seemed to come to a stop, and I held my breath. I pinched my eyes shut before jerking it off of my hand.

Samantha's gasp restarted my heart, and the allegro beat made up for lost time. I pressed my other hand to my chest, hoping to calm the sprint.

"What is it?" Dan sounded like his mouth was still full of food.

I opened my eyes and stared down at my palm. Tiny tendrils protruded from the bottom of the acorn. As I watched they extended toward my fingertips.

Roots.

It was growing roots.

I yanked the glove back on while my friends looked at me with a mixture of confusion, curiosity, and sympathy. Staring at my toast, I said, "Malcolm says it's a curse." Tears pooled in my eyes, and my words were broken. "That's all I know."

"You were cursed, and he's not here?" Samantha's eyebrows jumped up, hiding beneath her hair.

Cody's door shut, and soft footsteps padded across the carpet. "Hunting." He put his hands on my shoulders and gently kneaded my muscles. "What's up?"

"The acorn sprouted." I slumped forward.

"What's that mean?"

I pushed the napkin with my toast on it away and laid my head on the table. "That I'm screwed."

"It means the game has begun."

I jumped at the sound of Jax's voice. He chuckled, and this time I was able to pinpoint where it came from. "Morning, Jax."

"Morning." He appeared in the chair. An ornery smirk lifted his lips. "You didn't think we'd leave you alone. Did you?"

I waved my hand toward the door. "I figured we were being watched from the other room."

"With Kieran and the Nephilim—" he shook his head like that was the dumbest thing he'd ever heard "—assume one of us is always with you."

Cody stared into the fridge as if breakfast would magically appear. "Where're the others?"

"With Malcolm, discussing the phouka."

Samantha looked at me out of the corner of her eyes, then focused on Jax. "How bad is it?"

"Don't sugarcoat it." I folded my arms over my chest. "Just say it … whatever it is."

The smile he shot me was filled with approval and lit up his pale eyes. "All right." He leaned toward me. "In my many years, I have never once heard of someone besting Kieran. He plays to win."

The butterflies that had been flitting around inside of me seemed to die all at once. They plummeted, dragging my stomach down with them. Even so, I held Jax's gaze.

"I would like to see you best him. I'd like for you to be the first." Jax leaned back in his chair. He tilted his head as if he was listening to something. Then he winked at me before turning invisible again.

Cody sat next to me and poured cereal into a bowl. "Gotta eat, Dacia."

"Maybe later." I lifted my legs onto my chair and rested my head on my knees. There was no way I would be able to keep anything down. After a few minutes, I got up, threw my toast in the trash, and went to brush my teeth.

When I came back out Malcolm, Mavros, and Seth were waiting to walk me to class. Cash smiled at me, but it didn't reach his eyes. I knew he wanted to be with me to keep me safe, but I appreciated him guarding Cody in Liam's absence.

"I'll be okay," I said to him.

He nodded. "We're training after your class. You should take a granola bar or something with you."

Cody went to the cabinet and grabbed a couple of them for me. "Please eat." He shoved them into my backpack, then spun me around. "Come back."

That seemed to be the most common thing for him to say lately. I hated to make him that promise because one of these days, I wouldn't be able to keep it. I lifted my hand to his cheek. His stubble pricked my palm. "I'll do my best." I kissed him quickly, then slid my hand into Mavros'.

Seth took the lead. Malcolm and Mavros walked next to me, and I assumed Jax was behind us. We stepped outside, and the cold chilled me to the bone. The sky was filled with dark clouds that held the promise of a storm. Wind blew through the trees, knocking snow from their branches.

I edged closer to Mavros, relishing the warmth that wafted off of him. He wrapped his arm around me and tucked me against his side.

Thankfully, it wasn't that long of a walk to Quartz Building. As we made our way to the back of the classroom, Mavros never let go of my hand. My entourage seemed extra vigilant. Maybe it was because of my fear, or maybe they felt something was coming, too.

I pulled my backpack off and set it on the floor. Then I tugged on the fingertips of my gloves, pulled them off, and tucked them into my pockets. As I was unzipping my coat, the green glow from the acorn caught my attention. I grabbed my glove and shoved my hand back into it but not before noticing two leaves opening from a single shoot. I plopped down in my chair and held my head in my hands. Whatever this was, it wasn't good.

"What is it, Dacia?" Malcolm sat next to me.

I lifted my gloved hand up and rotated it. "The acorn is growing."

"Show me." His voice was low, but there was a dangerous edge to it.

I pulled my hand down and sat on it. The thought of taking the glove off again made my stomach flip. I tapped my temple with my right hand, opening up my thoughts to him. I let him see what my hand had looked like at breakfast. Then I showed him how the acorn had grown.

He stared at me. His dragon shone through his eyes.

I held his gaze until his eyes flicked to the side. My stomach dropped. I could only think of one thing that could drag his attention away. My head seemed to swivel without my permission. I didn't want to see Troy again. I couldn't stand the idea of looking into his smug face. I didn't want to listen to his hateful voice.

It wasn't Troy making his way toward me, though. It was Kieran. He sauntered through the classroom with a mischievous grin covering his face. His hair flopped against his brow with every step he took. His yellow eyes never glanced away from me. He pulled out the chair next to Seth and sat backward in it, facing me. "Miss me?"

"Miss me?" Rage burned inside of me. I jerked my hand out from under me and shook it at him. "You do whatever this is to me and then come strolling in here with that cocky smirk on your face and ask if I miss you?" I was half standing, leaning over my desk with my face right in front of his. "What did you do to me?"

He grabbed my hand, and there was no reaction from my guards. I looked around the room, but nobody was paying any attention to us. "What's going on?"

"They think we're being the perfect students, paying attention to whatever nonsense the teacher is blathering on about." He never pulled his focus off of me, never let go of my hand. "They can't hear us."

I narrowed my eyes at him. "What. Did. You. Do. To. Me?" The words were forced out through my clenched teeth.

Kieran didn't look phased at all. He shoved his hair out of his eyes and shrugged. "You seem like you could use some fun in your life."

"How's this fun?" I yanked the glove off and shoved my hand in his face.

His dark eyebrows pulled together, making his confusion seem genuine. "How isn't it? Games are always fun."

"If this is a game—" I sat down, forcing a semblance of calm "—what are the rules? How do I win?"

He rubbed his hands together. "Now, you're asking the right questions?" His yellow eyes seemed to sparkle. "The tree will grow. Leaves will cover it. Maybe a bird or two will nest in its branches." He tilted his head. "It's hard to tell with birds. They're a bit flighty." He reached out and grabbed one of my curls, holding it between his fingers. "Their color will change to the color of your hair, and then they will drop. If you haven't discovered how to stop it before the last leaf falls, you will be whisked away to Faerie to join me. If you figure out how to stop it, you win." He dropped my hair and stood, leaning down, he whispered in my ear, "No one's ever beaten me."

He bounded away, and Malcolm stared after him. "What just happened?"

"I learned the rules."

When class ended, my guardians hustled me out of the room. They surrounded me, keeping the other students from bumping into me. We stepped out into the hall, and I froze. Jax ran into me, and I fell into Seth. Malcolm and Mavros each grabbed one of my arms and jerked me back to my feet.

The whole time, I never took my eyes off of Troy. He stood in an alcove across from me. His arms were folded over his chest. His muscles were flexed, and his eyes were filled with hatred. Just like they'd been every time he came into my cell. Just like they were every time he had ever seen me. "You're being selfish."

Even with all of the people in the hall, with their chatter, their laughter, I heard him like he was standing right next to me. "How?"

"People are suffering because you won't come with me." He leaned against the wall and lifted his hand, examining his fingernails. "You should hear their screams."

I stumbled back against Malcolm. Troy was right. I could save three people, but I only cared about myself, about my happiness.

Malcolm swooped me up in his arms and carried me away from Troy, but I could still hear everything he said, "Begging you for help, calling out for you to save them. They put their faith in the wrong person."

I watched Troy over Malcolm's shoulder. Liam's, Diana's, and Olivia's broken pleas filled my head. Their cries tightened my chest and brought a painful lump to my throat. They didn't deserve this. I was the abomination. I was the one who had summoned and befriended a demon. I was the danger. They'd done nothing except try to protect me. Was I selfish for not returning the favor?

Malcolm's chest rumbled against my body. "Don't think it, Dacia."

"Think what?" I pulled my stare from Troy and looked up into Malcolm's face.

His fangs jutted out of his mouth, and his voice was all dragon. "You're not giving yourself up."

"It's my fault." I swallowed hard, but the pain in my throat didn't dissipate. I stared down at the ground, watching the snow-covered sidewalk race beneath Malcolm's feet.

He didn't set me down until we were in my apartment. Then he pulled my backpack off and set it beside the door. I started to walk away, but he spun me around and clutched my shoulders. "None of this is your fault."

"Yes, it is." I tried to step back, but he wouldn't let me. "I shouldn't have asked Liam to stay. None of this would have happened if I would have let him go." I dropped my chin to my chest and slumped forward.

Malcolm's hold on me faltered, but he didn't let go. "Even if you hadn't asked him to stay, he still would have been hunting Troy."

"You don't understand." I stepped closer to him, pressing my forehead against his chest. "How could you?"

He ran his hand down my back. The motion was jerky, making me think he was fighting his dragon for control.

The doorknob turned, and I grabbed hold of his sweater, clinging to him. He turned so my back wasn't facing the door, and I relaxed slightly.

"What happened?" Cash asked as soon as he stepped inside.

A hand clamped down on my shoulder, and Malcolm let go of me. Cody wrapped me in his arms, and I let him soothe me while I contemplated how to rescue Liam and the others. Unless I could figure out where they were, the only thing I could do was trade my freedom for theirs.

"Enough!" Malcolm roared. "We're training now." He grabbed hold of my hand, and Cody stepped away from me.

In the next instant, we were standing in a clearing with Mavros, Jax, Seth, and Cash. "What do you want, Dacia?" Mavros' voice was the low rumble of distant thunder.

"What do you mean?" My teeth chattered together. I heated the air around me, trying to stifle the cold.

He pointed up at the gray sky. "Flying or fighting?"

I didn't know what he meant by fighting, but if a battle with the Nephilim was looming, fighting was probably the best choice. "Umm … fighting?"

"Jax, Seth, you're with Mavros." Malcolm's expression was feral. "Stay human, and try to capture her. Dacia—" he turned toward me, and I couldn't help but wonder how long until Malus Tribulus stood in front of me "—do whatever you need to do to stop them. Don't let them take you away."

I put my hand on his arm. "Are you going to be able to watch this?" I kept my voice soft and tried to control my emotions.

"It won't be easy." He pinched his eyes shut, and when he opened them again, they were more human-looking.

I walked away from him, stretching my arms and rolling my neck. Unlike when I trained with Liam, I really didn't know what to expect. I strolled past my would-be attackers, and without meaning to, my muscles tensed, waiting for one of them to jump out at me.

None of them did, and I had to fight against myself to keep from looking over my shoulder. Whatever happened, I needed it to be a surprise. I needed to be able to keep myself safe.

Strong arms wrapped around me, lifting me off my feet. Jax. The Krav Maga movements came naturally now. I did what Liam had trained me to do, but when I hit Jax in the groin, he didn't let go.

A small seed of panic planted itself in the pit of my stomach, but instead of focusing on it, I thought about ice until my entire body was a frozen block.

Jax dropped me with a hiss, and I flew off.

"Again," Malcolm yelled. Filtered sunlight glinted off the onyx scales that framed his face.

Cash stood next to him, looking nearly as tense. I wondered what his role in this training session was. Was he here to keep Malcolm in line if need be?

Mavros grabbed me before I had a chance to turn around. It was as if I was held in a vice. I couldn't move my arms at all. He didn't lift me in the air. He just started walking backward, dragging me off.

I dug my heels into the ground, but I was no match for his strength, and without being able to get my feet underneath me, I didn't know how to use any of Liam's techniques. I sucked in a deep breath and tried to figure out what to do. I couldn't use ice against him. I knew what it did to him, and unless I had to, I would never willingly do that again.

An image of dragon wings popped into my head … only the wings.

They burst from my shoulders, knocking Mavros back.

As I fell, I pictured a precipice not too high above us. I disappeared and landed on my feet on the edge of it.

Four dragons and a demon lifted their heads, searching for me. "Dacia!" Malcolm roared.

I teleported to the middle of the clearing. "I'm fine, Malcolm." I stepped toward him. "I'm safe." *I was doing what I can. I can't use ice against him.* I sent him the image of Mavros' ruined arm. It still haunted me. *I can't do that to him again.*

Malcolm nodded at me. He'd been there. He knew what it had done to me to hurt Mavros like that. "Again."

I turned around, wiping my eyes as I went.

Jax charged at me. Dropping down, he slammed into me and lifted me over his shoulder. After the initial shock wore off, I pounded my fists into his back, hoping to hit his kidneys and make him let go.

"That'd be a good move if I was one of them." His steps didn't falter. He just kept running. "But I'm not."

I teleported us high in the sky, above the cloud cover. We freefell until I transformed into a dragon. He tumbled away from me, but I grabbed him in my talons and dove for the ground. I held him out in front of me and landed on my hind legs. Before I transformed back into myself, I stood him on his feet.

He patted my scales. "Well done."

They attacked me—sometimes in groups, sometimes alone—until the sun was a memory, its warmth all but forgotten, and millions upon millions of stars filled the sky.

Chapter 30

Kieran perches on the end of my bed, staring down at me. His sunny eyes seem to glow in the dark room. "Oh, the fun we'll have when you join me in Faerie." He flips off the footboard and lands on his feet.

"You haven't won yet." Holding his gaze, I sit up. I'm not willing to take my eyes off of him for even a second.

He prowls around the edge of my bed, stopping when he stands right next to me. "I always win, and besides, you'll love Faerie. There are no Nephilim there."

"What if I don't like it?" I bite my lip, pulling it into my mouth. "What if I want to come home?"

He cocks his head, looking at me like I'm speaking Greek. "Of course, you'll like it." He kneels next to my bed. "It doesn't matter, though." He shrugs his slender shoulder. "Once you eat our food, you can never leave."

"Well, I guess I won't eat then."

He lifts my hand and studies the growth of the tree. The first two leaves that had shot up are yellow and wilting, but a new branch is growing up between them with leaves sprouting off of it. "Darling—" he looks into my eyes with a wicked grin on his face "—if you don't eat, the ravens will feast on your flesh. They'll pick your bones clean."

My eyes shot open. I looked around the night-darkened room, starting right beside me where I'd last seen Kieran in my dream. I expected to find him watching me. Continuing my search, I met a pair of glowing eyes at the end of my bed.

I pressed my hand over my mouth, holding in my scream. My heart raced.

"What's wrong, Dacia?"

Malcolm.

Of course, it was Malcolm.

"Kieran." I rubbed my hands over my face. "I thought he would still be in my room when I woke up."

He leaned forward, clutching the arms of the chair. Scales covered the backs of his hands. "You dreamed about Kieran?"

"Yeah, I thought you were watching."

He walked over to the window and pushed it open. "I was watching. You were dreaming about Cody."

At the sound of his name, Cody sat up next to me. "He was in her head, and you didn't know?"

"No." Malcolm turned from the window. His lips were pulled into a snarl. "I saw you." His gaze trailed from Cody's head to his feet.

Cody wrapped his arm around me. "What'd he want?"

"He's looking forward to me living in Faerie with him." I closed my eyes. "I think I know a way to keep this from happening."

Malcolm moaned and leaned into the screen. "No, Dacia. Whatever it is. No. Absolutely not."

"Which is worse?" I threw my head back against my pillow. "Faerie or the sanctuary?"

Malcolm spun around and strode toward my side of the bed. "You will not give yourself up. You're not going to the Nephilim's sanctuary, and you are *not* going to Faerie." He pointed his finger at my face and then at himself. "You are staying here where we can keep you safe. You are *ours*."

He disappeared from my room, and a soft knock sounded on the door before it slowly opened. Cash came in. "What did you do to him?"

"I dreamed about Kieran, but Malcolm saw me dreaming about Cody."

Cash looked from me to the living room. "Mavros."

"I'll never get tired of dragons needing a demon." Mavros' silken voice came from the desk chair.

The bed bounced twice. I turned toward him. He was leaned back in the chair with his hands behind his head, and his booted feet were on top of the comforter.

"If Malcolm couldn't keep the dreams away, Mavros is your best bet." Cash looked down at Cody and me. "Do you want me to stay in here, too?"

I felt like I was standing in front of the classroom, giving a speech in the buff. Everybody was looking at me, and all of them wanted different answers. I tugged my hand through my hair, trying to come up with something that would appease them all. "Did Malcolm tell you to come in here?"

"Yes." Cash sat on the floor and pulled one leg up to his chest. "As riled up as he was when he left, I shouldn't defy him."

"How's this work?" Cody asked. "Is Malcolm like the alpha? Can you do whatever you want? Or do you have to do what he says?"

Cash pushed the door shut with his foot that was stretched out. "We are free to make our own decisions. Like with every group, it's best to have a single leader. We can't all be doing whatever we want. Malcolm is the oldest and strongest. He's also the most volatile right now, so we follow his lead. Now, get some sleep."

I had homework to do. I had to figure out how to save Liam, but it had been a week, and I needed to talk to Sarah, to fill her in on everything that had happened over break. She had waited long enough.

Malcolm hadn't returned from hunting, so Seth, Jax, Cash, and Mavros walked to Cacomistle Hall with Cody and me. Since it was Saturday, Alicia's desk was empty. I turned toward Seth, not sure of where Jax was. "If you don't want to come up, you don't have to."

"I will stand by your side until you no longer need me." He waved his hand, ushering me ahead of him.

I climbed the stairs, hoping that I would be able to talk to Sarah without having a panic attack. When I got to her office, the door was open, so I knocked on it as I stepped inside.

"Come on in," she said from one of the rooms at the far end. "I'll be out in just a minute."

The last time I'd been here, I'd been too on edge to enjoy the mountain view and the roaring fire. I sat down on the couch between Cody and Mavros and stared out at the scene. From here it looked like the world was a peaceful place, free of monsters, where my fear and anxiety didn't belong.

Some of the tension released from my shoulders. I slid my fingers through Cody's and rested my head on his upper arm.

When Sarah strolled out, I sat up. "Well—" she looked from my face to those with me "—I wondered when you would come to see me." She headed toward Seth and stretched out her hand. "I'm Sarah Aspen."

"Seth." He shook her hand.

She stepped back but kept studying him as if she was mesmerized. "Is your hair the same color as your scales?" A pink blush settled on her cheeks.

How does she know? He cocked his head and stared at me. The motion was similar to how a bird moves and reminded me for a moment of Aurelia.

I lifted my shoulders. *She knows what Malcolm and Cash and the others are. I suppose she assumes you are, too.*

"Yes." Blue scales shimmered along his cheekbones before disappearing.

"Magnificent." She sat across from me and smoothed her slacks out. "You can sit if you'd like."

Cash shook his head. "It's easier to protect her when we're standing."

With that sentence, all sense of security left me. The tranquility I'd felt disappeared. I looked outside. The shadows beneath the pine trees seemed dark and dangerous. The mountain peaks lost their serenity, appearing treacherous.

Cash reached over the couch and rested his hand on my shoulder. I jumped at his touch, but he held on, sending a peaceful feeling flowing into me.

"So … my break." I stared down at my hands, one gloved and one not, while I told her all the things that had happened since I left school for Christmas vacation.

She interrupted with a few questions here and there, but after I stopped talking, she remained quiet for a long time. Her gaze slid between me and each of my guards before settling back on me. "Where are Malcolm and Liam?"

"Malcolm's dragon is riled." I clutched Cody's hand a little tighter, needing his comfort. "My dream last night didn't help with that, so he's hunting."

She leaned toward me, stretching her hand forward, but she couldn't reach me across the coffee table. "Your dream last night?"

"I'll get there." I sucked in a deep breath. "Liam was taken by the Nephilim."

Her eyes widened. "Oh, no." She shook her head. "They're still after you, then?"

My throat seemed to close up. I wanted to talk to her, but the words wouldn't come. Dread like a thousand spiders marched up my spine. I stared at Sarah until my vision blurred everything together.

Cash's energy poured into me, but it was no match for my terror. Panic cut through it, leaving it in tiny pools that evaporated into nothing.

All I could hear was Troy's voice in my head. *Please, fall and break your neck. Save us all the trouble of dealing with you. Demon lover. Liar. You've no idea how much I'd like to beat the truth out of you. You might wanna sleep with one eye open.*

Dacia. Cash's voice mingled with Troy's, and for the first time in a long time, I heard his hatred, too. *I don't care what you call me, but if you say my true name out loud again ever, you'll regret it. I can smell your fear. You'd do well to remember it in my presence. You worthless human. Pathetic.*

I wrapped my arms around my stomach and leaned forward, but Troy's words didn't stop. *Liam sends his regards. At least he would if he could speak. People are suffering. You're selfish. You should hear their screams.*

Mavros threw his arm over my shoulder and pulled me into his side. His warm summer nights smell was intoxicating. I snuggled against him, wrapping my arms around him, loving his strength, his warmth, and his comfort.

The room came into focus, but Mavros was the only thing in it that I wanted to look at. The voices cleared from my head. I heard the fire crackling, Sarah's sharp intake of breath, Cody's pained moan, and Cash's growl.

Mavros threw his hands up in the air. "Back off, dragon. You couldn't get through to her, so I did what I could."

The spell was broken. "Oh, God, Cody." I pulled away from Mavros and wiped my hand over my mouth. "I'm so sorry."

Cody's mask was firmly in place. There was no emotion on his face, but I knew I'd hurt him. "I know."

How could I ever make this right? I wanted to reach out and take his hand in mine, but I was afraid he would reject me in front of everyone. "They're still hunting me," I said to Sarah without pulling my attention from Cody, without thinking about Troy. She shifted, but I didn't look at her. It wouldn't have mattered anyway. I couldn't see past the hurt in Cody's eyes. "They'll never stop."

A window slid open, and a cold blast of air slammed into me. I looked up in time to see Sarah staring at it in confusion. "Sarah, meet Jax."

Jax became visible for long enough to nod at her. His features weren't fully human, and when he spoke, the words were practically snarled. "I need to stay unknown to the Nephilim."

The color washed out of Sarah's face, and she stared unmoving at the space where Jax had been.

Cash, can you help me? I looked up at him, hoping that my emotions weren't too much for him and Seth to handle. *Take the edge off or make me angry. Something. Anything.*

He put both hands on my shoulders and sent a rush of calming energy through me. It crashed against my fear, like a wave against a rocky cliff. The spray washed away little bits of my terror. With each upsurge, my dread diminished. When the worst of my fear was gone, Cash stepped away from me.

I reached back, grabbed one of his hands, and returned it to my shoulder. "I'm going to need you for a little longer."

He didn't say anything, just sent a trickle of energy streaming into me.

Closing my eyes, I yanked the glove off of my hand. I opened and closed my fist, keeping my palm down so nobody could see it.

"Dacia." Cash's voice was low, but I could hear how much he was straining.

I sucked in a deep breath and opened my eyes at the same time I flipped my hand over. The tree had grown substantially. Roots extended to the very tips of my fingers. The top of the leader was close to an inch above my wrist, and several new branches covered my palm. I wanted to show it to Sarah, but I couldn't pull my gaze from it.

As I watched, new limbs broke through the bark, filling out the branches. Leaves pushed through the buds, unfurling like a butterfly emerging from its cocoon. My stomach churned. This was too fast. How long would I have until the leaves began to turn? How long until the last one fluttered to the ground?

Cody twined his fingers through mine and squeezed gently. "Dacia?"

I pulled my gaze from the curse and looked into his sapphire eyes. There was something in them, confidence or determination, that hadn't been there before. He didn't blink, didn't look away.

His jaw was set. "Not losing you to him."

"I have until the last leaf falls." I didn't pull my gaze away from Cody. I needed his strength for this. "If I don't figure out how to get rid of it by then, I'll be trapped in Faerie."

Chapter 31

"You've been cursed?" Sarah's voice shot up. She looked away from me before seeing me nod. "She's been cursed? How? When?"

"A phouka—"

Mavros cut me off. "Malcolm was watching her dreams. Somehow the phouka made him see something else."

"Hence the hunting," Seth said.

I dipped my head toward my shoulder but didn't contradict him.

"How do you get rid of it?" Sarah walked over and sat on the coffee table right in front of me. She cautiously lifted my hand and studied it, careful not to touch the tree.

"I've only been able to come up with one idea." I raked my fingers through my hair, hoping the three dragons with me wouldn't react the same way Malcolm had. "I could let the Nephilim take me." I looked into Seth's vivid blue eyes. "Hence the hunting."

The energy in the room seemed to change. The air felt charged, and all of my guards tensed. Cash's fingers dug into my shoulder, and Mavros pulled away from me.

"We'll find another way." Jax's voice came from near the window. From the sound of it, his features were probably even more dragon-like.

Sarah squeezed my fingers. "Don't decide yet. You still have time to come up with something else."

I stared down at the tree that was rapidly growing. Its bright green leaves rustled, blown by a breeze that none of us could feel. I wondered if I poisoned myself or stopped drinking if the tree would die, but if it did, its leaves would still fall. Would that still count? There had to be some way for me to beat this.

When I looked up from my hand, everybody looked away from me. Sarah patted my knee. "I'll see if I can come up with any ideas, too."

"Thanks."

She crossed her legs and folded her hands over her knee. Turning from me to Cody, she asked, "How is everything else going?"

"Fine." Cody shrugged.

I wished he would have said more. I wished he would have kept her focus off of me for a while. After my display earlier, though, I couldn't blame him for being quiet. I just hoped he would remember what it had been like for him when I'd controlled him. I hoped he would remember that I had no choice.

Sarah focused her attention on me again.

"I'm trying." I sucked in a big breath and blew it out noisily. "It's hard to concentrate on classes when I'm afraid Troy might show up. Every time I see him … it's like I'm in that cell again, with no way out."

Her voice softened. "I can't say I know what you're going through, but all you can do is the best you can, Dacia."

When I tried to respond, my lip quivered, so I just nodded.

She asked about the apartment and about Dan and Samantha. She genuinely cared about us, so I tried to focus on our conversation and not think about Mavros controlling me or Troy or Kieran capturing me.

Finally, she stood and smoothed the wrinkles out of her gray slacks. "As much as I enjoy your company, I have work to get done." She pulled me into a hug. "I'm here if you need me and even if you don't."

"Thanks." I looked over her shoulder and out the window. Fat flakes fell to the ground, distorting my view of the mountains.

Cody and I bundled up before leaving Sarah's office. Mavros took hold of my arm, guiding me down the steps. The door opened before we reached it, and I assumed Jax was holding it for us.

As soon as I stepped outside, the cold air seemed to seep inside of me. A shiver shot through me at the same time that a vision of Liam flashed through my mind.

His face was nearly unrecognizable, and his agony racked my body. I stumbled, falling to my knees before my guards could catch me, and screamed.

Mavros knelt in front of me, and Cody's hand ran up and down my back. "What happened?" Cody asked.

The pain sucked the air from my lungs and stole my voice. Clutching my head in my hands, I rocked forward, curling my body over my legs. I wanted to share my thoughts with the people surrounding me, but I was afraid I wouldn't be able to control my powers well enough.

"Where are you hurt?" Mavros' voice right next to my ear made me flinch.

The connection between Liam and me was broken. I gulped in a lungful of air, and my body shuddered. Pulling my hands away from my head, I pressed them to the ground and pushed myself up onto my knees. The cold air hit my face, and I realized I was crying.

"What's going on?" Cash's voice was the low rumbling of thunder that made me wonder how he was holding his form.

I stood, wobbling slightly. "Liam …" What had just happened? Could Nephilim send their thoughts? "I think he contacted me, but all I got from it was his pain."

"Get her to her room …"

I turned toward Jax's voice and stared right through him into the trees that lined the road. Snow clung to the branches, hiding the green needles beneath a white blanket.

"… before it happens again."

Mavros took hold of one of my arms and Cash grabbed the other. He dipped his head toward his shoulder. "Sorry, Cody."

"No worries." Cody shoved his hands into his coat pockets and started walking. "Get her back."

We only passed a few other students before Seth opened the door to the apartment building. It was a snowy, Saturday morning, and Cacomistle Hall and Pine Grove Apartments were on the edge of campus, away from most of the foot traffic.

Cash and Mavros hurried me up the stairs.

Dacia. Liam's voice was weak. His pain shot through me again.

My legs wobbled, but Cash slid his arm behind my knees and lifted me, jogging up the steps. At the same time, healing energy flowed into me. My thoughts cleared enough for me to respond. *Liam, where are you?*

Everything darkened, then I saw Diana and Olivia as if they were walking in front of me. They were dressed in solid black and moved from shadow to shadow, approaching a rundown building. A single streetlight fought against the night. It reflected off the twisted tin roofing that lay on the ground. Jagged pieces of glass clung to the window frames where they weren't boarded over. The door wobbled on only one hinge, making a screeching noise that pierced the silence.

They stood to either side of the door, and Diana held her hand up. She raised one finger at a time. When three were lifted, they slipped inside. They tread cautiously, peeking around every corner before moving on.

Bright lights filled the warehouse, momentarily blinding Liam. He threw his arm over his eyes, and light seeped in around it, allowing his vision to adjust. When he uncovered his face, the three of them were surrounded. Something slammed into the back of his head, and even though the pain that tore through me was just a memory, it brought tears to my eyes. He fell to his knees, and another hit made the world go dark.

I slumped back against Cash. My body shook from pain that wasn't mine.

Cash growled but held me as tenderly as if I was a fluffy dandelion blowball that he didn't want to break apart.

Cody opened the door to our apartment. Dan was sitting on the couch, leaning forward, staring at the TV with a controller in his hands. Russ watched us from an armchair. His amber eyes took in everything.

Cash walked in and set me on the other side of the couch. Then he knelt in front of me, keeping ahold of my hand.

Dan paused the game. His hazel eyes darted from concerned face to concerned face until they settled on mine. "What's up?"

"Are they back?" Samantha burst out of her room, rubbing a towel over her wet hair. She slammed to a stop, and whatever she had planned on saying was replaced with, "Oh, no."

"What did you see, Dacia?" Cash's eyes were completely amethyst except for the thin slit of his pupil. His fangs extended over his lip, but otherwise, he held onto his human form.

I squeezed his fingers. "I know where he is. That's all."

"If that was all, you wouldn't smell like that." Jax showed himself. Twisted horns sprouted from the top of his head, and purple scales lined his face.

My gut churned, and my heart raced. I tugged my gloves off and wiped my sweaty palms on my jeans. Terror made me contemplate doing what was right or doing what was best for me. "I—" tears filled my eyes and made a lump grow in my throat "—I could take us all there. I've seen it. We … we could save them."

ಜ355ಅ

Chapter 32
Planning A Jailbreak

*M*alcolm appeared in the middle of the room. "No." He stepped toward me and held his hand up in front of him in the stop gesture. "Don't even think about it."

"I—"

"Dacia, no." His voice was a warning. A line I didn't want to cross.

Now wasn't the time to discuss this. I needed to wait until the dragon was a little less prominent.

"How do you know what she's talking about?" Dan set the controller on the couch next to him.

Mavros tucked his hands into his pockets and shot me a sheepish grin. "He needed to know."

The apartment was too small for five dragons that were about to transform, one demon, and four college students, especially when one of them was me. Unless I could get my emotions under control, this wasn't going to end well.

I closed my eyes and focused on the mountain lake that had calmed me when I learned how to control my powers. The water lapped against the rocky shore. A gentle breeze blew my hair back. I tried to let the view pull the tension out of my shoulders, but I kept thinking about Liam, how weak he had sounded, and how much pain he'd been in.

There was no sense in trying to calm myself. I looked up at Malcolm, hoping he understood that I wasn't trying to argue with him. "He's in so much pain, Malcolm. We've got to help him."

"And, we will." He strode closer to me, and Cash stood up, blocking his path. He put his hand on Cash's arm and pushed him far enough to the side that he was standing right in front of me. His expression was hard. The tendons in his neck bulged, and when he spoke again the words were ground out through clenched teeth. "You will not."

I remembered him looking right at me even though I'd been invisible. I remembered his claws tearing through my back. My hands shook, and I shoved them under my legs to keep anyone else from noticing. "H-how will y-you get there without me?"

"You'll show me your memories."

My fear was making him more unstable. I could see the dragon looking out at me.

"Enough." Cash shoved Malcolm back and stood between us. "Quit scaring her."

"She needs to be scared." Malcolm glared down at me.

Rage burned away my fear. "You don't think I am?" I stood up and shoved my finger into his chest. "You don't think I'm terrified of what will happen if Troy captures me? How—" I was at a total loss for words. The dragons could taste my emotions. They could smell my fear. "How can you not know exactly how terrified I am?"

"You keep rushing into danger. You haven't even considered that this could be a trap." He flashed his fangs at me, but I was too angry for his action to scare me. "He won't let you go again."

"You don't think I know that!" I fisted my hands at my sides. My fingernails dug into my palms. "I don't want to go anywhere near him, but it's the right thing to do."

He wiped his hand down his face. "And, we'll do it. The demon will stay with you."

"Liam would come for me." My anger disappeared, leaving my muscles shaky. I plopped back down on the couch, leaning forward with my head in my hands. "I can't abandon him."

The hand that clutched my shoulder was unexpected. It was small and gentle. "He's right," Samantha said. "Stay here with Mavros, do your laundry, your homework, hang out with Dan and me, whatever. Let the dragons save Liam."

"He wouldn't want you anywhere near Troy anyway," Dan agreed.

I couldn't go on my own, and they obviously wouldn't let me go with them. I nodded. "Fine. When?"

"Right now, if you want us to." Cash looked at the others. "That okay with you guys?"

Jax and Malcolm nodded. Seth said, "Sure."

"Please be careful." I opened up my thoughts to them and shared every detail I could think of, hoping it would be enough.

Malcolm stared at Mavros. "She doesn't leave this building, and if she leaves this apartment, you don't leave her side."

"If only I took orders from dragons." Mavros narrowed his eyes, and black smoke rolled off his skin.

They stepped toward each other, and I moved between them. "Stop." I shook my head at them. "I might do my laundry, but I won't go anywhere else." I glared into Malcolm's bronze eyes. "You know Mavros won't leave me. You know he worries about me as much as you do, so get out of here and bring them back."

He dipped his chin to his chest. "You're right."

"If you need me," Cash said, "think my name, and I'll be there."

Except for Russ, the dragons disappeared all at once, and the room felt enormous without them looming over me. Cody grabbed hold of my hand and sat on the couch, pulling me with him.

"We were going to see if you wanted to go to Althea for lunch." Samantha brushed her fingers through her wet hair. "Maybe dinner instead?"

I chewed on my lip. I didn't want to tell her no, but if the dragons freed Liam, Troy would be even more desperate. "I—"

"No." Cody rubbed his thumb along mine. "I don't think that's a good idea. Don't let it stop you two, though."

Dan shot us a cheap imitation of his smile. "We can make something here if you want."

"No, you guys can go." I hated that my problems were always intruding on our friendship. "Maybe take Bryce and Cassandra with you. Then we can hang out when you get back. Laundry should be done by then. We'll find something here."

Samantha folded her towel. "Sure." She nodded. "We can do that. If they go with us, do you want them to come here afterward?"

"If they want." I shrugged. "I don't care. It's up to you." Realizing that I sounded distracted and unconcerned, I smiled at her. "It would be nice to just hang out for a change."

Russ left with Samantha and Dan. Up until now, none of the dragons had guarded them, but if the others were successful in rescuing Liam, we didn't want to risk retaliation against my friends.

Once they were gone, Cody and I grabbed our dirty clothes, and Mavros joined us on our journey to the laundry room. He held onto my arm as we descended the stairs. He kept watching me, but whenever I looked at him, he turned away.

Wondering if I had something on my face, I switched hands I was holding the hamper in and wiped my hand along my cheek.

We turned on the landing before descending another staircase, and he glanced at me again.

"What?" I stopped walking. "Why do you keep looking at me like that?"

Cody was three steps in front of us. He turned and looked up. A mask of indifference covered his face.

Mavros lifted his hands and took half a step back. "I'm waiting." He tilted his head.

"For what?" I couldn't take the guessing anymore.

"To have to catch you, to keep you from tumbling head-first down the stairs." He rolled his eyes. "I don't know if Liam will try to contact you again, and I can't heal you like Cash did, so I have to be ready to stop you from getting hurt even worse."

I felt stupid for questioning him. I should have thought of that. Liam's pain had toppled me twice. "Sorry."

"No need, Dacia." He took the hamper from me. "Let's just get this done and get back up to your apartment before something does happen."

Two washing machines were empty. Cody and I took both of them, sticking our light-colored clothes in one and our darks in the other. Then he turned to me and said, "Stay or go back to the apartment?"

The thought of climbing the five flights of stairs to our room was daunting. I felt pathetic for thinking it, but I was exhausted to the core. "Can we just sit here?" I pointed at the chairs.

"Sure, Dacia." Cody took my hand and led me over to them.

We watched the clothes tumble through soapy water without saying anything. My thoughts were on the dragons. I had expected to hear from them by now. Actually, I had expected them to be back with Liam, Diana, and Olivia within minutes of departing.

Butterflies twirled and fluttered in my stomach. I should have insisted on going with them. What if they didn't come back? I would have to go after them with Mavros as my only guard or on my own if he refused.

Mavros stood by the door, staring down the hall. Every so often, he looked over his shoulder at me, his expression impossible to read.

The washing machines beeped. Cody and I both got up and tossed the clothes into the dryers. When we finished, I said, "Let's go back."

"Sure." Cody brushed my hair off of my face and tucked it behind my ear.

I looked at the timers, then the clock on the wall. "We can get lunch." I waved my hand toward the dryers. "They should be done by then."

Mavros turned around, facing us. "You can't leave the building." He folded his arms over his chest. "As much as I hate taking orders, Malcolm was right about that."

"Fine." I tugged my hand through my hair, picked up my hamper, and glanced down the hall in both directions. Nobody was nearby. "Do you just want to teleport back?"

"Yes." Cody grabbed my hand and waited while Mavros took hold of my arm.

Our bodies stretched in and pulled out. Darkness filled my vision. When everything came back into focus, we were standing in my room.

I let go of Cody's hand and set my hamper down before I realized Mavros hadn't been holding onto my arm when we materialized. I spun around, but he was nowhere in sight.

"Where's Mavros?" Cody's eyebrows were pinched together.

Lifting my shoulders, I said, "I don't know. Probably here but invisible." I started toward the door, but Cody grabbed me and pulled me back against him.

He skimmed his fingers down my arms, then wrapped his around my waist, bowing down so that his head was on top of mine. "I gotta bad feeling."

I tucked my hands into his back pockets. "Yeah, me, too. It feels like something's going to happen soon."

"Promise you'll come back to me, Dacia." He sounded lost and desolate. "Even if you don't mean it, promise me."

"Oh, Cody"—the desperation in his voice made my heart break a little—"I will always do whatever I can to get back to you."

We stood like that for several minutes. Cody needed to hold me, so I let him. He stepped back and cupped my cheeks between his hands. "Dragons keep saying you belong to them, but, Dacia, you're mine."

I stood on my tiptoes and pressed my lips to his. The kiss was tender. It was about love, not desire.

When I pulled away, he slipped his fingers into mine and led me through the door. We walked past the humming refrigerator, and somebody wrapped their arm around my neck. At the same time, Micah grabbed Cody from behind.

Chapter 33

It's Over

The movements Liam had taught us were instinctual, but I fought against them. I wanted to throw my attacker off. I wanted to show him not to mess with me, but for now, I still had my magic. *Cash!* I thought at the same time that I teleported away.

My captor clung to me as we fell through the cerulean blue sky. Jagged mountain peaks rushed past us. The air was frigid.

"What the hell?"

Troy.

Of course, it was Troy. Part of me knew it would be, but having it confirmed seemed to stop my thoughts. I couldn't remember what I was doing. We were going to splatter across the valley nearly 10,000 feet below us. My body trembled. Whether from cold or fear or both, I didn't know.

He twined his legs around mine, pulling us closer together. His grip on my neck tightened, and black spots flickered at the edges of my vision.

No! Malcolm's angered roar shot through my head, clearing it.

Magic flared inside of me. Wings exploded from my shoulder blades. I snapped them tight, and the wind hit them, lifting me.

Unable to hold onto me now that I was a dragon, Troy bounced over my back and plummeted toward the ground. The scent of his fear hit my nostrils, and the mouth-watering aroma made my stomach growl.

Folding my wings in, I dove after him. The air rushed over my scales. I no longer felt the stinging bite of the cold. I narrowed my eyes on Troy's tumbling body.

His screams were a sweet symphony. The background music that played at a restaurant.

Fire burned in my belly, begging for release. I narrowed my eyes, targeting my prey. The flames grew hotter.

My dragon wanted this threat obliterated. I remembered Cash telling me he didn't share my fears because his captor was dead, and I wondered what it would be like. Would I quit jumping at shadows? Would I be able to sleep? Would the panic attacks end?

The idea of a world without Troy in it was irresistible. After what he'd done, he didn't deserve to live.

I kicked into my dive, making my body more streamlined, gaining on him faster. The air rushed past, exhilarating me.

The thrill of the chase brought the dragon's instincts out. Fire inched up my throat, preparing to be released.

Unbidden, thoughts of Draconian and Argentum flitted through my mind. Their deaths had freed me from their reigns of terror. Troy's would do the same.

He stared up at me. His brown eyes were dull, lifeless. Resigned to his fate, the fight had left him.

He was close enough that I could hear his blood pumping through his veins. I imagined it stopping. The freedom that would give me.

Then I remembered my sword piercing Draconian's heart, the life draining from his eyes, and his blood on my hands. Next, I thought about Argentum. I remembered feasting on his blood and power. I remembered how even after death, he had haunted me.

I remembered feeling like a monster, and I didn't want that.

Never again.

I lifted my head and blasted the flames into the clouds above us. Then I reached down and swiped Troy out of the air, clutching him in my talons.

His body was stiff with fear. "Wh-what are you g-going to do?"

Afraid I would flame broil him if I opened my mouth, I spoke the words directly into his mind. *That depends on you.*

He flinched, and when his eyes widened, I had to remind myself why I wasn't eating him.

I flew to a rocky outcrop and landed as gracefully as I could with him grasped in my talons. When I let go of him, he stumbled, falling to his hands and knees, then crawled a few feet away and threw up.

Malcolm. I sent the thought out to him, wanting him to know I was all right.

His answer was instantaneous. *Dacia, where are you?*

I need you to give me a few minutes. I knew the dragons wouldn't be happy, but I wanted to try to get through to Troy without them here. *Please.*

I'll try. The words were hard to make out, but it was more than I'd hoped for.

I sent him an image of where I was. *Wait until I say your name.*

Troy wiped his mouth off on his sleeve and pushed up off the ground. As soon as he stood, he started waving his hands in front of him. The scent of hope filled my nostrils. As bright as a sunny day, it wafted off of him. Before he could open a portal, I snatched him up.

The color drained from his face.

Holding him out in front of me, I pinned his arms to his sides, making sure he couldn't open a portal or stick a collar on one of my fingers like he had in my dream.

The valley floor was far beneath us. He kept glancing over his shoulder, looking down at it, and I realized that he probably thought I would drop him.

"You know I hate you, right?" The rich tone of my voice was still surprising to me. I loved this body, the strength and confidence it gave me. I stepped toward the precipice and stretched my arm out farther. My blue scales shimmered in the light, making prisms dance over his cheeks.

His brown eyes widened, and the intoxicating scent of his fear coated my tongue.

I blew out a puff of smoke, hoping to burn the aroma away. Then I held him out and relaxed my grip on him enough to let him slip but not fall. He clutched my talons. "You deserve it."

I turned so that his feet touched the ground, but I didn't let go of him.

"W-why?" He swallowed several times in quick succession. "W-why didn't you do it?"

I lowered my head until I was looking him directly in the eyes and enunciated each word so that he could not mistake what I was saying. "I. Do. Not. Want. To. Hurt. Anyone." The growl that followed my words surprised me, but I tried not to let it show. "I am not evil. Khione, Aurelia, Arion, and Rayne have all vouched for me. You can sense that I haven't fallen to darkness."

He shook his head.

"I know you can. Liam told me." Saying his name brought about memories of his pain. I pinched my eyes closed, fighting against the instincts that wanted me to kill Troy for hurting my friend.

"You're friends with a demon." His voice was flat like he was saying the words but no longer believed them.

"I am." I loosened my grip a little. "Isn't that a good thing?"

Anger flashed across his face, hardening his eyes, tightening his jaw.

I breathed in deeply. When he'd been afraid, he'd smelled like a tantalizing meal, but now, he smelled like something burnt and disgusting.

He glared at me. "Why would that be better?"

"He's bound to me." I pointed at my chest. "He's free. He could be terrorizing the world. Instead, he's helping me. He's not hurting anyone."

"He shouldn't be here."

Flames sparked in my throat, and when I talked, the air seemed to fan them. "Even if you kill me, he'll remain free, and you can't send him back."

His mouth moved, but no words came out.

Malcolm.

No sooner had his name left my thoughts than dragons in mostly human form surrounded me. A portal opened about fifty yards away. I expected to see Liam, Diana, and Olivia step out of it, but it was Vicki along with several other Nephilim that I didn't know. A black mist swirled in the air, and Mavros materialized next to me.

He bowed his head. "I failed you."

"You'll have to tell me what happened later." I couldn't afford to be distracted from Troy. Even though a lot of the fight seemed to have drained out of him, I didn't trust him.

When he saw the Nephilim, Troy slumped forward in my grasp. The smell of shame was like a freshly popped bag of popcorn. Delicious until I noticed that some of the kernels had been burned.

"I want you to remember something, Troy." I let my voice become more menacing. "I didn't want to kill Draconian or

Argentum, but they pushed me too far. Don't make me end you, too."

I released him, and he fell to his hands and knees.

Malcolm moved between us. His rage and loathing filled the air with a horrible stench.

"She could have killed me." The hatred disappeared from Troy's voice, and with it gone, my fear of him seemed foolish. He was just a man. A man who found happiness in other people's suffering … but still a man.

"Should have." Malcolm's words were a guttural growl, low and menacing. "I believe that's what you meant."

Troy's head bowed further. All of the fight had drained out of him.

The Nephilim surrounded him, and two burly men pulled his arms behind his back. When they had him secured, Vicki walked toward me. Her fear was tangible. I could smell it wafting off of her. I could see it in the rigidness of her posture. I could hear it in her elevated heart rate.

She had been kind to me. Without her, who knew if I would have been fed or had a cot to sleep on? It was possible that she'd been the reason Liam had been my guard.

I looked around, making sure that I wasn't in danger, and transformed back into my own body. Instantly, I missed the warmth of my scales. Mavros shrugged out of his coat and held it out to me. I pulled it on greedily, savoring his warmth.

Malcolm, Cash, Seth, and most likely Jax all moved within an arm's length of me. Even though I didn't sense any danger, they were vigilant.

"Hello, Vicki." I nodded at her.

"Dacia." Despite the fact that she said my name, she was focused on Mavros. Her dark eyebrows pinched together. "Your demon …" She shook her head. "I can barely sense that he's one."

I took a step toward her, moving so that I was blocking Mavros just slightly. "That's what Liam said." I pulled my bottom lip into my mouth. "Do you know how he is?" Before she could answer, I turned to Cash. "Is Cody okay?"

Mavros slipped his hands into his pockets and looked down.

My stomach plummeted. Why would he turn somber if everything was okay? "Cody?"

"He's fine." Cash put his hand on my shoulder. "He had Micah down on the ground before I got there."

I tilted my head to the side and looked at Mavros, waiting for an explanation from him.

"Yeah, you did good." The smile that he shot me didn't reach his eyes. "You did better than I did."

I let out a deep sigh. "Hold that thought, okay?"

Vicki's lips were pinched together, and she watched us like we were a conundrum that she wanted to solve.

"How's Liam?" I asked her again.

She shook her head. "I don't know."

"He'll live." Malcolm's voice was gruff. He grabbed hold of my shoulder. His fingers dug in through Mavros' leather coat, but I tried not to let him see any weakness. His dragon was too riled already. "Every time I leave you, something happens."

Not wanting him to think I was challenging him, I kept my eyes downcast. "I'm fine."

"Will you take me to Liam?" Vicki's brown eyes were glossy.

Cash nodded. "He's in our apartment."

"Not until I know what's going to happen to him." Malcolm stared at the Nephilim restraining Troy. His clenched fist shook, and the veins running up his arm throbbed.

Vicki followed his gaze. "He will be tried and found guilty." She shook her head and sighed. "It's such a shame. There are too few of us to be this divided."

"He will stay imprisoned?" Even though cobalt scales covered his cheeks, Seth somehow managed to keep his voice calm.

A bitter smile pulled her lips up. "He will be more heavily guarded."

The Nephilim pulled Troy through a portal, and I breathed out a sigh of relief that clouded the air in front of me. "I don't know if this is done, but I want to go."

I reached for Mavros' hand, but he pulled back. "Go with the dragons. I cannot enter your apartment."

"Why?" My chest tightened. I didn't need another problem. I didn't know what had happened to Sebastian or the other Nephilim who wanted to imprison me. I didn't know if this was over, and I still had to figure out how to break the phouka's curse.

Malcolm grabbed my hand. He was gentler this time, but his dragon was still too close to the surface. "Wards. They will have to be destroyed before he can enter again."

Cash held his hand out to Vicki. As soon as she took it, the two of them disappeared. Once they were gone, the rest of the

Nephilim created portals. I squinted against the bright lights, tilting my head away from them. In a matter of seconds, the Nephilim had stepped through them, and they closed up.

Mavros looked down at his feet as Seth took my other hand. Apparently, even with Troy in custody, the dragons weren't going to relax their guard.

Right before Malcolm teleported us, I smiled at Mavros, hoping he would understand that I didn't blame him for anything. I'd needed to be alone. I'd needed this to happen. Troy would never have tried to take me with Mavros or the dragons guarding me.

Cody was pacing away from me when I returned to the apartment. Russ sat on the couch, watching him. He never turned his head, but his eyes followed every step.

When Cody turned, relief washed over his expression, pulling the tension out of his body. "Dacia." He dragged his hand down his face as he walked over to me. "Thank God."

"He's gone for now." I lifted my hand to Cody's cheek. His right eye was swollen, and a bruise was beginning to darken the skin beneath it. "You're hurt."

He shrugged, then put his hand on top of mine. "It's nothing."

"What happened to Micah?" I looked around the room, but he was nowhere to be seen.

"Didn't expect me to know self-defense." He raised his eyebrow and grinned at me. "Threw him down, but—" he rubbed the back of his neck "—little more crowded here than where we've been. Got a hit in before the Nephilim took him away."

I stepped closer to him and leaned my head against his chest. "I'm sorry I left you. I didn't know what else to do."

"It's all good." He rubbed his hand over my head and down my back. His fingers faltered when they met Mavros' coat, but he didn't say anything about it. "He really gone?"

"Unless the Nephilim let him get away," Malcolm answered. Even though I was safe, his voice was gruff. He turned his attention to Russ. "Go. Watch over the others."

"Thank you." I pressed my hand to my heart.

Russ nodded before disappearing.

I knew that none of the dragons would leave me alone until Mavros could come into my apartment again. They needed to hunt, and I needed to get rid of the wards for them to go. "I need to see Liam."

Chapter 34

Healing Magic

$\mathcal{M}$avros stood in the hallway, leaning against the wall next to my door. His arms were folded over his chest, and his muscles were taut. His lips pinched together in a tight line.

I tilted my head to the side. "What are you doing out here?"

"Waiting." He raised one dark eyebrow as if in challenge.

Malcolm opened the door to his apartment and ushered me in. I turned and looked out at Mavros. "Coming?"

"Can't."

Cash looked up from the armchair. "They warded both rooms." The door shut, and he added, "He's going to be grumpy about this for a while. The Nephilim can't send him back to the Abyss, but it seems that they can keep him out."

"Surprised they didn't ward the whole building," Cody said.

Cash shook his head. "No—" he pointed at the doorframe where several of the angelic symbols had been drawn on it in what appeared to be Troy's gold-flecked blood "—he had to do that around every door and window. It would have taken far too long."

"So … where's Liam?" I wasn't ready to face him. If I'd never come into his life, he wouldn't be suffering right now.

Cash pointed to the doors on his right. "Olivia. Diana." Then he pointed to the left. "Liam."

"Good thing you guys don't sleep." Cody huffed out an almost imperceptible laugh.

Cash shrugged. "Yeah, sometimes the privacy's nice, though."

"Privacy?" I chuckled, but it lacked any humor. For a second, I was rendered totally speechless. "What's that?"

He shook his head. "Ha. Ha. Go see Liam."

"Is Vicki in there?" I pulled my bottom lip into my mouth with my teeth. I didn't want to interrupt the two of them. They deserved some time alone.

Cash nodded toward the other side of the room. "She's tending to Olivia right now."

"How bad are they?"

A low growl rumbled through his chest. "Go. See him."

Before I could say anything else or find another way to delay, Cody grabbed my hand and pulled me toward Liam's door.

Recalling all of the times Liam had helped me tightened my chest and made a lump form in the back of my throat. I never should have asked him to stay with me. I should have told him to stay as far away from me as possible. I knew Troy would never forgive him, especially after Liam hit me. Troy had thought he was winning Liam over to his side.

I couldn't bring myself to knock or turn the handle. I just stood in front of the door, staring at the wood grain without really seeing it.

Cody reached around me and rapped his knuckles gently against the frame.

"Come in." Liam's voice was weak, and as soon as the words were out, he started coughing.

My chin dropped to my chest. This was my fault. How could I face him?

"Dacia," Cash snapped at me, and I realized my emotions were too much.

Cody opened the door. Then he pressed his hand to the small of my back, guiding me into the room. The curtains were pulled closed, and the lights were out. It took several seconds for my eyes to adjust to the darkness of the room.

Liam had a couple of pillows propping him up. His chest was bare, and a blanket covered him from the waist down. Bruises and cuts covered every bit of his skin that I could see. His eyes were swelled shut. If I hadn't known it was him lying there, I wouldn't have recognized him.

"Hey." My guilt nearly swallowed the word up. I knelt on the floor next to his bed. "Can I touch you?"

His eyes moved beneath his eyelids, and he nodded. The movement was so slight that if I hadn't been focusing on him so intently I would have missed it.

I started to reach for his fingers, but the purple and black digits were taped together. I finally settled on his arm just above his elbow. Even though it was bruised, it didn't look as badly beaten as the rest of him. I closed my eyes and thought about life. Power, cool and crisp, filled my body, pouring from my fingertips into Liam.

He sighed.

The sound soothed some of my remorse, but like with everything else I'd done, I would carry this weight around with me long after my friends and family were gone from this world.

"Dacia"—Cody's hand clamped down on my shoulder—"think you can stop."

I didn't. I opened my eyes and stared at Liam. A faint light surrounded his body, reminding me of when the fairies had removed Mavros' taint from me.

He smiled at me. His gray eyes were clear and bright. The pain had been washed from them. The bruises and cuts had all healed. A couple of old scars still marred his skin, but even if I could take them away, I didn't know if he would want me to. Sometimes, they were reminders. Of what we'd been through. Of what we'd survived. And that we could do it again.

I stopped the flow of magic. "I'm so sorry."

"It's not your—" His back arched, and he shot up, knocking my hand loose. A pained cry tore from his lips.

The door burst open, and Vicki and Cash charged in. I scrambled to my feet, trying to get out of their way.

Vicki stared at Liam. Her mouth fell open, and her eyes widened.

At first, I thought she was surprised by how much better he looked, but I followed her gaze and saw the truth. Wings burst from the two nasty-looking scars on his back. They were magnificent. Tan and white like a barn owl's feathers.

He threw the blanket off his legs and jumped out of bed. We all backed away from him as he spun. His wings bumped against the nightstand, knocking the lamp and alarm clock to the floor with a loud crash. "What the hell, Dacia?" His voice was high-pitched. He shoved past us, striding for the bathroom, and slammed the door shut behind him.

"What did you do to him?" Vicki wiped her hands down her face.

I shook my head. "I just wanted to heal him. I-it was m-my fault. I, uh—" I tugged my hand through my hair, wondering if there was any way to fix this "—I just wanted to heal him." My heart thudded against my chest, the beat of a dirge. I'd wanted to make things better, but I'd made them worse instead.

"All of us are born with those scars on our backs." She didn't pull her gaze from the door while she talked. "It's as if our wings were cut off of us in the womb." She glanced over her shoulder at me before turning back toward the bathroom. "Could you heal us all?"

Cash stepped closer to me. "I don't know if that's a wise decision."

"Why?" Vicki spun around and glared at him. "You can fly." She jammed her finger toward me. "She can fly. Why shouldn't we be able to?"

His eyes flashed to his dragon's and back. "I didn't say you shouldn't, but we can hide our wings. Can you?"

"No." Liam stalked out of the bathroom. The tips of his wings dragged on the floor. "At least not yet." He smiled at me.

"Thank you for healing me, Dacia. Unfortunately, I won't be able to guard you with these."

"I'm so sorry, Liam." I couldn't look him in the eyes. I couldn't bear to see his disgust.

He walked over and tilted my chin up. "Don't be sorry. You healed me and gave me quite a gift."

"How ya gonna sleep?" Cody asked.

"On my stomach." Liam turned around and stared at the bed, rubbing his chin. His beard was longer than I'd ever seen it, but it still made the scratching sound it had when he'd been my prison guard. "They're gonna take some getting used to."

"It's crowded in here." Vicki opened the door and walked out into the living room. The rest of us followed her.

Liam pulled out a kitchen chair and sat with his arms folded over the back of it. "Gonna take a lot of getting used to."

Laughter came from the hallway, and I recognized it as belonging to my friends. Seth opened the door. "In here."

Samantha, Dan, Cassandra, and Bryce filed into the dragons' apartment. "Liam, you're back," Cassandra's voice rose excitedly.

Dan pointed at Liam's wings. "I think you meant, Liam … your back."

"Dacia healed me." He lifted his shoulder, and his wings bumped the table, knocking the salt and pepper shakers over.

Bryce walked around behind him. "When we played basketball, you had some wicked-looking scars."

"Nephilim are born with them." Liam didn't look like he was bothered by his wings, but from his earlier reaction, I assumed he was trying to keep from upsetting me.

Mavros moved so that he could see into the apartment. A crooked smile tugged on his lips as he looked from Liam to me again. "Interesting turn of events."

"Come here." I moved my index finger, beckoning him toward me.

He strode forward, stopping short of the door. "Your wish." He bowed. "My command."

"Do you trust me?" I held my hand out, but he didn't reach for it.

He shook his head, and my gut clenched in response. Why would he trust me? I had returned him to the Abyss to keep myself safe after he defied Argentum's orders. Then I did it again after he lent me his power. No matter what he did for me, I did wrong by him.

"Dacia—" he lifted his hand toward my face but stopped short of touching it "—I trust you. I cannot touch you while you're in there." He looked at the doorframe, and I wondered if the symbols were drawn on the outside, too.

I stepped into the hallway, followed by Malcolm's growl. "Get back in here."

"I need to touch Mavros."

Cody looked over his shoulder. His expression was filled with despair before he realized he hadn't slid his mask into place.

"To see if I can break the wards, Cody." I pulled my hand through my curls and realized I was still wearing Mavros' coat. I took it off and handed it to him. "Thank you. I would have frozen without it."

"Always, Dacia." He slid his arms into the sleeves. "I will always give you my coat. If I didn't have it, I'd give you the shirt off of my back."

"Thank you." I held my hand up again, hoping he would put his in it. "Right now, I need you to give me your trust. Can you do that?"

"Of course." He laid his hand in mine, and I turned it so the palm was facing up.

I thought about my dragon form, and my finger transformed until a talon extended from the end of it.

"What are you doing, Dacia?" Mavros' obsidian eyes flicked from my claw to my face.

"Trust me." The words were quiet, soothing, but Mavros' discomfort was palpable. I slashed my talon over his palm. Black blood pooled there. I dipped my claw in it, careful not to spill even a drop. I walked to the door and wiped it over the wards.

Mavros' blood sizzled, burning away Troy's.

"Can you step through now?"

Mavros tentatively inched toward the door, placing each foot gingerly before picking up the next one. The nonchalant look on his face couldn't mask the hope in his eyes. He took another step, and pain rippled across his features. Black mist wafted into the air.

I looked down the hall, hoping nobody was around to witness mine or Mavros' transformations. "Are you okay?"

"Don't worry about me." He lifted my hand and wiped his blood off of my talon. "See if you can help Diana and Olivia without giving them wings." The laugh that followed his words was off, but I pretended not to notice.

I slumped forward. "I need you, though."

"Not right now, you don't." His fingers trailed along my cheek, stopping at my chin. He tilted my head up. A sad smile tugged on his lips. "I'll be right here."

I walked into the apartment, glancing over my shoulder before I shut the door. Mavros stood with his hands tucked into his pockets and his head bowed. His usual cockiness had been replaced with defeat.

He lifted his head slightly and caught me watching him. "Go on."

I knew he didn't want my sympathy, so against my better judgment, I pushed the door shut and turned toward my friends. "So … how bad are Diana and Olivia?"

Chapter 35

A Mighty Oak

*M*agenta clouds blaze across the sky, reflecting onto the trees and mountains, casting a pink glow on everything around me.

"Storm's coming."

The voice shocks me. I didn't realize anybody was with me. I turn away from the sunrise to find Kieran standing next to me. "What do you want?"

He pushes his shaggy hair out of his eyes, but it falls right back down. "You, Dacia, in Faerie with me."

I roll my neck from side to side, hoping to ease some of the tension, but it doesn't work. "Why?"

"Why not?" The grin that he shoots me is carefree and wild. "You're powerful." He walks around me, looking me over from head to foot. "If you're in Faerie with me, your guardians will do whatever it takes to get to you. Think of all the fun I'll have."

I fold my arms over my chest and try not to give him the satisfaction of an argument. "So, this is more about them than me."

"No." He runs his finger over the oak tree on my arm. His touch is soft. The skin of someone who has never done a hard day's work. "This is most definitely about you and all the fun you'll bring into my life."

My eyes snapped open, and Malcolm growled from his position at the end of my bed. "Kieran?"

"Yeah." I tugged my hand through my hair before looking at the curse. The leaves were still green but for how long?

"I hate to say it, but we need Mavros in here."

I blew out a long sigh. "Well, if I wouldn't have given Liam wings, maybe Diana and Olivia would have let me heal them."

"Why would that matter?" Cody asked.

"If I could have—" I flopped onto my back and stared up at the ceiling "—they might be able to help Liam and Vicki take down the wards." There were no answers in the spackling. I kissed Cody on the cheek and climbed out of bed. "I'm gonna read for a while." On the way out the door, I grabbed my book.

Malcolm followed me into the living room. He sat on the couch next to me and wrapped his arm around my shoulders. "I might be able to keep him out if I'm touching you."

My eyebrows drew together. "Haven't you been?"

"You move, and my foot loses contact." He lifted one shoulder. "It's only for an instant, but that seems to be all he needs."

"Cody won't understand."

"He might not like it, but if it keeps Kieran away, he'll understand."

I opened my book and read the first paragraph four times before giving up. "How can I beat this?"

"We'll figure it out." He pulled my head onto his shoulder. "But, first you've got to sleep."

The End

If you enjoyed this book, please leave a review.

Without reviews, potential readers have no idea what they're missing out on. The plain and simple truth is, reviews sell books.

Please find the time to go online and leave a comment no matter how short. Something as simple as, "I liked it," helps put the book out where readers can find it and helps your favorite author be able to continue writing.

Acknowledgments

This may very well be the most difficult part of writing a book. I never know what to say in this part.

Of course, I am grateful for my husband because a lot of Cody's compassion and understanding comes from him. So, thank you, Jeff, for always being there for me, for caring about me, and taking care of me. Thanks for being you and for being mine!

I want to thank my kiddos, Jami and Jesse, for being great kids, for being my biggest fans, and for cheering me on. You filled the empty spots in my life, and I wouldn't know what to do without you.

My parents, Jim and Vicki Drews, taught me to reach for my dreams and always made me feel like they were attainable, so I need to thank them.

Anybody who follows my Instagram page sees how my cats support my writing. So to Bella, Galadriel, Merida, and Westley, thanks for being the inspiration behind some of the characters.

I would also like to thank Shreya Vijay. Your compliments and unending support always brighten my day no matter what I'm going through. I never thought I would be somebody's favorite author. Knowing that I am, makes it all worth it!

Thank You!

If you liked this story, you can join my mailing list.
Drop by my website MandiOyster.com
or if you have any comments,
shoot me a note at mandi@mandioyster.com.
I am always happy to hear from people who've read my work.
I try to answer every email I receive.

Facebook – https://www.facebook.com/MandiOysterAuthor
Instagram: https://www.instagram.com/mandioyster/
My web page – MandiOyster.com

About the Author

Mandi Oyster lives in Southwest Iowa in the middle of an enchanted forest where unicorns, fairies, and dragons abound. At least, that's what she assumes when she looks out into the trees. Her husband, two kids (when they're not away at college), four cats, and two chinchillas share the house with her. 

Besides being an author, she also runs her own editing business and works full-time as a digital prepress technician for a local printshop.

You can find her online at:
https://www.MandiOyster.com
https://www.facebook.com/MandiOysterAuthor
https://instagram.com/MandiOyster/

AND THE
PHOUKA'S CURSE

Book 7